Grey Dog

elliott gish

Grey Dog

Published by ECW Press
665 Gerrard Street East
Toronto, Ontario, Canada M4M 1Y2
416-694-3348 / info@ecwpress.com

Editor for the Press: Jen Sookfong Lee
Copy editor: Jen R. Albert
Cover design: Caroline Suzuki
Wolf cover art: "Canis Lupis var. Nubilus." Fauna boreali-americana, London, John Murray, 1829-1837, plate 3.
Deer cover art: "The Apara Brocket." Mammalia, London Printed for Geo. B. Whittaker 1827, plate 16.

This is a work of fiction. Names, characters, places, and incidents either are the product of the author's imagination or are used fictitiously, and any resemblance to actual persons, living or dead, business establishments, events, or locales is entirely coincidental.

LIBRARY AND ARCHIVES CANADA CATALOGUING IN PUBLICATION

Title: Grey dog / Elliott Gish.

Names: Gish, Elliott, author.

Identifiers: Canadiana (print) 20230571670 | Canadiana (ebook) 20230571697

ISBN 978-1-77041-732-8 (softcover)
ISBN 978-1-77852-262-8 (PDF)
ISBN 978-1-77852-261-1 (ePub)

Classification: LCC PS8613.I84 G74 2024 | DDC C813/.6—dc23

This book is funded in part by the Government of Canada. *Ce livre est financé en partie par le gouvernement du Canada.* We acknowledge the support of the Canada Council for the Arts. *Nous remercions le Conseil des arts du Canada de son soutien.* We acknowledge the funding support of the Ontario Arts Council (OAC), an agency of the Government of Ontario. We also acknowledge the support of the Government of Ontario through the Ontario Book Publishing Tax Credit, and through Ontario Creates.

PRINTED AND BOUND IN CANADA   PRINTING: MARQUIS   5   4   3   2   1

For Cael

August 17, 1901

The train shudders so horribly that this page will probably be impossible to decipher later. With every bend and bump in the track, my hand skates and jumps over this black book, creating blots and slashes in the paper. To my future self, should she try to read what I have written here: my apologies and Godspeed.

How old was I the last time I kept a diary? Thirteen, I think, or fourteen. A girl with her hair in braids, fresh and unbroken as new snow. I can scarcely recall now what I wrote about then, although it all felt terribly important at the time. Perhaps in a year or two I will reread this passage and encounter the same feeling that arises when I recall those youthful diary entries — a mixture of fondness and impatience, with a dash of incredulity that a creature so young and ignorant could call herself unhappy.

For I am unhappy. I am unhappy to be in my current position, stuffed in a hot and dirty train carriage next to an old woman who sleeps with her mouth wide open. (She snores as well, but I can scarcely hear her over the noise of the rails.) I do not travel well at the best of times, and the prospect of arriving in a new place, a place where I know no one and am familiar with nothing, means that I cannot even look forward to the end of my journey. Every teaching post I have ever taken has begun this way: an uncomfortable voyage, awkward greetings, a long, hard period of "settling in." This should be no different. But it is, it is! And I know why.

I found this book only a day or two ago, at the bottom of the wardrobe that my sister, Florrie, and I shared as girls. It was part of the haphazard bundle of her belongings that her husband had returned to my father's house, sandwiched carelessly between a sewing basket and a folded flannel petticoat. I picked the book up out of idle curiosity, thinking it might be one of the "nature logs" she and I kept together through childhood; but when I opened it, I found it blank, save for an exquisite border of flowering vines in blue ink on the first page, each bloom and thorn rendered in minute detail. A cardinal perched in the upper right corner, drawn so beautifully that it seemed about to take flight and escape the boundaries of the page. I recognized the artwork as my sister's even before I saw the dedication below in her outsized scrawl, so unlike my own cramped, minute hand.

> To Aidy, for when you are in the woods.
> Love always, F

I had to close the book then, for fear of smudging the ink. Into my satchel it went, hidden beneath a layer of fresh white handkerchiefs.

Father gave me only a smattering of details about my new post. I know that the town is called Lowry Bridge; that, properly speaking, it is not a town at all, but a village twenty miles away from the terminus in Portsmouth; that they are desperate for a teacher, and therefore not inclined to ask inconvenient questions about that teacher's past once she arrives, particularly if her father is superintendent of the district school board. This last he did not say to me, but he did not say it at tremendous volume.

"Write to us, Aidy," he said at the station this afternoon, his eyes blank, like those of a shark. The pet name made a liar of him. "Aidy" was what Florrie had always called me in moments of tenderness, and my father does not suffer from so vulgar an affliction as tender feeling. "We want to know how you are keeping."

This, too, was a lie. I said nothing, only chewed at the edge of my lip in a way that made him frown and reach out to grasp my hand within his big one, squeezing it hard until my bones rubbed painfully together. I stopped then.

After this interminable train ride, I shall meet a Mr. Grier at the Portsmouth station, the man in whose house I shall board. He is an acquaintance of my father's, although the circumstances under which they once met are unknown to me. He has a wife, presumably — my father would never allow me to board with him otherwise — but I do not know her name, nor anything else about the pair of them. Are they old or young? Is their marriage happy or miserable? Do they have children, and if so, do they love them?

This train churns the contents of my stomach into a sickly froth, but that churning is nothing to the knot that forms in it when I imagine the moment when the churning stops and my feet meet solid ground.

I shall send my parents news of the countryside, my classroom, the daily minutiae of a spinster's life in the middle of nowhere. Cheerful, dishonest letters, quite free of emotion and depth. Since Florrie's leave-taking, there is no one with whom I may share my real feelings, no place in my life for candour and misery, save between the covers of this black book. My truth shall remain trapped on its pages, while my happy little lies travel the world.

August 18, 1901

It was nearly two o'clock before I finally arrived in Portsmouth, bedraggled, dusty, and stiff as a corpse from hours spent upright in a train seat. After disembarking — and nearly losing my hat in the process — I scanned the platform for Mr. Grier, repeating to myself my father's brief sketch of him.

"A small fellow — rather stout — not much hair left, but what's there is red."

And indeed, there was a gentleman matching that description standing by the station door, a searching look on his ruddy face as he peered through the dispersing crowd. I met him with a smile, one that felt as limp and dispirited as I doubtlessly looked.

"Miss Byrd?" he called hopefully, starting forwards. Small he certainly was, his stoutness running to outright plumpness, with a thin fringe of ginger hair combed unconvincingly over his crown. He wore a shabby grey suit and moved so uncomfortably in it that I knew it to be his Sunday best. "Miss Ada Elizabeth Byrd?"

It was gratifying to hear my proper name on someone's lips again. After spending the past five months in hiding in my father's house, *Aidy* has come to sound more like an epithet than a pet name to me.

"Mr. Grier, I hope," I said, and reached out to shake his hand. (He looked a bit startled at that; perhaps ladies do not shake hands here?) "I am so pleased to make your acquaintance. My father has spoken most highly of you."

Highly was, perhaps, a bit of a stretch, but Mr. Grier's face flushed with pleasure. It was an uneven flush, the crimson mottled and broken like the flesh of an uncooked sausage.

Those were the last words we exchanged for some time, for Mr. Grier concerned himself chiefly with heaving my belongings into the buggy he had left tied at the front of the station, a venerable thing with a patched cover, pulled by a team of disinterested grey mares. It was not until we were both settled and on our way down the road that he spoke again.

"Well now, Miss Byrd," he all but shouted over the clatter of the wheels, "I must say we're all surely glad you've come."

There was nothing I could say to that that would not have been either a lie, insulting, or painfully banal, so I smiled vaguely in response. Taking that as an invitation to continue, Mr. Grier went on:

"I suppose your father told you about the bother we've had — trying to keep teachers and all? It's three we've lost in the last four years, one right after the other. The first two were young, right out of the teacher's college. They left to get married. Well, that's to be expected. Just wanted a year's salary to pay for their wedding doo-dabs, I suppose. But the last was an older lady, nice and steady. We thought we'd have hold of her for a least a few years." He shook his head, fiddling a little with the reins.

"Was she taken ill?" I ventured when he didn't offer anything further.

He shook his head again, looking gloomy. "No. Her mother. She got word that the poor woman had come down with pneumonia, and nothing would do for a nurse but her own daughter. Left in the night, right in the middle of the spring term, and the little ones were without a teacher again. When your father wrote and said that you were seeking a new post, I thought, *That's providence, sheer providence!* The Lord provides, Miss Byrd."

I don't remember what I said to that — perhaps nothing at all. Whatever it was, it was not enough to inspire Mr. Grier to further conversation, and we continued in silence for a discomfiting length of time. I was an exotic stranger to this man, a woman from (comparatively) far away, whose eyes had seen places and people that his had not. Why, then, was he not asking me questions? Was he of that breed of country men who have no interests beyond their own fields and barns? Or — and this was a dreadful thought indeed — had my father told him what had transpired at my former post, and had that knowledge discomfited him so that he felt he could not speak freely?

I tried to divert myself by admiring the scenery, but found myself with little to admire. The chief feature of the journey from Portsmouth to Lowry Bridge was the thickness of the spruces that lined the sides of the road, clustered so dark and close that, for a fanciful moment, I imagined them pressing in on us, swallowing the road and leaving the land untouched and whole again. Our own dust was behind us, and ahead more road and more trees, forever and ever, ad infinitum.

Presently Mr. Grier cleared his throat and said:

"I do hope, Miss Byrd, that you won't find Lowry Bridge too quiet. I understand that your last placement was in a bit of a fast town."

I managed not to laugh at that. Willoughby could, I suppose, be considered a fast town by someone from such a place as Lowry Bridge.

"Not at all, Mr. Grier," I said, as gravely as I could manage. "I was raised in a small town myself. They suit me very well."

He looked mightily relieved at that.

"Well, I'm glad to hear it," he said, "very glad indeed. I know some people don't hold with little places these days — nothing will do for them but to run off to a city as soon as they cut themselves free of their mother's apron strings. But we're a good town, for all we ain't big."

Aren't, not ain't, I nearly corrected him, before biting my tongue and saying nothing.

"We're small, but we have a town hall now," Mr. Grier went on. He seemed to gather steam as he continued, speaking more and more rapidly. "We have a church — Presbyterian, with a good, sober minister. His wife teaches the Sunday school. There's prayer meeting once a week for ladies. Even dances. I play at them from time to time, fiddling — jigs and reels and such." He looked at me sidelong, as though worried he had offended me, and added, "Not that you need come, of course, if you don't care to. I know a lot of people don't hold with dancing, but we have young people in town, and it's good for their spirits, my wife says."

"I've been known to dance a step or two." This was broadly true, although I have not done so for some time, and I have never done so well. "What about the children, Mr. Grier? What are they like?"

"Like?" that good man repeated, as though unsure what I meant.

"How many of them are there? Do they read well? What sort of games do they like?"

He looked a little blank. "The usual ones, I suppose," he replied, rather vaguely. "Hopscotch and jumping rope and such. My wife and I don't have children, you see, so I can't say that I know much about what they get up to."

He sounded wistful. I wondered if he and his wife had wanted children, if they were saddened by the lack of them, or if they were perfectly content as a pair. There has always been something markedly odd to me about childless couples. They seem too complete within themselves, twin chicks growing in a single egg. Marriages, I think, can work too well in uniting two people as one.

Thus sayeth the spinster, nearing thirty with neither marriage nor children under her belt.

The road wound on through trees and open farmland, brassy fields of wheat and barley nodding gently in the breeze. Occasionally a house or barn would pop up in the distance, lonely sentries standing in a haze of green and gold. I was keenly aware of every window we passed, imagining eyes behind the glass. Small towns are veritable factories of gossip, churning out thick black clouds of judgment that pall the landscape for miles around. How long before that cloud would hang over me?

"Tell me about Lowry Bridge," I said, more to distract my own nattering brain than because I was genuinely interested. Mr. Grier was more than happy to oblige. As we rode onwards, the road sloping gently down toward banks of the river, he told me more about the town than I could ever have hoped to learn. Founded nearly two hundred years ago by a healthy mix of Germans, Scots, and Englishmen; originally two settlements, each with its own name, both of which I now forget; named for the brothers who built the bridge that spanned the river, connecting the two original communities. The one on the northeast bank apparently has the reputation of being the rougher of the two. The southwest side of the river is where civilization dwells.

"And where is the school?" I asked him.

"Northeast," Mr. Grier admitted, rather sheepishly. "Land goes cheaper over there, on account of the trees being so thick on that side. Nobody wants to clear it. It ain't a *bad* part of town, you understand. The church is over that side, and the manse. It's just that some of the folks over there ain't quite like us. Coarse, like. They're poorer, so I suppose that explains it."

Looking at Mr. Grier's patched buggy and worn suit, I suspected that this was one of those small-town distinctions that are utterly incomprehensible to outsiders but taken as a matter of course by citizens. It was a neat line to draw in the sand, I had to admit. How easy it must be to know which folks are respectable and which are not, if you only need look at what side of a bridge they live on! (Mr. Grier himself, he hastened to assure me, lives on the southwest side of the bridge — that is, the *good* side.)

As we took a sudden bend in the road, the thick clusters of trees suddenly cleared a bit, and Mr. Grier interrupted himself to nod his head to the left.

"See there," he said, "that's Slade River."

And there it was, laid out amidst the trees and fields like a broad, flat ribbon. Having seen a map of the town, I know that Lowry Bridge spans a bend in the river; it flows from the north, then wends east, then turns south again, giving it an almost angular appearance, like the edge of a staircase. Beyond it rose a gentle curve of land, golden fields darkened here by stands of pines and there by little whitewashed houses. I could not make out the shape of the river in that moment, only the shining band of it sparkling in the afternoon light. A kingfisher skimmed across its surface, a brilliant azure flash against the murky greens and muddy browns of the water.

"Oh! How beautiful!" I exclaimed. My enthusiasm rang a little false in my ear, and perhaps in Mr. Grier's too, for he gave me a sidelong look that was very nearly askance. But I meant it.

"Well, now, I suppose it is," he said, almost grudgingly, but I detected a smile lurking at the corners of his mouth. It is impossible, I think, not to feel a little proud when one's home is found beautiful.

The road dipped farther down, the trees gathering closer again to its sides. Their shade was welcome after such a long time in the sun, and yet I found myself shivering a little in the sudden gloom.

"Cold, are you?" Mr. Grier asked, as though it were a perfectly natural thing for a woman to shiver in the middle of August. "Never mind. We'll be home soon, and Mrs. Grier will get a bit of supper in you."

The notion appealed to me. I had packed a little lunch to eat on the train, but it had not been much, and I was suddenly ravenous.

The Grier residence proved to be a two-story house of grey stone, set back a little off the main road in the shadow of a stand of sternly upright spruces, surrounded by a wooden fence daubed with grey-green moss and crusted with white lichen.

Orderly beds of dahlias and chrysanthemums grew on either side of the path, which led to sandstone steps and a door painted blister-red.

I stumbled, looking at that door, and not only because my legs were stiff with disuse from the journey, for there had been another red door, only a year ago, that had irrevocably changed the course of my life. As I looked at the Grier house, I felt that I could see *that* door laid neatly over *this* one — that I was in Willoughby again, watching that door open onto my ruin.

But, of course, when the door of the stone house opened, it revealed nothing but Mrs. Grier, neat as a packet of pins in a starched and ironed apron. Nothing else, no one else. I looked at the little woman — and *little* is the right word; she is several inches shorter than I — and felt blessedly relieved.

"Hello, Miss Byrd!" Mrs. Grier said, her voice brisk and high, like the peep of a sparrow. "What a pleasure it is to have you."

She strode forward to take my hand in hers, shaking vigorously. (Perhaps ladies do shake in Lowry Bridge after all!) Thus captured, I allowed myself to be led into the house, sat down, and fed.

Mrs. Grier is a short, sturdy woman, plain and scrubbed-looking, with a quick smile and quicker eyes. Even as she flits from place to place like a little bird, those eyes remain level and calm, watchful in a way that gives one the impression that she has seen everything that has ever happened. She is neat, almost aggressively so, and her house, with its framed samplers and plain, sturdy furniture, is neat as well, as though she has bent it to resemble herself out of sheer force of will. I liked her immediately and, as always happens when I like someone immediately, found myself incapacitated by shyness. My gaze dropped to the floor; I answered her bright, curious questions about my last post, my experiences as a teacher, the health of my family, in whispered monosyllables until the poor woman stopped trying to engage me in conversation. My appetite fell away in the wake of this new self-consciousness, and I found myself only playing with my food on my plate, chasing bits of bean and turnip in circles. Mrs. Grier must have noticed, for before she and her husband had finished their own meal, she turned to me and said:

"Miss Byrd, you do look pale. Why don't you go and have yourself a rest? I can take care of the dishes."

I was glad not to argue, for my head was throbbing, and the air seemed heavy and thick as syrup.

I expected to fall asleep as soon as I stumbled up the stairs and into my new bedroom, but at the sound of the door clicking shut, I found myself suddenly crackling with an odd surplus of energy, as one sometimes does when exhausted. The world seemed very bright and sharp, everything in it charged with special, obscure meaning. I walked around my new room, touching the objects in it. My trunk and carpetbag, pushed carefully into a corner. A wardrobe, oak. A low cot with a crazy quilt. A willow-back chair, upright as the spruces outside. A washstand with a white jug and basin. A rag rug near the door, fashioned in the shape of a rose. Walls papered with a dingy diamond pattern that was once blue and green but had long since faded to grey and greyer. A picture on the wall of the Sermon on the Mount, apparently clipped from a missionary paper, in which Christ boasts a scowl and a tremendous pair of whiskers. It is not the smallest room I have ever stayed in, nor the ugliest, but it has a plain-scrubbed look to it that suggests a cell in a nunnery.

At least it is not in the attic. I could not bear to sleep in an attic room again.

Mrs. Grier has left a candle by my bed (lamps, I have been told, are used only in the downstairs rooms here). It is by its light that I am writing, and by the little moonlight trickling onto my bed from the window, which looks out onto the trees beyond the Griers' farm. I can see other little windows scattered in the dark, welcome signs that I am not the only person awake and alive at this hour of night. Through the trees is the glimmer of the river itself, the constant, restless churn of its passing turned to silver in the moonlight. From here it looks less inviting than it did this afternoon, darker and cooler.

Diving into cool, dark water would be a blessing right now. I can imagine the pleasure of it, like slipping between a set of sheets on a winter's night: the shock of cold, the quick sink, the rapid warming of the body as the river accepts its gift. My new room is close. All the heat of the day seems to have risen and become trapped beneath the slanted ceiling.

August 25, 1901

The past few days have rushed by so quickly I've scarcely had time to breathe, let alone write. It is only now, alone in my little room, that I can sit and let my whirling brain come to rest.

I slept soundly that first night, a deeper sleep than I've had for many months, and yet when I woke up, I felt curiously unrested. As I stumbled down the stairs, yawning too widely for dignity, I felt that I could have happily stayed in bed for another twelve hours, sunrise or no sunrise. When I entered the kitchen, I saw Mrs. Grier bent over the stove, stirring something in a little iron pot that put me in mind of a cauldron. Twining about her feet was a small grey-and-white cat, its little face adorably fat, that added to the scene's air of "bubble, bubble, toil and trouble." It took one look at me and retreated skittishly behind the stove, its green lamp-eyes winking in the shadows.

"Good morning, Miss Byrd," said Mrs. Grier. Her bright calico dress was almost completely consumed by a voluminous apron — the old-fashioned kind, with sleeves. Not like a witch at all, really. "Sleep well?"

"I did," I confirmed, wavering between helping her at the stove and taking a seat at the table. She certainly seemed to have everything in hand, but I worried that if I sat down, she would peg me as lazy or demanding, and our relationship would thereby be strained before it even began. Having boarded with families before, I have learned that it always behooves one to assume that any action one takes might offend a person in the house. "I do apologize for rising so late."

"It's the trains." A sage nod accompanied this droplet of wisdom. "Travel by wagon, now, that doesn't leave you so wrung out. But the rails drain you." She stirred whatever was in her pot again, then lifted her spoon to take a quick taste, and I saw lumps of porridge sticking to its sides. "Sit you down, now, and I'll dish up some breakfast."

I obeyed — a little too quickly, perhaps, but the appetite that had deserted me the night before had come rushing back with the sunrise. The porridge, for which I usually have no taste, smelled delectable.

Mrs. Grier and I were not in a great state of comfort with each other at first. Our conversation came in fits and starts, punctuated by long silences and polite, vague smiles. I was still smarting over my awkwardness of the night before, and she, I believe, felt the unease that any housewife feels when a strange female intrudes on her territory. It wasn't until I complimented the magnificent dahlias in the front yard that Mrs. Grier really became animated. Flowers, it seems, are her passion, and she has nursed those dahlias as fervently as Miss Nightingale might a soldier. She let her tea grow cold beside her as she spoke, telling me all about how difficult it had been to track down the seeds for that particular species, how often they needed to be watered and the quality of soil they preferred, the prizes she had won for them in last year's fair, and so on.

Although I love wild things of all descriptions, I am cursed with the blackest of thumbs. The only successful interactions I have with flowers are in their natural environment, observed and unmolested. But I have boarded with more than one gardening enthusiast in my time, and so I knew at what points in Mrs. Grier's impassioned monologue to nod, to raise my eyebrows, to exclaim "is that so!" in tones of barely suppressed admiration. The conversation was so slanted in one direction that the cat — whose name, I deduced from Mrs. Grier's affectionate asides to it, is Cat — eventually came out from beneath the stove to sit upon the braided rug before it, though not without bestowing upon me a hard, suspicious glare. By the time Mr. Grier came in from outside, bringing a sticky gust of August air with him and soaking through with sweat, his wife and I were chatting with relative ease.

"I see you girls are getting on well," he said, sounding genuinely pleased. "Now, Miss Byrd, I was wondering if you'd like to come for a ride with me once you're through with breakfast? I have a few errands to run, and I thought maybe you might want to see the town. Meet some folks, like, before school gets into session."

Truly, in that heat I had no desire to see the town at all — or to do much of anything besides lie motionless on my little bed and nap away the morning. But Mr. Grier's expression was so eager, his voice so full of expectation, that I hated to disappoint him.

"Certainly," I replied, hoping I sounded more enthusiastic than I felt. "Just let me help Mrs. Grier with these dishes first, and then we shall see the sights."

And see the sights we did! For the next few days, life was a whirlwind of strange faces, strange names, strange houses where I sat and drank cup after cup of tea with beaming mothers, their stoic, docile husbands, and too many shouting, jumping children to name. I met the Perleys, the Agnews, the Woodrows; the Castles, the Thatchers, the Brewers; the Morices, the Barres, the Bensons. Family after family, large and small, all of them eager to meet the new teacher, touted as coming from "a big town" far away. There was, I perceived, a certain defensive edge to their reception of me, as though they expected me to turn my nose up at their lives and their children. I tried to disabuse them of this notion by playing up my own humble origins — a quiet childhood in a small town, a teacher's college education, a career confined to little schools in little places. I hope it set them at their ease, though I suppose only time will tell.

Of all the people I met during our rounds of Lowry Bridge, the one I liked the most was Mrs. MacPherson, the minister's wife. The minister himself I did not care for — a dull old man with a flat voice and hair sprouting liberally from his nostrils and ears, though not his crown — but his wife is a laughing, golden thing, all pepper and salt. She looks half his age, and when I sat with them in the manse sitting room, watching him smile vaguely at the little jokes she made and splash too much milk into his tea, I could not help but wonder what it was that drew her to him. Seeing the two of them together was like watching gay young Spring dance with grim and dour Winter.

We went to the other side of the river this morning for the Sunday service. The church is white with a delicate spire, perched on top of a little hill like a swan on a nest. Reverend MacPherson was, alas, just as dull in the pulpit as I had feared he would be — many dire warnings of hellfire and damnation, but no mention of grace or glory. Mrs. MacPherson, however, was a regular genius on the organ, playing even the most solemn hymns with admirable gusto. I wanted to speak to her after the sermon, but she was nowhere to be found. She had adjourned to teach the Sunday school, I was told when I asked after her, taking most of my soon-to-be-students with her.

"You'll want to see the schoolhouse soon, I expect," Mr. Grier said as we drove home from the service. We had lingered afterwards, and the roads were clear, all the dust of the wagons that had left before us settled back onto the road. "To set everything in order."

I agreed that I would, but in truth the thought made my heart sink a little. The last few days have been busy enough that I have been able to forget that soon I will be back in front of a classroom, staring into a sea of unfamiliar eyes. I became a teacher because, as a woman of gentle breeding, with no romantic prospects and too much fondness for books, it was the only respectable way for me to leave my father's house. The profession itself I find, at best, tolerable. In consequence, the rest of my life is likely to be, at best, tolerable.

That gloomy thought took hold of me as we drove down the road from the church, winding back into the trees that clustered around the river, and one of my black moods descended with the speed and force of a summer storm. I sat silently in Mr. Grier's buggy, letting myself be tossed to and fro by the motion of the wheels, seeing nothing ahead but a long, grim stretch of first days. Years of them, decades of them, until I eventually became too old and feeble to teach in even the smallest country schools. And then . . . what?

Now, back in my little room with my quilt pulled around me and Cat purring warm as a gin-jar on my feet — she has apparently decided that I am not an evil interloper, but just another piece of human furniture — I can feel my despondency abating. My window is open, and a little breeze tugs playfully at the curtains, carrying with it the distant sound of laughing foxes. They are alive, and so am I, and that, at least, is cause for hope.

"Happiness is an act of will." This was a pet phrase of Father's, one he especially liked to use when Florrie and I were sulking over some childish injustice. "If you are unhappy, it is no one's fault but your own."

Very well, then. I shall try to find some little bit of happiness here. It is not impossible, surely!

August 26, 1901

This afternoon I was finally able to do a bit of traipsing about in the woods. Mrs. Grier looked at me somewhat askance when I told her that I was going for a walk. She would not let me leave before wrapping a few thick slices of buttered bread in a clean handkerchief for me to take as a luncheon.

"I know you mightn't want to eat, it being so hot," she said, "but you bring that anyway, Miss Byrd. I won't have you starving to death before you start the term."

Hot it was, the air thick and wet as billowing steam, but I found myself feeling curiously invigorated as I made my way up the road and across the bridge, munching dutifully on bread and butter. I brought my pressing-book with me, as well a few specimen jars, which clinked and plinked in my leather satchel like music. The sound recalled happy memories of Florrie and I running about as children, armed with empty jam jars that we might use to trap any interesting plants or insects we came across. One day I used such a jar to catch a cricket at the zenith of its leap from a blade of wild wheat, and I remember how my sister beamed as I handed it to her, the little creature scrabbling frantically at the glass with its thin black legs.

I did not attempt to catch any insects today. Keeping to the road that winds throughout Lowry Bridge, I looked for any interesting flora that I could pluck and keep, darting now and then into the treeline to snatch up a promising shoot or flower. I grew bolder in these sojourns as the day wore on, wandering farther and farther into the trees in search of more enticing patches of green. It was not long before I had left the road behind entirely, forsaking the path of prim, bare dirt for the lush excess of the woods.

There is a hush I always feel when I wander by myself through wild places. It is not true quiet — the woods are always alive with the clicks and buzzes of any natural system, the sounds of thousands of creatures living and dying in close quarters. But beneath these noises there is a sort of verdant silence, a stillness so overpowering it steals the very air from my lungs. I found myself breathing with my mouth open as I walked, devouring the bouquet of odours proffered to me by nature: sharp pine sap, the drowsy scent of wildflowers, the warm rot of last autumn's dead leaves. The air was thick with bird calls; I could hear the cheerful whistle of a chickadee, the distant scolding of a family of blue jays, and, once, so close it made me jump, the harsh cry of a young crow. Beneath my feet I trampled bracken ferns, broom moss, catbrier, baneberry, starflower — names that sounded like nothing so much as ingredients in some fantastic fairy-potion. The sunlight trickling down through the canopy overhead seemed almost green by the time it reached me, strained through the gauze of a dozen different kinds of tree — black spruce, balsam fir, red maple. I knew the scientific names for all of them once, but the only one I could remember just then was *Betula papyrifera*, white birch. Florrie had read it in a book as a girl and laughed, saying that it sounded like the name of an opera singer.

"There are two Gods," she'd told me once, sotto voce in case our father heard her uttering such an impious thought. "There is the God of inside — the God of churches and prayer meetings and all that — and then there is the God of outside, the God that lives in the trees and in the dirt. And the insects, and the birds, and the things that eat them too."

And even though I had protested that surely there was one God only, sovereign over church and nature both, Florrie would not be swayed. If the same God was in charge, she argued, why did *inside* and *outside* seem so at odds? Why would we leave a sermon with our limbs heavy and our eyes drooping, but come in from a day in the woods humming with life?

I was still smiling at this memory when I caught a glimpse of something pale lying between the roots of a birch tree, cradled between twining white radicles. Thinking it might be some type of mushroom, I drew closer and knelt to take a closer look. A mushroom is always a useful thing to have on hand in a class-room, especially when contending with younger children. The fungal kingdom draws their attention, perhaps because there is a hint of the slimy and unspeakable about it.

My fingertips grazed its surface and found it smooth and hard to the touch. Not a mushroom, then. Nor was it a stone, for the thing felt fragile as an eggshell. I brushed dirt and dead leaves aside with one hand, uncovering more of it, then inhaled sharply as I realized what I had found. It was a tiny skull, rounded at one end and tapered at the other, boasting enormous empty sockets. An owl, not an adult, but an owlet, a nestling, fallen from its home while Mother went a-hunting and left to die on the forest floor.

I had to have it, of course. I could just picture it nestled on a bed of moss in one of my jars, glowing in the afternoon sun.

A gem cutter could not have handled a diamond so gently as I did that precious object, lifting it from the ground using only two careful fingers. It had a brownish cast, like ivory, and the thin arches of bone between the eyes made it look like the most delicate of carved trinkets, a souvenir from a distant land. All its flesh and feathers had been eaten away, leaving it bare. The wicked curve of its beak pricked into my palm.

"My goodness," I murmured. There is something curiously attractive about bones, and bird bones have a particular charm, being so light and little. "What a pretty thing."

Florrie would have loved it. I could just see her eyes lighting upon it, her pencil flying to produce a carefully rendered sketch of its shadows and recesses.

I stood, reaching into my satchel for a jar; and that was when I heard the noise. *Crack. Crack. Crack.* It sounded like a series of brittle twigs snapping in half under the pressure of a foot.

Slowly, slowly I turned, making sure to tuck the owlet skull safely inside my palm. Squinting through the greenish dim of the trees, I looked for any sign of moving, breathing life. There was nothing — just spruce after fir after maple after pine. The road, I realized, was nowhere to be seen. All around me was untouched forest, unbroken scrub. Even the trail I had left behind me seemed to have been swallowed in the thick of the woods, as though I had been picked up and dropped there by some unseen hand. How, I wondered, had such a thing occurred?

"Hello?" I whispered, my voice unnaturally small in the quiet beneath the trees. It occurred to me that the sound could have come from a bear, wandering through the woods in search of an evening meal, and I had to swallow several times in succession against the rising panic in my throat. *Were* there bears in Lowry Bridge? "Is anyone there?"

Nothing, just green and brown and grey as far as the eye could see. But . . . was there something rustling in the bracken? Could I hear the sly, slow movement of limbs somewhere beyond the edge of my field of vision?

No sudden movements, I reminded myself, no gestures that could give any wild creature cause for alarm.

Crack. Crack. Crack. I whirled and stared wildly about, all my care abandoned. Trees, trees, nothing but trees and ferns and thick layers of rotting mast, and no sign of any thing that could create the noise I had just heard. And then it came a third time, closer, louder: *crack, crack, crack.*

And then I felt it: *something behind me.* Breath upon my neck, coaxing up the little hairs until they stood on end. Eyes burning into the back of my head.

If I turned, I knew I would see it, but I could not make myself do it, could not force my body out of the fearful stupor that held my feet in place as though roots had burst from them to tether me to the dirt.

The birds were no longer singing. Every creature in the woods seemed to be holding its breath, watching, waiting.

It was going to touch me.

"Who are you?"

The voice came not from behind me, but to my right. It startled me so terribly that I couldn't help but shriek a little as I spun around.

Standing only a few feet away from me was a girl — a most unusual-looking girl. She had the long, coltish look of a child on the verge of adolescence, with thick, coarse hair that was probably gold in sunlight, but in the shadow of the woods was the murky brown of river water. Her jaw was sharp, her chin roundly stubborn, her mouth marked by a deep dip above the upper lip. The calico dress she wore was neatly patched, and short enough that her skinny legs looked longer beneath it than they otherwise might; her feet were bare and exceedingly dirty, as were her face and hands. Her eyes met mine boldly, with no sign of the reticence so common to girls of that age. They were no particular colour.

"You frightened me," I gasped, pressing a hand to my chest. My heart galloped merrily along beneath the skin. I felt foolish, the way I'd always felt as a girl when Florrie would creep up behind me and spook me with a loud noise or a tug on my hair. *Nervous, nervous,* she would say, and then pat my cheek to show she meant no harm. "I thought I was alone."

The girl seemed unimpressed by this statement. Her head tilted slightly to the side as she regarded me. "You're never alone out here. Are you lost?"

I was tempted to deny it in hopes of preserving some semblance of dignity but knew that would be foolish. "I'm afraid so," I replied. "I was looking for things to put in my specimen jars and wandered away from the road. Quite far away, it seems."

The girl made a dismissive little noise in the back of her throat. "As soon as I saw you wandering around," she said, "I knew you probably didn't know where you was. What's that in your hand?"

I opened my fingers and showed her the skull. A part of me feared that the girl would find it as enchanting as I had and try to take it, but I needn't have worried; she looked at it with blank disinterest.

"It's just a bit of old bone," she said. "What did you want that for?"

"So I can show it to my students," I replied, closing my fist. Her lack of enthusiasm was rather galling. "I'm the new teacher — your teacher, if you are as young as you look. Miss Byrd."

I extended my empty hand for her to shake, but the girl did not take it. Instead, she looked up at me through a thick fringe of dark lashes and said:

"It's this way to the school. You can get back to the road from there."

And with that she started walking, going at a clipping pace that soon left me breathless with the effort to keep up. Chest heaving, shirtwaist soaked through with perspiration, I scrambled after her up a steep embankment, wading through thick underbrush and weaving through stands of spruce and fir. I felt the whispery tickle of spiders racing across my neck but could not stop to brush them off. The girl did not bother to look over her shoulder and check that I was still behind her, and I found myself resenting the quick patter of her feet in the dirt, the ease with which she dodged outstretched branches and hopped over fallen logs, nimble as a goat.

"Could you please slow down?" I gasped at one point, but she spared me only a single disdainful glance over her shoulder; if anything, her pace quickened. There was no breath left in me to protest or insist. All I could do was stumble after her, panting like a she-dog.

The woods ended so suddenly that I scarcely realized the girl had stopped until I nearly ran into her. She darted out of my way with a curious kind of ducking grace.

"This is it," she told me, and nodded at the land before us. A clearing, thick with weeds and wild grasses, and there, at the heart of it, the school.

It was the smallest I'd ever seen, a squat little building whose siding and shingles had faded to a mossy grey. The windows were soft with dust, the roof spotted with swallows' nests. As I drew closer, I saw that the stovepipe poking its way toward the sky was blackened with soot, so dirty I was sure it had not been swept out for months. The only lick of colour on the whole thing was the door, which was blue — or had been, before time and weather had peeled off the paint in irregular patches, leaving bare wood in its wake.

The sight of it ought to have dismayed me — surely would have dismayed any other teacher, used to posts well-kept and -ordered — but I found myself charmed instead. The school-house did not look as though it had been built at all. Instead, it looked natural, a sprout that had matured not into a fern or a tree but a building. The wildflowers and long grasses growing up around it, nearly obscuring the wooden steps, only added to this impression. It was difficult to tell where the woods and meadow ended, where the walls and doors began. It was like the girl herself, a wild thing.

"I love it." I hadn't intended to say it aloud but did not regret the words when they left my mouth. I did love it — or at least the sight of it, nested comfortably in flora, drowsy and warm in the afternoon sunshine. Clearing my throat, I turned back to the girl. "Thank you for your help. I can't imagine how I became so turned around."

The girl shrugged. "It's a good thing I found you," she replied. A strange way to say "you're welcome!"

"I've given you my name," I said, stung by her dismissive tone. Though I am not of that class of teachers that thinks children must grovel before any adult they meet, it rankled to be spoken to with such evident disdain. "It would be good manners for you to give me yours. I would like to know what to call my rescuer."

A wry little smile twisted the girl's mouth. The smile had a curious effect on the rest of her face: while most children's smiles make them appear younger, hers made her strangely adult, a woman sewn into the skin of a girl.

"Muriel," she said. "Muriel Melville. I live just up there." She pointed down the path that led away from the schoolhouse, and I saw a rough little trail branching off it and winding away into the trees. "At the end of the Melville Road."

"Road" was something of an exaggeration. The trail looked like it would not fit two men walking abreast.

"Hello, Muriel." I extended my hand again. This time the girl took it, though without enthusiasm. I felt the scratch of a hangnail on her thumb. "I hope I shall see you again soon. You do go to school, don't you?"

"Sometimes," she replied, with another of those insolent shrugs. "When my old dad don't need me at home. Sometimes he wants me in the house, taking care of him, not wasting time in school."

"Your father doesn't want you to be uneducated, surely?"

The girl did not respond to this question, but that wry smile returned, and I was suddenly certain that I was being mocked. Why or how I did not know — even as I write this, I do not know — but the feeling was so strong that I found my hands clenching defensively into fists. Surprised by the force of my reaction, I deliberately relaxed my fingers, one by one, before I crushed the owlet skull.

"Maybe," Muriel said finally, with the air of someone making a great concession. "I'll see if he'll let me come, anyhow." And with that she turned and started running toward the path she had called Melville Road, moving with the same wild grace as she had in the woods, until she disappeared into the trees.

Mrs. Grier exclaimed over the mud on my skirt and the bits of moss in my hair when I returned. Nothing would do but that I would submit to a bath after supper and scrub every last particle of dirt from my body, and so I did, folding myself awkwardly into the little tin tub in the kitchen and soaking in lukewarm water for the better part of an hour. I found a spider floating in the water afterwards, its spindly legs curled tight against its body. I wonder if it fell from the ceiling while I bathed, or if it had the misfortune to attach itself to me in the woods. Cat remained on her mat by the stove through the ordeal, looking askance at this foolish creature voluntarily entering the water.

The owlet skull I placed safely in a specimen jar on my walk home from the schoolhouse. It is on my washstand now, gleaming in the candlelight, little shadows dancing underneath its empty eyes. No painted shepherdess or silver jewel box could please me more.

August 28, 1901

Mrs. Grier and I went up to the schoolhouse this morning to give it a good cleaning before class comes in again. I had meant to go alone, but Mrs. Grier would not hear of it.

"More hands make less work," she said, in her brisk little bird-voice. "That school has been empty since April, and I imagine the dust is inches thick on everything."

Perhaps the dust was not inches thick, but it was enough to make me sneeze heartily when I opened the door! The two of us set to our work with a will, sweeping out cobwebs from the ceiling corners and blacking the stove until it shined. Together we scrubbed the two rows of desks until only the most stubborn epithets remained, cleared the empty swallows' nests from the roof, pulled the weeds that choked the path and wiped both the schoolhouse windows clean with vinegar. I brought my map of the world to hang upon the wall, which Mrs. Grier regarded with interest, and my specimen jars to arrange at the edge of my desk, which she regarded with confusion (and, in the case of the owlet skull, not a little horror). When I tried to explain their purpose, her confusion only deepened.

"But why do you want to teach them those things?" she asked finally, after I had regaled her with tales of introducing my former students to the wonders of the natural world. "What use is it?"

The question is one that has recurred time and time again since the first time I picked up a pinecone on a walk as a tot. Pleased by its sturdy symmetry, I brought it home to examine it better, only to be soundly chastised by Father for filling his house with rubbish.

"But I wanted to look at it, Father," I had protested. I was very young indeed then; in a few more years, I would learn that protesting my father's will led only to a sound thrashing.

He had looked down his nose at me and replied: "To look at it! What on Earth is there to *see*?"

His voice rang in my ears as I said, "There is no end to the lessons that children may learn from the world around them, Mrs. Grier, and while those lessons may not be as immediately useful as arithmetic or spelling, they are beneficial nonetheless. A flower or a singing bird may teach them as much about the universe as a history book."

Mrs. Grier nodded at that, but uncertainly, as though she did not find my answer altogether satisfactory. I could scarcely blame her; I do not find it satisfactory myself, although it is the answer I always give when asked. The shameful truth of the matter is that my pedagogical habits are purely selfish. I teach natural history because I find it fascinating, and if I did not have something interesting to teach, I would go mad.

While we worked, I asked her about the Melville family, taking care not to mention my encounter with Muriel the day before.

"The Melvilles?" Mrs. Grier sounded greatly surprised. She was scrubbing the teacher's desk at that point, her hands with their rags moving so fast they nearly blurred. "Why, yes, they've been out there in the woods for years. A big clan in a little yellow house. Too little, really, for the number of 'em. Old Ed Melville rules the roost out there. He's got one bairn still young enough for schooling, Muriel. You'll see her when you start teaching — sometimes, anyway. They aren't much for education, that family."

I gathered from her tone that she did not quite approve of the Melvilles. They were, of course, from "the other side" of the bridge — the side where, her husband had said, people "ain't quite like us."

"How many of them are there?" I asked.

"Oh, heaven knows. Ed Melville's been married three times now, had children with each wife: the big boys by the first two, and poor Muriel by the last. His boys are almost all gone now. Gone West to chase gold, or else to sea."

I wondered what it was about the child that earned her the moniker "poor Muriel." Perhaps being the only girl in a sea of boys was enough to do it. "You said he had three wives," I said. "What happened to them?"

On bright days, there are times when a cloud passes so quickly across the sun that you can register it only as a blink of darkness, a momentary pause of light. Something like that happened to Mrs. Grier in that moment, her little bird's face crossed by a shadow so brief I could almost think it imaginary. "Died," she said. "They were young things, and pretty — Ed Melville has an eye for a pretty girl. But he can't seem to make them last."

And before me, between one breath and the next, was Florrie, laid out in her best dress, her pale hands folded on top of each other, a bruise visible at her temple beneath a whorl of hair.

Her husband stood over her, one white-knuckled hand gripping the edge of her casket. I looked away, blinking furiously, and applied myself to wiping the very real, very solid blackboard in front of me.

I cannot think about her too much. I cannot think about any of it too much.

In lieu of thought, I let myself be carried away by the mindless drudgery of women's work. The familiar motions of setting a school in order distracted me, and by the time Mrs. Grier and I crossed back over the bridge, I was, if not actually soothed, at least too sore and tired to think. I wanted nothing more than a meal, a cup of tea, and a good, sound sleep.

I have not yet described the bridge that gives this little town its name. One comes upon it suddenly, after a sharp bend in the path suddenly opens onto the wide stretch of the Slade River. It is a beam bridge of greying cedar, bordered on either side by cross rails. Underfoot, its timbers feel strangely fragile, as though any moment the wood will splinter and give way. I have been assured that the bridge has stood without incident for nearly a century, though that is hardly a comfort. All I can imagine is the rot creeping into the beams, year after year.

As Mrs. Grier and I crossed the bridge, I paused by the rails, looking from one side to the next. To my left, the river curved broadly away from the spruce woods into lush green farmland. I could see a hint of rolling fields, neat orchards, the barest gleam of a little white house in the distance. To my right, the spruces clustered close and thick, their shadows darkening the surface of the water. Just visible as the river bent again was an old grey watermill, lurking behind the trees. In the distance, the wooded hills rose to kiss the sky, the green of their leaves almost black in the fading light.

I gazed at the trees that bordered the northeast end of the bridge, the deep, greenish gloom of the woods beyond that seemed to swallow the road. For a moment I thought I saw something there: some flicker, some movement, something staring from the shadow of the trees. It tugged at the corner of my eye, needy as a child, but when I turned to look properly, there was nothing. Perhaps it was a deer, come to drink at the river, or a hare.

September 2, 1901

$\mathcal{I}$ woke early this morning, as I always do on the first day of school—as many of my pupils must do, too, come to think of it. The dawn had barely begun to break, and the sky outside my window was that hazy, delicate grey so particular to early autumn mornings. I lay in bed for as long as I could stomach it, watching the colour change to the faintest blushing periwinkle. It wasn't until I heard Mrs. Grier stirring in the bedroom across the hall that I finally forced myself to rise.

I wish that it were proper for teachers to wear their Sunday best to school. My nicest dress is a grey poplin, patterned with little white feathers and trimmed with edging lace; wearing it makes me feel like less of a dowdy spinster than the plain white shirtwaists and dark skirts that are my teacher's uniform. Still, I dressed neatly, and managed to convince my thick, stubborn hair to behave itself instead of sticking out at all angles in a colourless mass. By the time I came downstairs for breakfast I felt, if not actually handsome, at least presentable. Mrs. Grier seemed to agree — when I appeared in the kitchen, still a little blurry about the eyes, she looked at me with an approving smile.

"My goodness, Miss Byrd," she said, "don't you look fine this morning!"

"Very fine," Mr. Grier hastily agreed after a sharp look from his wife. I very much doubt that he noticed a difference, but I felt myself blush anyway. Of the two of us, Florrie was always "the pretty one," with her curls and quick, dimpled smile, while I was "the clever one" — a kinder way to say plain, bookish, not likely to be married. Compliments to my vanity are not things to which I am accustomed.

I ate my breakfast without tasting it. My stomach surged up and down with every breath I took; the palms of my hands were slick. I am often nervous at the start of a term, but never had I been so acutely disquieted. It has only been a few months since my disastrous year at Willoughby, and yet I felt as though I had never stood in front of a classroom before. I imagined a dozen pairs of little eyes on me, a dozen pairs of sticky hands fidgeting and drumming on desktops, and my skin fairly began to crawl.

Mr. Grier offered to drive me over the bridge, and so gallant was the offer that I felt as if I could not in good conscience refuse. We sat together in the buggy, my hands folded tightly in my lap to keep them from trembling. I saw Mr. Grier's eyes flick once or twice from the road to my face. For the longer part of the journey, he said nothing, but as we finally pulled up to the schoolhouse, grey and strange in the virgin sun, he turned to me.

"It's always like this the first morning," he said. "Every teacher Mrs. Grier and I have taken in, they're always riled as a cat on the first day. But it gets better, Miss Byrd. Every day it gets better. You just mind that."

His round, ruddy face looked straight into mine for a long moment. His eyes, I have noticed, are greener than they are blue, and they were particularly green that morning, the pale gold of the early sun settling in the irises. There was something lying beneath his words, a current of understanding that made me think that perhaps he knew my agitation came not only from it being the first day of school. I wondered, again, how much he had been told about my year in Willoughby. What did he know? What had my father said?

The half hour or so before my students arrived was agony. I paced the room, setting the things on my desk at different angles, wiping imaginary smudges on the glass, constantly smoothing my skirt and hair. But as soon as the door opened and the first little head poked inside, I found myself overtaken by another version of myself, a calmer, more competent Ada Byrd. This is how it goes, I find, every year — teaching seems an impossible task, too great a challenge for any mortal woman to undertake, until my students are before me. At that point my body takes charge, pushing my frantic mind behind it. I speak in my teacher's voice, walk my teacher's walk, make my teacher's gestures, and altogether behave differently than I did only moments before. I imagine a musician might feel this way, taking up an instrument to play in front of a crowd: one moment all shivers and nerves, the next in utter control of himself.

The day passed by in a blur. Fourteen students, ranging from fifteen years of age to a tot of five. Eleven different family names, although I am sure that in this small town most of those names are interrelated through marriage and blood. An even split between girls and boys, with most of the girls on the older side, most of the boys on the younger.

We did no real work this morning. Instead, I spent my time assessing each child to determine his level of competency. The results, unsurprisingly, were mixed. Most of them can read at least a little, excepting the very youngest, but the older children are not as easy with letters as they ought to be, and their spelling is atrocious across the board. Mathematics seem to be well understood by all students — a relief to me, as they are certainly not *my* strong suit — and their knowledge of geography is passable, although one little boy confidently exclaimed that the country I'd indicated on the map with my pointer was Scotland when, in fact, it was Madagascar. They were able to tell me who Napoleon was but had never heard of William of Orange, and their understanding of the natural world was very thin indeed. When I held up a specimen jar that contained a little trimming of glittering wood-moss and asked the children what it was, I was met with blank and incurious stares.

The thought of simply giving up all other subjects and concentrating solely on natural history is tempting. There is so much space in those childish heads that I long to fill with all the things I myself like best. But the school board wishes for them to know about geometry and the imports of Portugal and all manner of practical, uninteresting things, and so they shall.

It wasn't until the last child walked out the door at the end of the afternoon that I began to relax back into myself, prim Miss Byrd giving way once more to Ada Elizabeth. I sat behind my wide teacher's desk, looking down into the pits and gashes in its wooden surface, watching dust motes drift through the golden light. I felt, as I always do after a first day, wrung out as an old rag but also curiously satisfied. I had made it through the day, after all. That meant I could make it through those that followed.

Slowly, I gathered my books up in a pile, grunting a little at the weight. These were my own books, my Bible and my dictionary, the works of Wallace and Wood and Mrs. Brightwen and Thoreau, my Shakespeare set and a few slim storybooks to give as prizes to promising students, and when I opened the lid of my desk to put them away, I realized that there were books inside of it as well, a little stack of them that Mrs. Grier and I had somehow missed when we cleaned the schoolhouse.

I picked them up one by one, marvelling at this unexpected treasure. They were volumes of poetry, yellow-leafed and much spattered with stains. Keats, Wordsworth, Tennyson, Blake, all the old, familiar names from my days at the teacher's college. The books must have belonged to my predecessor, the woman who left so suddenly to tend to her sick mother. Had she been using these poets to teach the children of Lowry Bridge? Or was she one of those horridly romantic spinsters, spending her waking hours dreaming of the Ancient Mariner and the Lady of Shalott? When I try to picture her, I imagine a woman with that dried-out, greyish look so particular to old maids, prim and starched as a fresh shirtwaist, but I imagine as well a pair of large, wet eyes, moonstruck and wistful, suitable to a woman enamored of verse.

That unknown woman returned to my mind again and again as I set the schoolhouse in order, swept and tidied, prepared lesson plans for the following day, but thoughts of her flew from my mind as I locked the door behind me and set off home, my satchel slung carelessly over my shoulder. There was a smell in the air that thrilled me, a crisp, sweet scent of leaves about to turn and apples about to ripen on their branches. The long walk back over to the "right side" of the bridge felt like no long walk at all.

When I returned to the Griers' house, I found myself greeted with a marvellous supper, as well as a special treat: a sticky bread pudding, golden-brown and speckled with plump black sultanas.

"In honour of your first day, Miss Byrd," Mrs. Grier said, and doled me out a larger portion than I thought possible to eat. And yet, somehow, I managed it. Such rich, sweet foods have been hard to come by these past few months. Father never grew out of the belief that strong flavours will tempt a body to sin, and his table boasted no food more savoury than boiled mutton.

The clock downstairs just chimed the hour — it is nearly midnight! I must put this book away and get some sleep if I mean to go on as I have started.

September 10, 1901

 *M*y students have begun to be used to me, and I to them. The odd, stilted quality that marked my first week in the schoolhouse has all but dissipated, leaving us in a much friendlier state. True, every now and again I hear complaints that the way *I* do things is not the way Miss Webster did things, but I simply respond that I am *not* Miss Webster, and that the plaintiff must now mind *me*.

Miss Webster, I gather, is my predecessor, the poetry enthusiast. I have not been able to gather much intelligence vis-à-vis this lady from my students, although I have discovered that she was extremely lax in the areas of spelling and grammar. Consequently, I have been leaning on these subjects heavily, much to the children's dismay.

All schoolrooms have hierarchies, and this one is no different. The roost is ruled by a trio of young ladies: Effie Agnew, who is fifteen, and Anna Carlisle and Clara Brewer, both fourteen. Effie is the undisputed leader of the three, being not only the oldest and prettiest, with her blue eyes and smoke-brown curls, but the one with the sharpest tongue. The other two hang on her every word, particularly Clara, who seems to be rather looked down upon by her schoolmates. (The Brewers, I understand, are sniffed at throughout Lowry Bridge, being from the "wrong" side.) Of the three, Anna has the best head on her shoulders, though the disdainful attitude of her chums toward any kind of schoolwork seems to infect her from time to time. If I can break her of that, I may recommend that she go on to the high school in Portsmouth. Twelve-year-old Caroline Mason acts as a sort of tagalong and maid-of-all-work to these three. She is a thin, freckled little thing who, judging by her prematurely long skirts, is eager to be thought of as a young lady. She has a beau of sorts in thirteen-year-old Arthur Benson, the oldest boy in the school. He dotes on Caroline and is forever giving her little gifts of pencils and sweets and chews of gum.

Arthur is doted on in turn by eleven-year-old George Perley, a boy whose parents have clearly spoiled him a little too much; he has already thrown a temper tantrum over being told to finish his arithmetic. George has a sort of playmate in Winifred Benson, Arthur's nine-year-old sister, a wild, tomboyish creature who likes to join in with whatever games the boys are playing, rather than look to her fellow girls for company. Paul Miller is also nine, a skinny, surly boy whose ragged clothes speak to his homestead on this side of the Slade River. Eugene Castle is a delicate child and newly eight, prone to fits of asthma and nerves. He is advanced for his age, and I have already started him on the Fifth Reader.

Clarence Stewart and Matthew Perley are seven and six, respectively, and the best of friends. Matthew is George's brother, and Clarence some kind of Perley cousin; apparently the two of them have been thick as thieves since infancy, and rarely do without one another in the schoolyard. Matthew shows a few of the spoiled tendencies of his brother, but Clarence is sweet as a peach, and his influence tempers that Perley piggishness nicely. Peter Miller, the younger brother of Paul, is seven as well, and as cheerful as his older sibling is cross. He was pleased to tell me that he knew how to write his name, although when he demonstrated this ability on his slate, his surname was missing an *L*. The youngest of all, little Lillian Morice, is only five, a chubby, curly-headed thing whose round cheeks I long to pinch. She has some trouble with her *r*'s and pronounces my last name as "Buwd." The other children seem to feel a certain responsibility toward Lillian, and I have seen several of them help her with her lessons, unprompted. Her most valiant protector, oddly enough, is Winifred Benson, who hovers over the child with all the vigilance of a hen watching her chick. A curious thing to see in a girl so boyish and gruff — but then, I suppose the fiercest tigers make the best mothers.

I have said nothing about the place of Muriel Melville in this little feudal system. That is because, as far as I can tell, she *has* no place. At recess and lunch, she makes no attempt to consort with the other children; she shows no interest in the games the other girls play in their corner of the yard, skipping rope and scratching tic tac toe grids into the dirt, nor in the wilder, rougher games the boys (and Winifred) play in theirs. Likewise, the others avoid her. They do not approach her to take part in their games, or share their secrets, or help with schoolwork. Even her seatmate Caroline Mason, with whom she shares a copy of the Sixth Reader, does not speak to her.

The girl is a mystery that I have not yet solved, but the rest of my pupils are easy enough. George throws tantrums over his sums, but he is eager and engaged when any other subject comes up. Caroline is a hopeless speller, but able to memorize Bible verses and passages of prose in a blink. Clarence's penmanship is disgraceful, but he has a beautiful voice both when singing and when reading. They are good children. I hope that I may do right by them.

A curious thing happened last Sunday while the Griers and I were in church. It was a dreadfully warm day, and the prickling of sweat in my hair and down my spine made me fretful and annoyed. My mind wandered from the sermon, and my eyes wandered from the pulpit; I let them travel around the church, lighting on first one face, then another, until they landed on a person I had never seen before. A woman, not young, perhaps fifty or so, sitting alone in the pew directly opposite our own.

She was dressed very smartly in a dark blue dress and a hat frothy with feathers and silk flowers. I could not catch a glimpse of her face at first, only her dark hair, shot through with glittering threads of silver. But then she turned her head slightly, and I could see her properly.

Hers was a face one would not call beautiful, nor even pretty; it was pallid, with too firm a jaw and too thin a mouth. But she had a lovely nose, strong and Grecian, and the pale eyes that shone above it were the exact shade of a winter morning sky. They wandered the room, flitting from pew to pulpit and back again, until suddenly they lit upon me. I was too startled to look away and pretend that I had not been staring. We sat, our gazes locked across the room, for some long, slow minutes. I felt — oh, how strange it was! — somehow *vulnerable* under that pale and eerie stare, not a woman meeting another woman's gaze but a rabbit locking eyes with a circling hawk.

Then that thin mouth smiled, and suddenly I could look away.

"Who was that woman in the pew across from us?" I asked that evening at supper. It was a ham, cured with honey, and potatoes swimming in butter. I am thankful that Mrs. Grier knows how to keep a table; I have boarded with many a family whose pantries leave far more to be desired.

The Griers shared one of their married looks, speaking silently across the table with their eyes.

"That's Mrs. John Kinsley," Mr. Grier said at last. His voice, I thought, seemed unusually devoid of inflection. "The Widow Kinsley, as she's known."

"She hasn't been to church before, has she? I haven't seen her before."

"Well now, that may be so." I saw Mr. Grier sneak another look across the table at his wife. Mrs. Grier was eating steadily, her face betraying not a single thing, but I saw the knuckles on her right hand grow pale, as though she gripped her fork too tightly. "She doesn't come regular. Hasn't since her husband died."

In a town like this, it is the mark of a respectable woman to be seen in church every Sunday (and at prayer meetings on Wednesday evenings, held in the parlour of the aggressively respectable Mrs. Elijah Castle, mother of Eugene and proud owner of the whitest curtains in Lowry Bridge). Was the Widow Kinsley not entirely respectable?

"Does she live very far?" was my next inquiry. Perhaps that was why she did not often come to church.

"Far enough." Mr. Grier shifted slightly in his seat. "Out past the Melville place, on the other side of the bridge."

The wrong side of the bridge. Was this enough to make Mrs. Kinsley disreputable? I recalled again the richness of her dress, the stylish hat she wore. From what I knew of the town, the families living on the other side of the bridge tended to be poor. Mrs. Kinsley did not fit the bill.

"What happened to—"

But the end of my sentence was swallowed by the noise Mrs. Grier made in setting her cutlery down and standing up, scraping the legs of her chair against the floor. For just a moment her expression was so fierce I thought — I honestly did! — that she was about to strike me.

But as soon as I had registered her expression, it disappeared as though it had never been. Her friendly little bird face looked just as it always had, and she asked if I wanted tea.

We did not return to the subject of Mrs. Kinsley for the rest of the evening, and our talk around the fire was more halting than usual. It was not until Mrs. Grier read aloud from *The Pilgrim's Progress* that we all began to relax, tension dissolving under the familiar rhythm of Christian's escape from the City of Destruction and journey to the Wicket Gate.

I wonder, still, at Mrs. Grier's reaction. Of course, it could be that she was simply displeased that her husband was speaking about another woman, and one without a husband at that, but she has never responded in such a way to Mr. Grier talking about any other woman in town, even the ones he describes approvingly as "very handsome." Why would this woman inspire such a brazen display of pique?

Truth be told, I do not know why I had such a strong reaction to the woman, myself. Something about those pale eyes caught me and would not let me go. I feel that she is looking at me still, her gaze somehow finding mine across the silver band of the river.

September 13, 1901

$\mathcal{I}$ have made a friend!

At least, I believe I have. It may be too soon to tell.

This afternoon, as I began my walk home from school, I took it into my head to take a slightly different path. The one I usually take is a straight line to the bridge, but at one point the road branches out, winding away from the river awhile before merging again with its brother and surging back down to the water. The air was so fresh and warm when I emerged from the schoolhouse that I felt it would be a shame not to dawdle a little, and so, when I reached the fork in the road, I turned left.

The road curved up around one farm and back down past another, eventually leading me past the church. There it sat, sunning itself in the mellow afternoon light like a great white pelican, its steeple pointing the way to the sun, and there, some ways behind it, lay the manse, a neat little clapboard house with a sensible grey roof. From the road I could see sober rows of shrubs and flowers planted in the front, all of them utterly sensible and utterly dull. I was about to walk by when a voice called out my name.

"Miss Byrd? Hello there!"

And down the path from the manse trotted Mrs. MacPherson, the minister's wife, wearing a worn cotton dress and a disastrous straw hat. Her hands, from a distance, looked as enormous as the paws of a bear. As she came closer, I realized that she was wearing gardening gloves, caked with black soil.

"I saw you passing from my garden," she said, sounding a little out of breath. "And I realized that we haven't had a chance to speak yet, not really, so I thought I might catch you as you went by." She extended a hand for me to shake that was still clad in its double swaddling of glove and dirt. I took it as lightly as I could, trying not to work the grime into my own skin. She must have noticed how gingerly I gripped her, for she looked down, saw her mistake, and laughed.

"What a mess I've made of you!" she cried. Fishing in the pocket of her apron, which had probably once been white, she pulled out a handkerchief and offered it to me. It was scarcely cleaner than her hand, but I accepted it gratefully. "Would you like to come in? I was about to put the kettle on."

A host of excuses rose to my tongue, all of them proper and true. I was expected at home; I had compositions to grade; I needed to get my mending done that night, before Mrs. Grier took the washing in. But Mrs. MacPherson looked so bright-eyed and hopeful, so delightfully ridiculous in her straw hat, that what came out instead was, "I would love to."

As we entered the manse, stepping carefully over the little gravel path bordered by prim little shrubs, I felt that shyness that had gripped me upon meeting Mrs. Grier raise its head once more. What a hideous trick this mind of mine plays on me! When I find a person hateful or tiresome, I can say anything I like, but whenever I meet a person who I think might be a friend, I clap shut as firmly as an oyster. I sat mutely on Mrs. MacPherson's uncomfortable armchair, only nodding when she asked if I took milk and sugar, and kept my eyes cast away from hers, taking in instead the poky little sitting room with its threadbare settee and wingback chairs, the old oak whatnot shelf with its array of porcelain knickknacks, the ugly green carpet strewn with gargantuan pink cabbage roses. (The carpet, Agatha told me later, was a wedding present from one of the Reverend's aunts, and she dared not give it away, for fear of causing offence.) It felt like the den of an elderly aunt, one that always manages to imply that you have grown fatter and uglier since last you met. There was nothing in that room that looked like Mrs. MacPherson, with one great exception. In a little pine cradle at the end of the settee, there was a baby sleeping soundly, its fat little face peeping out from beneath a yellow blanket. I did not notice the child at first, and when I did I audibly gasped.

"A baby!" I exclaimed — and really, was it any better than mute shyness, blurting out something so obvious? "Is it yours?"

Worse and worse! Mrs. MacPherson did not take offense but laughed again. It was a lovely laugh, lazy and warm.

"My little Douglas," she said, pouring the tea into two cups painted with pink roses. "Named for his grandfather."

"Will we wake him if we stay in here?"

"No fear of that!" She ducked down to give the little pink face a quick kiss on the cheek. The baby stirred but did not open his eyes. "I heard so many horrible stories of new mothers who can't sleep a wink for their babies fussing, but I am lucky. He sleeps through the night, and most of the day, as well. Not a peep will he make until he gets hungry, and then, what a peep it shall be! He has a powerful set of lungs on him for such a little lad."

"How old is he?"

"Five months, nearly to the day. And what a day *that* was." She shuddered a little, as though recalling the whole nasty business. "Nine months of crying, and sickness, and fainting every time I got up too quickly, and then, oh! Two days in bed, and so much blood, and fuss, and wet . . ." She trailed off, her eyes suddenly looking inwards at some horror at which I could only guess, a hot, dark land painted red and black. I flinched — I couldn't help it. My thoughts turned, as they always do, to Florrie. I saw her laid out once more, her quick, clever hands stiff and still, their knuckles bluish-grey, and then I saw her as she must have been at the moment of her death, her sheets soaked russet-brown, the room stinking of human waste and thwarted life. That hideous bruise on her temple, raw as fresh liver.

I shook myself a bit to dispel the image, and Mrs. MacPherson seemed to do the same. Her gaze returned to her son, and her smile returned, though less readily than before. "And then there he was," she said, "loud and pink as a posy, and so, you see, it was worth it."

Was she saying that for my benefit, I wondered, or her own?

"I remember my mother and I going to visit one of her friends," I said, "only two days after her youngest son was born. Her husband was a physician and delivered the boy himself; afterwards, he gave the order that the whole room must be kept dark, and that his wife mustn't read, or sew, or have much by way of conversation. He would not even let her sit up, for fear of disturbing her health. By the time we got there she was wild with boredom. When we came into the room, she caught at my mother's hand

and hissed, 'The curtains — the curtains, Elizabeth! Let some light into this dreadful room before I go mad!'"

She had said other, less delicate things as well, but I was reluctant to relay them to a minister's wife.

"Oh, how old-fashioned!" Mrs. MacPherson cried. "If anyone had suggested such a thing to me, I would have torn my hair out. Or theirs."

"Mrs. MacPherson," I said, "somehow I can easily imagine you doing just that."

She blushed a little, looking pleased. Beneath the rising pink I caught a glimpse of a faint, faded spatter of freckles. The sight of them filled me with sudden delight. Perhaps, as a child, she had been a tomboy, running through the grass with her sun-bonnet flying out behind her by its strings, and those freckles were the last sign of her misspent youth. "Agatha, please. I do hate being called Mrs. MacPherson; I'm not used to it yet, and it makes me feel old, Miss Byrd, so very old!"

I told her that if she was to be Agatha, I was to be Ada, and she happily agreed.

That dreadful shyness still had its claws deep in me, and over the next hour I found myself so fiercely gripped by it that at times I could barely speak. Agatha, however, more than made up for my noticeable lack of loquacity by the liquid movement of her own tongue. She, like myself, is no native of Lowry Bridge; she came instead from a place called Bloomtown, several miles to the east. It was there that she met the esteemed Reverend MacPherson when he "took on" the parish. She was, I take it, very young when he began to court her — young enough that their romance was, if not an actual scandal, certainly kin to one. Her mother, she said with charming frankness, took her aside and asked her if she wasn't worried about suffering an "early widowhood."

"*Does* it worry you?" It was a bold question, informed more by curiosity than tact, but her frankness made me feel that I ought to be frank in return.

Agatha considered the question as she turned her spoon over and over in her tea, the little chiming noises it made against the porcelain like rain against a pane of glass. In his cradle, young Douglas whimpered faintly, then sighed.

"Sometimes," she said finally. "It seems a dreadfully lonely thing, to lose a husband. My father died when I was young, and Mama was never the same afterwards. But then, she and Father were childhood sweethearts; they knew that they would be married someday when they were only six years old, and neither of them ever had second thoughts on the matter. The Reverend and I aren't like that."

That is how she refers to her husband more often than not — "the Reverend." It seems a terribly cold address to a husband from a wife.

"Did you have other beaus, before you met him?"

She waved a hand as though swatting away the question. "Schoolgirl flirtations, here and there. Really, music was my first love. Papa's family is very musical, and I inherited the knack. We had a piano in the parlour, and I used to creep in while Mama was out and press the keys, over and over, just to hear the notes. Soon I began to realize that you could string the notes together, like beads on a string, and make up melodies — ditties — songs, eventually. When I was a bit older, I begged for lessons, and I was so persistent that I got them. I wanted — oh! so badly — to go to college and study music. To be a performing pianist someday."

"And then the Reverend came to town."

Agatha shrugged. "Well, after Papa died there was no money to send me anywhere. Besides, I don't believe that Mama ever truly believed I could be a musician. Or anything else, for that matter." She took a contemplative sip of her tea and added, "When the Reverend and I began courting, all I could think of was the wife of the minister we had when I was a child. I was terrified of her — she was so grim, so colourless! I don't believe I ever saw her smile. But every week she played the organ in church, and as soon as she sat down on that bench, she was all fire and spark. She *glowed*. I remember watching her hands as they flew up and down the keys, how quick and sure they were, and thinking that that was the only time she ever really seemed to be herself: sitting in front of an organ for a few minutes a week. On the day that Hugh proposed it was *her* face I saw, not his. I thought, 'If I can't be a musician, a real one, at least I'll still be able to play. I'll have those few moments a week. That should be enough.'"

She sounded wistful then. Her eyes are grey — have I said this already? If so, I will say it again. They are grey, decidedly so, without a hint of green or blue to tip them one way or another, like a thick fog on a summer morning, or the downy feathers of a tern.

"That was what drew me to him," she said. "That was why I said yes. But I have no idea why he deigned to court some little slip of nothing from a nothing town. I suppose I will never know."

If Agatha cannot see why the Reverend took a shine to her, I can. She is a pretty woman, of course, but there is more to it than that. Even in that moment, dishevelled as she was, streaked with dirt and with strands of red-gold hair plastered to her damp neck, there was a radiance to her that made that poky sitting room seem airy and light.

It was then, or around then, that the clock began to chime the half hour. I glanced at it and gasped aloud. It was 5:30 PM, well past the time when I ought to have been helping Mrs. Grier get supper on the table. Agatha followed my gaze and laughed once more.

"See how long I've kept you!" she said, standing up. "And myself, as well. I haven't even put the potatoes on to boil. You mustn't let me hold you hostage like this next time, Ada!"

My Christian name sounded different in her merry voice, younger and gayer. I found myself smiling absurdly as I rose to shake her hand again. We promised one another that we would meet again, and I felt that perhaps this was not the empty sort of promise that it usually is — that we would meet again, deliberately, and sooner rather than later.

Mrs. Grier seemed annoyed when I finally came in the door, too late to help much with supper, but her irritation soon faded when I told her where I had been.

"She's a giddy one, is Mrs. MacPherson," she said. I heard again that note of disapproval in her voice. "I won't speak ill of the Reverend, but he married too young, and that's a fact. Perhaps being acquainted with you will steady her some, Miss Byrd."

I must say, the idea of my friendship "steadying" Agatha is rather depressing. I wouldn't want that sparkling, lively presence of hers dampened by my own. I like her as she is, with her bear paws and silly hat and frank, schoolgirlish ways, and I hope — I very much hope — that there is something in me for her to like too.

September 16, 1901

This morning I received my first letter from Father. It was waiting by my breakfast plate when I entered the kitchen, the address written in a forced and heavy copperplate. As soon as I could, I excused myself from the table and took myself upstairs to read it in the privacy of my little cell.

The contents of that letter could have been addressed to a girl of fourteen, not a woman of nearly thirty. Father advised me to mind my reputation; to be careful of the company I keep; to be aware that rumours fly faster and further than the truth; and that, like a piece of paper, a woman's life may be ruined by a single damning blot. All this written in such a sermonizing tone that I felt I was back in the Griers' pew, listening to Reverend MacPherson warn tremulously of hellfire.

"I trust that you are mindful of how fortunate you are," it concluded. "To begin anew in a town that has heard no whisper of your indiscretion is a second chance rarely granted to a woman in your position. Be sure that you guard yourself *properly* this time, and that you take care to bring no shame to your mother and me in Lowry Bridge."

Mother, I noted, did not send her love. Perhaps she was elsewhere when he wrote it, just as she managed to be elsewhere whenever he raised his hand to his daughters.

I wanted to scream; I wanted to run; I wanted to fling myself onto the floor, howling like a child. Denied these vents of feeling by my dignity and position, I stormed up the road to school in a state of froth, stopping briefly on the bridge to kick at the posts. School was a veritable terror, with myself presiding as Robespierre. More than one child cried — most notably Anna, after I tore into her for forgetting her Reader — and poor Eugene Castle was so distressed by my wrathful tone and bearing that he could not recite the Bible verse I'd had him memorize the night before. He sat trembling in his chair, his face paler than usual, and whimpered.

It was that which brought me back to my senses at last. I forced myself to lower my voice, loosen my shoulders, and smile a little, but I fear it had no effect on my pupils, all of whom regarded me with dread and suspicion for the remainder of the day. I can't blame them, the poor things. When I get in a pet like this, I always know that I will come out of it feeling small and ashamed for how I carried on in its midst. That does not, however, ever seem to stop me from behaving poorly anyway. It was, Florrie had once told me, my tragic flaw.

"It's bad enough to have a temper," she said, patting my shoulder to take the sting out of her words, "but so much worse to be aware of how badly you've behaved when you're out of it. You can't properly enjoy a tantrum if you're always thinking of how silly you look kicking your heels against the floor."

I believe that the Griers noticed my wretched mood, for they were both very gentle with me this evening. Mrs. Grier pressed second helpings upon me as though they were cod liver oil, and Mr. Grier told me, in his awkward, kindly way, that there was a harvest dance coming up at the town hall — a yearly affair, apparently. He will be providing the music, along with a few other fiddling gentlemen in town. I ought to go, he told me, since I have been working "awful hard" and deserve a chance to "let my hair down."

Mr. Grier played his fiddle for us tonight, possibly to smooth my still-ruffled feathers. The songs were all slow Scotch ballads, plaintive and wild as the wind over the hills. They filled that dingy little room until the very fire in the stove seemed to snap and crackle in time with the music. As I listened, I felt the agitation that had made my heart pound and my fists clench slowly subside.

Mrs. Grier must have noticed the slackening of my body, the gradual leak of tension from my shoulders and back, for she reached out and gently patted my hand.

"Tomorrow is another day," was all she said; and when she and her husband retreated upstairs, I threw Father's letter into the fire, staying there to watch it burn.

She was right. Tomorrow is another day.

September 18, 1901

*A*utumn has begun in earnest now, and the leaves are beginning to turn. Soon they will fall and form thick piles of gold on the road, and I shall kick them up into warm and rustling clouds before me as I walk.

The term has continued without incident so far, save for the usual petty squabbles. Effie and Anna were for a few days merciless toward Clara, who, I understand, made the mistake of speaking to a young man to whom Effie had taken a shine. By the third day, the poor girl was so distressed by her exile to Coventry that she remained at her desk all through the lunch hour in tears. I tried to console her, but like most young girls faced with a dispute between chums, she was inconsolable.

"Effie will never forgive me," she wept. She is a plain little thing on the best of days, and at that moment, with her eyes wetly red and her nose dripping freely onto her desk, she was grotesque. "I know she's been setting her cap for Miles Putney, and I didn't mean to put myself forward, but in church I had to get by him in the aisle and I said, 'Pardon me.' That don't seem so bad, does it, Miss Byrd?"

"Doesn't, Clara," I corrected her, but then relented. "No, it certainly does not. After all, this is a free country, and I suppose a girl can speak to a young man if she pleases."

"But I *didn't* please!" Clara wiped her nose on her sleeve, leaving a long, silvery streak on the dingy blue calico. "Only I had to get by, and I couldn't very well just charge through like a bull, could I?"

"That would have been very improper," I assured her, and ventured a careful pat on the head. Clara's hair is very thin and fine, and the feel of the bone beneath it put me in mind of the owlet skull on my desk. "Perhaps I should have a word with Effie myself. She is behaving very foolishly."

Poor Clara bolted upright as though she'd been struck. "Oh, no!" she gasped, her watery eyes wide with horror. "No, Miss Byrd, please don't! She'd be awful mad at me if she thought I'd set you on her. Why, last winter Miss Webster scolded her for doodling on her slate, and Effie took it into her head that I told on her. She and Anna wouldn't speak to me for a week. And I hadn't even seen her drawing, so I couldn't have told on her. How could I, when I didn't even know? Please, Miss Byrd, just leave me to sort it out with Effie. I'm sure I can set it right if I try."

The next day, the pitiful thing came to school with a little white cake and a lacquered comb for Effie, offering them to her with the humble air of a penitent. Effie, after a long and pregnant pause, accepted, and lo, the three were thick as thieves once more.

Through careful questioning, I have been able to find out a little more about my predecessor, Miss Webster. It seems that she was a lax disciplinarian — this I discovered when little

Matthew Perley, cross at having to stay in through recess and finish his sums, declared that "Miss Webster never was as mean as you, Miss Byrd." (For which impudence the whippersnapper was kept in through lunch, as well.) She could not, I understand, handle "the big boys" (all of whom are gone now, either working on their fathers' farms or otherwise employed), nor deal effectively with Effie and her queenly airs. I suspect this may be why Effie has been the de facto ruler of the Lowry Bridge schoolhouse for so very long, and why poor Clara is so cowed by her. Aside from that, the children have told me that she did, indeed, enjoy poetry — that she liked to read pieces aloud, and that she had a certain elocutionary knack that they seem to miss. I have tried reading aloud from some of the volumes she left behind, but I can see my pupils' attention wandering, their eyes drifting to the window or falling to their slates.

Muriel Melville remains an enigma. I have detected a whiff of wistfulness about the girl at times, as though she longs to jump up and make a dash for the wilderness. And no wonder! When we met in the woods, she seemed to be in her natural element, as graceful and assured a beast as any I have ever seen. The confines of the schoolroom strip her of that easy fluidity. Trapped between four walls, she moves awkwardly, speaks rarely, casts her eyes about her with marked wariness. She acts like a girl forced under duress to learn her letters and is prone to fix me with a hard stare if I dare comment on a mistake she made in her spelling or sums. Mistakes she makes aplenty, so I am stared at with furious disdain for most of my working hours.

"Poor Muriel," Mrs. Grier called her. Poor Ada, I say!

I mentioned this to Agatha yesterday. I hadn't thought the two of us would speak for some time, but last Sunday she caught hold of me before hurrying away for Sunday school to say that she hoped we could see one another soon. And so I took the long walk across the bridge and up to the manse, half-afraid that she had changed her mind, only to be greeted enthusiastically by the lady herself and young Master MacPherson, this time awake and dandled happily on his mother's knee.

"The Melvilles are an odd paddling of ducks," Agatha agreed. She had not been in her garden that day, and so was not nearly so dishevelled. I found myself rather missing her hat. "When the Reverend and I first came to town we had dinner at least once in every house, and the Melville place was the queerest one by far. All that peeling yellow paint, and great lumbering boys filling up the place, shouting and growling at one another, with little Muriel nearly lost among them, serving, and then of course Edmund Melville at the head of the table, silent, barely moving. We were there for at least two hours, and I don't believe I heard him say a single word. All he did was look at us and smile."

She pulled a face in imitation of him, a grimacing moue that made me nearly double over with laughter. Douglas chuckled and thrashed in response to my laughter, and Agatha lifted one of his chubby hands to her mouth and chewed on it playfully, eliciting more delighted giggles.

I said, after a moment's hesitation, "Mrs. Grier told me that he's had three wives."

"So I hear." There was none of the puritanical disapproval one might expect from a minister's wife in Agatha's voice; indeed, she seemed almost enthralled. "He is the kind of man who uses up the women he marries, from what I understand. A veritable Bluebeard, with a chamber full of dead women in his palace."

There was an eagerness in her voice that I did not like. I had to look away.

The harvest dance will happen this Saturday, under what promises to be a great, glowing lantern of a moon. Mr. and Mrs. Grier seem to take it as a matter of course that I will go, and go I must, I suppose, though the idea fills me with as much dread as excitement. I am no longer accustomed to dancing.

The last dance I attended was with Florrie, almost three years ago, while I was at our father's house for the winter break. How did she gain his permission for us to attend? What was the occasion? I do not remember; I remember only my sister, pink and laughing, pulling me from my wallflower's nook for the square dances. I remember, too, her locking eyes with a man over the rim of her cider cup, flirting shamelessly across the length of an entire room. I thought nothing of it at the time. Nor did I think anything of it when she danced with that man, time and time again; nor even when, as the evening went on, she disappeared with him, only reappearing when our curfew drew near. On our walk home she was gay and giggling, her eyes glittering above round, flushed cheeks, smiling as though at some thrilling secret.

That is how I like to remember her, in those last moments when she was still herself, before the man who would become her husband leeched away her colour bit by bit. She told me nothing about her life with him — Florrie, who used to tell me everything, whose letters to me had been so thick with irrelevant detail that she would have to scrawl sideways in the margins to make it all fit — but I pieced together enough of her pauses and omissions to know what kind of man he was. What is that quote from *Othello*, what Emilia says about men?

> They are all but stomachs, and we all but food;
> They eat us hungerly, and when they are full,
> They belch us.

That quote ran circles through my head the last time I saw her. The change that marriage had wrought in her shocked me to my core: the thinness of her face, the dullness of her eyes, the blooming purple I glimpsed when she rolled up her sleeves to wash a dish, as thought someone had grabbed her wrist and squeezed. Her swollen stomach looked less like a sign of new life than the kind of horrible bloating one sees in pictures of famine victims, the body filling itself with air for lack of anything else to sate it. I sat with her in her husband's house, drinking tea she had brewed with trembling hands, and smelled the heavy stink of fear rising from her skin. My sister, who had never been afraid of anyone or anything, lived in terror of her husband.

I should have taken her away, then and there. But to where? I had no home of my own. The only haven I could offer was our father's house, and that was no safe harbour for either of us.

It was only weeks after that visit that a letter came from Father, calling me home for my sister's funeral. She'd had a fall down the stairs, he said, which had triggered an early delivery. She had died in the attempt to give her husband a child, and the child died alongside her without ever drawing breath.

A fall, the letter had said, giving no details of how such a fall could have occurred, how my graceful sister had been rendered so clumsy as to tumble backwards down a staircase she climbed every day. But I saw her in her casket, her hair not quite combed over the bruise at her temple, her husband standing over her as though he owned her even in death, and I knew.

I have no proof to support an accusation, no living soul who will support me. But I do not believe that my sister fell down that staircase. I believe, and always will, that she was pushed. Her husband, that Bluebeard, sucked the marrow from her bones before tossing them aside. She was eaten, then belched.

*M*y heart pounds and my cheeks are warm to the touch, although I have been sitting quietly on my bed for the better part of an hour. What a night this has been! What a gay and jolly time of it I have had!

Even as I was readying myself to leave for the harvest dance, I felt sure that I might change my mind at any moment. There is no mirror in my room, but I could picture my face with perfect clarity in my mind's eye even without one. A pale, plump oval, small eyes too close together, a mannish chin, crowded and overlapping teeth. Short-legged, thick-waisted, hair the colour of old dishwater. On most days I care little enough about these defects, but this evening I was horribly conscious of them as I donned my Sunday best. Even as I turned to come down the stairs and join the Griers in their little buggy, I fought the urge to jump into bed and pull the blanket over my head.

We approached the town hall under the honeyed gaze of the harvest moon. The building is not much to look at, little more than an old barn repurposed into a gathering-place. The doors were thrown open, light and music spilling out into the night. Mr. Grier muttered anxiously about the other fellows starting without him and trotted in without so much as a backwards glance at his wife as soon as he'd seen to the team, hoisting his fiddle case like a weapon of war. I thought that this might annoy Mrs. Grier, but when I glanced at her she wore a patient and tolerant smile.

"Bless him," she said, the very epitome of wifely indulgence. "Shall we, Miss Byrd?"

The hall fairly writhed with people, its floor a boiling sea of starched shirts and rustling calico, stomping feet and hooting laughter. They were at that moment engaged in a strip-the-willow, that odd, twining, weaving dance that is so very dizzying to look at; onlookers stood just outside the haven of the floor, staying close to the wall and watching the proceedings. The entire town, it seemed, had turned out for the dance, even some of the children. I saw a few of my students there, including the queenly Effie and the hearty Arthur Benson, mingling easily with the adults. Mrs. Grier was quickly swallowed by the room, and I was left on my own, staring like a deer frozen by a bright light. It was hot, the air laden with sweat and music. Everywhere I looked I saw bright eyes, gaping mouths, whirling skirts.

I was able, once, to attend such events because Florrie would come with me, acting as something between a bodyguard and an interpreter. She would keep the worst of the crowds away, and she would be sure to whisper in my ear if I was doing something wrong or saying something odd. To be in this writhing mass of people alone was too much by far; I quailed, ready to turn tail and run out into the blessed dark. But just as I made to do so, a hand clamped tightly on my arm, and a familiar voice said, "Hello, Ada! I am so glad to see you — I was worried that you weren't going to come!"

It was Agatha, bright-eyed and merry-faced, beautiful in her Sunday best. The lantern light brought out a reddish gleam in her hair.

And with that, I was taken firmly under her wing for the evening. Keeping tight hold of my arm, she took me round the perimeter of the hall, introducing me to those few townspeople I had not yet met. They were gracious, curious about this woman from far away and her business in Lowry Bridge; those with children were anxious to hear of their progress, and those without nevertheless had opinions to offer on the subject of education. I was pressed on all sides by eager eyes, probing questions, hands reaching out to firmly grasp and shake my own. It felt almost as overwhelming at times as that first frightening moment in the hall, but Agatha kept her steady pressure on my arm, seeming instinctively to know when to steer me from one person to another.

After some time had passed, the townspeople grew less interested in me, and Agatha and I were left alone by a long table laden with refreshments. She fetched me a cup of lemonade, and I welcomed its sweet bite as a salve to my throat, which had grown hoarse from answering so many questions. I drank it in one long swig.

"Is Reverend MacPherson not here tonight?" I asked her. Somewhere behind us, hidden by the shifting crowd, the fiddlers were playing something slow and mournful, a ballad about a woman drowned.

"Hugh does not approve of dancing." Agatha's voice, I noticed, was suddenly pitched lower, as though to thwart eavesdroppers.

"He does not think it unholy, exactly, so he will not foreswear it from the pulpit, but he does not think God smiles to see it done, either. He almost forbade me to come tonight. I had to promise him three times that I would not dance with another man before he would let me out of the house."

A little sigh blew past her lips. The music came to a stop, and with barely a pause, the fiddlers changed to a jauntier rhythm. An answering cheer came from the crowd, and the people rearranged themselves into pairs, hands clasping and boots tapping out an eager rhythm on the boards. Those not on the dance floor began to clap out a steady beat, keeping time for the dancers.

It was the clapping, I think, that gave me courage. Setting my cup down, I held out my hand to her and said: "Would the Reverend object to you dancing with someone who was not a man?"

Agatha looked at my hand blankly, as though unsure what it was, and I felt a shiver of dismay ripple through my spine, but then she laughed and extended her own hand, grasping mine tightly. She pulled me close. I could smell the rosewater scent she wore, billowing about her like a cloud.

"I suppose he wouldn't," she said, and we were off, her hand holding tightly to mine.

Everyone else in the room was dancing a high-stepping Highland schottische, and Agatha and I attempted to do the same, kicking up our heels in time to the clapping of the onlookers, but as the song went on and we became breathless and giddy, we lost our form. The schottische turned into a polka, which then became a waltz, which then became nothing more than a pair of silly women twirling about like spinning-tops, gasping with laughter at each turn. Neither of us led, in the end. My sides heaved with the effort of each inhalation; my head rang with music and the sound of stomping feet. The faces in the crowd blurred so that I could not read their expressions. The only face I could see was Agatha's, pink and pleased, her smile threatening to split it right in two.

The song ended all too soon, and we staggered to a stop, still laughing fit to burst. We tried to dance to another, but we were simply too breathless; we staggered to the edge of the room to catch our breath, grinning at one another like fools.

"That," Agatha panted, "is the first dance I have had since I turned sixteen. Well done, Ada!"

Well done! The words stayed with me on the way back to the Griers' house, a warm ache in the pit of my stomach. They are with me now.

The Griers and I crammed into the buggy for the ride home, a blanket tucked carefully around our laps to keep out the cool of the evening. After several minutes of silence, broken only by the jangling of bits and the dull clopping of hooves, Mrs. Grier turned to me and said, "You danced with Mrs. MacPherson, I saw."

I could not tell if her tone was disapproving or not.

"She said the minister did not want her to dance with another man," I said. "When I was a girl, we would often dance together if there were not enough boys to go around."

"Of course," she said, but her tone was rather thoughtful. "Well, it does her credit, I suppose, to shy away from taking a turn with men. That wouldn't be right for a minister's wife. But then, there are some that might say it isn't right for a minister's wife to dance at all."

"Nothing about it in the Bible," said Mr. Grier. It was the first thing he'd said since leaving the hall; up to that point he had just whistled under his breath, his foot tapping against the floor of the buggy. "Seems harmless enough."

Mrs. Grier hummed. The exact meaning of the hum I could not ascertain. Still, I found myself a little downcast after that. The minister's wife and the schoolteacher are figures of some authority in a little community such as this, and with authority comes the expectation of dignity, remove, a certain amount of distance. Perhaps I had not behaved well.

But now, back up in my little room, I can scarcely bring myself to care about such things. My feet twitch as they remember the steps they took, longing to take them again. I am filled with the sound of Agatha's breathless laughter, the pleased way she said, *Well done.* What chance have dignity and remove against *that*?

September 26, 1901

There are certain autumn days that seem bathed in gold —
days when the very air is sweet and heavy, the wind carrying
with it the delectable perfume of ripe apples and falling leaves.
Today was one of those days, warm and bright, with mellow sunlight above and drowsing earth below, and it inspired within me
what I thought was a singularly wonderful idea. As my students
trooped in and shuffled dutifully to their desks, I called for them
to stay in place.

"Keep your coats on, children," I said, "and your hats too.
We shan't sit in our chairs and learn today. We are going on a
nature walk!"

I said this with great spirit, hoping that my own enthusiasm
would lift them onwards and upwards like a rising tide, but I was
met with a sea of blank, uninterested gazes and a few scattered
yawns. Matthew Perley picked his nose and withdrew his finger
to inspect its findings with the weary gaze of a connoisseur.

"What's that, Miss?" he asked.

It took some time to explain the concept, and my students' interest was not particularly captured once they fully grasped it. Still, they understood well enough that they would get to spend their day out-of-doors, and that was enough to make them follow me into the woods, trailing behind me like the unfortunate children of Hamlin.

For all their initial indifference, the walk was a modest triumph. Some of the children remained unimpressed — Effie, for one, spent the entire day complaining loudly about how warm she was in the sun, and George skinned his knee on a log and set to wailing in tones more suitable to a boy half his age — but the rest of them warmed to the subject as we pressed on, responding with increasing enthusiasm to my impromptu lectures on the various flora and fauna we encountered. By the time we reached the bank of the Slade River, I believe that I had won them over, if not to the charms of natural history, then certainly to the charms of spending the day outside of the schoolroom.

At the water's edge, I let the children dabble their feet in the cool water, keeping a careful eye on the younger ones. Frogs were caught, minnows spotted and marvelled over, and Caroline's bonnet fell off her head and was carried far downstream before being rescued by the gallant Arthur. Lillian Morice found a toad, and was so enchanted by the warty creature that she attempted to scoop it up and bring it home with her, saying that she would make it a bed out of her mother's hatbox. When it wriggled away, she became so despondent that only Winifred could calm her. For all her tears, I could not help but smile — I recall Florrie and I doing the same thing once with a baby squirrel that had fallen from a tree, smuggling it into our father's house and trying to keep it as a pet. We made a nest for it of rags and scraps of paper, tried to feed it scraps we slipped up our sleeves at the supper table. Alas, we were sorely lacking in the veterinary arts. The poor thing died only a day after we brought it inside, and we buried it amongst our mother's cabbages, digging it up months later to examine the bones.

The one student left untouched was the one I thought would be most delighted by a ramble through the woods. Muriel's face showed nothing but boredom for the duration of the afternoon, and she stood well away from her fellow students, watching the proceedings from the shade of a willow. Her expression was one of strangely adult detachment, as though she were an old woman watching children play in the sun. Only at the end of the afternoon did she say a word.

It began when I gave a description of what we would be able to find in the river at different seasons, mentioning specifically the gelatinous clouds of frogspawn that would appear on its surface in March and turn into wriggling pollywogs. Young Clarence turned to me and asked:

"Miss, how do them eggs get into the water, anyhow?"

I blushed a little as I told him that the lady frogs laid them there, of course. I hoped that would be the end of it, but of course, it was not.

"But then, what happens to turn 'em into those little wiggly things?" his seatmate Matthew demanded then. "We have chickens at home, and when they lay eggs, sometimes they turn into chicks, and sometimes they don't. Why is that, Miss Byrd?"

Oh, horrors! I was torn between wanting to explain the workings of nature to an inquisitive young mind and knowing that explaining such a thing could well be considered indelicate. My mouth opened before I knew what to say, and I gaped foolishly at the boy, wondering how on Earth I could satisfy my requirements as a teacher and a lady at the same time. But before I could say a single world, Muriel spoke.

"The chicks is because you got a rooster," she said to Matthew, "and the frog eggs is because there are man frogs as well as lady frogs. Like men and women, and how you get babies."

This seemed to satisfy Matthew well enough, and he turned to continue his inspection of the river. But Eugene Castle, who was nearby and had overheard the exchange, turned to Muriel, his face agog with interest.

"My mother says that the doctor brings babies in his big black bag," he said. "That's how we got my baby sister."

Muriel looked at him then, the first time she'd made eye contact with another child that whole afternoon, and Eugene flinched at the expression on her face. Scorn, pure scorn.

"Your mother is—"

"Right," I broke in, desperate for the discussion to be over before it strayed into more unsavoury territory. "Right altogether, Eugene. After all, people are not like frogs, are we? It stands to reason that we get babies in a different way. Go play with the other lads, now."

This was good enough for Eugene, and he picked his careful, sidling way along the bank to the others. I turned to Muriel, shading my eyes with my hand to see her better. Her hair hung limp over her shoulders — she hadn't bothered to braid it that morning, it seemed, nor had she come to school with a bonnet or hat. Bareheaded, sunburned, she stared up at me with the same scorn she'd turned on Eugene.

"Muriel," I said, pitching my voice low so that the other children would not hear, "you must be a bit more discreet. Eugene is very young, and there are some things that he oughtn't know, not yet. Indeed, you are young, as well. There's no need for you to concern yourself with . . ."

But I could not say, exactly, what I meant. How could I, without crossing every line of delicacy? My blush, which had gone away, came back with a prickly-hot vengeance, and I saw Muriel's eyes land on my cheeks, as though they were drawing the blood to the surface themselves.

"Babies don't come in no black bag, Miss," she said, her voice the merest whisper, that strange smile that makes her look so adult flitting across her lips. There was, I fancied, a sly, conspiratorial note in her voice, as though she was thinking of a secret we two shared together — as though, in fact, she thought that I knew all about babies and the origins thereof.

Flustered, I called an early dismissal, and the students scattered very willingly. Every pair of cheeks was kissed pink with sun and good fresh air, and I fancy that I saw a certain spring in the steps of the children who had plodded dutifully into the schoolhouse that morning.

It certainly seemed that the outing had been a success. However, I found myself dwelling on my conversation with Muriel as I set the schoolhouse in order and crossed the river to the other side of the bridge, wondering about that look, that implication of shared knowledge. Why might the girl think that I myself have intimate knowledge of such things? What has she heard, and from whom?

I must not torment myself with such worries. Father was very firm with the school board when they offered me this post. He made it clear that certain things were not to be discussed, either amongst themselves or with the locals. There is no pressing need to panic, surely.

Agatha is hosting a picnic for her Sunday school students and asked that I help her put it on. For the sake of her friendship I agreed, but I must admit that I am not looking forward to the event. Every single Sunday school picnic that I have ever attended has felt at least three days long, an excruciating exercise in tedium. Even Agatha's sunny company may not be enough to save the day.

September 29, 1901

*I*s there anything more tiresome than a Sunday school picnic? If so, I cannot imagine it.

The day, at least, was a beautiful one, crisp and clear, without a cloud in the sky (I had, I admit, half-hoped that it would rain), and the field behind the church where it was held smelled sweetly of warm grass and the last of the season's wildflowers. Every child who attended the event seemed to bring with him a basket full of goodies, and all were quick to point out their own contributions to their peers and to me.

The only child who brought nothing was Muriel. Truth be told, I was surprised to see her at all — she rarely attends church, and never Sunday school, Agatha says — but I suppose the lure of abundant free food was enough to secure her attendance. She seemed more comfortable in this setting than in the schoolroom, sprawling easily across the grass beneath a sugar maple tree. It was just starting to turn for the autumn, and the light trickling down through the wine-coloured leaves gave the girl's face a warm glow, as though she sat in front of a dying fire. She did not join in any of the games, not the footraces, nor the ring toss, nor even the prim, ladylike games put on by the older girls that involved no effort likely to muss one's hair, but watched the proceedings from the shade, just as she had the day of our nature walk. Her eyes followed the movement of the other children with neither rancor nor envy. She looked at them as another child might watch birds weaving through the air, or a family of deer picking their way across a field. There was interest in her gaze, but no identification — or so, at least, it seemed to me.

It wasn't until the picnic was drawing to its close that a curious incident occurred. I was sitting on a blanket with little Lillian Morice and her protectress, Winifred Benson, helping the two of them make a daisy chain, when all at once the world seemed to grow unaccountably quiet. The lack of sound was almost a sensation, an electric tingle like the feeling in the air as snow begins to fall. I looked up from my lapful of flowers, wondering at the sudden hush, and saw someone I would never have expected to see at that picnic: the widow, Mrs. Kinsley, resplendent in a rose-trimmed hat and delicate pink gown, walking through the grounds.

Her pace was measured and slow, her smile utterly pleasant; she nodded here and there to the adults in attendance. Some of them nodded back; most of them looked away or frowned, and Mrs. Castle, in whose immaculate home I have attended many a prayer meeting, deliberately turned her back as the woman passed. Never before had I seen so fine a lady be so thoroughly snubbed. And yet, she did not seem to mind; she simply kept on strolling across the field, with the air of one determined to enjoy the sunshine and the fresh autumn breeze. Her destination seemed to be the maple tree where Muriel was seated. Beneath the shadow of the leaves, I saw the child slowly stand, her eyes fixed on the widow's face.

Next to me, Lillian gave a little hiccupping shiver. "Oh, Winnie!" she said. When I tore my eyes away from Mrs. Kinsley, I saw that she'd nearly crawled into Winifred's lap. "What is *she* doing here?"

Winifred snorted derisively, although I noted that her own eyes never strayed from the widow as she made her way through the field. "Never mind, Lillian," she said, her boyish voice clipped and short. "She's got too much money and not enough to do, so she just wanders about bothering ordinary people. That's what Da told me."

I longed to ask her what she meant, but I knew it would not be proper to ask one of my own pupils to pass on gossip. I reached over and stroked Lillian's soft brown curls, as one might pet a kitten. One of Winifred's arms tightened around the child's middle, making her squeak.

We watched Mrs. Kinsley pick her way over to Muriel's place beneath the maple tree. The girl stood still, following her approach with her eyes. Then, acting on a cue none of us had seen or heard, she stepped closer. I could see their lips moving, though not a word of their conversation came to me on the wind. Once, I was sure, Muriel looked away from the widow and toward me, her eyes seeking mine across the grounds and boring into me, unblinking as a lizard.

What was Mrs. Kinsley saying to the girl? Why was she looking at me? I could think of no answer to either question, could do nothing but stare back until Muriel turned her gaze back to the widow.

Mrs. Kinsley smiled and reached out one pale hand. The scene was too far away for me to really see any details, but my mind eagerly filled them in: the luxuriant softness of the skin, the fine articulation of those aristocratic fingers. Muriel looked at the proffered hand for what felt like a long time, then bent down and — this is the strangest thing in the world — brushed her lips against its knuckles, as one might kiss the hand of a queen, or a saint. It would have been an odd gesture from any child, but from Muriel it was doubly so. Cold, haughty Miss Melville, bowing and scraping over this woman!

"She's queer," Winifred muttered. Her eyes flicked up to meet mine, then returned to the strange pantomime beneath the tree. "Don't you think, Miss Byrd, that Muriel is queer?"

"No," I said, although of course I did. It *was* queer, all of it.

"That Mrs. Kinsley's a witch," Lillian said, wiggling a little in Winifred's lap. "Ain't she, Winnie?"

"There's no such thing as witches," Winifred replied, a little too quickly. I suspect that if I had not been present, she would not have been so swift to dismiss this theory.

"But she *is* a witch," Lillian insisted. In her voice now was the faintest shiver of glee. It is a delightful thing to imagine that there may be witches when you are young. "I heard someone say it. That's how her husband died. She witched him. She took a carrot root and drew his face on it and nailed it to a tree and then he died."

"Mr. Kinsley died 'cause he had a bad heart," Winifred said curtly. "Don't be stupid."

This was an unusually harsh way for Winifred to speak to her little charge, and I could see Lillian reel from the shock of it. Before her round blue eyes had time to fill with tears, I intervened.

"You aren't stupid, Lillian." I stroked her hair again, as much to soothe myself as her. "But Winifred is correct. Witches do not exist."

"My granny says they do." Lillian looked from Winifred to me, clearly baffled. "She says they're why milk spoils and storms come. It's witches, or the Devil."

"Lillian Morice, don't you talk about the Devil," Winifred said sharply. "It's the Lord's day."

Two rebukes in the space of a moment were too much for Lillian. She began to cry, noisy baby-sobs that attracted much attention from the other picnickers. By the time I had her settled again, and made Winifred apologize, and helped them finish their daisy chain, Mrs. Kinsley had disappeared. So, I noticed, had Muriel.

I did not mention our picnic's strange visitor when I returned to the Griers. I reported the usual news one brings home from a Sunday school picnic, instead: what pies and cakes the children had brought, who had won the footraces, which of the ladies had been wearing a new hat. Mrs. Grier was pleased to hear that the little queen cakes she had made were well received, and Mr. Grier showed interest in hearing how well Arthur Benson had done in the footraces.

"I'll be needing a new hired boy next spring," he said. "Young Perry Mueller is well enough, but he's leaving for Australia after the winter, or so he says. Maybe if this Benson boy is finished his schooling by then I'll hire him on."

I am trying to settle myself in for the evening, to read from the Bible or finish the lace collar that I have been working on as a Christmas gift for Mrs. Grier. But I keep remembering the widow sweeping through the field, mindless of the silence that suddenly fell as she approached, smiling like a woman with a beautiful secret. Of Muriel's lips, brushing that fine, aristocratic hand.

A witch, Lillian called her. But, of course, witches do not exist.

October 8, 1901

The autumn rains have begun, and what a miserable time we have all had of it! Every day, my students and I enter the schoolhouse soaked to the skin, our clothes heavy with water. Through the morning we shiver and sneeze our way through our lessons, huddling as close to the stove as we can. Gradually we dry out, our spirits rising and our steps growing lighter as we do, but then by the time we are really comfortable again the clock on the wall strikes three, and we must venture out into the wet once more. I have spent the past four days as damp as a fish, grumping and lumping my way through lesson plans and gradings. It really feels as though I might grow mould.

A saving grace: I was able to fill a shoebox with wet dirt and earthworms this morning and bring them into the classroom, as part of a lesson on invertebrates. The reaction of my students was decidedly mixed. Most of the older girls shrieked and drew back when they saw me touching the things, while the younger students were fascinated by the wet, wriggling mass of them. By the day's end, I had convinced most of the children to hold them in their hands, and Lillian was utterly enamored of them. She asked if she could keep them and pouted dreadfully when I told her no, I would be returning them to their homes.

"These worms live outside, Lillian," I told her, "just as you live with your mama and papa. How would you like it if some giant took you out of your house and made you sleep in the dirt, instead of your nice warm bed?"

At which Lillian glowered mutinously and said she would *like* to live in the dirt, she *would* — and anyway, she could fill her pinafore pocket with earth, wouldn't that be just as good? It took much petting and soothing from both Winifred and me for her to eventually acquiesce, and I saw her at noon squatting down to look at the patch of mud where I had freed the creatures, perhaps hoping they would come to the surface again so she could spirit them away.

I understand her fascination, of course. One of my earliest memories is of watching a curling mass of worms thrash through the dirt in the rain, stretching blindly in either direction, seeking the comfort of darkness. So alien, with no eyes nor mouth, and yet so very alive. They looked like little strips of raw flesh, brought to life by some eerie spell.

In the spirit of our squirming guests, as the afternoon drew to a close, I tried once more to read to my students. Since all my attempts at poetry have fallen flat, I tried a different tack today: Eliza Brightwen's *Inmates of My House and Garden*, an old favourite whose spine is cracked with love. Mrs. Brightwen has always been a darling of mine and of Florrie's too; hers may not be the most scholastically rigorous work in the field, but it is written with a gentle, inquisitive spirit, infused with fascination and respect for the natural world and its denizens.

I had not opened my copy of *Inmates* since Willoughby, but the words on their flyspecked pages were as familiar to me as they had ever been. I chose to read the chapter on insect observation, having always had a soft spot for creepy-crawlies. Perhaps it was my own enthusiasm on the subject, or perhaps it was simply that immortal childish impulse to sit up and listen at the mention of bugs and beasties, but the toothsome descriptions of sunflies and wolf spiders did the trick to hold their attention. Every time I looked up from the text, I saw upturned faces and wide, enraptured eyes.

I was halfway through the chapter when a slight noise by the door made me look up from the volume in my hand. There, standing in the doorway of the schoolhouse with her cloak dripping onto the floor, was Agatha, her grey eyes shining as she watched me read!

I made it through the rest of the chapter, stammering a little under Agatha's gaze. It is one thing to read aloud when the audience is comprised of children; it is quite another to have a friend watch you do it. But I managed and then called for dismissal. My students fled eagerly, barely noting the presence of their Sunday school teacher at the door. Indeed, Paul Miller was in such a rush to burst out into that grey, wet afternoon that he very nearly knocked her down! I rushed to the door to shout an admonition after him, but it was no good; he had already bolted up the road, his brother trotting far behind, pleading with him to go more slowly.

"Agatha, I am sorry," I began, but Agatha only laughed.

"Nonsense," she replied, perching lightly on the edge of my desk. Her eyes landed on my owlet skull in its little jar, and one hand reached out to touch the glass, fingertips light as a kiss.

I watched her pick it up and examine it more closely, certain that she would grimace in horror. To my surprise, she smiled at it, then at me, and put it down again. "They are children, and children *will* run, whether we wish them to or no. What a lovely voice you have for reading, Ada! So steady and calm!"

The blush started over my cheeks before she'd even finished the sentence. I found I did not know what to do with my hands.

"Not a patch on Miss Webster's, I imagine," I said, but Agatha shook her head.

"I daresay they enjoyed that book of yours more than the stuff she used to read. Winifred complained about her poetry readings in Sunday school last year, saying that poetry was even more boring than mathematics and that she would rather do a whole slate of sums than listen to one more poem about the springtime." She smiled again, rather sadly. "I told her that many children would be very happy to have a teacher read them poetry, and that I would have been one of them. I love poetry — it's so very like music — but the Reverend doesn't really approve of it. It is too often base, he says, and poets too often ungodly. He *will* stand for Hopkins, on occasion, but Hopkins was Catholic, so there are difficulties there, as well."

"I wanted to become a Catholic when I was a girl." Why I said this I do not know. Perhaps some contrary part of me wanted to shock her. If so, that part was disappointed, for Agatha only chuckled.

"So did I," she said. "I read some sensational novel about a nun and found the idea terribly romantic. I've never told Hugh that, of course. He hates novels even more than poetry because novels are lies."

It unnerves me to hear her call her husband by his Christian name. He seems the sort of man who oughtn't have one. Still,

I smiled, for there was a perverse thrill in knowing something about his wife that he did not. Agatha smiled back, then said:

"I have a confession to make, Ada."

"A confession? Perhaps you are a Catholic, after all."

That chuckle came again, and I felt exquisitely bold, to have dared to tease her and to have made her laugh.

"My confession is that I did not come here only for an afternoon visit. I came because I have a . . . well, a present for you."

"A present!" I echoed, rather stupidly. She nodded and reached into the seam of her skirt, rummaging briskly in the pocket hidden there.

"As a thank you for helping me with the picnic," she said. "This was the first event for the children that I'd arranged since Dougie was born, and I was so very worried about how it would go off. I loathe organizing such things on my own, and you — you made it easy, when I thought it would be a dreadful trial. So I thought I ought to show you, somehow, how very grateful I am."

With a flourish, she pulled a little shining item from her pocket and pressed it into my hand, her expression suddenly bashful.

It was a bottle — an exceedingly pretty little bottle, made of cut glass and tied at its neck with a pink ribbon. It glittered in the dim of the schoolhouse like a river in sunlight. When I tugged out the stopper, the unmistakeable smell of rosewater met my nose. Something about the scent felt strangely familiar.

"I made it myself," Agatha said. It could have been my imagination, but I swear I saw pink creeping along her cheeks. "Not the bottle, of course, but the scent, from the roses in my garden. It is the same kind that I wear. You and I shall be like sisters now!"

Sisters. No other word in the English language could have had the effect on me as that one did. My fingers curled tight around the little bottle as though to crush it, hot tears pricking at my eyes. I turned as quickly as I could, away from Agatha and toward the blackboard, which sported a cloudy smudge. The smudge was what I looked at, squinting furiously at it until the tears melted away. I taught myself this trick as a girl, as a way to avoid crying in my father's presence. Pick a point on the wall or the floor or the ceiling and stare, stare hard, until the urge to howl has passed.

"Thank you," I said finally, turning round. There she stood, rainwater still dripping down her cheeks, as bonny and golden as ever a woman was.

It came over me at all once then: the desire to throw my arms about her, draw her close to me and feel her soft cheek against my own. The longing was so fierce that I found my foot lifting from the ground, as though my body had already made up its mind to do it. But I remembered another cheek pressed against my own all those months ago in Willoughby, another pair of eyes watching me read. I could not give my thanks that way. It might not turn out right.

And then I had a thought of such perfection that I could not stifle a triumphant little chuckle. Turning away from Agatha, I opened my desk to reveal the little stack of books left behind by Miss Webster. My hand fluttered over that little collection of tomes for an undecided instant before settling on the second volume of Wordsworth's *Lyrical Ballads*. Of all Miss Webster's abandoned books, it was the least battered, the fabric cover worn only a little at spine and corners.

"I have something for you in return, Agatha," I said. The book was not really mine, of course, but her eyes had been so wistful when she spoke of loving poetry, their grey turned misty as a spring morning. I could not let her leave without giving her *something*.

"Oh, Ada, no," Agatha protested, but her hand twitched convulsively as I held out the book, as though she fought the urge to snatch it away. "I couldn't take your book from you!"

"Ah, but you see, it is not really mine," I said, and flipped it open to show her the title page. There at the top was Miss Amelia Webster's signature just as it appeared in every other volume, rendered in a fussy and tremulous hand. "Miss Webster abandoned it here before she left, and I very much doubt she will come back to claim it. Unless you want it to remain in my desk and gather dust, you'll give it a good home."

This, it seemed, was all Agatha needed to hear. She seized the book, rifling through its yellowed leaves with undisguised delight. Her eyes landed on a page here, a page there, gulping down lines of verse as eagerly as a man dying of thirst might gulp down water.

"'Song for the Wandering Jew,'" she murmured, her eyes alight, "and 'Poor Susan'! 'The Fountain'! Really, Ada, this is too much. I—" She paused in her eager perusal, frowning down at the slim little volume. "Why, what's this? It seems Miss Webster was in the habit of leaving notes for herself in her books."

Surely not, I thought. Wanton literary vandalism did not at all fit the image I'd had in my head of my predecessor. But when I looked, I saw that the page had indeed been defaced. There, squeezed between the gutter and the righthand margin of "Lucy Gray," ran the following words:

> no matter if I plug my ears it
> still calls to me

It was recognizably the same hand as the one that had signed the book, but it looked somehow scattered, as though Miss Webster had written it in a terrible hurry. Or in some state of dishevelment. I was curious about the words — I am curious still — but I was more inclined to be dismayed that my gift had been defaced.

"Well, what a terrible present I have given you!" I said, and reached out to take the book away, but Agatha laughed and pulled it out of my reach.

"A wonderful present, and you shan't have it back," she said. "You are a perfect strawberry, Ada Byrd."

It was the queerest and loveliest compliment I have ever received. I carried it with me all that long walk home, my shadow trailing behind me like a long black tail.

Now that I am home again, however, I find myself wondering more about that strange inscription. I have checked the other volumes, and none of them have been so defaced, although all bear the woman's simpering little autograph. Why that volume, that poem? Why those strange and unsettling words?

When I put on my nightgown tonight, I daubed a generous amount of Agatha's rosewater onto my wrists. I keep mistaking my own smell for hers, looking up as though she might be standing at the foot of my bed, watching me.

October 14, 1901

This morning, it seemed as though we might have finally been granted a reprieve from the rain. The sun rose watery-bright into a clear blue sky, and I made it to the schoolhouse without a single drop falling on me. The difference it made to all our spirits was remarkable. Even dour Paul Miller seemed more chipper than usual, raising his hand to respond to a question about the Battle of Hastings. (Was his response correct? Nay — but any participation from the boy is an improvement!)

Alas, our fortune did not hold. As the afternoon wore on, the sky began to dim, and by three o'clock, dark grey clouds had begun to roll in from the east, lowering and ominous above the trees. The children scattered as soon as they were dismissed, clutching their hats to their heads as they ran madly off in all directions.

I rushed through my end-of-day chores, hoping to take all my grading home with me and finish it in the safe, dry haven of the Griers' parlour, but even after leaving the sweeping for the next morning, I emerged from the schoolhouse into a veritable torrent. Cross, cold, and thoroughly dispirited (to say nothing of drenched), I began to tramp down the road, trying to use my leather satchel to fend off the rain. It did not work, of course, nor did holding my lunch pail above my head deflect the worst of the drops. A pretty fool I must have looked as I stomped through the mud, arms waving madly about like those of Don Quixote's giants!

I am in good spirits about it now, of course, being home and dry, but in that moment, I was in the blackest temper imaginable. A great many unladylike things did I mutter to myself, and when I heard the sound of an approaching team I only muttered more. It took all the strength I had to look up at the passersby, to nod and smile and wish them a good day. But look I did — look and then stare. For there was the handsomest matched pair of blue roan mares I'd ever seen, their coats shining silver in the rain; and there, behind them, was a clever little curricle with a gleaming black hood; and *there*, snugly tucked beneath an oilskin, was Mrs. John Kinsley!

"Good afternoon," said she. The pale horses against the dark buggy, her pale face against its halo of dark hair, all of it seemed apiece to me, as though *she* and *they* and *it* were all carved from a single great stone. "Dreadful weather, isn't it?"

It was, I realized as I stammered an agreement, the first time I'd ever heard her voice. It was low and soothing, the sort of voice one might like to hear read a bedtime story.

The widow's eyes swept over me, then up to the glowering sky. "It will get worse before it gets better, and you're already wet through. Would you like to take shelter at my home for an hour or so until the storm passes?"

I was about to demur, to tell her that I was expected by the Griers, but at that moment the sky seemed to split with lightning, a deafening peal of thunder hot on its heels. I fairly jumped out of my skin.

"That," I said, my teeth beginning to chatter, "would be lovely, Mrs. Kinsley."

She helped me up into her chariot, solicitous as a gentleman, and tucked the oilskin firmly in around us both before clucking sharply to her team. They set off at a leisurely pace, occasionally tossing their heads and letting loose a shower of droplets upon us.

I scarcely remember what we spoke of on the road. The rain, I imagine: the sheer volume of it, its suddenness. Truth be told, I was so wet and chilled that I could barely register what was coming out of my mouth, let alone what was coming out of hers. The scenery whipped by unseen, an indecipherable blur of greenery. It was not until we came up the long drive to the widow's house that I began to take things in again.

The widow's house is in the woods, flanked by silver birches and the odd crooked pine. It looks like what a painter from the city, having never seen a farmhouse in the flesh, might imagine one to be: a sweet little cottage, cozy as Marie Antoinette's Petit Trianon, with two stories, a porch lined with pillars, a cunning little gable flanked by two red chimneys. It is painted a very respectable white, with equally respectable grey slate for the roof, but scattered about its person are touches of the disreputable. There are little circular windows here and there, peeping out from beneath the roof like eyes. A later addition to the main house pokes out from the side like a long arm, impudently waving. At a first-floor window I caught a glimpse of crimson curtains, a most unwholesome colour for window hangings.

The house seemed to be winking at me, as though it knew I saw through its pretense of decency and cared not a whit.

Mrs. Kinsley drove the team up around the side, pulling up by the door in the newer addition. "I'll put up May and June for the night," she said, pulling back the oilskin. "Go in down the passage through the kitchen. The library is across the hall. I believe my girl has kept a fire banked there."

Hopping down from the curricle, I stumbled through the wet and mud of the yard until I got to the blessed dryness of the porch. The door, thank heavens, was unlocked, and I made my way through the indicated passage. It was exceedingly narrow, three feet wide at the most, and dim as a tomb. The doors that lined it were all closed, and I could only guess what lay behind them. A dairy, I imagine now, and a woodhouse, and perhaps a scullery, but alone, in the dark, they could have been anything.

I passed through the kitchen, crowded with smells and hanging pots, and into the main hallway. It was nearly as dark as the passage had been, but what I could see of it was grander, hung with elegant paper and bordered in handsome oak. One of its doors was open, and the kindest, friendliest yellow light spilled out of it. I lurched toward it and then found myself staring.

My wildest daydreams as a girl were of the day when I would have as many books as I pleased. Mrs. Kinsley's library looked as though it had been cut straight out of those childish fancies. Wood-panelled walls, richly gleaming in the firelight; comfortable chairs of plush red velvet, arranged cozily on either side of a terrestrial globe; a mantle of polished oak, on which sat a plaster bust of Athena, beautiful and severe. And the books! Shelf upon towering shelf of books, each with its own lead glass door, each full to the point of bursting with volume after precious volume.

What I wanted to do, more than anything, was tear the doors open and devour each one, gorge myself on words until my child-self was sated and content. Instead, I stood before the fire, turning slowly to dry myself on both sides, like a chicken roasting itself on a spit.

I was nowhere near dry by the time Mrs. Kinsley came in, quite damp herself. "My apologies for the wait," she said. "It takes a while to settle the horses on days like this. They are calm as captains on the road, but as soon as I get them back into their stables the thunder seems to spook them."

She dropped into one of the plush red armchairs with a sigh, indicating that I should do the same. I obeyed, but hesitantly — I did not want to stain that beautiful velvet. From a side table she picked up a bronze bell, summoning from goodness knows where an elderly woman with a face like a pickled walnut. Her "girl," I assumed, although the woman looked older than we two combined.

"Tea, Rebecca," she said, "and some iced buns, if there are any left."

Rebecca said nothing, only nodded and vanished in a manner most unsettling to me. Mrs. Kinsley turned to me and looked me up and down, just as she had in the road, her eyes all ice and morning skies.

"You are the teacher," she said. It was not a question. "Ada Byrd, isn't it?"

"You have the better of me, I'm afraid. I know you only as Mrs. Kinsley."

"Mrs. John Kinsley." A quick smile melted the severity of her thin mouth. "Norah is my Christian name. I was Norah Belsey, once upon a time, although my Belsey days are long since over."

Rebecca appeared again, this time carrying a silver tray. Two cups patterned with olive branches were set before us, the porcelain so thin I could nearly see through it. They were joined by a delicate teapot and milk jug, and then a plate of sticky-sweet iced buns. I looked at them and felt my mouth flood.

"Thank you, Rebecca," Mrs. Kinsley said, and without a word the woman disappeared again.

"She's a Lowry Bridge girl," the widow said, pouring a liberal splash of milk into her tea. "She's really too old to keep on now, I suppose, but I'm so used to her I should hate to have to train up another in her place. Country girls are always too independent. They make terrible servants. And worse wives, I hear. Have a bun, Miss Byrd."

I could not think of what to say in response to the rest of her statement, and so I obeyed and tried a bun. In that moment, cold and hungry as I was, it was the sweetest thing I had ever tasted. Mrs. Kinsley watched me eat it, her face smooth and impenetrable as that of the goddess watching us from her fire-side perch.

"I suppose you have heard," she said, "that I am a witch."

I choked on a mouthful of pastry. Only a hasty swallow and a quick gulp of tea saved me from a very undignified death.

"I beg your pardon?" I gasped after swallowing.

"A witch," Mrs. Kinsley repeated, her eyes crinkling with amusement. "No need to play innocent. I know what the children say about me, and I am not offended. Every town needs its witch, doesn't it? Someone to whisper about in the dark?" She took another sip of tea. "You must have had someone like that, Miss Byrd, when you were young. Some woman in your town who was just a little too strange, a little too old or wild or mad, for you to think of her as just a woman."

There had indeed been a woman like that in my own town, one who lurked at the edges of my child's mind in a most thrilling and satisfying manner. Her name was Jenny Carpenter. She was an old maid, a lonely creature who lived in a ruinous cottage and could often be seen wandering about without a hat, wringing her hands and muttering furiously to herself. She wore her grey hair in two braids, like a schoolgirl, and had yellow, splintered fingernails that looked as sharp and cruel as the serrated edge of a shark's tooth. Sometimes when she passed, we could hear her giggle, an eerie sound to come from such a wizened face.

I thought her a fiend, as did every other child I knew. It was a game we played, to see how close we could get to Old Jenny's door before losing our nerve. One little boy got all the way up to it one day and stood for several minutes on her front step before turning tail and bolting. And then, one cool autumn day while Florrie and I were walking home from Sunday school, I bested him: I knocked.

It was not something I planned to do before I did it. We passed by Jenny's wretched little house with its sagging porch and dirt-sugared windows, and the sight of it made me think of the boy who had climbed her front step, how admired he'd been after that venture. I was taken by a sudden urge to prove myself. Leaving Florrie by the side of the road, I marched down the path to Jenny's house, mounting the step and standing on that decrepit porch, its rotting beams creaking beneath my feet. One deep inhale to steady myself, and I rapped twice upon Jenny Carpenter's door with a trembling hand.

A moment passed, then two, with no sign that anyone had heard me, and I breathed a secret sigh of relief. But then I heard a cough from inside the house, and the sound of shuffling feet, and then the door swung open, bringing with it the smell of mildew, and I saw Jenny Carpenter standing there, swaying slightly as she clung to the doorknob.

She was naked. I could see the sallow skin hanging loose around her belly and thighs, the low swinging of the flesh on her upper arms. Her hair was not in girlish braids that day, but hung limp over her bony shoulders, yellow-grey and dirty. I stared at her, unable to look away from the wrinkled brown tips of her swaying breasts, the shadow of her mossy cleft. She smiled at me, displaying teeth as brown and broken as her nails.

"Pretty girl," she mumbled, shuffling forwards. One hand stretched out toward me, the sharp fingers reaching for my face. I could smell her unwashed body, her urine and sweat. And then that hideous giggle, that unnaturally youthful sound, and I turned and fled, snatching Florrie up from the side of the road.

I had not thought of Jenny Carpenter for many years. I did not like to think of her now.

"This is a beautiful library," I said, for the silence had stretched on for too long, and she was beginning to look at me rather quizzically. "That is Athena, isn't it, on the mantelpiece?"

"Indeed, yes," Mrs. Kinsley said, her pale eyes flicking over to the goddess's place on the mantelpiece. "Parthenos herself. I thought her my particular patron as a girl."

"Did you study the classics?"

Another of those quick, melting smiles. "Not formally. But I read whatever I could get my hands on about the Greeks. I loved the stories of Olympus, all those gods squabbling amongst themselves. I wanted to go to Greece for my honeymoon, but John never did care much for travel." A little sigh escaped her, as though the thought of that lost honeymoon still bore weight. "It was the only time he ever refused to indulge me. Even this house was an indulgence of his; it was our summer house, built for me after we were married. He had another wife before me, and in his will, he left the rest of his estate and his business to the children from that marriage. This house is what was left to me — the house, its land, and the horses. And the books, of course."

"Have you read them all?"

"Not yet. A little more than half, by now. I peruse them at my leisure, and often give them away once I have finished with them. I gave one to your predecessor, in fact — Miss Amelia Webster."

That name galvanized me. I sat straighter in my chair as though pulled upwards by a string. "You knew Miss Webster?"

Mrs. Kinsley nodded placidly. "She often came to visit me in the evenings after school let out. We were the same age, you see, and of sympathetic temperaments. I thought of her as a friend."

A veritable tidal wave of questions rose to my tongue then — about Mrs. Kinsley, about Miss Webster, about their evenings together in that pretty, lonely house. But Mrs. Kinsley suddenly rose from her seat, cocking her head.

"The rain has stopped," she said, and so it had. The relentless drumming on the roof and windows had ceased as though it had never been. "And it is growing dark outside, Miss Byrd. No doubt someone will be looking for you."

I stood and said that I would walk home, wanting to get a little fresh air before supper, and Mrs. Kinsley did not try to dissuade me. She reached out and clasped my hand, her skin warm and dry where mine was still clammy and cold.

"I am glad we have met," she said. "Perhaps you could visit again sometime."

As I started down the lane, the mud sucking eagerly at my shoes, I looked back over my shoulder at Mrs. Kinsley's house. The windows that faced the road were all dark, gazing blankly down at the world. The clouds had thinned, and I could see the dusk spreading like a stain, a couple of winking stars floating in the sky above the trees. I stood there, that damp chill still settled in my bones, and felt the sheer emptiness of the coming night pressing down on me.

When I came through the door, Mrs. Grier seemed to assume that I had waited out the storm at the manse with Agatha. She made a few remarks to that effect over supper and then over the dishes.

Finally, I felt myself forced to say: "In fact, it was not Mrs. MacPherson who rescued me, but Mrs. Kinsley. She saw me walking in the rain and let me stay in her house until it passed."

Mrs. Grier gave me a long, steady look, her mouth thinning to a line. She looked a little like Mrs. Kinsley just then — regal, aloof.

"Mrs. Kinsley, is it," she said, in a voice that clearly said it certainly oughtn't be! "Well, now. I hear the summer home is pretty fancy. I've never been, of course."

"She's never had you over for tea?" The thought was frankly baffling. Lowry Bridge is a small town. Neglecting to let a neighbour into one's home could only be an intentional slight.

"Never," Mrs. Grier replied, her voice brittle and bright. Her hands, sunk deep into the sink, rattled around beneath the suds. "Mrs. Kinsley is a breed apart. Stands to reason that she would only have a taste for certain people."

Those words were innocent enough, but I understood their import. I found myself flushing warm all over with irritation, my hands clenching tight on the drying rag as though it were a neck they'd like to wring. She did not see me do it, thankfully, and the rest of the evening passed without incident. Still, I cannot help but fret over her words now, in the privacy of my own room.

Why is Mrs. Grier so set against Norah Kinsley? Is there some bad blood between them? Or does she simply suffer from that most provincial of afflictions: fear of a woman alone?

October 17, 1901

A scandal took place in the schoolyard today, recounted to me in detail by several horrified witnesses. Apparently, at recess Caroline Mason and Arthur Benson were seen standing very close to one another, several yards away from the other children. There were smiles, bashful glances. There may have been handholding. There may even — so a very indignant Winifred insisted — have been more.

"He *kissed* her!" the girl told me, looking utterly horrified. "Right on the cheek! And they ain't even married, Miss Byrd!"

Married, indeed, they are not. I knew I would have to have a word with Caroline about such an indiscretion, and so I asked her to stay behind at dismissal. Once the last student had fled through the door and into the autumn chill, I told her to tell me what had happened in the schoolyard.

"Nothing," she said very quickly, but scarlet immediately began to travel up her neck and across her cheeks. Caroline is a child who blushes easily. It was probably adorable when she was a child, and will be very becoming when she is a young lady, but now, in her betwixt-and-between state, it looks quite silly. "We wasn't . . . we was just talking, Miss. We didn't do nothing wrong."

Wincing at her grammar, I told her that even so, it would do well to be more reserved in her behaviour toward Arthur. Absurd though it felt to cross-examine a twelve-year-old, I knew it had to be done; a young girl's reputation is as fragile as ice on a water bucket, and just as liable to break and melt away. Caroline nodded along, although I could not tell if she truly understood what I was trying to say. Perhaps a girl as young as she could not yet comprehend the gravity of the situation, was innocent of the burden laid upon her shoulders by virtue of her sex.

"I didn't kiss him, Miss," she said, but her denial this time was more hesitant, her eyes a little dreamier than they'd been before. As though she were thinking back on the events of the day, lingering over a sweetly whispered word, or the brush of a thumb along the back of her hand. "But—"

"There mustn't be any *buts*, Caroline. You know how to behave properly, I hope — you have listened to your mama and Mrs. MacPherson enough to understand that some things are not for little girls to do."

"Ye-e-es." Caroline drew this affirmation out into a thin and wavering line. "But . . . my ma met my pa when she was thirteen, and they got married pretty soon after. He must have kissed her, don't you think?"

There was much I could have said in response to this, although I chose not to. Thirteen and married! How unbearably medieval!

"Be that as it may, Caroline, you and Arthur are *not* married, and so I must remind you to act like a lady outside of my classroom as well as inside of it. You will mind your reputation, or I shall have to pay a visit to your father. Is that clear?"

This threat was only so much hot air, designed to make the girl mind more than anything, and it did the trick. Caroline agreed that she would behave herself, although she did so with a wounded, reproachful glance that stayed under my skin long after she'd left. It reminded me of a girl I knew when I was young — a school chum in whose bed I'd spent the night, just once, when I was thirteen.

Her name was Helen. She had black curls, so round that I spent my school days longing to stick a finger inside one and wear it as a ring. The curls were natural, not achieved by way of rags or hot pokers, and the night I slept in her bed they spread appealingly across her pillow as we lay in the dark and whispered to one another about all the things young girls have on their minds. She asked me if I'd ever been kissed, and when I said no, never, she said she hadn't either, and wondered what it was like. Her sister had a beau, and she knew that *they* had kissed, for she had seen them do it.

I don't know who came up with the idea. It may have been Helen. It may have been me. Regardless, we hit upon the notion of trying out this kissing business. She leaned over me, the ends of her dark curls brushing against my cheeks. I could not see her face beneath the shadow of her hair, could not imagine what expression she might be wearing as she gazed down at me. Feeling queer, I lay still and waited, my chin tipped up toward her.

It seemed to take an eternity before her lips brushed mine, bringing with them an unfamiliar heat, a taste of honey and salt. The sensation was not unlike the times that I had lain in the dark and practised kissing upon the back of my hand, imagining it to be the mouth of some unknown, unseen person. And yet, it was not like that at all. I could feel her pulse beating, as though my mouth touched not her lips, but the paper-thin skin over her wrist. A strange tide rose within me, stirring the currents of my blood. It made me gasp, and my mouth opened under hers, blooming like a wet rose. My tongue extended past the edge of my lips, seeking.

That seemed to spook her. She reared back like a startled horse, and I could see the ends of her curls swaying in the darkness, a faint impression of black upon black. Her eyes I could not see, but somehow I knew that they were peering down at me, searching for proof of some untested hypothesis. I could imagine her expression now: wounded and mistrustful, like Caroline's, brimming with reproach.

Helen shook her head, as though waking from an unpleasant dream, and lay down again on her side of the bed. A full foot of space separated our bodies.

"Don't see what all the fuss is about," she said. I remember that distinctly, and the strange little tremor in her voice as she said it. "Let's go to sleep."

Go to sleep she did, almost immediately, while I remained awake in the dark beside her, one hand straying up to my mouth. I was acutely aware of her warmth, her smell, the sound of her deep, even breaths. The gulf between us rebuked me. I thought of how she had started away from me, as though I had done something extraordinary and irregular. I felt, that night, like a freak.

That was my first kiss, if such a thing even counts as a first kiss. My second occurred sixteen years later, under very different circumstances. But I will not think of that, not right now.

I do not recall what happened to Helen, if she is married now, or a widow, or a spinster, or dead. We were not friends after that night, that I know.

October 20, 1901

*I*t is Sunday now — the parlour clock just chimed the midnight hour — and in just a few short hours I shall have to rise for the usual Sabbath routine of breakfast, Bibles, and church. I ought to be asleep. Instead, I have spent these last few hours lying in bed, waiting for sleep to find me, all for naught. I must write down what happened this evening, I think, before I will be able to rest. And before this candle stub gutters out completely, leaving me in the dark.

Saturday evening saw me walking over the bridge and up to the manse for a late supper with Agatha. The Reverend was there, of course, but the Griers were not; Mrs. Grier had been taken with a sick headache, and Mr. Grier, it seems, is reluctant to partake in any social situation without his wife by his side. I had feared that I would feel terribly old maid-ish, dining with a married couple alone — that I would be intruding on their intimacy like an unwanted chaperone.

Happily, this was not the case. Agatha kept up a steady flow of conversation, asking after my students, and chuckling at my recounting of Effie's brief feud with Clara; I in turn asked her about their behaviour in Sunday school, and was amused to learn that George Perley once asked her where Cain had found a wife, if there were only him and his parents alive on the whole Earth after he murdered Abel. (This was the kind of thing I often wondered myself in Sunday school, though I was never bold enough to ask.) Occasionally we paused so that the Reverend could interject a question or observation — more of the latter than the former, it must be said, and most of them on such subjects as the nature of sin, forgiveness, Godliness, and so forth. Very edifying conversational topics, to be sure, but somewhat out of place at the table.

"You must forgive Mr. MacPherson," Agatha said to me after the fifth (or was it sixth?) such digression. "He spends so much time in the pulpit that he sometimes forgets where he is and starts sermonizing over supper."

She said this with a laugh, and no trace of malice, but the Reverend frowned at her, very sternly, and her laughter faltered. He took no notice of either of us from that moment forward but sat and ate his dinner in silence, his grey brows lowered ominously. Our conversation was not so easy after that, nor our laughter. For the rest of the evening, she darted glances at his thunderous face, her own contorted with anxiety. The night, which had been so gay and full of promise, was spoiled.

I made my excuses soon after supper, pleading an early morning and lesson plans still to go over. The Reverend made no attempt to keep me — indeed, he barely acknowledged my goodbyes — but Agatha insisted on walking me down the lane, saying that she did not want me to be alone in the dark.

"He does get cross when I tease him," she said as we started walking, her arm threaded companionably through mine. It was a cold night, and it did us both good to draw closer together. "I know I oughtn't do it, but I simply cannot help myself. All that talk of sin and hellfire." I felt the sigh that went through her. "I suppose it is to be expected, being the wife of a minister. Sin and hellfire are the orders of the day."

"Is it terribly hard?"

Agatha considered the question in silence. Our shoes squelched a bit in the mud left by the autumn rain. From either side of the road came the chirruping song of autumn field crickets, as beautiful in its way as the cry of a fiddle.

"Sometimes," she said finally. "He doesn't approve of novels. I must hide them in my hope chest and wolf them down when he is gone, like a child gorging himself on sweets while his mother's back is turned. That is hard. Or when the children in Sunday school ask questions about hell, and they are so frightened, and I must answer the way *he* might. Or when we had to come here, because it was the only parish that wanted him, and I knew no one, and I had Douglas all alone . . . Yes. It is terribly hard sometimes."

In that moment, I acted without thinking. Withdrawing my arm from Agatha's, I reached down and took her hand in mine, squeezing gently. Her palm was very warm, her fingers delicate as the wings of a sparrow. It seemed to me utterly natural to do this, and just as natural to say:

"I'm glad you came here, Agatha."

There was more that I wanted to tell her: that I was grateful to have her as a friend; that she was the last thing I'd expected to find here in Lowry Bridge; that I wished she did not have to hide her books or worry about teasing her husband. But it all sounded silly in my head, and not really what I meant to say at all, and so I simply held her hand.

She smiled, squeezing back, and we continued in companionable silence until we reached the bend in the road. There she said she must turn back, for the Reverend would be waiting for his tea. I watched her slowly fade into the darkness, her pale dress first becoming a smudge, then a stain, then nothing at all. The thought of her trotting back up to the manse, waiting on her irritable husband and anxiously checking his face for signs of displeasure made me sigh.

I turned to continue walking, struck by the utter stillness around me. No wind blew through the trees; no dogs barked in the distance; no owls called from the heart of the woods. The clouds overhead had gathered thickly in the night, and there was no moon to light my way. The world was dim and full of shadows, the road barely visible in front of me. I took one step forward, then two, then stopped.

The crickets had stopped singing.

I saw no one, heard nothing, but a sense unbound to any bodily mode of perception screamed a warning deep within my guts. It was an instinct more than anything, some intuition left over from the days when man was prey to anything with teeth and claws. I felt with my entire body that there were eyes in the dark, hungrily tracking my every movement.

"Hello?" I called, remembering the day that Muriel had startled me so. Perhaps it was her, or some other young person, hoping to frighten the new schoolteacher as she made her way home. Perhaps it was a local man out cutting wood or checking his traps, wondering what a respectable lady was doing on the road so late at night. Or perhaps there was an animal hiding in the trees, choked with the same fear that held me frozen in place.

No answer came to me, and though I stood and waited, no one emerged from the deeper shadow of the trees. Presently my heart began to slow. After a few moments I was able to move again, although I did so cautiously, one foot at a time. A child may know that there are no monsters under the bed, waiting to grab his ankles, but he will take a running leap onto the mattress anyway, just in case.

"Nervous, nervous," I whispered to myself. My voice was brash and jocular, like Florrie's used to be.

I barely noticed the first one when it hit me. It felt like a small object, a twig or a pebble, thrown against my left shoulder. The second one struck the back of my neck, and that made me pause and turn, squinting into the darkness. The third one struck my face, and I reached out to catch it as it fell, raising it to my eyes to look at it. A spiky black insect, its long legs working feebly as it struggled to recover from its headlong crash into my cheek. A name came to mind unbidden, as clear in my mind as though I had just read it in a book: *Gryllus pennsylvanicus.*

"A cricket?" I whispered, puzzled. I let the thing drop to the ground, looking up, and then

then they were upon me by the dozens, the hundreds, uncountable numbers of tiny black bodies hitting my face, my chest, my legs. They flew directly into me as moths might a burning lamp, the air filled with the soft whirr of their rustling wings. It was like being pelted with handfuls of living gravel. I shrieked, waving my arms frantically around my head in an attempt to beat them off, but they kept coming in thick black waves, bouncing off my torso and limbs, catching in my hair and the folds of my dress. When I crumpled to the ground, I felt their bodies burst wetly beneath my knees and feet, heard the hideous crunch of their exoskeletons giving way beneath my weight. The eighth plague, the desolation of Egypt, clouds of locusts descending on fertile ground and stripping it of its green, its life! I covered my head with my hands and waited to feel the sting of the creatures biting into my flesh, laying me bare as the shores of the Nile.

As soon as I did this, the pelting stopped. The sound of thousands of wings moving in unison disappeared, replaced with that eerie silence. And then, gradually, the singing of the crickets returned, as bright and lovely as before.

After a moment I lifted my head and looked down at myself, then around me. There were no crickets clinging to my dress, no insectile gore waiting to be scraped off my knees or skirt. I lifted a hand to inspect my hair, and found it similarly free of vermin. The road beneath my feet was, so far as I could tell, clear. It was as though it had never happened at all.

Somehow, I managed the walk back across the bridge to the Griers' house and went straight upstairs, latching my bedroom door behind me and shutting the window tightly. When I took off my clothes, I shook each item carefully, waiting to see a dead insect fall onto the floor. None did, not even a segment of a leg or a tattered wing.

The clock just struck half past one. I must go to sleep. But I feel that if I close my eyes, I will feel those terrible spiny bodies hailing down on me once again, hear the terrible crackle of them beneath my feet.

To calm myself, I am recalling what I know of the habits of field crickets. They can fly, of course, and they have been known to swarm during mating season. They sometimes throw themselves against bright objects, as so many insects do. This strange occurrence could be easy enough to explain, well within the bounds of nature.

Far less easy to explain is their disappearance, the lack of evidence on my person, on the ground. They were there, then they weren't, and I was alone once again with the black trees and the black sky. And those eyes in the dark, watching me.

Perhaps tomorrow I shall ask Mr. Grier if this is a thing that occurs regularly in Lowry Bridge, if he or anyone he knows has experienced a similar onslaught of insects or animals. Sometimes wild creatures adapt habits particular to their regions. It is possible, I suppose, that this is simply something that happens here. There is a kind of logic behind the movements of all wild creatures, inscrutable though that logic is to mankind; nothing occurs in the natural world that cannot be understood through patient observation. No matter how strange this interlude was to me, I know that there is a way to make sense of it. I have simply not discovered it yet.

But where did they go? Why was there no trace of them once the onslaught ceased?

I must go to sleep.

October 31, 1901

 $\mathcal{T}$ oday being Hallowe'en, I cancelled lessons for the second half of the day in favour of a little party. After lunch, I had Arthur Benson and George Perley help me push the desks back against the wall, leaving a great open space in the middle of the schoolhouse. (I could have managed to do so on my own, but Arthur was eager to show off how strong he was in front of Caroline, and George, of course, was eager to show Arthur the exact same thing.) On my desk was a spread of tarts and cookies, kindly provided by Mrs. Grier; the water barrel was filled with scarlet apples, and the children bobbed for them, coming up with flushed and dripping faces. We played pass-the-apple, trying to keep a bright red "sweet" balanced on forks without using our hands, and the girls tried the trick of looking in the mirror to see if they could catch a glimpse of their future husbands. All of them lined up to do it, using a little cracked hand mirror from Effie's desk — all, of course, but Muriel Melville.

"You're supposed to do it in a dark room, of course," Effie said scornfully when no future husbands appeared. "It doesn't work when it is light out."

"If it only works when it's dark," retorted Clara, with a rare flash of spirit, "how are you supposed to see if there's anyone in the mirror at all?"

And though Effie sniffed and tossed her head and looked very superior, she had no answer to *that* question.

At the supper table this evening, I finally got up the courage to ask Mr. Grier about the habits of wild things in the region, if he has ever noticed any strange behaviours from animals or insects. Perhaps he thought that it was idle curiosity on my part that led me to ask, or perhaps he was simply in the mood for a bit of yarn-spinning, but for the rest of the meal he entertained myself and his wife with tall tales: deer so thirsty at the height of summer that they drank the river dry, owls startled by passing hunters into flying backwards, bears that shaved themselves pink and donned trousers in order to pass as men and gain access to barrels of sugar in the general store.

"What about insects?" I asked him, interrupting an anecdote about a chicken his grandfather owned that had turned into a rooster overnight. "Bees, spiders, crickets . . . have you known them to act strangely here?"

Mr. Grier scratched his scalp through his thinning red hair, his brow furrowed in thought. "Well, now, I can't say I have," he admitted. "The bees swarm sometimes, of course, and we had a tremendous wasp nest out behind the Hall one year. Taller than a man, it was, and wider than one too."

"But the wasps themselves behaved normally?" I persisted. I hoped that he would say no — would tell me that the insects in these parts are prone to rise up and swarm for no reason, that it is a mystery all have experienced and none have solved.

But Mr. Grier nodded, assuring me that yes, the wasps behaved just as wasps always do, bothering ladies at picnics and stinging horses and generally being nuisances. He told me of another nest they had built beneath the eaves of the church one year, how a child had thrown a stone at it and caused a terrible panic as the indignant insects stormed out en masse, rushing the congregation in search of the ne'er-do-well that had attacked their home. And then he asked why I wanted to know, if it was something to do with "that natural stuff" of which I am so fond.

It was an opportunity to tell them both what happened. I opened my mouth to do it — the words were on the tip of my tongue — but just as they were about to come out, a thought occurred to me. I could describe the behaviour of the crickets, certainly, but how on Earth would I explain their disappearance? I pictured their faces as I told them that the creatures vanished, that there was no trace of them on the road or on myself, and imagined their expressions changing from interest to confusion to concern. They would pass from one to the other one of those veiled, complex, *married* looks. They would question my experience of the event, the reliability of my account. They might think me mad.

Instead I smiled and said yes, that was it exactly; I was teaching my students about how the habits of animals differ from one region to the next, even within species, and was hoping for some examples specific to Lowry Bridge. The Griers both nodded, satisfied, and the meal continued as usual.

So: I have no explanation yet for what happened on the road. I say "yet," because of course there must *be* a rational explanation.

It is dark now, the house quiet as a cemetery. From where I sit on my bed, scribbling awkwardly into my lap, I can just see out my window. There is nothing to see, of course, but a sliver of sky, and the uppermost tops of the trees blotting out the stars. My window is open once again, even though it is getting colder in the evenings, and I can hear the singing crickets now. One half of my mind is listening attentively to their song, waiting for the moment when it stops.

Sleep has not found its way to me yet tonight. Indeed, my rest has been so disturbed these past few weeks that I am nervous to go to sleep at all. It seems that every hour or so I wake up with a start, bathed in perspiration and panting in the dark, my eyes moving of their own accord from one side of the room to the other, searching. But for what?

November 6, 1901

The first cold snap of the autumn has arrived, and we are depleting the woodpile in earnest now, keeping the schoolhouse stove roaring throughout the day. This morning I came in to find the water bucket skimmed over with a thin layer of ice, delicate as fairy glass. The crickets have at last stopped singing, dead for another year. That, at least, is a relief.

Relief or not, the quiet has troubled my sleep. Last night I woke up damp with perspiration and choked with fear, startled out of a dream whose plot evaporated as soon as my eyes opened. I could recall nothing but the feeling of being watched, of running and being chased by something that I could not see. Sleep eluded me after this rude awakening, and I was drowsy and irritable all day, shorter with the Griers than was altogether polite, sharper with my students than was altogether necessary. I found myself distracted, as the day wore on, by the specimen jars on my desk, the owlet skull shining softly in the afternoon sun.

We'd had a skull, Florrie and I: a doe's skull, sleek and pale, that we'd found grinning up at us from the floor of the woods behind our father's house. It was one of the objects that Father found the day that he looked in our shared wardrobe and found, carefully hidden beneath a pile of winter scarves, the various flotsam and jetsam the two of us had collected on our jaunts into forest and field, painstakingly sorted into jars and make-shift pressing-books. These objects he gathered up and placed in a row on the white marble of the sitting room table, like convicts in a line, before calling us in to see him. I was twelve or so, Florrie eight.

Where was Mother that day, I wonder? Lying down with a headache, perhaps. She often was when such things occurred.

Each item he took between two outraged fingers and shook at us, demanding to know why we had kept them, for what purpose, to what end. The bones of the squirrel we'd dug up from our mother's garden. A ragged snakeskin found abandoned between the boards of a picket fence. A number of Florrie's drawings, including one he brandished repeatedly of a hare's corpse, its abdomen eaten away by vermin, its spine brutally exposed. We had found the carcass in a field and examined it for hours, disgusted and transfixed. This picture he looked at again and again, until with a sudden, furious gesture he tore it in two. I felt Florrie's hand spasm within my own at the sound of it, as though it was her own flesh that he ripped, not paper.

My teeth worried at my lower lip. I tasted blood.

"You dirty little beasts," he said, and his voice as he said it was no louder or more violent than it ordinarily was. It may well have been quieter. "What is this trash?"

It was my responsibility to speak up, to explain, to defend our little collection and the passion that had inspired it. But my words withered and died as he turned his gaze upon me, my tongue limp and dry within my mouth. It was Florrie who stepped forward, Florrie who thrust her chin up and planted her feet, ready to fight.

"It isn't trash, Father," she said. "You see, we—"

But her words were lost as he raised his hand with its cut switch. That dread instrument came down again and again upon her, a jagged lick of lightning, and the sound of its passage through the air freed my feet and loosened my tongue. I tried to thrust myself between the two of them, to take the blows upon my own shoulders. I begged him to stop, telling him that it was not her fault but mine, that I had forced her to draw every picture, that I had collected all the objects myself. He could not hear me. She was screaming too loudly.

When he had finished with her, he turned the switch on me. His face was a perfect blank. He could have been thinking of anything.

The jars he broke, one by one, at our feet; the drawings and pressing-books he threw into the stove, the bones he crushed beneath his heel. And then, as so often happened, he pulled us both down the corridor toward the cupboard under the stairs. Its door was half the height of a man, slanted to accommodate the slope of the stairs, an iron lock on its outside. The shape of that lock is etched permanently into my retinas. When I close my eyes, a little whiteish-green picture of it seems to float before me, like the afterimage of a light. He unlocked the door with the brass key he kept always in his pocket, and then pushed us into the yawning dark.

"Here you are," he said, framed by the light behind him so that we could not see his face, "and here you will both stay until your mother calls you to bed. Use this time to beg God's forgiveness and ask Him to make you better little girls."

It may have been my child's imagination, but I thought that I heard a tremor in his voice as he said this — as though he really did hope that God would reach down from heaven to touch Florrie and me, turning us into the kind of little girls who would never collect animal bones or stare, transfixed, at a rotting carcass.

Florrie and I curled together like twins in the womb, my arms carefully wrapped around her middle. Her curly head fit just under my chin. The darkness inside of the cupboard was miles away from the wholesome dark of the night sky; it belonged entirely to the God of inside, not the God of outside.

"If I hadn't drawn the hare," she whispered. We always whispered in the cupboard. "If he hadn't seen that, Aidy, maybe he wouldn't be so angry."

"It was my idea to dig up the squirrel," I whispered back. It hurt to talk; my lips by then were little more than ragged flaps of well-chewed meat. "And I should have hidden the skull better."

Her hand found mine again and squeezed it tight. She and I shared a bed in those days, and whenever I began to thrash and murmur from a nightmare, she would find my hand and grasp it tightly, whispering my name over and over until I woke up. Her voice wove its way into my mind, her hand pulled me from my hideous dreams. In the daylight I was her protector, but at night, she was mine. I could always follow her out of the dark.

I wonder sometimes if Father remembers that day, the sound of breaking glass and tearing paper, the force with which he threw us into the cupboard and slammed the door. Did it make as strong an impression on him as it did on me? Or was it, to him, an ordinary day?

Mother never did come to get us that night. It was not until the next morning that we were rediscovered in the cupboard, curled up like mice in a nest. We were hauled out and onto our feet, dusted off and given breakfast, sent along to school. The remains of our jars and Florrie's drawings were gone, vanished into the air like so much gossamer.

November 12, 1901

Yesterday morning, a red-faced Eugene Castle was marched into school by his mother, she of the prayer meetings and white curtains, a lady of middling height but formidable stride. She strode up the aisle and as a greeting demanded: "What is this filth you've been teaching my son?"

The question was asked so violently and at such volume that I almost laughed. Fortunately, I caught myself in time.

"I must confess my ignorance, Mrs. Castle, as to what you refer," I said, as gravely as I could.

"Don't you play the fool with me, Miss Byrd!" she said, even louder than before. Poor Eugene flinched as though she had raised a hand to him, looking miserably at the schoolhouse floor. Those children already at their desks watched with fascination. "At table last night, my Eugene asked me about babies — said that he knows they do not come from the doctor's black bag! When I asked him why he would ask such a dirty question, he told me that you have been teaching him about how creatures multiply! That the children have been getting up to all kinds of devilishness, tramping through the woods and gathering insects and playing about in the river, instead of learning their letters! I won't have it, Miss Byrd; I simply will not. It's paganism, sheer paganism!"

My first reaction to such a charge was not, as it would become, annoyance or anger; instead, I found her immoderate display of righteous indignation rather amusing.

"Mrs. Castle," I said, "I'm afraid you have misunderstood. There is nothing paganistic about anything I have been teaching the children. I am simply—"

"Showing them dead things! and bringing in handfuls of worms!" she said. With every word she advanced on me a little bit, and with every advance on her part I retreated a single step. The hard edge of my desk struck the small of my back. "These children don't need to know about frogs, Miss Byrd! It is spelling and sums and the Bible they need, not all this nasty stuff. And a Hallowe'en party! Why, you've all but got them burning the wicker man! When Mrs. MacPherson hears what you have been up to—"

"Mrs. MacPherson knows, and approves," I said, a little too sharply to be strictly polite. Perhaps this was disloyal to Agatha, but if I was to drink hemlock, let it be in good company! "As a minister's wife, it is her duty to show the children how to admire the beauty of the Lord's creation through Scripture. I am trying to do the same thing by helping them to understand the workings of that creation. See, here—"

I reached blindly behind me to take up one of my specimen jars. I meant to show her one that housed a pretty sample of moss found by Eugene himself on our last ramble, but alas, fate was against me; the jar that I picked up and thrust in front of her small, round eyes was the one that housed my owlet skull!

Mrs. Castle's mouth fell open, making little gasping motions like a landed trout. One of the children let out a hiccupping giggle before being loudly shushed by his seatmate. I put the jar down hastily on the desk behind me where she would not see it, but the damage had been done.

"Well!" she cried at last. "I do not know what to say, Miss Byrd, but that I am astonished — I truly am! That you would keep such a thing on your desk! That you would show it to children! You stand there bold as brass and tell me you have no truck with heathenry, and yet here you are waving this . . . this witch's trinket under my nose!"

The woman was, I thought, going to run out of exclamation points if she didn't use them more sparingly. I felt my jaw starting to clench and my hands trying to work themselves into fists.

I spoke slowly to ensure that my voice would not tremble when I said: "You are a Christian, are you not, Mrs. Castle?"

"You ask me such a thing," said she, quite swollen now with indignation, "after coming to my house every week for prayer meeting! Yes, Miss Byrd, I am a Christian — no one, I hope, has ever had cause to doubt that of *me*!"

"And you believe in the Bible, from beginning to end? You believe that God said, 'Let the waters bring forth abundantly the moving creature that hath life, and fowl that may fly above the Earth in the open firmament of heaven' — and that, so doing, He saw that it was good?"

"Don't you quote Scripture at me, you young guppy," she snapped. Her face was very red, little flecks of spittle building in the corners of her mouth. "I should think I know my Bible — I daresay I have read it more often this very week than you have all your life!"

"Then you agree," I said, "that God created the bird to whom that skull belonged, and therefore the skull itself. That when I show it to my students, I am doing nothing more than showing them that which God Himself has created. That I am encouraging my students to take joy in the world that their Lord created for them all. That I am, in fact, engaged in a particularly Christian endeavour, with not a whiff of the pagan about it!"

I confess that I started this little speech louder than I meant to, and that I only became louder still as I went on; by the last word, I was fairly shouting. That final syllable rang out in the now-silent schoolhouse, clear as the little brass bell I ring at lunchtime.

However, loud as I was, I did not intimidate Mrs. Castle. She drew herself up to her inconsiderable height, ominous as a thunderhead.

"This will not stand, Miss Byrd," she said. "Be sure that I will be informing the school board of your conduct. I don't doubt but that they will have something to say."

And away she swept, leaving poor little Eugene half dead with embarrassment and the rest of my students wild with delight at having witnessed such an entertaining fracas. It was the work of nearly half an hour to get them to mind their lessons and set to their work, and for the rest of the day I caught them looking up at me with new curiosity. Once I looked up from my desk and saw Muriel levelling a gaze at me that I could not interpret — it was imbued with her usual disdain, but there seemed something else lurking in its depths. A hint, perhaps, of respect.

I had thought that perhaps that would be the end of it, but when I went to call on Agatha tonight, she seemed utterly dejected. "I have had mothers coming in and out of the manse all day," she said wearily, her head leaning against the arm of her ugly settee, "all with 'serious concerns' about what Mrs. Castle tells them is going on in your classroom. Heaven knows what exactly she said! All she passed on to me was that you are some kind of pagan Hypatia, and that you won't stop until the children of Lowry Bridge are dancing naked in moonlit glades."

I felt the sick tide of a headache starting in my skull. "What a lot of fuss over some worms and bones! What on Earth is the matter with these women? Do they honestly think that God hates for children to become less ignorant?"

"I really believe they do." Agatha sighed. "Many of them take 'children must be seen and not heard' far more to heart than they ought. That Mrs. Castle is the worst of them. Poor Eugene simply can't please her in church, it seems — every time he comes in for Sunday school his arms are covered in red marks. She pinches him to make him sit still."

I left her in a rather bitter mood. It is hardly the first time I have experienced resistance from a parent, but the opposition has rarely been so loud and visible as this. I wonder if Mrs. Castle truly intends to write to the board? I pray she will not. After Willoughby, I am hardly in a secure enough position to argue my case with them.

I received an invitation to dine with Mrs. Kinsley today, a fine distraction from all the goings-on. The widow actually sent a note to me by way of Muriel Melville, who thrust it roughly into my hand at the end of the day and then raced away before I could offer my thanks. The note was courteous, but brief.

Miss Byrd,

If you are so inclined, I should like to have you for supper on November 16th at six o'clock. Rebecca's meals are as good as her iced buns, and I am in the mood for company.

Sincerely,
Norah Kinsley

I dread telling Mrs. Grier whose company I shall be keeping, but I intend to accept her invitation. It shall do me good to think about something other than the Mrs. Castles of the world for an evening, I think.

November 17, 1901

So wary was I of Mrs. Grier's response that I only told her over breakfast yesterday morning that I would be spending the evening at Mrs. Kinsley's house. She hid her displeasure a little better than she did last time, murmuring something about me doing exactly as I pleased, but her mouth tightened, and her teacup clattered fiercely every time she set it down. Still, she did not prevent me from going.

(And how, exactly, could she have prevented me? Did I think she would lock me in my bedroom, chain me up in the cellar? Be sensible, Ada!)

On my first visit to Mrs. Kinsley's house, I had been too cold and uncomfortable to feel anxious, but as I walked up the lane to the summer house yesterday evening, I found my stomach churning and my hands tangling up in one another for want of anything to occupy them. As I set my hand on the gate, I was awash with a sickening conviction that I would not be able to speak at all when I passed over the threshold — that some eerie, undefinable *thing* would shut my lips completely, and Mrs. Kinsley would be so annoyed by my reticence that she would banish me from her table. Only with a tremendous act of will did I manage to grit my teeth against the vision of myself upright and mute in Mrs. Kinsley's dining room, growing paler and paler as I strove to speak, and push on toward her front door.

I needn't have worried. Even if I *had* somehow found myself mute, I am sure that Mrs. Kinsley would have wheedled speech out of me regardless, for she spent the entire meal asking questions. Over Rebecca's excellent braised chicken, she asked about my students, their habits and manners; she asked about my life with the Griers; she asked about the parents of Lowry Bridge and how we were getting on. It was this line of questioning that led me to mention my tempestuous interview with Mrs. Castle. Mrs. Kinsley seemed sympathetic, but wholly unsurprised.

"There are many fine things about Lowry Bridge," she said, "but Edith Castle is not one of them. Nor are her friends, Christian though they claim to be. The mothers of this town are a close-minded and commonplace lot. The ones I dealt with when I was a teacher were the same."

Mrs. Kinsley had been a teacher! I tried but could not imagine her standing at the front of a classroom, plainly dressed and armed with a pointer. The widow must have seen something of my astonishment in my expression, for she chuckled.

"Did you think that I materialized fully formed in this house?" she asked. "I have a past, Ada, just as you do. Just as everyone does." She took a contemplative sip of wine. (Oh, yes, we scandalous two had wine — a nice red, rich as blood and very sweet. I had only one glass, not wanting to smell of it upon returning to the Griers, but still, it went to my head.) "I taught for years before I met John. I wasn't old when we married, not as such things are reckoned now, but I was certainly closer to thirty than twenty. People used to poke fun at him for that — make jokes about him 'taking an old maid off the shelf.' He was fifteen years older than me. A widower. Rich."

Her eyes drifted thoughtfully to the lamp in the centre of the table, the dancing flame pulling lustfully at the wick. All was quiet, save the sound of Rebecca crashing about in the kitchen.

"You must have loved him very much."

Mrs. Kinsley looked at me then, one eyebrow raised. "Must I have?" she asked, a smile tugging at the corners of her thin lips. "Perhaps I did. I certainly loved that he seemed to care for me. It is a very seductive thing, knowing that someone wants you; it is almost as good as getting what you truly desire."

I swallowed and thought, all at once, of my bed in Willoughby, the feeling of sweat and spit drying on my skin, a trickle of salt running down my naked legs.

"I had become resigned to my lot as a spinster by then," she said. "My mother had stopped asking me when I was going to find a husband. Everyone took for granted that I was a lost cause, beyond all hope of normalcy. When John began courting me, I felt . . . triumphant. Perhaps I flaunted it a bit. My family certainly thought I did. My sister was so annoyed that she went around town telling anyone who would listen that I did not care for him at all, that I was only marrying him for his money." She shrugged. Her slim, aristocratic frame made the gesture look perfectly elegant. "The money helped. I was tired of being poor. But more than that, I was tired of being pitied, of being treated like a child who'd never grown up."

Such thoughts have run through my head many a time, word for bitter word. "Isn't it queer," I said, made bold by her boldness, or perhaps her wine, "that people will think an unmarried woman all but a child, and yet give her jurisdiction over their own children's education? One would think they would consider her unfit for such a task."

"One would," she agreed, another chuckle bubbling up in her throat. "I have often thought that spinsterhood combines the worst of childhood and womanhood — all the helplessness of the former and all the duties of the latter. Widowhood, on the other hand, has much to recommend it. A widow may do as she pleases, for she wears the respectable cloak of marriage about her shoulders still, and yet, she has no one to fetter her independence or dictate the company she keeps. If all women could be widows without marrying first, I think that there would be not a single woman in the world who would choose a living husband over a dead one."

This I have transcribed exactly from memory, for every syllable of the extraordinary statement etched itself into my brain immediately. It was not a *proper* speech by any definition of the word, and yet I found myself liking Mrs. Kinsley more for it, and for the ironical smile with which it was delivered.

After we had finished our dinner, nothing would do for Mrs. Kinsley but that we retired to the library for tea and a plateful of Rebecca's excellent scones with jam and clotted cream. There she insisted that I pick out a book from her collection — to keep, she clarified, not to borrow!

It would have been polite to demur and insist that I could not take a book from her, but to do so would have been anathema to my very nature. I found myself nearly salivating as I gazed at the rows of spines before me, each title an alluring siren's call. I wanted all of them, not just one! But there was a volume that called to me more than the others: a copy of John Henry Comstock's *Introduction to Entomology*, complete with Mrs. Comstock's excellent engravings and illustrations. I was surprised to find such a book on Mrs. Kinsley's shelf, but altogether glad. It would be useful, I thought, in the context of a natural history lesson, and useful as well in putting to rest those questions about crickets that have been nagging at me. I slid it from the shelf and felt the weight of it in my hand, greedy for the knowledge it held between its covers.

"Mrs. Kinsley," I began, but the widow shook her head.

"Norah," she said firmly, bestowing upon me one of her rare, warm smiles. Her hand caught up mine and squeezed it.

Was I really to call her by her Christian name? Such a thing seemed impossible.

"I cannot thank you enough for this," I said, and I meant it sincerely. "What a treasure you have given me! If ever you want anything from me, I hope that you shall ask for it."

What was the look in her eyes then? Some flicker — some flash — some sudden turn of light and shadow, like the gleam of a fish under water. I had hardly seen it before it disappeared, but something about it made my stomach twist. I took a step back under some pretext, turned my head in a pretense of looking at the titles crowding the bookshelves. The look unnerved me, made me experience a sensation like the chill that is said to mean a person is walking over one's grave. And yet, it was not unpleasant — not entirely.

As I walked home, I could not rid myself of the notion that something was trailing alongside me in the woods, just beyond the edges of my sight. I stopped several times and called out into the darkness, asking if anyone was there, but no one made themselves known to me. It was not until I stepped off the bridge and onto the other side of the river that the feeling abruptly stopped, like a candle suddenly blown out. A dog, I imagine — some stray living in the woods who caught the warm smell of fire and food wafting from my skirts.

Perhaps Mrs. Kinsley does expect me to call her Norah. I shall make an effort to do so, although the thought is daunting. She is so very imposing that I have caught myself thinking that she has always been her current age, born a woman of fifty rather than a baby.

Agatha was not in church this morning, and when I asked the Reverend as to her whereabouts, he made some vague mention of her being laid up with a terrible cold. I was scarcely surprised once I recalled how listless she had been at our last meeting, how her head had drooped onto the arm of the settee. I must visit her this week; the poor thing must be going mad with boredom, cooped up with only Douglas and the Reverend for company!

November 22, 1901

*T*hat little beast. That dreadful, *dreadful* girl!

This afternoon, after I'd rung the bell for dismissal, Muriel Melville remained seated at her desk. This was such an unusual occurrence — she is usually the first to bolt out the door — that I thought at first there was something wrong with her and asked if she felt ill.

"No, Miss," she replied. She sat in a curious attitude, her head half-cocked, like a dog listening for his master's voice, and she sounded distracted, even nervous. "I have something for you."

She reached into the depths of her pitted wooden desk and pulled out a bright bundle of something. Pulling herself to her feet, she trotted up to the blackboard and handed them to me, ducking her head as though the act embarrassed her.

It was a bouquet of flowers — not real ones, but ones so cunningly made from bright scraps of cloth that they looked almost real, attached to "stems" of thick black wire. There were cabbage-roses fashioned out of calico, daisies of deep blue velvet, demure freesias of buttery sateen. Each stitch was tiny and perfect, each petal exquisitely formed.

"Oh!" was all I managed to say after a few moments of speechlessness, and then again, "Oh! how lovely! Did you *make* these?"

Muriel cast her gaze down to the floor, one bare foot (for she still runs about with no shoes, even in this cold weather) scuffing at the floor. "Yeah," she mumbled.

"All by yourself?" I did not mean to sound incredulous, but it was almost impossible for me to think that such a wild, ungainly child could have sewn with such delicacy and care. My disbelief seemed to sting the girl; she looked up then, meeting my eye.

"Yeah," she said again, defiantly this time. "The widow taught me how. I'm good at it. Sewing and that. I *am* good at some things, Miss."

"You certainly are!" Lo and behold, a tiny smile played upon the girl's stubborn little mouth. "These are beautiful, Muriel. You are clearly very skilled with your needle. Do you make such things for your father and brothers, as well?"

It was the wrong question. The smile disappeared. Her eyes dropped back down to the floor, and her shoulders stiffened, as though they suddenly bore some tremendous burden.

"Dad'll want me," she mumbled, or something along those lines, and before I could say anything further, she dashed out the schoolhouse door, letting it slam shut behind her with such force that a little trickle of dust fell from the ceiling.

Well! I stood there like a statue, in a state of surprise not only from her gift but from her abrupt departure. Then, gathering my wits back about me, I set to finding a jar in which to place the flowers, setting them at the very edge of my desk, opposite the owlet skull, where the petals would catch the light. The delicacy of the work was even more appreciable in the shaft of afternoon sun coming in at the window. No two blossoms were alike in shape, fabric, and colour; no one pattern had been wholly repeated. The variety of design spoke to the girl's ingenuity, to the thought put into her gift, to the secret kindness in her child's heart. I had, I thought, grievously misjudged her. Perhaps there was still time for us to be friends of a sort. Perhaps, in the morning, we two could start anew.

A bouquet of false flowers has no scent, but as I admired Muriel's handiwork, I found my nostrils flaring as they caught the faintest trace of a smell. It was a salty, metallic tang, like the enticing reek of the sea. It was familiar, and yet I could not place it. I leaned forward toward the blossoms, burying my nose in those artificial blooms, and the smell grew stronger — and stronger — and yet again stronger. And then, my face still pressed to the bouquet, I felt a wetness on my skin, and a sensation of something not made of cloth — something that felt distinctly meaty, and hairy, and *animal*.

I could scarcely bite back a scream as I leapt back. A hand, applied to my face, came back thickly red and wet at the fingertips, and I knew at once why the smell had been familiar. Reaching into the centre of the bouquet, I groped blindly amongst the wire stems until I found the offending object. So gory and bedraggled was the thing in my hand that it took a moment or two before I could fully comprehend what it was.

Not an object at all, but a *tail* — that of a squirrel or some other bushy, creeping creature, its fur matted with blood, the tattered end of its severance oozing scarlet into my palm. It was still warm.

I have handled my share of dead animals over the course of my time as a natural history enthusiast, but this was different. That the thing had been included in the bouquet, that it had come to me from one of my students, disguised as a gift, made it far more ominous than any of the bits and pieces I had ever picked up of my own accord. Swallowing a hot tide of vomit, I pinched the thing between two fingers and threw it out into the dead yellow grass in the schoolyard. Afterwards, I scrubbed my hands and face clean with water from the rain barrel, shaking as much from shock and betrayal as from the chill of the water.

The flowers I threw down the privy, too incensed at the sight of them to admire them any longer, and then, out of the most morbid curiosity, I looked for the tail where it had fallen. I wanted to identify it, to know what kind of animal Muriel had so cruelly mutilated. I wanted, as well, to make sure that it was what I had seen, that I had not mistaken a silken blossom or ersatz cattail for that nauseating horror. However, I was unable to find it on the ground where I had dropped it, nor anywhere else around the schoolhouse. Perhaps some animal dragged it away while I was cleaning myself off. Or . . .

It did not occur to me in the moment, but now I recall the crickets on the road outside the manse, how they disappeared after those few hideous moments in the dark. I do not like to think about them, I do not *want* to think about them, but I can scarcely help it.

I shall say nothing to Muriel about this, not even to rebuke her. Let her observe that the flowers are nowhere to be seen and draw her own conclusions; let her not see how this rattled me, how easily I was taken in by her shy, schoolgirlish offering. I do not want her to know that she got the better of me. Her, or anything else.

November 28, 1901

Agatha still suffers dreadfully from a cold, so Mr. Grier drove me to the manse after supper this evening, his little cutter making quick time across the first snow of the season. He was, I thought, unusually quiet as we crossed the bridge, and when he handed me down (as he will insist on doing, no matter that I can easily climb down myself), he seemed to flinch away from my touch. I stared after him as he drove away, my feelings rather wounded. What, I wondered, had I done to him, that he should treat me so strangely?

This question weighed so heavily on my mind that I ended up recounting the story to Agatha, forgetting entirely my plan to regale her with the tale of Muriel's vile bouquet. The poor thing was in no fit state to comfort me. Her cold is a particularly nasty one; she scarcely got through two words together without pausing to sneeze.

"But, Ada," she said when I had finished, "did no one tell you? Mr. Grier has a particular horror of illness — he probably did not want you to come and see me at all. You know, of course, that the Griers are childless?"

Her face twitched and contorted as she spoke, and no sooner had the last syllable died than she let forth another mighty *haitch-choo!* I said yes, of course, and passed her my handkerchief.

"Well, they were not *always* childless. Many years ago, long before the Reverend and I came to Lowry Bridge, they had a son. His name was James, I believe, but then again, it might have been John, or Joseph. I heard his name only the one time."

This was such a startling piece of news that I had to look away for a moment to properly absorb it. A child! A little boy, running about that orderly house, knocking pictures askew and treading crumbs into the rugs! It was impossible to imagine.

"What happened to him?" I asked, but, of course, given the shape of the conversation, I feared that I already knew.

"I scarcely know the story myself," Agatha said, handing me back my handkerchief. "Only whispers. As it was told to me, when the boy was six or so, he went out to play one evening and did not return when it grew dark. A search party was called, but they could not find him; it was Mrs. Grier herself who did. She went across the bridge and deep into the woods, and there she found him, curled up tight beneath a tree. He was chilled to the bone, half-mad with delirium. Some sickness, it seemed, had come over him very suddenly, and left him too bewildered to find his way home."

Her face, I saw, had that same eager look it had had all those weeks ago when she had recounted Edmund Melville and his many wives. Her eyes shone over her reddened nose, as though she were recounting a fantastic scene from a sensational novel and not a real event in the lives of real people. It did not become her, this passion for tragedy; it made her pretty face suddenly, unaccountably ugly.

"Did the Griers not call a doctor?" My voice was a little sharper than I had intended. I hoped, I think, to dim that eager look a little, to make her recall that the boy she spoke of really had existed. It worked; she seemed to come back to herself a little, her eyes losing their look of unseemly interest.

"They did," she said. "But of course, the nearest doctor is in Portsmouth, and he was attending a difficult birth and could not leave. It was three days before he could come back to Lowry Bridge, and by then—"

"It was too late," I guessed, and Agatha nodded. "Did Mrs. Grier tell you about him?"

"Oh, no, certainly not. She does not speak about him — as you know yourself! No one else does either, out of respect. Someone told Hugh when we first came to Lowry Bridge, and Hugh told me." She threw a cautious glance over her shoulder at the door leading to the hallway. The Reverend's study was close by, and the walls of the manse are thin, very thin. "He said it showed how important it is to resign yourself to providence, submit to the will of the Lord. I didn't disagree with him, of course. But if that happened to Dougie, if he were taken from me like that . . . I would not be able to resign myself. I would hate God, hate Him enough to burst. Hugh would be angry if he knew — he already thinks I am too impious. But I can't help it."

She coloured and looked away, picking at a loose thread in the blanket on her lap. That unsettling avidity was gone from her face, replaced with defiance and shame in equal measure.

Her son slept in his cradle at the end of the settee, his face contorted in a frown that made him look like a little old man.

In those first few dreadful weeks after Florrie's death, there would come every so often a blissful moment of amnesia. The memory of my sister's passing would slip my mind; I would think of things that I wanted to tell her, or show her, or ask her, when I saw her next. And then, on the heels of such thoughts, would come the realization that I couldn't, that I never would again, and the world would fall suddenly, sharply away from me.

In those moments, I hated God. Enough to burst.

"I think," I said, and paused a moment to clear my throat, which had gone curiously thick. "I think, Agatha, that most people would feel that way about the loss of a child. If God is all-knowing, all-loving, He knows they feel it — and doesn't mind. How could He, if He was the one who gave them the capacity for feeling in the first place?"

Agatha's chuckle in response was a bit watery. "I'm sure you are right. Still, I don't like to think of Hugh ever finding out. I fear his version of God is not so lenient as yours."

Naturally not. The Reverend's God is the God of inside through and through, the God of stifling churches and ugly carpets. *He* has no truck with lenience.

Agatha let loose another mighty sneeze, and I offered my handkerchief again, and the conversation turned, quite naturally, to more ordinary things. She intends to put on a Christmas concert soon, held in the church just a few days before the feast itself. That such a thing would fall to the minister's wife and not the teacher surprised me, but she assures me that it has long been a tradition in Lowry Bridge; they have often passed a year or two without a teacher, but rarely any time at all without a minister's wife.

I gave her my promise that I would help her with this project. Goodness knows why — I enjoy Christmas concerts as much as I enjoy Sunday school picnics. Agatha has simply bewitched me; there can be no other explanation.

As I helped Mrs. Grier in the kitchen tonight, I watched her from the corner of my eye, looking for some trace of her great loss, some sign of the sorrow that she must feel to this day over her lost boy. She was her usual brisk self, giving me orders carefully phrased as instructions, smiling occasionally when I told her about the goings-on in my classroom. Smiling, but not laughing. She does not often laugh, I realize now.

We all sat together in the parlour after supper, Mrs. Grier at her sewing, Mr. Grier listening intently as I read aloud from a week-old newspaper. I let my eyes wander as I read, examining with new eyes the trinkets on the polished corner shelf, the faded prints hung over the mantelpiece. I was looking, of course, for some sign of the child, but again there was nothing. There is only one photograph in the house, and it is of the Griers in their wedding suits, hands clasped tightly as they stand unsmiling before a colourless background.

When I retreated to my bedroom for the night, it was as though I had never seen it before. Its ordinary lines and contents had been utterly transformed by Agatha's revelation. There are only two bedrooms in this tidy little house; mine, I realized, must have belonged to the boy when he was alive. The wardrobe had once held his clothing, the floor had once sounded with his little pattering feet. He had once stood on his tiptoes to peep out the window. Perhaps even the bed

No, that is too morbid a thought. Surely mine cannot be the bed the child died in.

A sudden, ferocious need for proof of the boy's existence gripped me. I looked in the wardrobe, under the rug, beneath the washstand, for any sign that a child might have lived in that room. It was the same kind of mania, I suppose, that came over me in the bedroom I had once shared with Florrie when I came home from her funeral, frantically gathering all the bits of her I could find there. Notes in her hasty and imprecise hand, pen and ink drawings of butterflies and birds, pictures she'd cut out of magazines, a hair ribbon she'd dropped between the bed and the wall. The act had soothed me, as much as I could be soothed at the time.

There was nothing in the room to indicate that the Grier boy had ever existed, not so much as a lost marble or stray handkerchief. His parents have wholly blotted him out. But why? Was it an offshoot of their grief, this need for annihilation? Or was it something else?

I have almost made my way through *Introduction to Entomology* by now. It is an interesting book, if a trifle dry, but I regret that it has taught me nothing about crickets that I did not already know.

December 6, 1901

*F*ather was here.

December 7, 1901

I was so stupefied yesterday that I could only manage a single
sentence. Today I am steadier, but bitter. Oh, very bitter!

The day had been quite pleasant, before. My students behaved
themselves, and a few made strides in their lessons that pleased
me. Peter Miller's spelling has improved, and Clara Brewer wrote
a composition ("On Ambition") so unexpectedly eloquent that I
began to wonder if I have been underestimating the girl all this
time. We spent the latter half of the afternoon practising our
songs for Agatha's Christmas concert, and the sound of childish
voices filling the schoolhouse with music put me in a marvellous
humour that lasted all the long walk home. When Mrs. Grier
called from the parlour that I had a visitor, I entered happily,
thinking that Agatha had come for tea.

All my good humour drained away when I saw *him* sitting
stiffly on the divan, one of Mrs. Grier's finest teacups clutched

in his hand. His eyes beneath their tremendous brows were round pebbles of slate.

"Father," I said, my voice little more than a gasp. In a novel, I suppose I might have swooned.

Father got up and kissed my cheek. He wears his whiskers unfashionably long. They scratched me.

"Hello, my dear," he said. Smooth as cream, his voice. It was just as smooth the day he came to collect me from Willoughby before term was out, the day he told me that I had cast a permanent shadow over the family name, ruined myself like a common slut. "How have you been keeping?"

I can scarcely remember what I said, then or in the moments that followed. For what purpose had he come to Lowry Bridge? Had Mrs. Castle sent her threatened letter to the board? Had he come to discipline me himself? There was no cupboard under the stairs in the Grier house, but . . .

My teeth began, of their own volition, to gnaw at the edge of my lip, worrying at a loose bit of skin. Father saw it and frowned, but in the presence of a stranger, he said nothing.

After a few moments of awkward conversation, Mrs. Grier excused herself, retreating to the kitchen on some pretext and making a point of shutting the door firmly behind her. I badly wanted to shout, "No, please! Don't leave me alone with him!" — but, of course, one can scarcely say such a thing about one's own father.

I have never liked to be alone with him, even at the age when little girls are meant to adore their fathers. His gaze reaches into me and rips out whatever peace I have made within myself, leaving me open and empty and raw.

"You look healthy," he said at last.

Every syllable that my father utters requires a translation, for he never says what he truly means. Here, what he meant was: "How fat you are! No wonder you are still unmarried, with no prospects, at the age of nine-and-twenty!"

"I feel healthy here," I replied, rather stupidly. "It is the country air, I think."

"Hm, yes! It is charming," said he.

Which translated to: "What a miserable hamlet this is! But then, what other kind of place would have you?"

"My-my students are doing very well," I said, grasping desperately at conversational straws. Oh, why can I never find the strength to speak to my father with unguarded honesty, as so many daughters do? Florrie could — Florrie never let him bully her as he does me. She spoke the truth and shamed the Devil, every time. "There are fourteen of them. The youngest has just learned how to write her name."

"Fancy!" Father said, raising his eyebrows.

Which translated to: "I don't care a fig about your students, and well you know it!"

"And I have made a friend," I blundered on. "Mrs. MacPherson. She is the minister's wife" — this last thrown at him desperately, in hopes that it would assure him that I was not running voluptuously wild.

"The minister's wife," Father repeated, his eyebrows still raised as though he very much doubted that there was any truth to what I said. "Well, well."

Which translated to: "Enjoy *that* while it lasts. Sooner or later she will discover what kind of woman you are!"

We sat in silence, he sipping his tea with no evidence of enjoyment, me letting my hands twist and pluck at my skirt. I pulled at it too hard; there is a pucker in the fabric now. My mouth is puckered too, with sores left from my teeth. I cannot help but run my tongue over them.

"Why are you here?" The words escaped me in a hideous rush of sound. I had not meant to say them. They were as sudden and uncontrollable as a sneeze.

"I had business in the region," he replied, not missing a beat. "I thought it would be a pleasant surprise for you if I stopped in for a visit before continuing to Portsmouth to catch the train."

Which translated to: "You know why I am here. I am here because I do not trust you not to disgrace yourself, and I wanted to see with my own eyes that you hadn't yet. I am here to make you realize that I can appear at any moment and drag you home by your hair. I am here to pound into your head, as a hammer might a nail, the knowledge that I am always watching."

Watching me, as I was watched that night on the road by whatever *thing* stood in the dark. As I had been watched in the woods, the hairs rising on the back of my neck. I spoke loudly to cover my own thoughts.

"If you are worried about me, Father, you really needn't be. I am getting on very well here. In fact, I think I may remain in Lowry Bridge for some time."

Which translated to: "Leave me alone, old man! A father who truly loved his daughter would not spend all his time reminding her of her mistakes, or making her feel like a silly baby unworthy of trust or forgiveness. But then, you don't love me — you never did — you have never loved anything but your own blessed reputation. Get out of this house, you miserable toad — get out, before I throw the mantle clock at your head!"

Father nodded thoughtfully, as though weighing the wisdom of my words. Then he reached into his jacket and pulled out an envelope, sliced neatly open at the top. My first thought was that my fears had come true, and Mrs. Castle had barraged him with angry correspondence regarding my teaching methods.

Then I saw the return address on the envelope, written in a careful, looping hand: *Willoughby*.

"This came for you," he said. "I read it, of course. Do you want it?"

How sick I felt then — how weak — how full of loathing! I looked at Father and saw him as he had been the day that he came to take me away from my former post, his nose wrinkled as though he could not stand the stink of me.

"No," I replied, as evenly as I could. I tried not to look at the hateful thing. Why had it been written? What in God's name could either of them have to say to me now, months after the miserable affair was finished? And which of them had written it? Was that return address in *his* hand, or *hers*? I could not tell, not from where I was seated, and I would not give him the satisfaction of leaning forward to see.

Father nodded at the stove, where a merry fire was burning. "I shall burn it, then," he said. "Since you do not want it."

He got up and fed the letter to the fire, his movements slow and deliberate, as though waiting for me to cry out in protest. But I did not — I sat, mute, and watched it burn through the grate of the stove. I fancied that I could see the words inside the envelope turn from black to white, hotter by far than the flames that consumed them. He waited there by the stove until the thing had been reduced to ashes, all the while looking at me. His face was empty and placid, a lake on a windless day.

It was always empty, his face. His expression never changed, even when he took his switch to Florrie and me as children. That hideous length of wood would strike our hands, our backs, our thighs, again and again until our legs would no longer bear us, and we would crumple in a stiff and trembling heap to the parlour floor. He would watch us fall with nothing on his countenance to betray any human feeling, nothing in his eyes that made him look like a father beholding his daughters. Nothing but barren cold. My teeth dug deep into my lip, remembering.

Once the thing had burned, he stepped over to me and ducked down as though to kiss me again, but stopped only inches from my face. Those stony eyes of his locked on my teeth, worrying at my lip, and he frowned. Reaching out with one hand, he grasped my jaw, digging into my yielding flesh. So firm and painful was his grip, so thick and hot his fingers, that I imagined the print of his thumb forever burning itself into my mandible, a Mark of Cain seared into the very bone. Only when I released my lip did he release me and straighten, looming over me just as he had loomed over me as a child.

"A nasty habit," he said, impossibly tall and stern. "Keep well, Aidy. A father worries about his daughters, you know."

This required no translation. My father worries about all the things he owns.

That night at dinner I crackled with nervous energy, fumbling and dropping my silverware, letting my cup rattle noisily against its saucer. My hosts could see that I was agitated; Mr. Grier seemed a little flustered by it, and left before dessert, muttering that he had to go see to the hogs. Mrs. Grier has been markedly cool to me since my visit to Mrs. Kinsley but melted when she saw how badly I had been shaken. She slipped me an extra piece of seedcake with my tea, telling me that she did not need my help for the rest of the evening.

"I daresay you have work to be done," she said, "and precious little time to do it in! We can't expect you to fritter your time away with us every evening."

I did go up to my room for the night, but I could not work — I could not write — I could barely even think. All I could do was pace back and forth, crushing my fists against my head and chewing the inside of my cheek until I tasted copper. There was nothing inside of me save my father's words, the ones he said and the ones he did not have to say, twisting and turning in the whirling currents of my soul. When I closed my eyes, I saw little red spots, spinning in time to the thudding of my heart. They looked like rubies, spilt across black velvet.

That is in the Bible, isn't it? Something about a woman's virtue, its price being above rubies. I knew it once. I suppose it is fitting that I no longer do.

If Father had wanted to ensure that I did not repeat the mistakes I made in Willoughby, he could have burned the letter himself, unread, and never alerted me to its existence. He came to Lowry Bridge with that envelope in his pocket, already knowing its contents, and showed it to me to remind me of my transgression — to make sure I still felt the burden of my sins.

What had the letter said? I cannot help but wonder, though I know the wondering will do more harm than good. If it were *he* who wrote it, I scarcely care. But if *she* did — if something moved her, after all this time, to write to me — God help me, what could she have had to say?

I crept down to the parlour last night after the Griers went to bed and poked at the ashes in the stove. No legible fragments of the letter remained, thank goodness. I shudder to think of what might have happened if Mrs. Grier had found some scrap of it.

December 10, 1901

$\mathcal{M}$rs. Grier has not asked about Father. I know that she wants to — I feel her, every so often, to be on the verge of asking — but each time, she manages to stop herself before the words come out. When I winced to feel the salt on my meat burning my lip at supper, she slipped me a little tin of home-made salve, whispering that it might help the sores. It *does* seem to help, although it smells odd.

To divert myself, I have been trying to throw myself whole-heartedly into work. All my students' compositions have been marked; every stocking I own has been carefully darned; the corners of both the schoolhouse and the Grier residence are resplendently empty of dust and dirt.

Agatha's upcoming Christmas concert is proving to be a worthy distraction, as well. We two spent the evening sewing costumes for the Nativity scene yesterday; an old blue tablecloth of hers is serving as Mary's hood and cloak, while Mrs. Grier has thoughtfully donated some sheets that are well past mending to be made into the robes of Joseph and the shepherds. (One *does* have a pretty pattern of pink rosebuds on it, but it has been so often laundered that from a distance they are barely visible.) Pasteboard and gilt paint will serve as the headdresses of the Three Wise Men, with dressing gowns for robes. The whole production promises to be singularly adorable. Agatha's cold is much better now, and this past Sunday she took her place once more at the organ, playing each hymn with renewed gusto.

Our winter examinations shall be held next Wednesday, on December 18. I received notice some time ago that two men from the board, a Mr. Gannis and a Mr. Ammerman, will be coming to oversee the proceedings. I hope that they will be pleased with the progress the children have made, though at the moment I find myself caring more that all my students know the words to "God Rest You Merry, Gentlemen" than whether they can spell "quixotic" or recite all the capitals of Europe.

There is only one whose academic progress worries me, and that is Muriel. The girl simply will not attend her lessons, and when asked to recite a Bible verse or figure a sum on the blackboard, she acts as though she has been forced into performing a tedious and repellant chore. She acted similarly when I caught her on her way out the door this afternoon and asked her if she would like some extra tutoring before Wednesday. She answered with a wordless snort and a toss of her dark gold head.

"You needn't be disrespectful, Muriel," I said, sharper than I'd intended. Ever since the incident with the tail in the flowers, I have felt myself ill at ease in the child's presence, uncomfortably aware that she bested me in a game I hadn't known I was playing. "I only want you to do well. Don't you want to prove that you know as much as any other girl your age?"

Oh, the look she gave me then! The faint, queer smile on her insolent face!

"I know enough," she said. Just three words, but all of them laden with tremendous weight, as though whatever knowledge she bears on her thin young shoulders is both a burden and a boon.

With that strange pronouncement, she breezed past me and out the door — really breezed, like a wind with no concern for the leaf batted about in its wake.

I fear that someday I shall have to strap that child, loath though I am to do so. Being struck as a girl left me deeply averse to corporal punishment, and I find I can't look at the little switch in my desk without getting nauseous. Thus far I have not had to take it out, even to bang for order. (I can shout very loudly when the need arises.) But a day may come when nought but a whipping will do the trick.

December 14, 1901

$\mathcal{I}$ begged off my Saturday chores today in favour of spending the afternoon with Agatha, putting the finishing touches on the costumes for the Christmas pageant. Much of our time was put to making cottonwool beards for Effie, Anna, and Clara, for they are the lucky three chosen by Agatha to play the Wise Men!

"Effie was furious," Agatha told me, her smile markedly mischievous. "She wanted to be Mary, of course. But I told her that the older a girl is, the wiser she becomes, and so it was only right that she and her friends play the Magi."

It is little Caroline Mason who shall be playing Mary, with her beau Arthur as Joseph. The shepherds shall be played by George and Winifred; Lillian, Matthew, and Clarence are to be sheep, as are a few younger children whose names I do not know, with headdresses for ears and little tails tied to their behinds; Eugene, poor lad, shall play the donkey; and the Christ Child himself shall be played by Douglas, who will likely sleep through the entire event, just as he did through all our labours today.

"Mind, I say *play*," Agatha said, "but we must be ever so clear that the Nativity scene is not a play. Plays are sinful, I have been told, and as the concert takes place in the church, I must be careful not to offend Mrs. Castle and her ilk. Especially given that I have made her son the donkey. Have you heard from her again?"

"Not a peep."

"And has she written to the board after all, do you suppose?"

I was sewing a little lamb headdress for Lillian when she asked this, my needle moving busily in and out of a length of whiteish rag to form a sweet little pointed ear. In my mind's eye, I suddenly saw Father standing over me again, brandishing that mysterious letter. I faltered; my hand jerked too tight, and the thread pulled and snapped, ruining my neat line of tiny stitches.

"Perhaps," I said after a moment. My voice, I thought, was smooth, but not smooth enough, it seemed, for Agatha looked up from her own handiwork, her forehead wrinkling with concern.

"You aren't still worried about her, are you, Ada?" she asked. Her voice was very gentle, as though she spoke to a nervous dog, cowering beneath a chair. "Mrs. Castle's bark is fierce, but she has not yet proven to have a bite. I doubt she will say a word. What *can* she say?"

She smiled then, as though to encourage me to do the same; wanting to oblige her, I did, and told her that she was likely right.

"Of course I am!" she declared. "The mothers in this town may complain about you, Ada Byrd, but you mind *me*, not them. You are a good woman, and they can all go to . . ." She faltered, her eyes straying to the sitting room door.

"Heaven," I supplied quickly, for the benefit of her husband's ears, should they be pricking. Agatha giggled. That giggle lifted my spirits, and I found it easier to settle back to my work, my thoughts dimmed for the time being.

I walked home as the sun began to sink down beneath the trees, trudging rather than trotting; I have not been sleeping well, and a day of squinting down at shepherd's robes and false beards had driven my weariness deeper into my bones. But when I drew near to the bridge and the frigid rush of the Slade River, I found the most delightful scene to distract from my fatigue. In a sugar maple tree was a little family of chickadees, hopping from one bare branch to another, cocking their little black-capped heads and winking their bright bead-eyes.

Florrie loved chickadees. A flock lived in the woods behind our father's house — a *banditry*, rather, that being the proper name for a group — and as a girl she mastered the art of standing with her hand outstretched, a scattering of breadcrumbs on her palm, breathing so slowly she scarcely seemed to breathe at all. After enough time had passed, a chickadee would fly down from the low branches and perch boldly on her hand, snapping up a few crumbs before launching itself back into the tree. On one occasion, three landed at the same time, and Florrie was so delighted that she laughed aloud, startling them into panicked flight.

My sister was never still in her ordinary life. She was a fidgeter, a hair-tugger, an inveterate shuffler of feet and twiddler of thumbs, as prone to sudden dashes as a squirrel. But when we two went into the woods, she suddenly ceased to be a creature of perpetual motion. If she found a plant or mushroom that she wished to draw, she would sit motionless before it for hours, only the frenetic movement of her pencil showing that she was a living girl and not a statue. A glimpse of a grazing deer or a hare fleeing through the underbrush would stop her in her tracks, her lively eyes following the creature until it disappeared.

I tried holding out my hand, but none of the birds came to me. Perhaps by springtime they will trust me enough to approach.

December 18, 1901

*W*inter examinations are over, and how thankful I am for that! This morning I could scarcely eat for nerves, and when I stood in front of the class to introduce the two members of the school board who had come to observe, my voice audibly trembled. I was half-convinced that each and every one of my students would suddenly prove to be utterly incapable of reading, writing, or 'rithmeticking, and that Mr. Gannis and Mr. Ammerman would come away from the experience certain that I could not teach a fish to swim.

The children did very well for themselves. True, some times tables were incorrectly recounted, some words ingeniously misspelled, but most of the children performed at the appropriate level, and some beyond it. When we spoke after dismissal, both Gannis and Ammerman seemed pleased, although I did notice the latter's eyes lingering with some distaste on the owlet skull on my desk.

"Your students are further along than we'd expected, Miss Byrd," said Mr. Gannis. He is a short man with a luxurious ginger moustache that grows over his top lip, making it look as though he has no lip at all. "It seems that you are doing well here. I must admit, I had worried that—"

Mr. Ammerman — tall, dark, unbecomingly slender — interrupted with an apologetic cough, a thing I had not known could be done apologetically. "We must inform you," he said, "that the board has received a number of letters from a Mrs. Elijah Castle regarding your abilities as a teacher. She seems to think that you have been filling the children's head with heathenism, rather than facts. After what we have seen here today, we must conclude that she is mistaken. Clearly, the children are learning all that they need learn. We shall write to Mrs. Castle and assure her that we have investigated the matter, and that we have not found you wanting."

This was a gratifying thing to hear, and I admit that it put a spring in my step to imagine how Mrs. Castle would react to such a letter.

There are still a few days left of the term, but I intend to use them for rehearsal for Agatha's concert. There are still a few challenges for us to face, not least of which is Effie's steadfast refusal to wear her cottonwool beard.

It has been snowing these past few days, a fine and powdery snow that is lovely to look at but dreadful to be out and about in. The children love it, although a few have complained that it isn't any good for making snowballs. Snow angels, however, they have managed. When they come in from recess, the whole schoolyard is full of them, eerie, watchful things with wings poised and alert. I don't like to walk between them when I leave at the end of the day. A foolish part of me thinks that I may see one move.

December 20, 1901

It was ordinary at the beginning. I must remember that. I rose, dressed, had tea with the Griers, walked to school through the snow under a lead-grey sky. I was thinking only of Agatha's concert later that day and hoping that my students would do well. Nothing more.

I let school out early so that the children could prepare at home for the concert, and supper was early too; Mrs. Grier knew that I wished to leave early and hurry up to the church before the general populace arrived, to help Agatha with any last-minute preparations. I wolfed down cold mutton and bread, then tore upstairs to dress myself in my Sunday best, ripping at the buttons on the bodice of my grey poplin in my haste. My fingers were shaking as I did it — misplaced nerves, I thought, my body reacting on behalf of my students. That, too, was the reason I gave myself for the anxious state in which I found myself after crossing the bridge, my frequent glances behind me, my dim perception that there was movement somewhere beyond the edges of the trees. It was not until I came in view of the church, its windows golden in the growing night, that I found myself able to breathe steadily again.

The pews had been decorated with red ribbon and little boughs of pine, garnished here and there with sprigs of holly. Despite these unexpected concessions to jollity, the building hummed with tension. The very air seemed alive with the noise and bustle of children, anxiously reciting to themselves, singing, whispering to one another. Agatha sat at the bench of the organ, her tawny hair arranged into a delicate chignon; it looked so soft as it gleamed in the lamplight that I found myself longing to touch it. She was wearing her best as well, a high-necked gown in a delicate robin's egg blue, with puffed sleeves and a dripping collar of Venetian lace. Even in my grey poplin, I immediately felt dowdy and plain next to her. But I didn't mind — or barely did, once she caught my eye and waved.

The next hour was a blur of minute adjustments, last-minute costume alterations, and the occasional childish nerve-storm. It was not until the pews began to fill with what seemed like every person in Lowry Bridge that we were able to herd our singers to the side, hushing them sternly every few minutes. Within a very short time, the church was filled, the air warm and thick with hushed conversation. I spotted the parents of many of my students, and those brothers and sisters too young or too old to participate in either songs or pageant. Even Mrs. Castle, that paragon of virtue, sat primly next to her husband in their usual pew, her little eyes drinking in the scene before her. Perhaps she hoped that my involvement in the concert would doom it to failure, and she would be able to cite this as proof of my ineptitude to the board.

The concert did not precisely go off without a hitch — Winifred's recitation of "In the Bleak Midwinter" had its share of mispronunciations, and Lillian forgot the words to "The Holly and the Ivy" mid-line, causing her to burst into tears and run to her mother — but the children sang as well as they could, and the most egregiously off-key were easily covered by Agatha's organ-playing and Clarence's clear, sweet voice. Even the Nativity scene went well, with Caroline proving to be a demure and serene Mary, and Arthur a suitably protective Joseph. Effie finally condescended to wear her beard, which made her mutinous expression appear sober and high-minded. The little ones made adorable sheep, all of them waggling their heads and behinds to make their woolly ears and tails twitch, and occasionally letting out a too-loud "baa!" that echoed marvellously through the church. The only thing that took away from the scene was our less-than-godly Christ Child, for little Douglas was fussy all evening. When his mother read aloud the line, "So they hurried off and found Mary and Joseph, and the baby, who was lying in the manger," he opened his mouth wide and let out a mighty wail that drowned out the next line.

At the end of the Nativity scene, the children in their costumes all stood to sing "O Holy Night." The high ceilings of that hushed, sacred place gave the children's voices a weight and echo they had not had during rehearsals in the schoolhouse. The music created a new world around us, one of grandeur and emptiness, black skies frosted with quivering stars. I could imagine the shepherds in their fields falling in terror and awe, shielding their eyes from the visions lighting up the sky.

"Fear not," angels always say. But how can a body help but feel fear when confronted with such proof of life beyond our ken?

I closed my eyes to better feel that vastness pressing down between each intake of breath, the expectant stillness running behind those words like a great, slow river. And I heard something else.

There was a sound *beneath* the music, like a half-heard whisper in a crowded room, like the rustle of an unseen animal making its way through the underbrush. I strained my ears to perceive it more clearly, but the more I tried, the less able I was to distinguish it from the sound of the children singing. I shook my head to clear it — pawed at my ringing ears — and Mrs. Grier leaned over to catch my eye, her expression inquisitive. Was there something the matter, did I have a pain of some kind?

Fall on your knees, implored a sea of childish voices, and beneath them something else implored me too, a sound as plaintive and incomprehensible as the cry of a loon.

What did I say to Mrs. Grier? I do not know — an intimation of some indelicate physical complaint that gave me leave to slip out of my pew and into the aisle, chasing that curious noise toward the doors of the church. The closer I got to the outside world, the clearer the noise became, and yet I could still not make sense of it. At the doors leading to the porch I hesitated, sparing a glance back over my shoulder at the children, arrayed by height order in front of the pulpit; at Agatha, playing the organ with her eyes tightly closed; at Mrs. Grier, who stared back at me in turn, looking vexed.

Bareheaded, coatless, gloveless, I slipped out onto the frigid porch, that unknown sound tugging me insistently forward.

He knows our need, the children sang, *to our weakness is no stranger*, and the music was cut short by the closing of the porch door. For a moment I stood there, gathering my courage up around me, and then with a shiver emerged from that vestibule and into the holy night.

The sky had been clear at sunset, but now the air was thick with falling snow, the edges of the world blurred under a flurry of moving particles. Still, I could see well enough to discern the shape of the manse, one of its first-floor windows warm with light. I could see the uneven black hem of the treeline, dark against the dark.

"What is it?" I whispered, my breath steaming out from my mouth in a silver cloud. I half expected to hear the night itself answer me, perhaps instructing me, as the children had, to fall on my knees.

And then, through the obscuring haze of drifting flakes, I saw something new: a smudge on the unbroken white beyond the path, something small abandoned in the virgin snow.

The sound that had been pulling me forward stopped. The world was cold and utterly silent.

It felt like a dream I was having.

Slowly, carefully, I stepped toward that unknown object. One step at a time, one breath at a time. The shape resolved as I drew closer, growing more and more familiar until I saw it for what it was.

The chickadee lay upon the snow, black feet as gnarled and barren as winter branches, grey tongue protruding from open beak. There was no depression beneath it. It did not seem to have tumbled from the sky, or to have landed and then tumbled forward into death. It looked, instead, as though it had been carried to that very spot and placed so gently onto the snow that not a single flake had shifted, but there were no prints leading to it, no sign that any living creature had placed the poor thing there. Its eyes were open and dull, no longer bright little black beads but clouded marbles. They could not see me. Surely, they could not.

Eyes in the dark. There are always eyes in the dark.

I looked into those eyes and saw the three chickadees crowding onto Florrie's open palm, her startled, joyful laugh at the sight of them and how they had taken flight, leaving her empty-handed, her eyes straining after them as they vanished into the trees.

"What is it?" I whispered again, and felt myself begin to tremble.

I heard it again then, that sound that had throbbed beneath the music and pulled me into the snow. Two syllables more familiar to me than any in the world, and yet pronounced in a voice so strange and alien that my teeth began to chatter. It sounded as though it came from the trees itself, from the earth, from the dark and lowering sky. It made my very bones ache.

Ada.

"Miss Byrd?"

The voice startled me. I stumbled and fell, barely catching myself with the palms of my hands. A sudden flood of light, warmth, and noise filled the dark. The song was over. People were clapping.

"Miss Byrd?" My name again, this time in a voice I recognized, utterly earthly, tinged with worry. Mrs. Grier, come to find me after my hasty exit. "Are you alright?"

I rested on my hands and knees, staring at the spot before me where the chickadee had been. The bird was gone. The snow was smooth and unbroken, save where I had fallen. No trace of it remained. Like the crickets. Like the tail in the flowers.

With great care, I pulled myself up from the ground, dusting the snow from my palms and skirt. The lamps that burned behind her left Mrs. Grier's face in darkness, and I could discern only the vague shape of her against the light, but I fancied that I could see her expression anyway: wary and unsure, a bird who has spotted an approaching cat.

I went back inside the church. I praised my students, all pink-cheeked and pleased from applause, shook hands with their parents. Made conversation and laughed politely at jokes. Hugged Agatha tightly and told her it had been marvellous, simply marvellous, and watched her flush with pleasure. By the time the Griers and I started home, I had all but forgotten the bird in the snow, that strange voice calling softly to me, until Mrs. Grier laid her hand upon my arm.

"Are you certain you are alright, Miss Byrd?" she murmured, so low I had to strain to hear her over the sound of the runners on the snow and the jingling of the horses' bits. Her hushed tone brought the vision of the chickadee back to me in a sudden rush, and I blinked fiercely again and again to dispel it.

"I am fine, ma'am," I assured her once more. "I felt a bit sick before — the church was so very warm. But the winter air has done me good. See, my cheeks are quite rosy now."

Perhaps they were indeed rosy, or perhaps I simply sounded sprightly enough to convince her. In any case, she did not ask me again. Indeed, she said nothing to me for the remainder of the evening, other than a quiet goodnight at the foot of the stairs. And now here I am, warm in bed, with a candle burning away the dark, Cat settled on my feet with her tail pressed to the tip of her nose. The day has become ordinary again now that it draws to a close.

But I feel those clouded eyes upon me now, staring at me from the darkness beyond my single candle. I see my sister's cupped hands, three chickadees crowded onto them, her face alight with joy and wonder, and I wonder what it was that called my name on the other side of the bridge. Was there truly something there in the dark, coaxing me into the snow? Or am I simply

Simply *what?*

December 29, 1901

I have tried to write many times since my last, rather muddled entry. Every time I pick up my pen, I end up putting it back down again for lack of anything to say.

Christmas was pleasant enough. We allowed ourselves to stay in bed an extra half hour and lingered at the breakfast table, our tea grown cold long before we felt obliged to get up and go to church, where Reverend MacPherson waxed philosophical on the wages of sin and the price of . . . something. I used to be able to recount sermons nearly word for word — Father would force Florrie and I to recite them back to him after church, to prove we'd been paying attention — but I seem to have lost the knack.

I went to my father's house last Christmas. It was, of course, the first Christmas since Florrie's death, and the mood, which in that house is always oppressive at best, was worse than usual. In past years Florrie would whisper the occasional joke or favour me with a well-timed grimace or roll of her eyes. Now there was no one to force a little light and laughter into the room. I remember sitting there at dinner, staring at the utensils clutched in my fists as though they were wholly alien in design, wondering what the point of it all was. "Food was ash in my mouth" — I can't recall where I read that line, but it rang through my head all that day as I struggled to swallow mouthfuls of tasteless grit.

Food was not ash in my mouth this year. Mrs. Grier roasted a fat little goose and stuffed it with apples and walnuts, cooking potatoes in its fat until they turned crisp and brown. After our pudding, a rich and filling tipsy laird made with a recipe supposedly passed down from a Highland ancestor, we exchanged presents. Mrs. Grier seemed pleased with the lace collar I made for her, and Mr. Grier accepted the handkerchief I'd embroidered for him very solemnly. (He did everything solemnly that day — I think he feels it to be the proper Christian attitude toward the holiday.) The two of them presented me with a lovely silver comb and brush, as well as a little hand mirror. I received these first two gladly, since my own comb has hardly any teeth left, and the bristles of my brush have largely fallen out. The mirror, however, I have placed beneath my bed with the glass turned to the wood. I have no desire to look at my own face.

My nightmares have intensified since that strange happening outside the church (for *happening* is the only word I can ascribe to the event). I do not remember them — I seldom remember dreams — but I wake in the middle of the night with a scream dying on my lips, my hands gripping the blankets as though I fear they will be ripped from my body. I blink upwards into the dark, thinking that I can see things moving there, waiting for them to pounce. They never do; the villains I imagine prowling through the night disappear just like the chickadee did, the tail, the crickets.

Sometimes I find myself reaching for Florrie's hand.

They make me tired, these dreams. I am glad that there are still so many days left of the break. I feel that I could sleep a thousand years.

January 1, 1902

*T*he first of the year. Well past midnight. No real "Hogmanay" celebrations in this house, but the Griers and I managed to stay awake with hot toddies and song until the clock struck twelve, and Mr. Grier played "Auld Lang Syne" on his fiddle for the look of the thing before we all stumbled off to bed. I thought that I would fall asleep as soon as I lay down, but I found myself roused into wakefulness by the noises coming from the Griers' bedroom. If I closed my eyes, I could imagine that I was back in my attic bed in Willoughby, my ears attuned of their own accord to the sounds of marital congress drifting up the stairs.

I am awake entirely now, no trace of sleep left in my veins. I am thinking of the summer of 1900, of my arrival in Willoughby one cold, wet afternoon only months after Florrie's death, of all that happened to throw my life off course and send me skittering into this strange, small corner of the world. And I am thinking, beneath these thoughts, of *her*, standing in the doorway of that plain little farmhouse where I was to board, one hand on the latch of that red, red door. A beacon on the threshold, pulling me forward.

She was tall, broad-shouldered, carrying with her the scent of warm earth and fresh bread, the tang of woman-sweat. Wisps of dark hair struggled out of her braid, curling like smoke on the damp of her neck. My age, or near enough. Her eyes were a reddish sort of brown, deep and rosy. They were warm, those eyes; I felt that I could put my hands to them and drive the chill from my fingers.

"You must be the teacher," she said, and smiled, and as that smile travelled from the centre of her mouth to its corners, I felt a strange unfolding within myself, as though my soul had opened up like a letter, waiting to be read.

I will not say her name now, although I said it any number of times then. I tapped it out in Morse code against the wood of my desk. I whispered it into the thick suffocation of a pillow, stillborn and swallowed by goose feathers. I wrote it on the attic wall with my finger and imagined that the letters would appear when the air warmed in spring, as though they had been inscribed with invisible ink.

The house belonged to her husband, a local man whose farm was just prosperous enough to allow him to "put up" a teacher for a year, but she was its mistress, and every room within it bore the mark of her hands. They had churned the butter on the kitchen table, tatted the lace on the mantel, sewn the quilt that lay across my sorry little attic cot. I thought of that whenever I smoothed it over my legs: that she had made it, that her fingers had pulled the thread between each faded patch.

She was not pretty, not as such things are usually reckoned. Her hands were coarsened from hard work and harsh soap, her skin browned from the sun. There was nothing delicate about her, nothing dainty. But there was grace in her assured stride, the movements of her powerful arms. It made me giddy to watch her draw a bucket of water from the well or hang a sheet out to dry. I greeted each morning with a queer, unsteady eagerness, hurrying down the stairs in hopes of having time to speak to her before leaving; I rushed through dismissal and came straight back from school in the afternoons, rejoicing at the sight of that red door. I liked the way she threw her head back to laugh, giving herself over entirely to mirth; I liked how her eyes widened with interest when I described my natural history lessons, the questions she asked about the world that betrayed an active and curious mind. Once, prompted entirely by her own line of inquiry, I haltingly recounted Mr. Darwin's theories of natural selection and evolution, nervous all the time that she would censure me as an infidel. Once I had finished, she tilted her head to the side in thought, considering.

"Well, I suppose that makes as much sense as anything else," she said finally. "My cousin breeds horses, and he chooses studs in the same way — which ones are hardiest or fastest or have the best temperaments. It isn't in the Bible, of course, but that doesn't mean it isn't so."

And she placed the tips of her fingers upon my hand as though in thanks, bestowing upon me a smile that was almost as much of a thrill as her touch.

I have no memory of meeting her husband when I first arrived. Meet him I did, I'm sure, but there is a sort of hole through those early days in his shape, the kind that might be burnt through a photograph with a lit cigar. My memories of *him* do not properly begin until a blustery November evening in her parlour, cold rain lashing in tiger-fury at the glass.

On such evenings, after she had put their children to bed, she often asked me to read aloud, just as the Griers do — it is, I think, the curse of an educated woman to always be reading to someone or other. At her request, I had chosen my Brightwen, for she had seen *Inmates of My House and Garden* on my bedroom table, and her interest had been piqued by the title. Although my voice was given over entirely to the book, my eyes kept straying from it to *her*, sitting by the fire and frowning in concentration over Mrs. Brightwen's words. The frown created a deep, stern wrinkle between her brows that made me shift in my seat, fascinated by the barely perceptible movements of the muscles in her face, the way the shadows danced over her features. It was not for some time that I realized that she was not the only person in the room pinned by another's gaze — that *he* was watching, not his wife, but me.

Her husband was neither dark nor handsome. He was nearer to Father's age than to mine or hers, his thin face dominated by a beaky nose and a prodigious moustache that curved around the corners of his mouth like the handle of a suitcase. The only beauty in that craggy visage was in his eyes, which were wide and brown. They looked, I thought, a little like hers.

Under their penetrating attention, my voice faltered. I saw him note it and smile.

My attic room was directly over their bedroom. I lay awake that evening and listened to the mysterious creaks and groans of their lovemaking, my fists clenching and relaxing in time to its brutal rhythm. Her long, low wail of pleasure carried to my ear as clearly as though she writhed in bed beside me, christening my bedclothes with her sweat. I could see her there somehow, her strong legs tangled in my white sheets, her eyes shining beneath half-mast lids. What if she were to reach out to me?

What if she were to lay her hand upon my throat, my cheek, my breast? What might happen then? What *could*?

Only a week or two later the scene repeated itself, the three of us crowded into the parlour on a cold and stormy evening. This time her husband and I listened to *her* read, for I had a wretched headache. She chose as her material a much-loved copy of *Little Women*, that tale of girlhood dreams thwarted by dreary woman-hood. The book was one I had hated as a child, much preferring the adventures of Alice, or Princess Irene and her loathsome goblins. But her voice seemed to raise the story up, elevate it from truculent claptrap to real pathos. When she reached the chapter in which young Beth dies in her bed, free from pain after months of suffering, I found myself gasping aloud, tears starting in my eyes. I had, I think, neglected to remember that the insipid dear does not survive the novel, and so had no chance to gird my loins for a scene in which a beloved sister passes on.

She saw it happen — sprang from her seat — closed the book and came to my side, asking me if I felt ill, or had a pain. Her hands took mine and warmed them between her long, strong fingers, as though she thought I might freeze to death.

"No, no!" I cried, although the tears were still coming. I could not help them. "No, it is just . . . it is so very sad."

She looked at me for a long moment, a little half-smile play-ing about her mouth. I caught the smell of her again: yeast, earth, perspiration.

"You sweet girl," said she, and leaned in to press a kiss onto my cheek.

It was a gesture more familiar than any we had shared before. My head felt warm and not quite attached to my neck, as though it might float away like a balloon. The kiss landed very near to the corner of my mouth. I almost turned my head so that she might catch my lips with hers. Madness — madness!

I was sitting, all this time, on the settee next to her husband. His eyes followed her as she got to her feet and told us that she would retire for the night, since the book was "making Miss Byrd so very troubled." And retire she did, bidding us both goodnight and leaving me and her husband alone in the parlour.

One expects a husband to go to bed with his wife. He always had before. But on this night, he remained in his seat, his craggy face mired in thought, and lit a pipe. The room filled with the comfortable, leathery scent of tobacco.

"The wife hates it when I smoke," he said, puffing away. "Says it makes her curtains smell. Well, a man's got to be a man, hasn't he?"

So obvious, now, his intentions. That strange question; the remark about the drapes; the brutal, careless way he referred to her as "the wife," as if she could belong to anyone. I should have made my excuses, retired to my attic bed, and locked the door behind me.

Instead, I looked at his eyes, so like hers that I could almost believe he was her twin, and found myself mapping her face onto his as the air between us filled with blue smoke. His mouth looked a little like hers, I thought, with the creases at its corners, and the nose — couldn't that proud, strong nose be hers, if I squinted?

My head hurt dreadfully.

He finished his pipe and set it aside, then reached out and grasped my hand. It felt like hers, but larger, thicker at the tips, black dirt rimming the splintered fingernails. His grip was tight, almost painful. He looked at me, then at my hand, and pressed it close to his lips.

"Got to be a man," he said again, and then he lunged, his hungry mouth pressed against me, his fingers digging deep into my flesh. I felt his tongue against my lips and gasped; he took that brief opening as an invitation and thrust it inside. My mouth was full of him, his spit thick with tobacco and tea, his crowded teeth pressing against mine. He thrust me down upon my back, my head striking the wooden arm of the settee, a sharp echo of the dull ache inside my skull.

This, then, was my second kiss, nothing like the one I had shared with Helen. His mouth was huge, wet, and sour. The weight of him crushed the breath out of my lungs. But I found myself thinking of his wife, how close our faces had been only minutes before, how near her mouth had been to where his now licked and chewed. A shudder tore through me. That seemed to spur him onwards, and he shoved himself insistently forwards, his hands tugging at my skirt. He was trying, I realized, to pull it up over my hips.

I stopped him. It took several attempts before I managed to get him off — I believe he thought at first that it was some coquettish game, that I wanted to put up a show of resistance before giving in to his advances. Finally, I managed to push so forcefully with hands and knees that he pulled himself into an upright position, red-faced, bright-eyed with want. He sat there, breath ragged in his throat, and looked a question at me.

"I must go to bed," I said. It was the only thing I could think to say.

I climbed the stairs in the dark, pausing on the landing outside of the bedroom where she slept. The sound of her breath came through the door, followed me up the stairs. All night I felt that I could hear it, her exhalations shivering on the shell of my ear, and I trembled.

I should have been ashamed to look him in the eye the next morning, but it was *her* gaze I had trouble meeting, thinking with a jolt of how she had kissed my cheek and drawn my hand between hers. That *he* had kissed me scarcely seemed to matter; the memory of his sour taste and sliding tongue evoked nothing but a faraway indifference, as though it had happened to some other woman, long ago. But her lips upon my skin, the press of her cheek, the way I'd seen her face laid over his . . .

That mattered. That had happened to me, and I had felt it. I thought she must have too.

But she did not blush or avoid my gaze. She kept up the same cheerful patter as she always had, was as kind and solic-itous as she had been the day before. I thought at first that she was pretending, putting on a brave face in front of her husband. But the longer I watched her bustling back and forth in the kitchen, setting out plates and doling out porridge, the more I began to think that, unlike me, she was not caught on the whirl-ing eddies of some new and startling emotion — that she was able to speak and behave normally because, as far as she knew, *nothing abnormal had occurred*. She had thought nothing of kissing me, touching me, calling me "sweet girl." What had been meaning itself to me had, it seemed, meant nothing at all to her.

How to explain the shame that rose in me when I realized this? How to explain that that shame led me to another — that the next time her husband cornered me, I did not fight him off, but *let him have me*? I cannot explain that to anyone, least of all myself. But after that day, I ceased to struggle. I let him suckle at my throat. I let him trace my ear with his tongue, huffing wet heat onto my neck. I let him slide his hand between my legs, scrabbling at what he found there.

If I closed my eyes, I could imagine someone else in his place, a different hand touching the places that he had touched. It was the best I could do, the best I could have. And so I became an adulteress.

What a curious, old-fashioned word that is. It seems ill-suited to these modern times, like scold's bridles or the stocks.

Details of the days that followed come to me in sudden, vulgar bursts, like a nasty oath that, once heard, floats to the top of the mind again and again. The sound of his feet on the attic stairs. The sharp probe of his fingers inside of me. His rough hands pulling my nightgown over my head, so eager he did not notice when the fabric caught and tore. The noise I made when he broke into me, the animal movement of his spine. The water-stain on the ceiling shaped like the head of a deer that I stared at while he moved in me, committing its form to memory until the urge to howl had passed. Blood on my thighs and on my sheets, black in the little light coming in from the attic window. It felt like a dream I was having, the kind of strange, licentious dream that comes hand in hand with a sickly fever, and in that dream, I could turn the body on top of mine into someone else's. Softness instead of hardness, sweet instead of sour. In the dream, I could transform him into her.

It was a dream until the night that I looked up and saw her there, white-faced, watching us. The attic door gaped open onto a darkness as complete as that of the cupboard under the stairs, the night sky over the woods, the back of my own eyelids. He had forgotten to lock it.

Those rosy eyes met mine and held them, a thousand emotions playing in their depths. Shock, yes, and betrayal, and hatred too — but did she take in the spectacle of the two of us, my body moved by his passion like a twig bobbing in a river's current? Did her gaze, for a moment, slide down the length of my body, lingering on the places where it joined his? Did she, in doing so, feel a twinge of pleasure?

Her name rose to my lips, unbidden; I could not help it. Nor could I help the movement of my hand as it stretched toward her in the dark. For a moment I saw, or thought I did, her mouth moving as though she whispered my own name back to me.

But that sweet sound was blotted out by a long, deep groan as he reached the agony of his bliss. He collapsed onto me, panting hard, licking a little at the sweat on my collarbone, a dog lapping water from a hole. Only then did he turn his head; only then did he realize that she was there, watching. So intimately were we connected that I could feel his muscles stiffen.

"My dear," he said, pulling away from me. I could not stop the sound that tore out of my throat as he hurriedly disentangled himself, and she flinched as though I'd struck her with a closed fist. "My dear, please—"

She let out a little cry and disappeared down the stairs in a flurry of splintery creaks. He cursed and chased after her, dragging my blanket around him like a royal robe. I was left alone upon the bed, sweat and slime slowly drying on my skin. The deer head spot on the ceiling gazed down at me in judgment.

It took three days for Father to come and collect me. In those three days, she did not speak to me once, nor even look at me. If I entered a room, she left it. I could hear her crying as I lay in my bed at night, my fists clenching in time to the rise and fall of her sobs.

On the morning that I left, I looked back at her house as it began to dwindle behind me, that red door shining in the winter sun. I saw the curtains flutter in the downstairs window, as though she were watching me leave. Shivering, I whispered her name again and again to warm myself, feeling the weight of it on my tongue. My tongue, which had known the taste of her husband, which would never know the taste of her.

God help me, *he was not the one that I wanted.* The shame of my dishonouring I can bear, my status as a fallen woman I shoulder without complaint, but that knowledge dogs my every step, its hot breath on my neck. I let him touch me, because I knew where his hands had been; I let him have me, because I could not have *her.*

The Griers are still awake. I have heard the fervent creaking of their bedstead, like a ship in a storm, and, once, her voice crying out in ecstasy. "Glenn! Glenn!" It sounded very loud in this quiet house.

Glenn is Mr. Grier's Christian name, although I seldom hear her use it. Mrs. Grier's is Holly. How strange, that I have never mentioned that before.

January 5, 1902

$\mathcal{Y}$esterday evening saw me make the long trek across the bridge to Mrs. Kinsley's house again, for that fine woman sent word on Friday that she would like to have me over for supper.

When I relayed this to Mrs. Grier, she pressed her mouth into a thin line, but said only:

"If you really want to go, Miss Byrd, I suppose I can't stop you. Just mind you are back before seven. I will need a hand with the mending."

That "mind you are back" irritates me in hindsight. Mrs. Grier is many things to me, but a mother is not one of them, and her child I am not. What right does she have, really, to tell me to *mind*?

The walk up the road to Mrs. Kinsley's is pleasant in autumn, but proved to be even prettier in the silvery haze of a winter afternoon. The river is frozen now, its current locked in place until the spring thaw comes, and I found that my footsteps echoed differently on the bridge as I crossed to opposite bank. The trees were fringed with icicles like cunning glass teeth, the shadows beneath them blue as the heart of night. Few other people seemed to be out and about; I heard little noise from the houses and farms I passed on the way, saw no one looking out their windows. It seemed as though I had stumbled into a great void leeched of colour: the pale sky above me empty of birds and clouds, and all around me white snow, black fences, white fields, black trees. The world seemed to be waiting for me to speak.

It made me nervous, this queer hush. It felt too much like the silence that precipitated the crickets, the electricity that crackled on the night of the concert.

Perhaps it was this that left me out of sorts; or perhaps it was my exchange with Mrs. Grier; or perhaps I was still melancholy from my New Year's ruminations. Whatever the case, I was unusually terrible company for the widow that evening. Every question she asked me I had to ask her to repeat. Every opinion I offered her seemed half-formed and childish. My conversation was so dull that the lady asked me, very kindly, if I was sick.

"For you have not touched your duck, Miss Byrd," she said, "and I happen to know that it is sublime."

"Oh! Not sick at all, ma'am," I said hurriedly. "No, I am only a little tired. It *is* delicious."

"Tired? Have you not been sleeping?"

"I have," I replied hesitantly, "after a fashion. That is to say, I fall asleep very well — only I have found myself waking up frequently in the night of late. Starting awake, in fact, very violently."

And I described to her, stumbling over my words, the dreams I have had, those dreams I can scarcely describe upon waking, but which, on recollection, seem to involve the woods. The woods, and something in them, watching me. Mrs. Kinsley listened with apparent interest, one finger tracing the rim of her wine glass.

"Do you never recall these dreams?" she asked. "I mean, truly recall them, from start to finish?"

"Never in detail, no. I wish I could. Perhaps they would be less frightening then."

"Perhaps," Mrs. Kinsley murmured. She looked at something I could not see, far beyond my head, and then said, rather abruptly:

"We never had children, Mr. Kinsley and I. John always said he didn't mind. It was companionship he married for, not babies; he had children from his first marriage and didn't want any more. But I wanted them, and I minded dreadfully. There were a few times when I thought . . . but it never turned out to be true. After a few years of that, my hopes rising high and then crashing down, over and over again, I became quite wretched. I couldn't help but think of all those people who'd pitied me before for being unmarried, how they must pity me still. I cried over it."

I tried and failed to picture Mrs. Kinsley crying. I could no more imagine such a thing than I could imagine her ripping off her dress in the middle of one of Reverend MacPherson's interminable sermons and dancing a polka down the aisle of the church.

"John thought that a holiday might do me good," she said. "That was when he decided to build the summer house here in Lowry Bridge. He got the land cheap — it's all cheap, this side of the river. He had it built in secret, keeping it as a surprise for me. He didn't even tell me where we were going when we went to catch the train, although I kept asking. I was a little afraid that he was taking me to an asylum. Or an exorcist, perhaps."

My laughter died in my throat as I looked at her. She was, I saw, quite serious.

"That first summer here . . . oh, it was horrible. I was lonely and sick. I thought again that we were to have a baby, and then found out we weren't. My nerves were raw as meat. I couldn't stop weeping at the littlest things — burnt supper, a cut finger, the sound of a child crying in the distance. I found myself walking every day to the river, staring into the water, thinking of how easy it would be for me to fall in. One wrong step and over the edge of the bank I would go, and that, I thought, would be the end of my troubles.

"I was not sleeping well, of course. I hadn't been sleeping well in the city either, but now I would toss and turn half the night, rising in a more advanced state of exhaustion than if I hadn't gone to bed at all. And when I *did* sleep, I would have dreams, terrible dreams. Dreams that, like you, I could not recall upon waking. All I remembered was fear — something had been chasing me, and sooner or later, it would catch me."

The edge of the table pressed against my ribs. I realized that I had been leaning forward, as though my body was trying to drag me closer to her, through some strange magnetism of the flesh.

"I decided one night that enough was enough," Mrs. Kinsley said. "As soon as I was certain that John was sound asleep, I crept out of bed and into the library, and settled down to read until morning. I wanted to fend off sleep, and dreams, for as long as I could.

"It didn't work. No matter how hard I struggled to keep my eyes open, they *would* fall shut, and eventually I could not open them again. I was so exhausted that I fell asleep right there in John's chair. And I began to dream, just as I had all summer. But this time, I was awake inside the dream.

"I was in the woods, and I was running. My breath came upon me in pants and bursts. My eyes stung with tears from the wind. My cheeks were lashed by branches, striped with blood; my hair kept catching on things, bits of it pulled out by the roots. I was running, I felt sure, for my life; there was something behind me in hot pursuit, so close that I could feel drops of spittle falling from its open jaws. I did not know what sort of creature it was — I could not see it — but I knew that it was fearsome, and that it wanted me between its teeth.

"I came at last to the bank of a river. In the dream I recognized it as the Slade River, the very same river to which I had recently been so very drawn. I cannot swim in my waking life, nor could I in this dream, and yet something in me told me to dive off the bank and into the water, crossing to the opposite bank. Somehow, I knew that I would be safe there. The thing that chased me, whatever it was, would not follow me across the river, to the other side of the bridge. Vampires cannot cross rivers, you see, nor fairies."

She paused then and took a moment to cut off the tiniest sliver of duck. It seemed to me that she spent more time chewing it than such a small piece required.

"Under I went," she continued finally, "splashing and thrashing my way through the water, dragged down toward the muck by the weight of my sodden skirts. My feet caught once or twice in slimy tangles of river weed, and I thought I would drown, but each time I managed to kick myself free and struggle onwards, until I pulled myself, choking, onto the other side. I lay there on the bank, eyes closed, breathing in deep, sweet lungfuls of air.

"When I finally got to my feet, I looked back across the river. It was a bright day, all sunshine, with the warm smell of hot grass on the wind, and so I could see clearly the thing that had been after me. It was a dog, a massive one, at least as high at the shoulder as a young horse. I could not identify the breed, but it had nothing of the lithe, beautiful lines of the wolf about it: its head was heavy and square, its jaws as powerful as a steel trap. Looking at it, I could almost hear my bones cracking under its teeth. Its only beauty was its grey coat, all silver and shadow. I could imagine what it had looked like as it ran after me, the way the light would have moved over that beautiful fur. Like mercury, like the moon.

"There was something familiar about it. In the dream, I did not know precisely what it was, but that realization — that feeling of having seen it before — left me suddenly without fear. The creature seemed less menace than mystery. Dripping, dappled with mud, I found myself raising my hand to it, as though in salute. I could see its eyes follow the gesture, but it did not move. It did not even seem to breathe.

"I knew then, as one knows in dreams, that the animal would not leave its station on the riverbank until I returned to the other side. It would stay there forever, like a thing of stone or steel, unless I stepped back into the water and swam across to meet it. And I knew, in the same way, that that was exactly what I was going to do.

"I took a deep breath — I prepared for the shock of the water — and then I sat up, breathless and quivering, in my husband's chair."

This was Mrs. Kinsley's story, as far as I can remember it. Some of the details may be muddled, and the wording is certainly not exact. But then, it never is when one recounts a conversation after the fact. It is the essence of the thing that is important, and that, I think, I have captured here.

"Why do you suppose the dog seemed familiar?" I asked. "Was it because you'd had the dream before?"

"I thought so, at first," Mrs. Kinsley said. "But then I recalled a book I'd owned as a child, an insipid collection of moral tales for young people. There was a picture in it that I always anticipated with mixed dread and delight, not wanting to turn the page and see it, and yet unable to think of anything else. It was a woodcut of a foxhunt. At least, I always supposed that the wretched creature being pursued was a fox, although whoever had created it didn't seem to know exactly what a fox looked like. It looked a little like a cat, and a little like a squirrel, and a little like a child with a tail. But the beast in pursuit was demonstrably a dog, a great brute with slavering jaws and dead black shark-eyes. Its teeth were mere inches away from the tail of its prey, and one felt, looking at the picture, that in a moment the poor creature would be swallowed whole. The picture terrified me, and yet I longed to see it, every time. That dog was the very image of the one I had seen in my dream, poised by the side of the river." She shook her head. "It's funny, isn't it, the things that frighten us as children? They are so silly when we recall them as adults, and yet, they never really lose their power over us."

Jenny Carpenter, her hiccupping giggle. The cupboard under the stairs, the floating after-image of the lock on the door. My father's eyes, his hands.

I asked, "After you saw it, did you still have dreams?"

She smiled, her pale eyes glinting in the lamplight like ice. "I did," she said. "But I did not mind them as I once had. A monster seen is a monster that can be dealt with. A monster hidden beneath a bed or inside a wardrobe cannot."

With that, she deftly turned the conversation toward other matters, and I, still a little dazed, followed like an obedient pet. But for the rest of the evening, I found my mind drifting back to that image of the grey dog on the riverbank, quiet as a stone. When I walked back to the Grier house in the dark, I caught myself looking at the trees out of the corner of my eye, waiting for a glimpse of silver fur, slavering jaws.

January 13, 1902

*S*chool is back in session with a vengeance now, all my pupils louder and rowdier for their time away. Several of them opted to bring their Christmas gifts in for show and tell on the first day back, a tradition the school has apparently kept for years. (Miss Webster, I am told, was all for it.) Lillian Morice has a fine new doll, sent to her from "the city" by some well-to-do auntie, which she has brought to school not only on the first day but every day since school came back in session. She sits it up next to her on the bench during class, for all the world as if it were another child, and shows it the malformed letters she scratches out on her slate. The poor thing is already grubby, its cunning little kid shoes more grey than white.

It seems that Effie's Christmas present was being allowed to wear her hair up. This gift has gone, appropriately, straight to her head, and she has become more of a saucebox than ever.

When I told her this morning to stop whispering and attend to her geometry, she tossed her head and said: "Well! but, Teacher, I won't ever really need to know geometry, will I? After all, *I* shall be married someday. It's only old maids who need to understand about angles and idioms and things like that."

Imagine, please, the little smirk on her face as she said it, and the half-hidden snickers of her seatmates. Imagine, too, how my veins burned in response to such a sting.

"That is true, Effie," I replied, as kindly as I was able. "Your future husband surely won't need you to calculate the area of a triangle — although I dare say he would like to know that his wife isn't such a dolt that she confuses an *axiom* for an *idiom*."

Was this cruel? Perhaps, but it shut her mouth very effectively, and I took pleasure in watching the blood rise in her cheeks as she bent her head over her slate.

It has snowed very hard for the past few days. Every time I leave the schoolhouse in the afternoon, I find myself walking home through a swarm of white bees, swirling so thick on the wind that I can scarcely see where I am going. Sometimes it becomes hard for me to even make out the shape of the path before me, and I must keep an eye to the trees on either side of me to ensure that I do not accidentally walk into the river. Mrs. Kinsley was right: it would be easy, all too easy, for an accident to happen.

A part of me is keeping an eye out for something else, as well. I do not want to see it, whatever it is; I do not look forward to the day that I look up and catch a glimpse of some strange thing watching me from the trees. A dog, like Mrs. Kinsley saw, or something more terrible still.

I looked at myself tonight while undressing, quite by accident. I never mean to do it; I hate to see the doughy plains of my unswaddled flesh, the body that time has already started to ravage. Age is making me shapeless, loosening the skin on my arms and pulling my chin into a soft pile of sag. The lines that separate me from the world have started to fade. I am losing definition.

When I look at myself, I see Jenny Carpenter, her body laid over mine, the details of her ageing flesh impressing themselves into my own, as though I am in the process of becoming her. If I am not careful, soon enough I will find myself wandering the road with my hair streaming in the wind, giggling to myself. A veritable witch.

January 17, 1902

A strange discovery! While making my bed this morning, I reached a little farther under the mattress than I usually do to tuck in the sheet and found my fingertips brushing paper. Curious, I pulled it out, and found that it was an envelope, folded but not sealed, and addressed to a Mrs. Frederick Webster. Tucked inside was a letter, written in the same fussy and tremulous hand that wrote the inscription on the book of poetry I gave Agatha:

> no matter if I plug my ears it
> still calls to me

The letter is unfinished, so far as I can tell, and tantalizing in what it does not say. I read it quickly this morning before leaving for my walk to the schoolhouse and puzzled over it all day, barely noticing the ebb and flow of lessons.

April 1, 1901

Dear Mother,

~~I This is I will not I hope that~~

I am sorry that my last letter was so odd. I could tell from your reply that you were disturbed by it, and with good reason. The strange things I have seen seem to have turned me strange as well.

The spring semester will end soon, and then I will come home to you ~~if~~. The school board wants me to stay another year, but I know that you were displeased by my acceptance of this post, and that the distance between us is a hardship given your health. This is the reason I shall give them, nothing more. I do not wish to shame you with my "silly fancies," as you call them. ~~But they are~~

~~The dreams~~ My students keep well, and I am meeting Mrs. Kinsley for dinner this evening. I hope to ask her

And there it ends. I must assume that Miss Webster hid the letter away, intending to finish it, and then forgot — or perhaps could not find the words for what she wished to express.

I puzzled over this letter all day, wondering at those crossings-out, the thoughts that trailed off into nothing. By the time class let out, I had decided to use the envelope to contact Miss Webster myself, simply crossing out the "Mrs. Frederick" and adding "Miss Amelia" above it. The letter I wrote was brief, saying only that I am the new teacher here in Lowry Bridge, that I have witnessed strange things during my time here too — though I was careful not to mention any particulars — and that I am curious about the circumstances that led her to leave Lowry Bridge. I asked, too, about that ominous inscription from Agatha's book, what *it* said when it called to her.

I managed to smuggle this letter out to the pile left on the table by the back door for the postman, hidden snugly between a letter bill and one of Mrs. Grier's dutiful missives to her sister. Hopefully Miss Webster will send a reply and my curiosity will be at least a little sated.

I received a letter from Father today. More sermonizing, more admonishments, more commands. I cast it directly into the stove with the rest of the kindling. I do not think I shall reply.

January 23, 1902

*B*ad dreams last night. I woke just as the clock struck three and could not fall back asleep, came downstairs to breakfast in a low and sullen mood. I trudged through the snow to the schoolhouse this morning with my head in a thick grey fog. Everything was suddenly maddening; to stand in front of a roomful of children and teach grammar and mathematics seemed like the greatest conceivable waste of time. The shine was off the world.

So distracted was I by my own misery that I became snappish and mean, barking questions and orders so rapidly that my students scarcely knew which way to turn. No one was safe from my tongue, not even little Lillian Morice, whose new doll I took away when she could not tell me how to spell "boat."

"A great girl like you, still playing with dolls!" I said as I shut the offending toy away in my desk. "You ought to be ashamed."

I could see the tears quivering at the edge of her lashes. They hung there only a second before dropping silently off it and sliding down her little round cheeks. I saw reproach in the eyes of the other children, although they sat in silence, not daring so much as a twitch.

The exception, as always, was Muriel. The girl watched me with complete equanimity, her hands folded on the desk in front of her. There was not the slightest flicker of apprehension in her expression. I do not want my students to be afraid of me, but in that moment, I found it tremendously irritating that she could watch me so coolly, utterly untroubled by any potential consequence for her bold gaze.

"Have you finished your sums, Muriel?" I asked.

"No, Miss," the girl replied, without so much as a blush or a blink.

"Why not?"

"Didn't want to."

"You didn't want to? Do you suppose, then, that all the other children have finished their work because they wanted to? Do you suppose it is not because students are meant to obey their teacher, or because—"

"I don't *suppose* nothing," Muriel snapped, and then, as an afterthought, "Miss."

For the first time, I found my fingers itching for the switch inside my desk. I did not reach for it, of course. If I have learned anything over the years, it is that when you find yourself longing to strike a child, you must make doubly sure not to do it.

"I am very displeased with you, Muriel," I said. My voice had all the warmth and care of an iron file. "You may be sure that I shall speak to your father about your conduct."

Muriel did not justify this with a response. Go ahead, her expression seemed to say, speak to him at length, tell him everything I have and have not done, all the Bible verses I have not memorized, all the games I have not played. You'll tell him, shall you? And I shall watch!

I had only half-meant it when I said I would come and speak to her father, but as I started my walk home this afternoon, I found myself convinced that the idea had merit. Perhaps a scolding from Ed Melville would hold more sway than anything I could say to the girl. By the time I came to the steps of the Grier house, I had determined that taking myself up to see Edmund Melville was the wisest course of action.

When I told the Griers my plan tonight at the supper table, both seemed unsure of its wisdom. The Melvilles, I was made to understand, were the only people in town not to invite me to dinner upon my arrival for a reason — they are not, as Mrs. Grier so delicately put it, "a terribly sociable clan," and do not take kindly to strangers on their land. Still, it must be done.

I must admit, too, that I am curious about the Melville place, and about Edmund Melville, of whom I have heard only the vaguest, strangest things. From what queer tree did Muriel fall? What sort of vine could bear such a vulgar and insolent fruit?

Agatha did not come to prayer meeting at Mrs. Castle's house last night. I wonder if she has taken ill again.

January 26, 1902

It was late afternoon by the time I marched up the road to the Melville place yesterday, refusing Mr. Grier's offer of a ride across the bridge. The house was as Mrs. Grier had described it to me: yellow and ramshackle, too small for all the life it contained, its frozen yard overrun with shrieking chickens and their leavings. As I approached the door, a white-muzzled dog heaved herself up off the floor of the porch, barking lustily. Her sagging grey belly and scarred nipples indicated that she was the mother of untold generations of puppies. She did not seem dangerous, but I halted anyway, not wanting to encroach on her territory.

"Hello, old thing," I said to her, and her ragged tail wagged twice. Behind her, the door to the house opened, revealing Muriel in a grease-stained apron that was far too big for her. The room beyond was dark.

"You're here to talk to Dad about me, I suppose," she said, scornful as ever. She looked at the dog, perhaps thinking me too cowardly to walk past the elderly animal. "You can come in, you know. She won't bite."

Come in I did, bestowing a few pats on the dog's head as I passed. She snuffled amiably at my hand and trotted inside behind me, bumping her nose against the crease of my knee. "What is her name?" I asked.

"She don't have a name." Muriel's voice was flat. Although she did not look back at me, I imagined that expression on her face again, the one that made her look so strangely adult. "Dad just calls her 'the bitch.'"

I stumbled slightly, as though she'd thrown the word in my path and tripped me with it.

The Melville house smelled of tobacco and unwashed linens. The walls, bare of pictures or paper, felt strangely greasy to the touch; the floor was dirty, strewn with mud and wandering balls of dust. The door opened directly onto the "front" room, all mismatched furniture and dim corners, dominated by a large fireplace in which a stove had been placed as a concession to modernity. The fire there burned low, despite the chill of winter. The dog brushed past me and lay down upon the floor in front of the stove with a sigh, her poor, stretched belly draped like a length of cloth upon her legs. A dark and narrow staircase at the back of the room rose to an unseen second floor through a hole in the ceiling.

In my time as a teacher, I have been in poorer houses than the Melville house. I have visited families in tumbledown shacks, climbed stairs to cramped second-floor apartments, descended into dingy cellars where rats made merry in the corners. This house was not the worst I'd ever seen, nor even close. And yet, as I let my eyes rove from corner to dingy corner, I found myself fairly aching for Muriel. The force of my sudden sympathy surprised me. Such a profound lack of cheer, such an absence of colour and life! What must it be like for the child, growing up in such a house?

"Where is your room, Muriel?" I asked, hoping that she might indulge me in some conversation, but Muriel just jabbed a finger upwards, as though pointing to heaven itself.

"Attic," she said, sounding suddenly more childish, her fingers tugging at the edge of her apron. Her eyes would not meet mine. Did she see the critical wandering of my eyes, casting judgment on her home and its contents? Or was she merely afraid of what I might say to her father? "I got to get supper on. You sit on the bench, Miss. I'll get the two of you some tea."

The two of us? Muriel disappeared through the kitchen door, leaving me puzzling over her words. I moved to sit down on the threadbare divan, let my eyes wander around the room — and could scarcely suppress a shriek. In an armchair by the fire, so thickly bundled in blankets that I had first taken him for a lumpy antimacassar, was Edmund Melville!

He was far older than I'd imagined; his face was more wrinkle than skin, his eyes sunk deep into his head. Blue eyes, full of snapping, sparkling life, all the more vivid in contrast with his aged body. He followed my every movement with those eyes, taking me in just as I had taken in the house and its contents moments before. He smiled at me. His mouth was full of holes.

"How do you do," I said, rather confusedly. I stood, extending my hand for him to shake; when he made no move to shake it, I sat again, slowly. Mr. Melville watched me do it, and from his mouth came an impish little giggle.

"You're the teacher, eh?" he said. His voice, like his eyes, was startling in its vivacity. It was unusually high, boyish instead of mannish. "The one with the animal name? Bear, or something?"

"Byrd," I replied, wondering if I should extend my hand again. "Miss Ada Byrd. And I must tell you, sir, that I have come to—"

"You're older than I thought you'd be," he said, cutting me off as neatly as Mrs. Grier might snip a bit of thread. "Younger than the last one, though. That Webster woman, all shrivelled and dried up like a bit of salt fish. No juice left in her."

This extraordinary statement, made in the most ordinary tone, made colour rise to my cheeks. I pressed my back teeth firmly together, grinding down until I felt pain crackling in my jaw, before replying.

"I never had the privilege of meeting Miss Webster, I am afraid." Oh, how carefully I formed those words — how bland and pleasant I made my voice, uttering them! "I understand she was a wonderful teacher in her own right."

"Read 'em poetry, the girl said." Ed Melville shook his head. "What's the good in that, eh? What help will poetry be to her once she's grown?" Those bright blue eyes fixed on me steadily, lit with a distasteful light. I felt as though they were peeling off my clothes, layer by layer, and then beyond that skin, and blood, and muscle, leaving me bare to the very bones. "You do the poetry, now?"

"Rarely, sir," I said, warm and mild as a cup of cambric tea. "My personal interests lie in the world of natural history. Plant life, insect life, that sort of thing. Animals too."

"Animals, is it?" He looked at me with renewed interest. "You see the bitch there, eh?" He pointed to the dog, who seemed to know she was under discussion. Her tail thumped once against the muddy floor. "Fine beast. Nearly eleven now, almost as old as the girl. How many times do you suppose she's whelped?"

I was sure at first that I had misheard him. "I . . . I beg your pardon, Mr. Melville?"

203

"Whelped, girl. Dropped puppies." That giggle again, so incongruously young. "I'll tell you — nine. Nine litters she's had over her life, nine times been used as nature intended. Just like my old mam. She had nine children before she died, meself included. Didn't know how to read, didn't know about poetry or what have you. She dropped her puppies and fed them and then she shrivelled away. The bitch there'll do the same, sooner or later."

I sat frozen in my seat, my hands awkwardly tangled together in my lap, and wondered what on Earth I could say to this. Had he spoken with any trace of innuendo in his voice, the slightest leering hint of impropriety, I would have known exactly what sort of response to give: a sharp rebuke, a firm shake of the head, a retreat into spinsterish disapproval. But he made his disgusting proclamations in such a carefree, boyish way, as though discussing the weather, or the health of his crops. Was he unaware of the unseemliness of the conversation? Or — and this I think more likely — was he all too aware of it, and eager to hide behind affect to obscure his aim of discomfiting and disturbing me?

Desperate for distraction, I glanced around the room again, hoping for something to take my mind off this ghoulish old man. Most unexpectedly, I found it on the mantel. A burlap mantel scarf dangled there, the rough cloth clustered with embroidered flowers blooming on a green thread vine. There was something terribly familiar about the design; the flowers on it looked very like those that Muriel had given me, the ones I had thrown into the school privy. The ones that had concealed the tail.

"Did Muriel make that cloth?" I asked, pointing to the scarf. Although it was beautifully done, the sight of it was strangely pathetic. It was not enough to brighten the room, only to make everything else seem worse in comparison.

"Eh," Mr. Melville agreed, jutting his bony chin up out of his nest of blankets. "She's a good hand with a needle. Patches our trousers up every time we have a hole. A good thing, for a gal."

As though her father had summoned her, Muriel entered the room that very moment, bearing two dirty mugs of tea. These she set on the ground at our feet, and she knelt to do it, first in front of her father, then myself. She moved with her eyes fixed to the floor, her head hanging limp as a flag on a windless day. In her own home, scornful, haughty Muriel Melville was as docile as a servant.

Was Muriel treated by her brothers and her father as a kind of "little mother," made to tend to the house and its residents as a wife might? Was her sullen behaviour at school a reaction to this burden, a way for her to declare herself a child and not a maid-of-all-work? The thought troubled me, not only for all it said of the quality of the girl's life, but what it said of my own perceptive powers, that it had not occurred to me sooner.

"The mantel scarf is beautiful, Muriel," I told her, and she did look up then. Was it my fancy, or was there a little spark of pleasure in her face?

"I got the stew on," she mumbled, and disappeared back into the kitchen.

"She's a good girl," Ed Melville said, raising his cup to his mouth with a quivering hand. Dribbles of tea fell onto the antimacassar, blotting the faded wool. "Does dinner and breakfast every day, for me and for the boys. We get our own lunch though, now she's schooling." This said in the long-suffering tones of a man making a great sacrifice!

"I hope that Muriel's domestic responsibilities do not get in the way of her schoolwork," I said, seeing the chance to begin. "I understand that you lost your wife several years ago. You must miss her dreadfully."

At this he gave a thoughtful little hum, a droplet of brown liquid trembling at the edge of his lip before beginning its descent down his chin. "She was young," he said, "young and pretty. Shame the girl din't turn out pretty, but then, she en't grown yet. There's still time." That odious giggle, fast becoming the most hateful sound in the world to me, burbled up from his throat for a third time.

I took a long sip of tea to steady myself, trying not to notice the strange, greasy aftertaste it left in my mouth. My smile felt tight as a cinched belt as I replied, "Pretty is as pretty does, sir. I have always thought — and I am sure you will agree — that it is more important for young girls to develop their minds and their characters than to be merely decorative. Mortal beauty is silver, and will tarnish, while knowledge is gold, and will not."

Of course, I was not at all sure that he would agree, but I did hope that airing this lofty sentiment would shame him into pretending to do so! It did not work; he only smiled, as though at some tremendous private joke.

"Gold," he said, and snorted. "Silver," he said, and followed it with a noisy gulp of tea. "Hogwash," he said, and laughed enormously. I could see down the red tunnel of his gullet.

"In fact, what brings me here, sir," I said, gripping my cup so tightly I felt in danger of cracking the handle clean off, "is Muriel's mind. She does not seem to be interested in any subject. She cannot recite Bible verses. She will not come to the board to solve mathematical problems. She refuses to read aloud. She barely passed her winter examinations, and at this rate will not pass the spring ones. She is clever, I believe, or would be if she applied herself, but I am afraid that, with her current lack of effort, she will not be able to move up to the next Reader at the end of the year."

Such dire pronouncements have worked well for me in the past, for no parent wants to think of his own child as a failure. But Ed Melville only shrugged and slurped up another mouthful of tea.

"Readers," he said, the way another man might say *fairy tales*. "They drop the puppies, and then they die. You talk about natural history. What's more natural than that?"

I looked into his merry eyes, so unlike his daughter's, and I remembered suddenly the exchange between Muriel and me in the summer when I'd asked if she attended school. Surely, I'd said, her father didn't want her to be uneducated?

How little I had understood.

"We disagree, I think, sir," I said, my diplomacy straining at its seams.

"Eh," Mr. Melville agreed and struggled to his feet, still wrapped in his antimacassar. One step closer, then two, then three, until he stood less than three feet from me, blinking down into my face. I could smell his breath, old food mixed with new rot. His eyes moved over my face, my body, and I fought the urge to cross my arms over my chest, to cover myself with my hands. My skin crawled from the dirt of him.

"Younger than the last one," he said again. His tongue poked slyly out from between his cracked and ancient lips, sliding along to collect any remaining drops of tea. "Still have a few good years left in you."

One hand reached out from beneath the antimacassar, thin-skinned and liberally spattered with liver spots. The fingers trailed through the air by my face, as though he meant to caress my cheek, but had misjudged the distance. From her place on the floor, the dog lifted her head, watching the movement of his shrivelled arm.

"You en't pretty," the Melville patriarch said. "Still, the wife's been gone for some time. Could be it's time I took another."

The sentence hung in the air between us, an almost tangible thing. I imagined his gummy mouth suckling at my breast, his rough, veined hands kneading my flesh, and felt the gorge rise in my throat.

"I think I take your meaning, sir." There was no warmth left in my voice now; I was not mild. "But I fear I must decline."

Ed Melville shrugged. Turning in the direction of the kitchen door, he bellowed his daughter's name until she hurried in, still clutching a wooden spoon clotted with gravy. Her eyes remained on the ground as she slipped her father's arm around her shoulders, taking his weight.

"He'll want to be taken up to bed now," she said. Was there a note of apology in her voice, or was that only wishful thinking? "He gets tired. You go, Miss."

I watched the girl all but carry her ancient father up the stairs, grunting a little as he put his weight on her. Ed Melville glanced down at me once more before he disappeared into the gloom of the second floor; one bright blue eye closed in a saucy wink.

That blue eye saw all there was to see of me. I felt uncovered, picked over in a way that felt not only vulgar, but *hungry*. Was he picturing me splayed obediently beneath him, like the three wives he had sent to early graves? Was he imagining himself my conqueror, the dog to his bitch?

As the bedroom door closed overhead, I fled that hideous house for the blessed outdoors, breathing in deep lungfuls of frigid air as though it could somehow cleanse me of the Melville patriarch's stink. I clung to the post of the porch, thankful to be away from that awful giggle, those bright, observant eyes.

"Vile," I whispered and realized that I was trembling.

Mrs. Grier had been right to say "poor Muriel." To live in such a place, raised by such a man, must be nigh unbearable. No wonder the girl runs through the woods like a wild thing. No wonder she seems wise about things that should be beyond a little girl's ken. She is an adult before her time, a child bent forcibly into the shape of a woman. What sort of life did she lead out here in this isolated house, I wondered, with that malicious old lech as a father? Did he look at his own daughter as he had looked at me?

I wanted to run back inside and find the girl, scoop her up and carry her to safety. Instead I gathered my wits about me, took a deep, cleansing breath, and started to walk home. The dark crept up behind me as I passed over the bridge, the sun sinking with unnerving rapidity behind the black line of the trees. It was not until I was back inside the warmth and safety of the Grier house that I began to breathe easily again.

The Melville house still sat heavy on my mind when the Griers and I filed into church this morning. I had hoped to speak to Agatha after the service, recount the whole sorry business to her from beginning to end, but she was not at her usual seat in front of the organ. The congregation sang without accompaniment, warbling and not quite on key. After the first hymn, I stopped singing. I do not like to hear my own voice without music to cover its faults.

Perhaps I would not have told Agatha about the visit even if she had been there. I did not tell her about the chickadee, after all, or the tail, or the crickets. Or the dreams that leave me trembling in my bed, bereft of any memory that might explain my racing heart.

February 6, 1902

After not seeing her at prayer meeting again last night, I took it upon myself to visit Agatha at the manse this afternoon. To my consternation, my knock at the door was answered not by her, nor the Reverend, but a little woman with a face like a wrinkled apple, her thick white hair pulled into a tight knot at the back of her neck. She was, it transpired, Agatha's mother, called by the Reverend to Lowry Bridge to look after Douglas while Agatha was ill. She needed her rest, her mother warned me as she ushered me through the door, and although I was welcome to visit briefly (this said in less than welcoming tones), I mustn't make her excited while she was unwell.

"Unwell" hardly began to cover it. Agatha lay in her bed, terribly pale and thin at the cheeks, with deep violet shadows beneath her beautiful eyes. Although she struggled into a sitting position when I came in, it looked as though it hurt her to do so.

There was a smell in the room that I could not place, familiar and unpleasant.

"Ada," she said, and I heard a scratchy thickness in her throat, the kind that comes along with too much time spent crying. "I am glad to see you."

I rushed to her bedside, reaching for her hand. It felt thin in my grasp, like the paw of a lifelong invalid. "Agatha, what has happened?" I demanded, squeezing her fingers (perhaps a little too hard — I saw her wince and released them at once). "How did you become so ill?"

"Oh," said Agatha, softly, and then, louder, "oh! Oh, Ada — I was going to — we were to have . . ."

But she could not finish what she was trying to say. Instead, she buried her face in her thin hands and began, noiselessly, to weep. I watched the tears slip through her fingers and fall onto the Tree of Paradise quilt spread over her bed, pattering darkly on the pale squares. My mind hummed along, connecting the spaces she'd left between her words, filling in the emptiness with what meaning I could parse from her voice, her face, her tears.

I sat at the foot of the bed, careful to keep some distance between our bodies. I was terribly aware as I did so that it was *her* bed I was sitting on, not just any bed — that this was the place Agatha came to every night to sleep, to dream, to entertain the Reverend's rough and ugly kisses. I could picture them there together, his nude and grizzled body hunching over hers, her slender legs pulling him tightly in until their bellies met. I shook my head to dispel the image, glad that my friend could not see the flush creeping up my cheeks.

"Were you," I asked, keeping my own voice very quiet, "going to have a baby?"

A little hitching sob; a single nod from a head still cradled in her hands.

"And it was a miss. Oh, Agatha!"

I reached out then to touch her shoulder, which felt painfully sharp through her nightgown. What I really wanted to do was pull her to me, gather her up in my arms, and rock her, back and forth, as one might a child, but I was too shy, still, to touch her in so familiar a way.

"Hugh was angry," she whispered, and though I could not see her face, I could picture its expression: wounded, hunted. "He has been sleeping in his study. He says it is for my own good, that he does not want to chance hurting me somehow, but I think he is doing it to punish me."

It was then that she looked up, her face salt-raw and wet. Her expression was not quite what I had pictured. It was wounded, true, but there was reproach there, and indignation, and a kernel of something else. Anger, perhaps.

"I'm sure he isn't," I said, though I was not sure at all. "He is disappointed, I am sure, just as you are—"

But Agatha shook her head so furiously that my words stopped as though she'd plugged my mouth with cork. "But I am not, Ada!" she cried, the words tearing brutally out of her lovely throat. "I'm not disappointed at all!"

And then the tears began anew, and I could no longer help myself: I put my arms around her, clumsy as a boy, and drew her close. My nose pressed into her hair, and I breathed in the smell of roses that lingered still on her skin, even through the smell of illness and blood.

Blood. *That* was the scent that had seemed so familiar, that thick, nauseating, clotting smell I remembered from three hours spent in the privy at my father's house, less than a year ago. The pulsing and wrenching deep inside as flesh pulled from flesh, the sickening sound of an unwelcome stranger falling out of my body and into the muck heap. It had only been a month or two. I hadn't even been sure until the day I woke up to pain and gore on my sheets. His seed had found purchase in my body, like a weed in dirt, and the sprout of our illegitimate union was being pulled up by the roots. That was what it felt like: something had been grasped and wrenched, without mercy, from inside of me.

I did not look down while it was happening. I did not want to see.

I'm not disappointed at all. I had misread completely her expression; it was not anger that lurked beneath her other feelings, but guilt.

Three hours in the privy, moaning piteously and breathing stink as that alien creature fell away from me, and when I limped back across the yard to drag myself back to bed, I found Father standing on the rear porch, watching my slow journey toward the back door. Twice I stumbled and nearly fell, overwhelmed by the pain in my belly, the weakness in my legs. He did not start forward to catch me. Blank eyes. A merciless, immobile face.

I could have told her all of it then.

"My mother had them," I said instead. Always a coward. I spoke directly into the softness of her hair. "Between my sister and I, then after her. Perhaps before me too."

"How many did she have?" Agatha asked, snuffling into my shoulder. I felt the wet there, from her eyes and her nose; I did not mind a bit.

"Eight?" I guessed, after a moment of silent counting. "It is hard to say — I did not understand it at the time, you see. All I was told was that Mother was ill, very ill, and that I mustn't bother her. I would see people leaving her bedroom with bloody linen and thought it was just what happened when mothers became ill. When my sister was born, I supposed at first that it was just Mother getting sick again. Nobody told me otherwise until they brought me in to look at her."

I saw Florrie then as vividly as I had seen Agatha and the Reverend's marital tableau moments before: my sister as a baby, with an apple-sized head and squinting eyes, wrapped tight in a yellow blanket. How strange she had looked to me that day when they placed her in my arms, squashed and ruddy and displeased, squalling at the indignity of the world outside the womb. As I held her, her little hand came loose from its swaddling. Somehow, it found my finger; somehow, she knew to squeeze it tight.

My sister as a baby, and then grown, cold, in her casket. I closed my eyes and tightened my grip on my friend. After a moment Agatha made an anxious little sound in her throat and told me, half-laughing, that I was smothering her. I pulled away at once, shuffling back to my place at the foot of the bed.

"I feel so unnatural," she said, and her eyes filled with tears once more, though they did not spill. "Aren't women supposed to want as many babies as their arms can hold? Wasn't I supposed to be glad, that I would have another? But oh, Ada, I was miserable at the thought of being in that condition again. It was so hard, with Douglas. And then, when it . . . when it stopped, when I felt it all coming out, I felt so very relieved. Hugh knew, I think — he could see it in my face when the doctor left. He thinks, I am sure, that I did something to make this happen. He is so angry with me, and why shouldn't he be? I . . ."

She shuddered, looked away as though she could not bear to meet my eyes. When she spoke again, her voice was little more than a whisper. I could scarcely make out the words.

"I bought pennyroyal tea after Dougie was born. I read somewhere that it . . . fixes things, if you need them fixed. It's in a sachet in the wardrobe. Hugh thinks it is potpourri."

Those words filled the air between us. She met my gaze again, her own filled with that complicated mixture of emotion: guilt and defiance, pain and relief. I drew in a deep breath, remembering again the stink of the privy, that alien thing falling out of me and into the dark, and reached out to put my hand upon her knee. She jumped a little at the touch.

"Whatever happened, Agatha," I said, "God didn't stop it. Doesn't that mean that it was His will?"

A theologian could have easily torn such a trite statement to pieces. I suppose the Reverend would have, had he been there. But I could not look at Agatha and say anything less; I could not see her there, so thin and pale, so burdened by upset, and do anything but comfort her.

"The wages of sin," Father said to me that day as I dragged myself back from the privy, and he would not let me draw a bath for myself, would not let me go back to sleep. He had me come down to dinner that night with him and Mother, even as I shook and bled through my petticoats, even as my fingers trembled so violently they could scarcely grasp my knife. He would not let me go to bed early, either, but kept me in the parlour with him, reading from the Bible. Judges 19, the story of the Levite and his concubine, a woman thrown to a howling and ravenous mob, ravaged, left for dead. He had me stand before him and read it over and over until my voice gave way, blood dripping down my leg and staining forever the carpet in front of his chair. It ruined my petticoat. I had to take it out to the yard later that week and bury it under the cover of moonlight, like a murderess.

The God of inside condemns Agatha for failing to want another child. But the God of outside knows about traps, and the animals that will chew through flesh and bone rather than stay in them.

I stayed with Agatha for an hour or so, and I believe that my company may have helped her, at least a little bit. By the time I left, her eyes seemed dry, and her smile, though still unsteady, looked truer than it had.

"It will be alright, won't it?" Agatha asked me as I stood to go, reaching out to grasp my hand. The touch made an odd little shiver chase itself up the tangle of nerves in my spine.

"It will be alright," I promised. I looked her in the eyes when I said it and made my voice teacher-firm, and she nodded, and smiled again, and looked as though she believed that what I said was true.

Who knows? Perhaps everything *will* be alright, somehow.

February 11, 1902

*I*t is my birthday. I forgot until this morning when I began to write the date upon the blackboard along with the day's lesson, and the realization so took me aback that I faltered in my writing. I stood very still, my hand frozen in midair, the chalk barely touching the blackboard, until one of my students — I believe it was Anna — called out:

"Are you alright, Miss?"

Which made me start, and twitch, and the chalk in my hand scraped against the slate with an unholy shriek, and the whole class cried out in protest, and so I came back to myself.

My birthday. And not just any birthday, but my thirtieth, a year that marks a woman as, decidedly, no longer young. A woman who is a spinster at thirty, Mother used to say, will be a spinster all her life — this with a little sigh and a shake of the head, as though to say more would be too embarrassing for the spinster in question.

Birthdays were not a thing much celebrated in my family when I was younger. Father, of course, did not look kindly on such frivolities as cakes and parties, and Mother followed his wishes in that respect as she did in all others. But Florrie and I would always do something for each other. We would make one another little gifts of hand-copied poems and tatted lace, raisin cakes and apple tarts, or we would do each other's chores, or make up a song and sing it, or write secret notes to be tucked under pillows and into satchels. On one occasion, unbeknownst to me, she stole away my best handkerchief for several weeks, working it over in those rare moments when we were not together. She returned it to me on my birthday, with great fanfare, and I saw that she had embroidered in its corner a cunning little rabbit, curled up with its eyes closed, as though sleeping.

This black book, of course, was to have been her gift to me the year that she died. The thought of that last gift pulled at me all day, distracting me from my students and the lessons I had so carefully planned. I imagined her buying the book on some excursion to the market, hiding it from her husband and drawing the fanciful cardinal design on the first page by candlelight while he snored obliviously beside her. She'd mentioned in one of her letters that she could not easily sleep while in a delicate condition. What a relief it must have been to have some task to keep her up, rather than the incessant kicking and writhing of her murderer's child growing in her belly!

I had promised to go see Agatha after school let out and to take supper with her in the sitting room, where her mother has set her up to recuperate now that she has gained a little strength. Go see her I did, but my conversation was utterly lifeless, and I ate without really tasting my food. I felt as if I were floating a thousand miles away. So distant and vague was I that at length she asked:

"Ada, dear, are you ill? You look terribly drawn."

Her eyes were wide with concern, and I so hated to see her in any such state that I tripped over myself to say, as reassuringly as I could, "No, no! I am fine, I truly am. It's only — it is my birthday today."

Her expression changed not to relief, as I had hoped, but to dismay.

"Your birthday!" she exclaimed, clutching her hand to her breast like a girl in a pantomime. "But you should have told me! I would have made you a cake — a present — or wished you many happy returns, at least! Do the Griers know?"

"No," I replied, rather alarmed at the thought that she might tell them, "and you mustn't say anything either! I don't want them to make a fuss."

"Fuss," she said, struggling to sit up, "is precisely what a birthday is for. Really, Ada, you must allow people to make a fuss over you occasionally! Did you never have birthday parties when you were a girl, or dinners, or anything?"

Her face was so earnest, her voice so full of puzzled affection, that I found my mouth opening and spilling out a torrent of words — stories of the sad, stilted birthdays I'd had at home, the ritual Florrie and I had made of celebrating in secret, the last gift of this black book that I had found bundled amongst those belongings her husband had sent back to my father's house. Agatha listened in silence, aside from the occasional murmur of dismay or pity. When I had finished, exhausted by the force of my disclosure, she reached out and gathered one of my hands into two of her small, thin ones. This gesture, so like that doomed one from Willoughby, almost made me start back in alarm, but then I looked at her eyes, their soft grey so unlike those rose-brown ones that haunted me still, and I made myself relax. This was not *that*, of course.

"So many unhappy memories," she said. "We must make a better one."

And we did. Agatha's mother brought us raspberry cordial and seedcake, which we toasted over the fire and smeared with dripping butter until our lips were shiny and soft. Curled up together on that ugly settee, we whispered and shrieked like girls, reading one another snippets from ladies' magazines and playing an altogether too raucous game of snap. (That Agatha owned a deck of cards at all was a great surprise to me — what a thing for a minister's wife!) Luckily the Reverend is away for several days on some urgent business or other, else we would have disturbed him and kept him from his very important thoughts. We certainly disturbed Agatha's mother; she came back in once or twice to remark, disapprovingly, that Douglas was still asleep, and that we would do well to mind we did not make too much noise and wake him.

"And what if we do," Agatha said after her mother had retreated into the kitchen once more. "Let him join the party!" She said this, however, in a whisper, either because she did not want to wake the baby or because she did not want to be scolded again.

It was great fun, but as the evening drew on, it became clear to me that Agatha's strength was flagging. When the clock struck eight, she let out a great sigh and rested her head against the arm of the settee, her eyes already fluttering shut.

"Happy birthday, Ada," she said, speaking in that drowsy half-whisper so particular to those about to fall asleep, and indeed, in a moment or two she was snoring gently, her soft mouth slightly parted. At some point in the evening, she'd thrown her legs carelessly over my lap; they lay there still, pinning me to my seat, and she sprawled out across the cushions like a boy lying in the sun. I sat there and watched her for some time, knowing that I had to leave but loathe to disturb her. A few strands of red-gold hair straggled over Agatha's forehead, and I reached out to push them back. Her skin was warm to the touch.

The weight of her body upon me, the slight hum of her breath in her throat, the firelight playing across her face, all induced in me a queer and dizzying contentment. It was rooted in my body, this feeling, a matter of the flesh as much as the heart. My breast felt as though it strained against an iron band. Little jolts of feeling chased themselves up and down my arms, as though they were preparing to do something. Reach out for her, perhaps, and pull her close.

"You pretty thing," I murmured, keeping my voice low. I did not want to wake her.

So soundly asleep was she that I hardly disturbed her when I slipped out of the house and into the snow, bringing its warmth with me for my walk home. I felt no fear even when I passed the doors of the church where the chickadee had fallen, or the place where the crickets had set upon me so many weeks ago. There was no room in the world for beasts prowling the night, things watching me from the trees, eyes in the dark. My mind was full of the sight of her in gold, sleeping in the firelight with her legs thrown over mine.

February 14, 1902

*I*t happened again. God help me, it happened again.

Today was a long, dull Friday, the kind of grey winter day that stretches on for so long it feels like three sewn together, end to end. All my lessons were flat and flabby, squashed lifeless by the weight of the hours. I kept my eye on the clock for most of the day, and I noticed several students shifting in their seats to sneak surreptitious glances at it over their shoulders before turning back around to face the blackboard. I pretended not to see, glad that their lack of enthusiasm had translated into listlessness instead of mischief. It was not quite three o'clock when I called for dismissal. I expected the usual race for the door, but the children took their leave as limply as they had taken the entire day, trudging lifelessly through the snow to the road.

On my birthday, I had promised Agatha that I would come and see her again on Friday afternoon, and so I did, after setting the schoolhouse right and writing Monday's lesson on the black-board, but I was in a strange state of mind as I walked toward the manse. A large part of me felt as sluggish as I had all day, ready to curl up in a stupor and wait for winter to end. But there was another part — smaller, but no less insistent for that — which longed to make noise, to stamp and shout, to run screaming through the woods and throw myself headfirst into the river. My footsteps seemed to jar loose a kind of rising wildness, rattling about inside of me like pennies in a jar.

"What is happening to me?" I whispered once, stopping to catch my breath, and I waited as though I expected the trees to answer — as though I expected once again to hear that thing, whatever it was, call my name. But I heard nothing but the wind ruffling their bare branches, and, once, the distant sob of a loon.

By the time I reached the manse, I was jumpy as a flea. I sat in Agatha's uncomfortable sitting room chair, my fingers curling and clenching on the arms. My feet shuffled violently in place on the ugly carpet as I tried to speak of calm, ordinary things: my students, the weather, Douglas's recent attempts at standing on his own. My eyes kept straying to the darkness outside the window, flickering from Agatha's face to the hushed beating of snow against the glass. (For it had begun to snow again by now, the kind of driving snow that makes the night thicker and more oppressive.) One part of me — the larger part, again — was there in the manse, making polite conversation with Agatha and thanking her mother every time she filled our teacups. The other was outside, in the black.

I tried to act natural, to smile and nod when smiles and nods were called for, but perhaps I did a bad job of it; or perhaps Agatha was simply tired, and no longer cared for conversation. Her head began to droop, and she rested her cheek against the arm of the settee with a yawn and said, "Ada, I'm sorry — I can barely keep my eyes open! I must be very poor company."

I tried to protest, but she would have none of it. Her eyes half closed, she pointed to the little bookcase in the corner with the lead glass doors.

"Perhaps you could read to me?" she suggested. "I know it's a bit childish, but I do like to be read to when I am not well. Mother used to do it, but her eyes are not what they used to be."

Reading aloud again! Would I never be free of this onerous duty?

"I am afraid I am no elocutionist," I said, but Agatha smiled.

"Nonsense! I heard you reading to your students, remember? You do it splendidly." And she pointed to the bookcase again, a little more insistently this time.

What choice had I? I made my way to the bookcase and opened the doors, letting my fingers trail over the cloth bindings. The slight indentations of the letters made me shiver. Most of the books were works of theology and collections of sermons; the novels Agatha loves so much are all hidden in her hope chest, away from prying, pious eyes. The only volume on the shelf fit to be read aloud was the Wordsworth, the one I had given her. Slowly I pulled it free from its resting place, wincing at its familiar water-stained cover. Riffling through its yellowed pages, I chose a poem at random, reading with all the feeling and animation of a clockwork doll.

So automatic is my response to words upon a page that reading scarcely feels like a thing I *do* now. It is an involuntary reaction to print, like a hiccup, a response I can neither control nor stop once it begins. As I read, I felt the tightly coiled springs of my body gradually loosen, my spine softening in that uncomfortable chair. My feet slowly ceased their restless shuffling, and my hands, which had at first gripped the book so tightly, began to relax their hold. Two poems I read, or three, or four, skipping blithe as a lamb through the book, and then I came upon the page where Miss Webster, my predecessor, had written that strange declaration:

> no matter if I plug my ears it
> still calls to me

The poem where this phrase had been written was "Lucy Gray," a piece I had read before, but never with any especial interest. Now I found myself lingering over each line, chewing them slowly as one does meat. The story of the girl lost on the moor after her father sends her into the snow with a light to guide her mother home . . . how it reminded me of Mrs. Grier's poor child, the son she had lost. I saw *him* in place of Lucy as I read the poem, though I had no idea what the boy had looked like. Red-headed, perhaps, like his father, with his mother's quick step and knowing eyes. When I came to the line:

> And many a hill did Lucy climb
> But never reach'd the Town.

I had to pause, closing my eyes against the enormity of it, until Agatha asked in a low, sleepy voice if I was feeling well.

I was fine, I assured her, and went on.

My eyes, once open, wandered again to the window. The snow had tapered off a little, a few last straggling flakes speckling the darkness. I could see the great expanse of white in front of the manse, with only vague humps and valleys to mark where Agatha's flowers slept. Beyond it, the road, and beyond that, the woods — always the woods.

But there was nothing standing there, nothing to see, no one calling my name, and so I continued reading, my voice quite steady.

In the poem, Lucy's grief-stricken parents search the moor for her, and are on the verge of giving up, when at last her mother sees her footprints in the snow. They follow the prints across the hills, through an open field, until they come to a bridge — a bridge that, in my mind, looked remarkably like that unsteady structure spanning the Slade — and there the mystery of the missing child balloons from an ordinary tragedy to something stranger and wilder:

> They follow'd from the snowy bank
> The footmarks, one by one,
> Into the middle of the plank,
> And further there were none.

I said this line in as dramatic a tone as I could muster, and on the last syllable, just as though it had been timed, it happened: a knock on the door of the manse.

I must have jumped or cried out. I know that I dropped the book, for it landed on the floor with a mighty thud. Poor Agatha, whose eyes had been below half-mast, started upright in her seat.

"What is it?" she asked, her voice wild in the way of a woman startled out of a comfortable doze. "Ada, what is wrong?"

I did not answer; I could not. The knock came again, a light and merry rapping like that of a girl coming to call on her sweetheart. Or a child teasing its mother.

"There is someone at the door," I said. These words came out in barely a whisper, and the dryness of my mouth made my tongue stick strangely to its roof and click. I was intensely aware of every part of my body: the blood pounding hotly in my veins, the nerves plucked and thrumming madly, the limbs that seemed to have suddenly become rooted to the floor. For I could not move. I could only stare in horror at that door, waiting to see the knob turn.

"Someone at the door?" Ada frowned. I did not see it, but I heard it in her voice. "Surely not. On a night like this, and so late!"

"But the knock," I said desperately. I was almost pleading, I realized, on the verge of begging on my knees for someone else to experience what I was experiencing, to assure me that what was happening was happening, that I was not — oh *please*! — going mad. "There was a knock, Agatha, surely you heard it!"

Agatha's frown deepened. "There is no one knocking, Ada."

The knock came again at the end of her sentence, again as though it had been carefully timed, and this time I felt sure that there was an edge of mockery to it. Whatever was on the other side of the door could hear her and knew that she was deaf to whatever noises might come from it. It knew it could get up to whatever mischief it wanted, and I would not be believed — I would never be believed!

The anger that sparked in my breast at that moment spurred me to my feet. The anger was unexpected, but bracing in its sudden, righteous burn. How dare this spectre, this thing, torment me! How dare it mock my terror, my pounding heart, the hairs that stood up on the back of my neck! I was at the door — I had hold of the knob — I had it flung open with a hoarse and incomprehensible shout!

Beyond the doorway was the snow, and the road, and the woods. Nothing more.

Agatha shouted something behind me, some word of alarm or reproach, but I scarcely heard it. Unburdened by hat or coat, I stepped over the threshold and into the snow.

"Coward!" I screamed. "Watch me from the shadows, will you? Whisper my name? Knock in the middle of the night? Come out and look me in the eye!"

In the distance a dog began to howl, its voice twining with mine. I stood with my fists clenched, squinting into the darkness in search of some sign of whatever it was that had lured me out beyond the warmth of Agatha's sitting room. There was nothing, no sound but the dull thud of my own heartbeat in my ears, no feeling but the shivers rippling through my skin like the waves of an earthquake.

There was nothing there. And then, in the space of a breath, there was.

The hare regarded me from its place in the snow, its long ears pricked upwards as though it, too, could hear the pounding of my heart. Its lower jaw moved slightly as it chewed something, a stray shoot or clover somehow left untouched by the winter. The tips of the ears were black, the hind feet long and slender. Its thick winter fur was scarcely less white than the ground beneath it. A snowshoe hare. *Lepus americanus*, the same species that Florrie had drawn hollowed out in death, all those years ago. The drawing that had enraged our father.

Any natural animal would have fled my approach, but this one did not flinch, did not so much as blink its dark eyes as I stepped toward it. Shivers rattling my jaw, I knelt in the powdery snow before it, my skirt soaking through almost immediately. The hare sat placidly and chewed, pale and still in the cloudy moonlight.

"The hare upon the green," I murmured, remembering again Lucy Gray's wild, lonely death on the moors. The hare was within my reach now. I was so close I could have stretched out my hand

and placed it on its head; indeed, my arm rose as though I meant to do so, though the movement scarcely felt voluntary.

The creature's head jerked violently at my hand's approach, and it spat something onto the snow. Next to that white fur, on top of that white snow, it looked almost black, a little worm lying in a spreading puddle of slime. But it was no worm, I saw as I leaned down to look, nor was it a piece of clover. It was a little scrap of flesh, rounded at one end and ragged on the other, sodden with blood and spittle.

A tongue. The hare had chewed off its own tongue and spat it out at me, a grotesque offering.

The gorge rose in my throat. My stomach revolted. I turned to vomit into the snow, greasy strings of spit and bile dangling off the edge of my lips and blowing in the wind.

When I had finished, I scooped up a handful of snow to rinse out my mouth, swishing it through my teeth and spitting. My vomit lay in a jellied pile, a stain on the smooth white sheet of the world. Another wave of nausea overtook me, and I looked over at the dark line of footprints behind me to steady myself. A rope for a drowning girl, flailing wildly in the sea.

Agatha stood in the doorway of the manse, an expression I had never seen before on her dear face. Her nails dug into the wood of the doorframe; I fancied I could hear the particles cracking beneath them. From deeper within the house, I heard the thin wail of baby Douglas, roused from his sleep by all the noise and fuss, and the voice of Agatha's mother, shouting what was it? Were there robbers? Was there fire?

I wanted Agatha to come to me, to kneel beside me in the snow and stroke my hair, to tell me that everything would be alright and call me a perfect strawberry. But she did not.

"Ada," she said, then stopped. She took a step back from the threshold, farther away. She looked at me as though she did not know who I was. Or, worse, that she knew me, and wished she didn't! "What are you doing?"

It almost did not surprise me, when I turned to look, that the hare had disappeared, and its tongue with it. The snow was once again unbroken, my own footprints its only imperfection.

When Mr. Grier came to collect me, Agatha told him, very stiffly, that I was feeling ill, and that I ought to be taken home to rest. She stood well apart as I gathered my things and mutely made my way to Mr. Grier's cutter. Even after the door closed behind me, I could feel her eyes on me through the window, watching me recede into the distance.

(Come now, Ada. You know by now that they were not *her* eyes.)

Mrs. Grier was inclined to fuss when I came home, but I begged her off, saying that I was only troubled with a migraine, and had to lie down for the remainder of the evening. Lie down I did, but I have not been able to sleep. Every time I try, I see that hideous scrap of flesh on the snow, and my eyes snap open like paper fans. My candle scarcely does any good; the light deepens the shadows and makes me more afraid than I would be without it. Even so, I will not blow it out.

Is it some disorder of the mind that causes me to see things, hear things, that then vanish as though they never were? As a rational woman, I can think of no other explanation. Madness, or something like it, must be the only scientific way to account for these monstrous visions. But I remember the impact of the crickets crashing into me, the warmth of the blood oozing from the stump of the tail in Muriel's flowers. I *felt* those things. Surely madness cannot explain *that*.

February 16, 1902

After sleeping for most of Saturday, I woke this morning rested and, if not cheerful, at least calm enough to sit at the breakfast table and make polite conversation. I could push myself to say, "Please pass the butter" and "Might I have more tea?" and "I suppose it may snow today, a little." I dropped nothing, smiled when smiling was called for, heard no strange sounds. In church, I was able to sit quietly, my hands folded in my lap like a pious schoolgirl in a print. I was able to find my place in my prayer book and my hymn book. I was even able to listen reasonably attentively to the sermon, although it was a very dull one.

Agatha was in church for the first time since her miss, still looking a little worse for wear, and evidently too sick to play the organ, as we again had no accompaniment to our hymns. Once or twice during the singing she turned and looked searchingly through the crowd. Every time she did, I averted my eyes and examined my hymn book or turned slightly to look at the patches of pearl grey sky visible in the high windows. I could not imagine what might happen if our gazes should lock. Nothing good, I felt. Nothing at all.

Mrs. Kinsley was at church again today, looking very stylish in a new grey suit and a broad-brimmed black hat, a smoke-rosy pigeon wing adorning either side of its crown. *Her* eye I tried to catch, but she seemed intent on the sermon, and after the service she swept through the doors without a single glance at anyone in the congregation.

I lost track of Mrs. Grier in the general press of people scrambling to leave the church before the clouds, which were low and dark, emptied themselves upon us. For several moments I vainly searched for her in the throng of Sunday best, smiling and nodding to those of my students and their families that smiled and nodded at me.

And then, through a gap between this person and that, I saw Mrs. Grier in the neat little brown dress she saves for church, clutching her prayer book to her chest. I could glimpse only a little of her plain, sensible face, but it was enough to see that its expression was one of worry and that her mouth had worked itself into a thin, tight line. She was speaking to someone, it seemed, and about a matter of no small importance.

This I saw, and then the crowd shifted and thinned like milk in water, and I saw who she was speaking to. It was Agatha. Her face, still pale and thin, was the very picture of gravity, and she appeared to be speaking with some vehemence, the words volleying forth from her mouth as though she were barely able to contain them.

Her eyes lifted from Mrs. Grier's, and in the space of a sigh found me. They met mine only for the briefest instant before Agatha dropped her gaze, her cheeks staining with rose, but that glance told me everything I needed to know. Her grey eyes were lit, as they had been twice before, with a peculiar and prurient light; there was a look there of unsightly interest, as though she were all agog at some lurid tale in a magazine.

She was speaking to Mrs. Grier about me. She was telling her what had really happened on Friday night — that I had acted like a madwoman, and that she, Mrs. Grier, had better look out.

I kept my face calm, my demeanour pleasant, and held up my end of the day with aplomb. (But *wasn't* Mrs. Grier a trifle more reserved while we prepared supper? *Didn't* her gaze shy away from mine?) It was not until I was back in this awful little room that I let my worries bubble and burst. There were tears and cries muffled with the help of a fat pillow. My teeth found the swell of my lower lip and worried it, ripping fresh tears in the pink skin there. The pain gave me a fleeting moment of relief.

What had Agatha said to her? What does Mrs. Grier know? Does she think, perhaps, that I am overworked, a little nervous? Or does she think me, as I begin to think myself, quite mad?

February 20, 1902

*M*ore bad dreams these past few days, more nights that have seen me start awake and stare at the ceiling with a shuddering heart, waiting for some unseen thing or person in the dark to take hold of me. Exhaustion has left me worn and limp. I could blame what happened today on that, perhaps. If I wanted to. If I did not know better.

This whole week has been grey and stormy, but this morning the sun shone with a vengeance, making the icicles drip onto the soft piles of snow. Winter, it seemed, had decided to dress up as Spring for her own amusement. The children bolted outside as soon as I rang the dinner bell, leaving me alone in the schoolhouse for the first time in several days. I used the time most unwisely, rereading Thoreau's *The Maine Woods* at my desk as I ate my little meal of bread and butter. I should have prepared for the rest of the day's lessons, or swept or stoked the fire, or done anything to make myself useful, but instead, I sat and gloried in that singular philosopher's recollections of the wild nature of his homeland.

So transported was I by his words that I almost forgot to ring the dinner bell again and summon the children back inside. When I finally did so, and the whole host of them came trooping back inside, I was most displeased to see them followed in by another figure — a familiar but most unwelcome personage.

"Miss Byrd," said Mrs. Castle, in tones of distinct triumph. Poor Eugene sidled out from behind her, slinking to his desk with his eyes fixed firmly on the floor. "I trust you are keeping well."

I felt the colour rise in my cheeks. Her sudden appearance had flustered me, made me feel somehow *caught*, like a child found picking lumps out of the sugar bowl. In confusion, I stood, grasping at the edge of my desk and nearly knocking my owlet skull in its jar off the table and onto the floor.

"I have come to inform you," she said, "that I shall be sending another letter to the board, very soon."

Another letter! I felt my stomach twist with dismay. "Is there some matter you wish to discuss with me, Mrs. Castle? Perhaps, if you have any complaints or questions, we could—"

"No! Nothing," Mrs. Castle replied. The corners of her mouth tugged upwards in a little smile. "Nothing, at least, that I should like to mention in front of the children. They are *so* impressionable."

I heard the sibilant current of a whisper starting somewhere at the back of the class at that, like the half-heard hiss of a snake in the grass. My cheeks burning even hotter, I pounded my fist on my desk for order.

"Mrs. Castle," I said, speaking in my hardest, firmest teacher's voice, "I must tell you that I haven't the faintest idea what you are trying to say."

"I daresay you do not," Mrs. Castle replied, and that smile of hers grew. The urge to slap it off her face came upon me so sudden and strong that my palm fairly itched. "We are a simple people in Lowry Bridge, Miss Byrd — simple, decent, and God-fearing. We expect those charged with the education of our little ones to be the same in all respects. If it should reach anyone's ears that a teacher has not behaved properly, if it should be discovered that her conduct has been unladylike, or un-Christian, or *wanton*" — this pronounced distinctly and with that same thrill of triumph running through it — "how can we trust her with our children?"

Wanton. The whispers started again at that and did not cease when I pounded my fist again. Only when I got to my feet did my students fall silent. Fourteen pairs of childish eyes were trained on me, as well as Mrs. Castle's; I felt the weight of them there behind the rampart of my desk, staring out into what, in that moment, seemed like an army at banner against me.

If it should reach anyone's ears that a teacher has not behaved properly . . . For a moment I wondered if Mrs. Castle had somehow heard about what happened in Willoughby. But then I thought of Agatha watching me from the doorway of the manse, her eyes as she murmured to Mrs. Grier in church. Had she, then, told others about the knock that never was, my flight into the snow? Had she, in essence, told the entire town that I was going mad?

I looked at Mrs. Castle, squat and loathsome as a toad, and a little bubble of laughter rose in my throat. I tried to swallow it, smother it, to match my expression to the gravity of the situation, but the laughter fought against me, and I found myself making helpless, muffled sounds even as I turned away to calm myself. My legs trembled with the strain. I stepped away from my desk and faced the blackboard, desperately trying to control myself, but it was no good; reaching behind me, I groped desperately on my desk for the bell and rang it, hard and fast.

"Recess," I choked, although they had just come in from their dinner, and rang the bell again, the clang sounding out in that quiet room.

My students did not need to be told twice. Out they rushed with many an excited whoop, leaving the schoolhouse silent and cold. Still choking, I turned to face Mrs. Castle, who still stood in the aisle, looking frankly amazed.

"Miss Byrd," she began, "what on Earth—"

But I could no longer abstain. By that time the laugh had been trapped so long that it came out as a series of sharp and painful gasps. I leaned against the blackboard, desperate for air but unable to properly inhale. Bursts of formless noise tore from my throat, and I let one hand pound weakly on the board, neat rows of numbers smearing from the wet of my hand. Mrs. Castle's feet sounded upon the floorboards, as though she had taken an involuntary step backwards.

"Why are you laughing?" she demanded, and then, louder, "What? What is it that you find so very funny, Miss Byrd?"

I could not reply. Choking, I fought vainly for control of myself, paroxysms of laughter ripping through me and leaving me weak. Tears rolled down my cheeks, as much from the lack of air as from humour, and I felt them drop without ceremony to my breast and stain the cotton of my shirtwaist. It was like the kind of fit that comes when a marvellous joke is told, and the mirth becomes so powerful it hurts. My stomach ached with it.

What was the joke? I do not know. I only know that I could no sooner have stopped myself than I could have sprouted wings and flown.

I heard Mrs. Castle's footsteps retreating farther, and then the rattle of the door as she fumbled with the latch. Her voice was thick with revulsion, she declared:

"Be sure that this shall be in my letter too, Miss Byrd. The board will know *exactly* how you have behaved today."

The door opened and then slammed, leaving me to howl like a wounded dog in the empty schoolhouse. The room filled with the sound of my shrieking laughter. It pounded against the windows, rattled the door.

Slowly, slowly the laughter died down, and I was able to draw in several deep lungfuls of air. My mouth worked like that of a landed fish as I struggled to inhale comfortably. Shoulders heaving, muscles clenched, I stood with my forehead pressed against the blackboard, waiting for my breathing to even out.

"It *is* funny, isn't it, Miss?"

The voice caught me off-guard; I let out a little cry of alarm as I turned, my breath still ragged in my throat. Muriel Melville sat unmoving at her desk, her hands folded in front of her, the very picture of a pious little schoolgirl. But there was that gleam in her eye, the one I had seen a few times before, and as she looked at me, taking in my flushed cheeks, the sweat on my brow, she smiled.

That the girl had seen me in such a state felt like too much to bear. I looked at her, so smug and so comfortable, the only student who could bear witness to my strange fit, and my hands longed to open my desk drawer and take out the hated switch. I wanted to strike her, not just on the hands, as any teacher might, but on the face, the head, the spine. I wanted to break a board across her back. I wanted to pull her hair out by the roots. I wanted — good God! — I wanted, I think, to kill her!

"Go outside, Muriel," I said.

The girl stood and put on her worn woollen wraps, leisurely as a dandy. I watched her not, I now think, as a teacher ought to watch her charge, but as one might watch a wasp in the room.

Muriel paused by the schoolhouse door, her hand kissing the wood, and looked me in the eye. Her smile was still in place. It made me think of tails; it made me think of tongues on the snow.

"The way they carry on," she said. "Behave yourself. Learn your times tables. Keep quiet, don't laugh, don't run, read your Bible, spell your words. Be good, have babies, then get buried."

They drop the puppies, and then they die. I remembered that day in the Melville house, that ugly afternoon when I understood, finally, her place in her father's household, her purpose in the world as he saw it.

"Go and play," I said, fainter this time. I badly wanted to sit down, but I felt that I could not while the girl stood there. I did not want her head to be higher than mine.

Muriel did not do as she was told. She looked at me from her height, and I realized suddenly that her head was higher than mine already. She had grown taller over the last few months, and I had not noticed. She was well on her way to becoming a woman.

God help her. God help all of us.

"Get out," I said, a little less faintly. "Get out of here right now, or you will catch it, Muriel Melville."

Her smile deepened. She showed her teeth.

"They think it's all that matters," she said. "They think that's all there is."

But we know better, don't we? her expression said. *You and I know how much more there is out there, in the wide, wild world.*

Before I knew it, the blackboard eraser was in my hand, and I hurled it at the girl with great force. It struck her shoulder in a great puff of pale dust. "Get out of here!" I screamed. There was a brief lull in the noise outside, as if the children were struggling to recognize where the sound had come from. "Get out, go home, or the woods, or wherever it is you go! I want you out of my sight!"

The eraser striking her shoulder made an impression. She frowned and looked down to brush away the chalk dust with her hand, then wiped her hand on the door, leaving a trailing white smear. Shaking her head, as though my fit of temper had disappointed her, she pushed the door open and disappeared into the bright white afternoon. I sat limply at my desk, my hands flat on the wooden surface, and breathed in deeply through my nose, out from my mouth in a damp little cloud.

Gannis and Ammerman said they would not take Mrs. Castle's letters into account. Will that still be true when she tells them what happened today? Or will her account of my hysterical laughter be enough to convince them that I am unfit for my post?

The end of the recess period came and went, and eventually the students came to realize it; I did not ring the bell to summon them. They trooped back into the schoolhouse, pink-faced and pleased as pigs in muck. All except Muriel, who had disappeared — to home, or wherever it is she goes.

February 22, 1902

After church this afternoon, feeling in need of a rest, I went upstairs to have some time alone in my room before supper. I must have climbed the stairs more quietly than usual, walked down the hall with a softer step, for when I opened the door, I found Mrs. Grier there, unaware that I had entered the room. She stood with her back to me, bent over something on the washstand.

It was my book — *this* book — the book that has borne witness to all the madness of these past few months. And, dear God, she was reading it!

A strangled sound escaped my throat, a perversion of the greeting that had half-formed there already, and Mrs. Grier jumped and turned around. When she saw me there in the doorway, I saw the colour slip from her cheeks.

"Miss Byrd," she said, her voice falsely cheerful. Her stance shifted slightly as she spoke, her arms spreading out a little wider. To block my view, I suppose, of the washstand. "I was just coming up here to see if you had anything that needed washing. It is laundry day tomorrow, you know."

So it was. Monday is the day when she ordinarily does the washing, and I saw that she did have a basket sitting by her feet, already heaped half-full of shirts and socks. She had at least come to my room innocently enough. Before she'd caught sight of this book and decided it was hers to peruse at will.

In that moment, I could think of nothing but Father discovering our little collection at the bottom of the wardrobe, the fury with which he had turned Florrie's drawings into paper ribbons and our collection jars into so much crushed glass. Our attempt at creating a world for ourselves, separate from the one we shared with him, had infuriated him; he had thought a violation of that world a just and proper punishment for our sins. Now here I stood again, watching someone access my private world, with no word of consent from me.

What had she read? My account of the other day's encounter with Muriel? The description of the incident at Agatha's house, or the thing calling my name outside of the church? Or had she glimpsed only more pedestrian content — my unflattering portraits of my students, my fits of mood and temper, the sordid tale of my deflowering in the Willoughby attic room? I tried to measure the likelihood of each scenario by examining her face, but I saw nothing more expressive than its lack of colour, and a look, barely perceptible, of guilt.

Perhaps it was that look which unleashed my flood of temper. Father had not felt the least bit guilty for what he had done; I suspect he had no idea there was anything to feel guilty about. Mrs. Grier's awareness of her own wrongdoing gave me permission to acknowledge that I had, indeed, been wronged. I felt . . . not *enraged*, that is not the right word. The right one, perhaps, is *outraged*. My body was on fire, every nerve crackling and burning with *how dare?*

My hands clenched into fists as I looked at Mrs. Grier, standing awkwardly beside my bed. Just a brief squeezing, over almost before it began, but I know she saw it, for her eyes flicked down to them before snapping back up to attention.

"No, Mrs. Grier," I said finally. My voice shook a little; I found that I was trembling. The furious indignation flooding my body left me lightheaded, almost drunk. "Nothing here need concern you."

She took my meaning, I think — I hope — and nodded, stooping to retrieve her basket. She came toward the door, then hesitated, for I had not moved. Her eyes lingered on my face, as though trying to solve some riddle based on the coordination of my features.

"You know," she said finally, "I think I should be alright to get supper going on my own today. It's just stew I'm doing, nothing fancy. Maybe you could have a nice, relaxing afternoon, Miss Byrd?" She offered me a thin little smile.

She was trying to appease me. I found I liked the idea of being appeased.

"Yes," I said, after a long pause, in which her smile thinned considerably. "Yes, Mrs. Grier, I think it might be nice to have an afternoon to myself. Perhaps I will write for a while."

I put more emphasis on the word *write* than was strictly necessary. It was gratifying to see her flinch, though she gained composure again quickly.

"Just so," she said, and resettled her basket on her hip. "Well. I'll call you when the supper's on, shall I?"

I nodded, and finally moved aside. She scuttled away as fast as she could, barely escaping with her dignity.

I can no longer keep this book in my room, of that I am certain. This is no safe place for it. It must remain on my person at all times, or at least within arm's reach, so I may easily snatch it away from anyone who tries to touch it. My satchel, perhaps. That way it will come with me to school, and I can carry it with me any time I leave. I shall cover it with a few things — a handkerchief, a few old letters, some pencil stubs and a pair of gloves. The extra weight may be hard to bear every day, but I would rather a thousand times bear that than wonder when Mrs. Grier will thumb through the pages of my brain again.

I do wonder what she read.

I wonder what Agatha told her.

February 28, 1902

*W*hen I arrived home this evening, Mrs. Grier was at the door to greet me.

"There's a letter here for you, Miss Byrd," she said and passed me a flimsy and battered envelope. I stared at it blankly. The address clumsily inscribed on its front was in a thin and trembling hand that I did not recognize; there was no return address. Could it be from Father? Did he guess that of late I have been feeding his letters directly into the stove as soon as I see the postmark, and hope to get the better of me this way?

I nearly did the same with this one. But curiosity got the better of me, and I stole up to my room after dinner to read it in privacy. The penmanship was very poor, and I could scarcely read what I have transcribed here, to the best of my ability.

To Miss Byrd (so called),

Some weeks ago I received a letter from you that was addressed to my daughter Amelia Webster. It was a shock to read such a thing and me with a bad heart too but I thought it only decent to reply so that you will not write again.

Amelia was my youngest child and the last of her sisters to live here as the others are now set up in households of their own with husbands, babies, etc. She was never the kind of girl that any man wanted to marry and so I had determined that she would be the comfort of my old age. I am a widow and greatly troubled with physical complaints such as gout, rheumatism, cataracts, so cannot keep my house in the order it once was in.

Amelia became a teacher as we needed some income to maintain the household after the death of her father. She often accepted teaching posts in other towns but I was always very clear that she must not work so far that she could not come home on the week ends and see to the housework, take me out for my shopping, and read to me. However two years ago she received an invitation to teach at this junction of yours, Lowry Bridge. I did not want her to take the offer but her father's death had left us wanting and she made up her mind to go against my will and without my blessing. She did not seem to care that her poor mother would be left alone and helpless for the

Lord knew how many months which I thought was very ungrateful after all the trouble I had bringing her up. The Bible says that a parent must not spare the rod or else the child will be spoiled. Well I did not spare the rod but my daughter was spoiled anyhow!

For the first month or two Amelia sent me letters and they were very ordinary. She told me about her students, the weather, the people in the town, friends she made. One of these was a well-to-do woman who by her description sounded no better than she should have been. I told her to mind the company she kept and pray to God to make her a good and obedient girl but she must not of listened to me as her letters soon became very queer. She said there were noises in the woods that made her afraid and that she saw things that were not there. She said there was something watching her always. She said it called her name. I suspected she had taken to drink and when she came home for Christmas, I no longer had any doubt about it as she was so odd and thin. I came up behind her once and said her name and she jumped from her seat and screamed as though I had stuck her with a pin. When she saw it was only me, she started to cry and I said what do you have to cry about you silly girl. Oh oh you wouldn't understand she said and then would not speak to me for the rest of the day, even when I came on with a sick headache and needed her to read me the newspaper.

I do not know the exact meaning of the inscription you mentioned though I would guess that it is something Amelia wrote while under the influence of liquor. What a disgraceful indulgence for a child of respectable parents! I would ask her if that is so if she was here with me but she is not for she never returned home after her term was up. Why she would lie and say that she was leaving to tend to me in illness I do not know as she was not interested in tending to me before her time there despite all my maladies. Her last letter to me came last spring and was so muddled and strange that I could not make sense of it. She said again that she was being followed, something was after her, she could not outlast it, other things that I do not remember. I did not keep it but fed it to the fire for it was a disgusting sign of her decline into wanton habits.

I have received no more since that letter and am forced to conclude that my daughter abandoned her position to fall into a life of anonymity, drink, and despair. Where she is now and what her circumstances are I do not know. Since she no longer cares enough about me to come home or even write, I no longer consider her any child of mine and would not have her darken my door step even if she did return. I have a girl now hired to look after me and she is a better nurse than my Amelia was although she is an Irish and full of strange dirty habits as her kind always are. So I ask you Miss Byrd to refrain from sending me any more letters regarding my daughter as I have no more information to give you and no desire to hear the girl's name again.

Cordially,
Mrs. Frederick Webster (nee Rachel Horvath)

After reading this I sat for some time on my bed, stunned. The letter lay open on my lap, fluttering a little in the breeze that came in through the window. Fresh and brisk, carrying the scent of melting snow and new flowers.

My predecessor never made it home. The sick mother had been a lie, a ruse to free her from her post. She made her excuses, and then . . . what?

Mrs. Webster could be right, nasty, crabbed little soul though she seems to be. Her daughter could have been seduced by vice and dissolution, taken to drink, strayed from the righteous path. Perhaps her disappearance was no disappearance at all, but an attempt to flee from the grip of the mother who so clearly had too firm a hold on her. Daughters have disappeared before for just these reasons, even sensible, settled spinster daughters. It is possible.

It is possible. But, of course, I do not believe it.

March 3, 1902

This morning at breakfast Mr. Grier remarked that he thought a storm was coming.

"Red sky in the morning," he said, ladling a generous second portion of porridge into his bowl, "shepherds take warning."

I looked at him questioningly, for the sky was grey as a dove, solid with thick, soft clouds.

"Sunrise," was his explanation. "Very early this morning, when I was feeding the cows, I saw the sunrise. Just a bit of it, mind, around the edges of the clouds, but it was red as an apple. Redder. We'll have a storm tonight, is my guess."

I must admit, I put no stock in his words. March has so far come in as lamby as a month can come, each morning gentle, each wind the barest current in the air. It has been unseasonably warm, and much of the snow has melted, shrinking back beneath woodpiles and in the shadows of trees. It felt far too much like spring to countenance the thought of some late-season blizzard blowing in to cover the world again.

The weather was fine all day — not overly warm, but certainly not cold, and with no thickening clouds or lowering skies to indicate a coming storm. By the time I dismissed the children, I was confident that I could spend an extra hour or so putting the school in order and reviewing the next day's lessons.

I have said before that teaching is not and has never been my calling, but I have always found it satisfying to tidy a schoolroom after its students have left it empty for the day. I took the broom and swept the debris out from between the desks, dusted off the windowsills and brushed the ashes back into the stove, rearranged the books upon my desk until they stood in a neat little tower, their edges carefully lined up. Not until I finished did I realize that the light had changed — that the room was suddenly much dimmer than it had been — that the sky outside the window was no longer dove-coloured but dark as a bruise, and thick with falling snow.

Mr. Grier was correct in his prediction. A storm was upon us.

No matter, I thought at first, I can easily walk home in the snow. But I had only to open the door to realize that that was not the case. The cold sliced brutally through my thick winter coat, and the flakes fell so thick and fast that I could scarcely see a foot into the schoolyard. The lonesome howling of the wind scarcely faded when I shut the door again. The schoolhouse seemed to shake with every gust. It still does now as I sit at my desk, writing by lamplight.

I cannot walk anywhere, that much is clear. I would either freeze to death or stagger off the path and get lost in the snow, never to be found again. (Like Mrs. Grier's son — like Lucy

Gray!) I shall have to remain here, in the schoolhouse, until someone comes to retrieve me, or — and this seems more likely, given the ferocity of the storm — until the snow stops falling and I am able to leave the building without risking my life.

I do not savour the thought of it. Being on this side of the bridge after dark is not an opportunity I relish at the best of times, and this is scarcely that.

Still, I have my books with me, and a little dinner left over in my tin pail, and if I am here all night, I can use my coat as a blanket. There is plenty of wood by the stove, plenty of oil in the lamp. The door locks and is locked. There is no reason to fear.

7:58 PM

The clock on the wall says that it is not quite eight. I had to watch it very closely and count the seconds to make sure it was keeping time, for it feels as though I have been trapped inside this building for far longer than four hours.

Within the first hour, I had finished all I meant to finish for tomorrow's lessons. By the second, I had eaten the bit of dinner left over in my pail (just a biscuit and a little cold chicken, not nearly enough to quiet the grumbling of my stomach). I have spent the last two hours shifting this way and that in my chair, before finally deciding to plant my feet upon my desk and stretch my legs. Hideously unladylike, but then, who is here to see it?

The building is trembling like an aspen leaf. It has occurred to me before that this schoolhouse is a flimsy sort of structure, but I am realizing it anew tonight. The cold seeps through every gap in the boards, every crack in the plaster, and even though

I am keeping the fire well-fed, I can see my breath in the air before me. I already have my coat pulled close around me and may stir to get my hat and scarf off their peg by the door.

The children have a spelling bee this Friday. Perhaps I can look for some particularly tricky words in my Chambers dictionary to challenge them.

abstemious, adj. Temperate; sparing in food, drink, and enjoyments.

aeromancy, n. Divination by means of atmospheric phenomena.

ambuscade, n. A hiding to attack by surprise.

antelucan, adj. Before daylight.

The lamplight is caught in the specimen jars that line the edge of my desk, turning the glass to honey and gold. The warmth of it seems to make the fire burn a little brighter.

9:24 PM

The storm has not abated, and I have resigned myself to spending the night here. I have made it to the *D*s.

drawncansir, n. A braggart.

dysphagia, n. Difficulty in swallowing.

The wind continues to howl. A strange thing — sometimes it sounds far away, as though it has moved a great distance, and then, moments later, the building will shudder as if from a terrible blow, and the wailing of the storm will suddenly be as loud as though someone were standing beside me, whispering in my ear.

I have written MISS BYRD IS HERE in the frost on the window with my fingertip just in case someone comes by to collect me. This way they will know that I have sensibly hunkered down inside and won't waste time tramping through the woods in search of me. I doubt, however, that anyone shall come. It is so very wild out, the storm so fierce that it feels as though some great, invisible hand is reaching down from the sky to shake this little building as a terrier might a rat. Sometimes I swear I see the shadows on the owlet skull move, as though it, too, is swaying in the wind.

9:42 PM

hebdomadal, adj. Weekly.

humiliate, v. To make humble.

There is something outside.

I have tried not to hear it pacing around the schoolhouse in a circle. It is the wind, I have told myself, or the crackling of the fire, or my own imagination, playing nasty tricks. But just now whatever it was stopped in front of the door.

It did not try to open it. At least, it did not try very hard. But I heard the hinges rattle, just a little, as though something pushed on it gently from the other side. A test, perhaps, of its strength. I looked up from the dictionary, my finger still tracing down the column of definitions, and let my eyes rest on the door.

All quiet, all still, save the howling of the wind and the scouring of the snow.

Then the rattle came again, louder and more insistent. Beneath the noise of the storm, I thought that I heard someone speak in a voice softer than the faintest whisper. I could not make out the words — I did not want to — but I could hear enough to know that it was the voice that had called my name in the church those months ago, luring me out into the cold.

Ada.

I will drown it out. I don't want to hear. I don't want to see.

hydropathy, n. The treatment of disease by water.

hysterical, adj. Affected with hysterics or hysteria.

10:01 PM

*S*hould I cry out? Will that frighten it, as noise is said to do for wolves? Or will that attract its attention further?

It could be a wolf, outside the door. How comforting, to think that it could be only an animal!

minikin, adj. Small.

misdoubt, v. To suspect.

I know that it is not a wolf.

What will I do if I end up alone in the dark, with that thing waiting for me?

10:08 PM

Can it come through walls?

mollify, v. To assuage.

If it could, it would be in here already.

It would be such a relief to have it inside with me. To see it before me, tangible and real, something I could put a shape and name to, instead of the unseen fiend that knocks on doors and whispers my name. If only I could see what it is! But I dare not go to a window, to say nothing of going outside. I

The door is rattling again.

monition, N. An admonishment.

10:28 PM

The voice is louder now, soft and gentle, speaking in a lilting singsong that reminds me of the skipping rhymes my students chant on the playground. Sometimes it seems to me that there is not one voice, but many, speaking in such perfect unison that they blend into one sweet and continuous sound.

I still cannot make out the precise words being said. Thank God for that. The less I hear, the less tempted I will be to creep up to the door and press my ear to the crack.

The dictionary is still open on my desk. I have been reading words aloud, in hopes of drowning it out, but to no avail. I have tried the alphabet, poetry, passages from the Bible, nursery rhymes, all to draw that whisper from my ears. It should work — the voice is so quiet I ought to be able to overpower it easily — but no matter what I do, the sound curls in the air like the smoke from a pipe, soft and insidious. It seems to be coming from everywhere at once.

Perhaps I will sing. Perhaps that will drown it out.

10:47 PM

I can hear it scratching at the window. Not the one I have written on, but the one on the other side.

I heard a story once of a man who lived in a room a floor above a woman with whom he was enamoured. He had never spoken to her, nor even seen her face; he had fallen in love with the sound of her voice, which was low and clear and perfectly modulated. Each night he would lie with his ears pressed to the floor, desperate to snatch up any sound made by his beloved, scratching frantically at the floorboards in his anguish and agony, until one night he scratched so hard and so deep that the floor gave way beneath him. He fell on top of the woman, crushing her. She died instantly, as did he, and so they were introduced.

I told myself that story aloud just now to fill the silence. As I did so, the scratching stopped, as though the thing outside listened too. Now that I have finished, it has started again.

11:14 PM

It prowls from one side of the schoolhouse to the other, running what sounds like fingernails against the weathered grey siding. It digs fruitlessly at the glass. It pushes itself up against the door again and again, each time a little louder, each rattle a little closer to the final one. There are shadows playing on the windows, shadows of shapes I do not recognize, neither animals nor men.

The urge keeps rising in me to get up, move to the door, peep out into the snow. Such a thing would be madness. I must not. But oh! I should be so much less afraid if I did! It is as Mrs. Kinsley said: a monster seen is a monster that can be dealt with.

Is that what it is, the thing that prowls outside? Is it a monster? Is it that fearsome grey dog to which she alluded, the one that haunted her dreams?

The lamp is burning low, very low. Soon the oil will be gone.

11:20 PM

The fiend. The villain. Why must it torment me with these stupid games, these tricks and fancies? Why must I sit here, shivering and afraid, watching the shadows and the frost on the windows while it toys with me?

I must listen to it. I must find out what it wants.

11:43 PM

If anyone is reading this — if this book is found in my place, or alongside my body — let it be known here and now that I, Ada Elizabeth Byrd, was no madwoman. I have doubted that in the past few months — I doubted it even today — but I have spent this evening listening to the sound of some unseen creature circling me, a shark in the water, drawing ever closer to a little fish. I cannot accept that the thing exists in my imagination only. It is real — it is following me — it whispers seductively inside my head, teasing me with a slippery tongue.

I am so frightened that I can scarcely draw breath, so chilled I can barely grasp this pen, and yet, beneath cold and terror, I feel a tremendous sense of relief.

I may be doomed. But I am not mad.

11:51 PM

I understand the whispers now. The sounds have come together to create meaning, a sudden, blessed revelation so sweet it nearly made me cry out, as one might at the soothing touch of a cold cloth on a wound.

Ada, it says, that alien voice crooning my name like a lover. So gentle, so soft. It is red-brown eyes in the firelight. It is the gentle weight of a body on top of mine. *Sweet girl. Beloved. Open the door. Let me in.*

March 5, 1902

All day yesterday, I kept sitting down with my pen in my hand, determined to write. Every time I tried, I found myself frozen before a blank page, unable to think of how to start or what to say. My mind was still frayed by that wild night in the schoolhouse; I could barely sit still for two moments together without springing up and pacing, barely speak to anyone without dissolving into a babbling mess.

In this moment I am sitting up in bed, a lit candle burning in the window, my quilt tucked neatly in around my feet, a cup of tea balanced on the washstand. Cat sleeps on my feet, a reassuring weight. I am calm. Calmer, at any rate: my heart beats only a little faster, and I can blink the tears away now, when they come. And so, I think, I can begin.

The lamp sputtered out just as I wrote that last line in the schoolhouse, and I had only the gentle glow from the grate of the woodstove to cast any kind of light at all. I could not see the clock. I could barely see my hand in front of my face. I sat there in the dark, my eyes straining keenly to see again the outline of the door. I fancied I could still perceive its every detail, from the dull gleam of its hinges to the rust on the latch to the faint, white smear where Muriel had wiped her hand only days before.

Ada, it said, *open the door*, and I found myself rising, taking one clumsy step forward with cold-stiffened limbs, then another. The time that elapsed between every breath seemed to shrink and stretch simultaneously, an hour gone in a blink, a second stretched out to the length of a day, and then I stood before the door, my hand resting on the chill wood.

The thing stood on the other side of the door. I could feel it there, still and expectant, beyond that thick barrier of dead oak. There was a tugging in my belly that seemed to draw me forward, as though it called to me not only with its voice but with something else, its very presence drawing me as a magnet does iron.

Ada. Such longing, such need infused into those two cajoling syllables! No one had ever said my name in such a way. No one had ever wanted me so much. *Come to me. I am waiting.*

My fingers quivered as my hand slowly rose, their tips kissing the ice-cold iron of the latch. But as I did so, I felt the door tremble again, as though something leaning against it had drawn in a deep, shuddering breath in anticipation of some long-desired delicacy, and my senses came back to me. With a half-wild cry, I turned and ran back to the safety of my desk, huddling beneath it with my coat pulled over my head. A child might pull a blanket over his head in the same way, thinking to outwit the monsters beneath his bed. From my sanctuary, I could hear the door shaking terribly, as though the thing were throwing itself at it in a fury, and I closed my eyes to pray.

But I could not pray. Instead, as I shrank beneath my desk with my eyes shut tight against the dark, a memory came to me — one that I had not thought of in many years.

In the memory, I am ten. Florrie is six. We are walking on a footpath through the little woods behind my father's house, and I can just see the grey peak of it through the trees ahead. We are walking home from school, and Florrie has convinced me to take what she called the "secret path" between our school and our home. Her hand is in mine, but she leads the way, pulling me along behind her like a trailing flag.

We were expressly forbidden to take the secret path. I think that that was why Florrie liked to do it so often. Even as a tot, she was gleeful at the prospect of trouble, eager to flaunt a broken rule beneath our parents' noses. I would scold her sometimes, but my heart was never in it. She was my braver, brighter self, the girl I wished I had been at her age — the girl I wished I could be even at the age I was then.

She had taken the lead, as I say, and was prattling on about something that had happened at school — or perhaps a birthday party she was to attend — I hardly remember. What I do remember is her suddenly skidding to a stop, and her grip on my hand tightening.

"Oh, Aidy," she said. Her voice, which a moment before had been so carefree, was suddenly heavy. "Look."

I stepped forward to look, keeping hold of her hand. My gaze swept from side to side; then up into the canopy of the trees; then down at the path by our feet.

It was a crow. Something, or someone, had torn one of its wings off, and it lay weakly in a pool of its own blood, staring up at the blue cracks of sky between the leaves. Its beak was open, its chest heaving. It was too exhausted to caw, too exhausted even to move when I squatted down next to it aside from a sort of shivering sideways tremor.

I placed a finger on its head. It was very soft and very dirty. It did not seem to care if I touched it or not.

"Can we help it?" I remember her saying that, and I remember her face when I turned around, so anxious and so pale. Whatever I had thought to say died as soon as my eyes met hers.

I said yes, of course, it would be fine. If Florrie just went ahead, I would make sure the poor bird was alright. She hesitated, but when I repeated myself in my firmest voice, she nodded and trotted off down the path toward home, confident that I would be able to fix it. I was the older sister, and an older sister could fix anything.

I waited until her footsteps faded and I could no longer see her curly head bobbing along on the path before I stood. My first thought was to simply abandon the creature and come after her, armed with a lie to soothe her troubled heart, but when I looked down at the straining, panting thing, I knew that this would be impossible. My second thought was to find a rock and put it out of its misery. But when I scrabbled in the underbrush in search of one, I found nothing big enough to do the deed.

The crow let out a breathy, exhausted squawk, the first noise I had heard it make. Its one remaining wing fluttered uselessly. I could not leave it there any longer. It was suffering. I was suffering, watching it.

Drawing in an unsteady breath, I inched closer to the animal and slowly positioned my foot over its head. It fluttered again and let out another of those awful squawks. It knew — I am sure of it to this day! — what I was about to do.

I put my foot down, as hard and as quick as I could. I'd hoped that if I was fast enough there would be no sound, no resistance, but of course there was: a crunch, a wheeze of air escaping lungs, a terrible oozing squelch. Gore on my shoe that I found the next day, despite all my efforts to scrape it off into the dirt as I ran.

Florrie never knew what I did that day. Even years later, when she was old enough to know better, she always referred to it as "the day Aidy saved the crow" — for I told her, when I caught up with her, that I helped the poor bird up and put it into a tree, that I was sure its wing would heal with time. She must have known when she grew up that I did nothing of the sort. She must have guessed at what I'd had to do. But she never mentioned it.

I tried to recall the part of the woods we were in, the dress Florrie was wearing, if it had been spring or summer. Those details seemed to be flushed out of my mind. But I remembered her hand in mine, and how faithfully she had turned to continue home, confident that I would be able to sort it out.

What a dreadful responsibility. To have a bright little face turned up to you, shining with trust, and know that whatever happens next is your burden to bear, and yours alone.

This thought followed me into my dreams as, impossible though it seems, I fell asleep. Though I was curled up tight as a child in the womb, freezing, listening to that thing scratch at the windows and doors, exhaustion overtook me and I slept, waking up with a start now and again when the wind howled loudly, or the door rattled particularly hard. Each time, I swore to be more vigilant; each time I fell asleep again, only to wake up at the next noise, the next gust of wind.

What woke me finally and completely was the sound of a voice — not the voice of whatever had been awaiting me outside, but an ordinary voice, one that I knew. I crawled like a bear from the cave of my desk, stiff all over and bleary-eyed with tiredness and nerves. The sun was shining at the window. No strange shapes drifted past the glass; nothing pushed at the schoolhouse door, calling me out. And then came that ordinary voice again, in tones of high distress, "Hallo! Miss Byrd! Are you alright?"

It was Mr. Grier. Never had I been so pleased to hear him say my name.

The cold and the soreness of my limbs made my movements clumsy, but I managed to get myself upright and thrust both arms into my coat, fumbling with the buttons. I caught up this book and my school satchel, jammed my hat upon my head, and threw open the door to the schoolhouse. It felt almost wrong to do so, as I had spent so much of the evening determining that I would not, under any circumstances, open the door. But what a relief to feel that watery sunshine upon my face, the icy kiss of the breeze upon my cheek!

Mr. Grier was there in his little cutter, his face lively with concern. He waved frantically at me, as though there was a chance that I would not see him. The schoolyard had been transformed into a barren tundra, the schoolhouse roof liberally fringed with vicious icicles. I could scarcely see the shape of the woodpile at the side of the outhouse.

"Miss Byrd!" he called again, still waving. "Mrs. Grier was that worried about you, she sent me out to fetch you as soon as it turned light again. She didn't sleep a wink last night — not a wink, no word of a lie. I told her, 'Now, Holly, Miss Byrd's a clever lady, she knows not to leave the schoolhouse in weather like this. She'll be cozied up in there all night safe as anything, you mark my words.' Nothing would do for her though, but that I would drive out to find you first thing. She gets nervous, you see, about . . . about the night, and the cold, and people wandering out in it."

Their son, I thought, and saw again the child as I imagined him, crying forlornly in the woods. Red-headed, like his father.

"Thank you," I said, and I must have sounded hysterical, for he looked uneasily away and muttered that it was no matter, Miss, nothing anyone wouldn't have done, given the circumstances. "May we — oh please! Might we go home? I can come back to school, I know, once I have had something to eat. I will call class in a little late, that's all."

This was not an attempt to be brave or self-sacrificing on my part. Ridiculous though it seems now, the adrenaline that had flooded my body in the wake of that awful night was so tremendous that I really thought I would be able to simply carry on and treat this day like any other.

"Well, if you're sure, Miss," Mr. Grier said, but there was an unmistakable note of approval in his voice. "I dare say Mrs. Grier will fight against it, but I think if you feel fit to do your work, you should do it. Idle hands are the Devil's playthings, that's what my old mother used to say."

I was about to step out into the snow, feeling almost cheerful, almost good, now that the hideous night was over, but as I lifted my foot over the threshold, I looked down and froze. There was something on the step that I had not seen before.

Ada, be truthful. Otherwise, what is the point of any of this?

The something on the step had not been there a moment before. I had not overlooked it. I had not mistaken it for something else. It was nowhere one moment and somewhere the next. A limp black object, roughly triangular, with soft, ragged edges.

My body realized what it was before my mind did. My legs lost their strength; I crumpled to the ground in what must have looked like an exhausted swoon, half inside and half out. Mr. Grier, still up in his cutter, started to see me fall, his mouth open in consternation.

"Miss Byrd! What is the matter!" he said — or something like that. I saw his mouth moving, but the words came to me as though from a great distance, devoid of all meaning and shape. They were only sounds. They did not matter.

What mattered was the crow's wing, dark as night, soft as silk, lying on the schoolhouse step.

What happened after that? I scarcely know. I could not speak; I could not move; Mr. Grier had to carry me up to the sleigh and lay me in it like Moses in his cradle. I believe he drove me home, gave me over to Mrs. Grier. I assume Mrs. Grier put me to bed, perhaps after asking me questions and realizing that I was in no fit state to answer.

These things must have happened, but I do not remember them. What I remember is waking up — or coming to myself, perhaps, for I do not think I slept — and being told that I had had, in Mrs. Grier's words, "a bit of a turn," and that I might do better to just lie down for a bit. And perhaps, if I cared for one, they could call a doctor . . . ?

That I would not allow. I was still not quite in possession of myself, and if, in that state, I let anything slip! well. What conclusion could that good woman come to but the one that I myself dismissed only last night? I was only tired, I told her, exhausted from my night in the schoolhouse. I told her this as firmly as I could, meeting her eyes squarely with my own, trying to compose my face in such a way that I looked as sane as possible.

I know of the conditions that await women in madhouses. I have read the horrific accounts of women with their hair shorn or sewn to their heads, plunged into freezing cold baths, tied to filthy beds and left to rot. That shall not be my fate. I will let the thing take me in its jaws first.

Mrs. Grier did not believe me. I could see it in her face. But she was too polite to say so, or too nervous, and so she did not press the matter. After giving me a bowl of broth and a crust of bread, she left me alone with my thoughts.

The crow's wing. I can count on the fingers of one hand the number of people who have heard that story, and not a one lives in Lowry Bridge. If it knows this, what else could it know about? Has it heard my silent lamentations about Florrie's death, my dishonouring in Willoughby, the petty cruelties of my father? What other memories has this unseen beast carded out of the tangled wool of my mind?

If I could cut my time here short, I would do so in a heartbeat, walk the twenty miles to Portsmouth and catch a train to — oh! Anywhere else, any city, any country, any continent, so long as it took me away from this hideous town. But if I leave a second posting in a row without finishing the year, I shall be hard-pressed to get another. I have no other skills, nothing to offer the world but my ability to teach. Women of my station and temperament are bred to the task of education, as horses are to the bit.

In the morning I will return to the schoolhouse, satchel in hand, ready to pick up where I left off on Monday. My day will be full of spelling and mathematics and geography. I am ready to work. But that readiness stretches over a vast black pit of terror. The smallest misstep will end in an endless fall into the dark. Whenever I am on the other side of the bridge, I am in danger of hearing that voice again, that beguiling, invisible something that beckons me forward to my doom.

I must be careful.

It is the bridge that makes the difference, the passage over running water. Isn't that always the case? Vampires cannot cross it, Mrs. Kinsley said, nor fairies.

March 13, 1902

I am being careful. I am speaking when spoken to, smiling when appropriate. I have said nothing of what happened in the schoolhouse, or the manse. Or anywhere else. I keep my eyes ahead of me when I walk to work in the morning and when I walk home in the evening, ignoring the rustlings on either side of me, the half-heard whispers that drift out from the woods. But this evening . . . this evening I may have ruined it all.

I set my oldest students to writing compositions on the theme of courage today. This gave me an hour or two of peace while I helped the little ones with their writing and the middle graders with their multiplication sums. That, I confess, was the reason I gave them the assignment.

After supper, when Mrs. Grier and I had cleared away the dishes, I sat in the kitchen and looked over what they had written. I was only skimming the pages, not reading them, but the odd sentence leapt to my eye.

"Courage is when you are not afraid of things or when you are afraid of them you don't let them boss you because you are stronger than they are."

"Many historical people had courage. Alexander the Great was one. So was Anne Boleyn and Richard the Lionheart."

"I think my mother has the most courage of anyone I know because she sassed the old minister once and he did not dare say anything back."

I was still chuckling a little over that when a soft knock came at the kitchen door. Up I got to answer it, just as though it was my own house, and when I opened it, the smile on my lips shrivelled like a worm in sunlight.

"Hello," said Agatha. Her own smile was a little forced. "May I come in?"

I have seen her, since that awful night outside the manse, only in church; she has not been well enough to be up and about town, does not come to prayer meetings or make social calls. I scarcely think she was well enough to come to me tonight, for she seemed very pale, and when I offered her a seat at the table, she all but collapsed into it. (I did not ask her to come into the parlour — Mr. and Mrs. Grier were both there, and I felt that I did not want to speak to Agatha in front of them.) I sat across from her, the compositions still fanned out in front of me.

"Would you like some tea?" I asked presently. I could not think of anything else to say.

Agatha shook her head. "No, thank you," she replied. Her voice was softer than usual, warier. That combined with the new thinness of her cheeks gave her an air of weakness, the sickliest fawn in a herd of deer. "I cannot stay long. I've left Douglas with Mother, and she's had a wretched headache all day."

For a few halting moments, we discussed her mother, her son, the Reverend, the state of her house, the state of her body. It was almost like one of our old conversations, the ones that flowed so easily and were so replete with simple, easy affection. Almost, but not quite. What had happened lay between us like a great glass wall.

Finally, Agatha drew in a deep breath and said, all in a rush, "Ada, I need to speak to you about — about that night, at the manse."

There it was. The glass wall cracked but did not shatter.

"I am sorry," I said, choosing my words with care, "if I upset you. I did not mean to."

"You didn't upset me," Agatha started, then paused and shook her head. "Well, no, I can't really say that's true. It was very upsetting and very strange. I've felt queer ever since it happened. Have you?"

I didn't respond to that. How could I? I have felt queer for months now.

She reached out and placed her thin little paw on my hand, gently, carefully, as though laying a blanket on the grass. "Ada, please talk to me," she said. "You are my friend — the truest friend I have in this place! I can't bear to think of you suffering as you did that night. I want to understand what happened, and to help, if I can."

Her voice was sincere, and those dear grey eyes were sincere as well. I wanted to sink into that sincerity, to lean forward and embrace her, to whisper to her all the hideous, horrible things that had happened since I came to Lowry Bridge. I imagined the relief of unburdening my soul to her, and it was enough to make me want to weep.

But then I saw Agatha as she had been that day in church, the eager light that had burned in her eyes as she'd told my secrets to Mrs. Grier, and I felt my heart turn cold.

"What did you say to her?" I asked.

A little wrinkle of confusion appeared between Agatha's brows. "Who?' she asked. Again, her voice sounded sincere; again, her eyes did as well; but now, I felt certain that she knew precisely what I meant.

I did not want to say her name, for fear of being heard. Instead, I jerked my head in the direction of Mrs. Grier's voice, which carried over from the parlour as she read aloud to her husband from some agricultural newspaper.

I saw the flush start up on Agatha's cheeks immediately, more noticeable than ever where illness had left her skin so translucently pale. "Nothing," she said. "That is, not much. I told her that something seemed to have caught you off-guard — distracted you — taken you out of yourself. Oh, I can't remember how I said it! I was so worried, Ada, you must understand—"

"You shouldn't have said anything at all," I said. "It was not your business."

I scarcely recognized my own voice, forming those words. It was harsh, low, almost a growl. Ada Elizabeth Byrd does not speak that way to anyone. Ada Elizabeth Byrd is a mouse.

Agatha flinched, as though I'd threatened to slap her. Her gaze dropped to the table, her eyes tracing the letters on the composition nearest to her. It was Effie's. One of her wobbly sentences jumped out at me: "Courage is important because without it no one would ever have done great things and great things are important to make civilization great."

I pulled the composition toward me, sliding my hand back from Agatha's as I did so.

"You had no reason to speak to her," I said, my voice trembling with feeling. "All it did was make her poke around in my room, and look through my things, and treat me like the madwoman in the attic."

Agatha looked so thoroughly crushed at this that I almost took it back. "I'm sorry, I didn't mean it, please don't be angry, let's just be friends again, as we were before" — oh, I longed to say it. But I found that I longed to be angry just a little bit more. After all, didn't I have the right? She'd abandoned me, gone running to tell tales as soon as I did something she didn't like!

"You live with her," Agatha said, her voice much more subdued now. "She sees you every day. I thought if you were in some kind of trouble—"

The laugh that escaped my throat was louder than it had any right to be. It rang out in the still, dead air of the kitchen. Across the hall, the low buzz of Mrs. Grier's voice faltered, then picked up again, more slowly.

"Trouble!" I said. "And exactly what kind of trouble do you suspect me to be in, Mrs. MacPherson?"

Even then, in the midst of my rage and hurt, I believe that I truly wanted her to guess. Telling her what was happening was too enormous, too frightening a task for me to even contemplate. I couldn't think where to begin. But if she were to somehow arrive at the right conclusion herself, through perspicacity or luck, I would not even have to try.

But, of course, she didn't. She just shook her head, weary and bewildered.

"I don't understand you, Ada," she said. "Do you realize how frightening it was to watch you that night? You insisted that you heard something that wasn't there. You burst out the door as though chased by a demon. You screamed so loudly that the next day the neighbours asked what had happened. I had to tell them a story about my mother dropping a log on her foot at the wood pile."

"How awful for you," I said — no, I sneered. "My apologies, ma'am, for being such a terrible inconvenience, with all my strange carryings-on. I should hate to be a bother to such an important person as the minister's wife."

That wasn't what she meant. I know it now. I believe I knew it then too. But I could not help myself. A hurt animal will bite, even when someone is trying to dress its wounds.

"You are not listening to me," Agatha said, now sounding truly pained. "I don't care about inconvenience, Ada, or what people think — I care about you! If you are having some kind of attack of nerves, or—"

An attack of nerves! As if I were some hypochondriacal old woman, lying in bed and trying to wring out droplets of sympathy from callers! I looked at Agatha and felt that I suddenly saw her stripped bare, exposed as an animal whose pelt had been stripped away in one brutal pull. Her kind words, her concern, her entreaties, all lay at her feet like a shed skin. What was left was pink and withered and ugly. I did not like it. I did not like *her*.

"Get out," I said, and stood so suddenly and violently that my chair fell backwards onto the floor with a terrible clatter. "Get out of this house. You think I don't see you, you charlatan? You have pretended to be my friend all these months, wiled your way into my heart, and now, now you come here and tell me that I am — what, mad? Sick? You—"

I came round the table at her, practically spitting in my fury, and grabbed hold of her arm. Tightly, tightly, my fingers digging into her flesh so deeply that I knew she must be bruised, and yet she did not cry out, only whimpered slightly, shrinking away from me into her chair. Tears welled up in her soft grey eyes, spilling slowly over the edges of the lids and turning the lashes wet and dark. Somehow my other hand found its way into her hair, working the rough silk of it between my fingers. It was the first time, I dimly registered, that I had touched her hair, although I had sometimes thought of what it might feel like to lay my hand upon her head. To run my fingers through that soft length as though it were my own.

"Do you want me in back of some asylum's wagon, dragged off into the night?" My voice was quieter now, coarser. I whispered to her as a cutthroat might his captive, before driving home the knife. "Will you come and visit me when they have shut me away? Peep through the bars into my cell and watch me writhe on my bed of straw, and thank God that I am there and not yourself?"

She did not answer, did not move, only stared up at me, her body stiff with fright and shock.

"You bitch," I said — yes, I did! She flinched at the word, and my hand tightened its grasp on her hair. "You care nothing for me. You never did. You only want something thrilling to think about, something to fill the gaps that you can't fill with your baby and your music and your stupid, secret novels. If you breathe a word of this — a word—"

I was standing over her for this, panting and hot, my face so close to hers we were nearly cheek to cheek. A bead of perspiration rolled down through the part in my hair and dropped onto her, mingling with her tears.

What would it taste like? The thought occurred to me in a voice not quite my own.

My fingers gripping Agatha's arm even tighter, I leaned in and let my tongue protrude from my mouth. It slid up her cheeks like a hand up a skirt, greedily caressing. My own taste bloomed upon my tongue — my taste, and hers too, salt matching salt. Agatha twisted and tried to wrench herself away from me, finally uttering a cry of dismay.

"Ada, don't — you are upset, you are confused — let me—"

My teeth rested upon her cheek. I salivated at the thought of breaking through that paper-thin skin to the flesh beneath, soft as a fruit, sweet as a peach. It would have felt utterly natural, in that moment, to bite.

But then a gentle knock came on the kitchen door, and Mrs. Grier's voice calling uncertainly to ask if we were sure we were alright? — and my head turned to the source of the noise, my grip loosening just a little. Agatha sprang up from her chair, wrenching herself away from me. She lost several strands of hair in the process, leaving me with a handful of reddish gold. Scrambling out of my reach, she put the kitchen table between us, her bosom heaving wildly. Her grey eyes were dark with fear, roses blooming on her thin cheeks. Even in my fury, I could not help but see how beautiful she looked, shaking with confusion and disgust, her hands out before her as though to ward me off.

My fingers twitched. I wanted to touch her again.

"We are fine, Mrs. Grier," Agatha called, her voice wavering only a little. Her eyes were trained on me, as they might have been on a mad dog whose chain has slipped. She took a step back, then another. A third and she was nearly at the door. "I am leaving, that is all."

We could both feel Mrs. Grier hovering at the door, her presence nervous and inquiring, before we heard her footsteps retreat into the parlour, leaving us alone.

"You *are* sick, Ada," Agatha said, and now her voice trembled a good deal more, and her hands as well. "I worried that you might be before, and now I know — you are sick, and you are mad."

It looked as though she was about to say something more, and the trembling in her hands increased, but then her courage must have failed her, for she turned on her heel and left, slamming the kitchen door behind her. I was alone again with my grim little pile of compositions, my sad, wilted handful of her hair.

I tried to return to my work, breathe calmly, finish my grading, but I could not. My body and mind were both in a riot, and I could scarcely see straight to read the compositions, or hold a pen to mark them. In the end, I threw them into the cookstove to burn. And now here I am in my little room, writing by the guttering light of my single candle, and remembering how they tasted, her tears and my sweat commingled. Her flesh yielding beneath my hand. Her skin between my teeth. Under the layers of cloth that keep my flesh hidden from the air, I can hear my stomach growling at the thought.

March 14, 1902

I woke with the taste of salt on my tongue this morning, strands of red-gold hair still clinging to my dress. All the feelings of fury and ill-use that had raged within me before I laid myself down to sleep were gone. All I feel now is a rising tide of nausea, and the burning agony of shame. How I spoke — how I behaved — the language I used! It is tempting to believe that it was all a dream.

But I am not to be permitted that delusion, for this morning Mrs. Grier asked, in that hesitant way she has adopted over the past few weeks, if all was well with Mrs. MacPherson? Only last night she heard what she thought might be raised voices coming from the kitchen.

I assured her, rather woodenly, that she was mistaken, and we had merely been having a spirited debate. What topic I put forward as the purported topic of this "debate" I do not know. It does not matter. Mrs. Grier clearly did not believe me.

At first, I thought to go to Agatha's house and beg her forgiveness — on my knees if I had to, on her ugly sitting room carpet! I almost set out to do it after class, made my way up the road toward the manse before abruptly changing my mind and turning in the other direction — and then turned around again, and yet again, and so on, until I had wasted nearly an hour pacing back and forth over the same little stretch of road, earning myself more than a few strange looks from passersby. Finally I gave up and walked home, so engrossed in my own misery that I barely felt the weight of the woods.

An apology would mean nothing. Even if she accepted it — and why should she? — she will never forget how wild I was last night. She will always remember my tongue against her cheek and my teeth digging into her skin. I cannot forget it myself, although I have tried.

March 21, 1902

Caroline Mason said today that Denmark was bound in the south by Greece, such an egregious error that even the smallest children knew to titter. She blushed furiously at their laughter and at my wordless frown. It was the same bright, ugly flush that had made her so suddenly unappealing when I spoke to her, all those months ago, about her behaviour with Arthur.

"I guess that isn't right," she mumbled, and her fellow students rustled and tittered again, as drawn to that rush of blood as a shiver of sharks might be.

On other occasions I have scolded them for behaving in such a way, telling them that it is our duty as Christian people to never rejoice in the misery of others. But today I felt I could not do it. Truth be told, there was a part of me — a very large part — that wanted to laugh at Caroline too. A sudden current of savagery had risen in me, something that thrilled to see the child redden and lapse into silence. I recalled the picture she'd made as Mary that Christmas, pretty and demure at the side of the Christ Child, and how Arthur had loomed over her like a possessive Colossus. Her birthday was last week — she is thirteen now, the same age as her mother when she was married — and he gave her a hair ribbon, which she wears every day, although it is cheap and badly dyed.

Someday, I thought, she and Arthur would be married — what other fate could await them in such a town as Lowry Bridge? They would marry, and he would bear her away to the bridal bed, and then — oh! What miseries she would be party to! The wild indignities of coupling, the mess and the hurt; the grotesque shifting and swelling of her body as another formed inside of it, like a monstrous Russian doll; and then the gore of childbirth, tearing and stink, the rending of her body in two as something else forced its way out of it, just as something had forced its way into it nine months before. How little Caroline Mason would blush then! Blush, and howl!

It was not funny. And yet, I found myself smiling as I turned back to the blackboard. Some strange and horrible part of me, a part that I am sure did not exist before I came to this place, felt satisfied.

Mrs. Grier drew me a bath tonight. I watched the steam unfurl from the little tin tub for almost an hour, trying to work up the nerve to undress, but every time I began to unbutton myself, I found that my fingers would not move.

"Come on, old girl," I muttered, and willed my fingers to take up their business yet again — and yet again found that they would not. My fingertips hovered over the slick black buttons of my shirtwaist, a hairsbreadth away from touch. I thought again of

Caroline, my brutal vision in the schoolhouse, the way the blood had risen in her cheeks. Of Willoughby, his rough hands tugging my nightgown over my head. Baring me. Flaying me alive.

I sat on a kitchen chair and waited for the water to cool, then splashed my face and hair so that it looked as though I had washed. A minute deception, enough to keep me safe from Mrs. Grier's sharp eyes.

Eyes in the dark. Always something looking on, waiting.

Cat watched me from her place by the cookstove, her tail lashing occasionally against the sanded floor. Her belly has grown plump these past few weeks. She shall have kittens soon, very soon.

March 23, 1902

Saturday evening saw me walking up the road to Norah Kinsley's house, bent nearly double against a screaming wet wind. By the time I knocked on her door, I was damp and shivering, the cold of a not-quite-spring evening settled deep into my bones. Mr. Grier might have driven me there, I suppose, if I had asked him, but I did not want to subject myself to his wife's reaction, and so I did not ask. Although — who knows? — she has been handling me so delicately of late that perhaps she would have offered to do it herself.

Perhaps it is only in hindsight that I feel a shiver of unease when I think of the door of the summer house opening, Rebecca a silent, watchful guard on the threshold. Perhaps in the moment I felt nothing at all. But no — even though I am writing this a day after the fact, the hairs on my arms stand at the memory of it, and a lump thickens in my throat as I retrace my steps through that dark hallway to the library door. It felt colder inside the house than outside of it, of that I am sure, and in the shadows I thought I saw things moving, sly sideways gambolling shuffle like capering imps. When I turned my head to look at them, as quickly as I could so that they would not escape me, there was nothing to see.

The library door was just barely open, a crack of light and warmth spilling out into the hallway. I pushed the door open; it seemed to move slowly, as though some unseen force pressed back against its hinges. But open it eventually did, and I bit back a noise of surprise; for there sat Mrs. Kinsley, and beside her, hunched in one of the red velvet chairs with a sewing basket at her feet, sat Muriel Melville!

"Hello, my dear," Mrs. Kinsley said with a smile. "No, no, do come in!" — this because I hesitated, unsure if I should intrude on this cozy little scene. "Muriel and I have finished for the day. Don't be shy, Miss Byrd. Rebecca is about to bring in our supper."

Picking up her basket, Muriel rose and gave the widow a clumsy bow, then turned and brushed past me on her way out the door, barely acknowledging me.

Mrs. Kinsley watched her go, then turned her cool blue gaze on me. "She comes here once a week or so for sewing lessons," she said, in response to the question she read in my expression. "It is my duty, I think, to teach her. Certainly she has no one else who will do it, the poor, motherless thing. All alone in that house full of boys! It really is a pity." And she patted the empty armchair beside her, encouraging me forward.

After the grey bluster of the outside world, I had been looking forward to the warmth of the library fire, the pleasure of sinking into that deep red armchair. However, I found that once I had settled into that seat, the warmth somehow did not touch me. Shivers raced over the surface of my skin, and the chattering of my teeth was almost as loud as the crackling of the wood in the grate as the flames licked it up, ardent as a lover. The chill and bluster of early spring seemed to have settled into my very soul. The widow saw me shivering, and frowned.

"Heavens," said she, "what a state you are in! Here, let me help."

Solicitous as an angel, she took my unresisting hands and clasped them between her own, rubbing as one might rub a stillborn puppy to coax it back to life. Her hands were soft, the skin fair and unmarked. They were the hands of a woman whose life was easy, who had put work behind her, but on the fingers I felt the slight bumps of what might once have been calluses, ghosts from a life that had been all drudgery, all grey. Like mine.

The woman in Willoughby's hands had been rough, coarsened by a life of lye water and wringing the necks of chickens. I had felt the calluses on her fingers that night that she had drawn my hands between her own, had imagined them in place of her husband's. Now, with Norah's hands enveloping my own, I felt a sudden, surprising tug, as though those hands had pulled at a rope tied tight around my middle, and then, fast on its heels, a hot bloom of shame. I started back in my seat, feeling scalded, and pulled my hands away from hers.

Mrs. Kinsley looked at me, her expression placid as ever, and said, "You seem nervous tonight, Miss Byrd."

Nervous! Of course I was nervous — had been nervous for months — could scarcely remember the last time I had *not* been nervous. But I attempted to smile, and replied that I was perfectly alright! Only cold and damp.

Mrs. Kinsley shook her head only once, a smooth, slow motion like the inexorable turn of a screw. My eyes strayed, of their own accord, to that bust of Athena on the mantelpiece, her hooded eyes cast down in serene severity.

"Ada," the widow said, "I am no fool. I can see the way your eyes dart around the room, the tremble in your fingers" — and here she caught up my hands again, pulling them close to her eyes and examining them. My fingers were indeed trembling, minute quivers chasing up and down each digit. "Your voice is not your own, nor your expression. Something has happened to you, and if you do not tell me what the matter is, I shall be forced to guess."

Nothing was the matter, I insisted, nothing at all, but my tone, or perhaps my face, must have been unsatisfactory, for the widow continued to press me. Had something happened with my family? With the Griers? With my students? The older girls, perhaps — they did like to run in packs, she knew. Or perhaps it was one of the boys, not yet grown and already thinking himself a great strong man. Or even the youngest, for those still new to the rigours of a classroom might get themselves worked up into a dreadful state, and be impossible to manage—

"For God's sake!" I howled at last, my protest so loud I drowned her out entirely. "It is none of them, none of them — stop asking me, Norah, I can't bear it!"

It was, I realize now, the first time I had ever used her Christian name.

Mrs. Kinsley drew herself up and back in her seat. For a stomach-turning moment, I thought that I had mortally offended her — that for the second time in the space of a month, I had lost myself a friend. But then I saw that the corners of her mouth were turned up, and that she was regarding me, not with shock or displeasure, but with what seemed to be *pride*.

"That," she said, "is the first time I have seen you respond to something as a human being and not a lady."

Before I could draw breath to reply to this extraordinary statement, Rebecca came trudging into the room. Her silver tray bore plates of tiny smoked meat sandwiches and two glittering crystal tumblers of strawberry cordial. The two of us watched in silence as Rebecca set these delicacies down, placing each plate and glass on the table between us with exaggerated care.

When she had finally left the room, Mrs. Kinsley turned to me. "So it is not your students," she said, reaching out to pick up her glass of strawberry cordial. It winked like a jewel in the firelight. "Nor the Griers, nor your family. What is it, then, Ada, that has set you so out of order?"

It would have been easy to lie. I am well used to lying by omission — by deflection — by the veiling and dismissal of truths. But when I opened my mouth to speak, I was all at once aware of how deeply tired I was. Every lie that I had told had drained me of another ounce of vigour, sapped me bit by bit of energy and drive. I reached into the dark bag of myself and found it empty of everything but the truth.

I told her everything. The incident with the crickets — the tail in the flowers — that beckoning voice I had heard outside the church on the night of the Christmas concert — the knock on the door of the manse — the letter from Miss Webster's mother — the thing that prowled around the schoolhouse — the crow's wing on the doorstep — even, through a haze of shame and self-loathing, my hideous fight with Agatha, the feeling of my teeth on her skin! Mrs. Kinsley listened with equanimity, only punctuating my story with the occasional murmur of assent, as if to say, "Yes, my dear, I hear you — I understand — go on, do."

When I finally ran out of breath and came to a stop, I expected her to look at me with reproach and disgust, or to tell me I was mad, or to laugh, and exclaim over what a fine joke I had made. Instead, she regarded me steadily over the rim of her glass and asked:

"Did you know that I was the last person in this town to see Amelia Webster?"

This was so unexpected that I sat there with my mouth agape, vulgar as a fishwife. I shook my head and, wanting something to do with my hands, reached out for my glass of strawberry cordial. It was very thick and very sweet, coating my mouth with a taste I experienced, confusingly, only as *red*.

"She was a lonely woman," Mrs. Kinsley said. Her voice was measured, slow, thoughtful. "Lonely, and romantic, and very clever. That, I think, was her downfall. It does not do for a woman to be too clever. John used to say, 'You're too quick by half, Noddy, that's why you were left on the shelf so long.'"

I took another sip of cordial and placed my glass back on the table. My movements were careful and small, my breaths shallow, like a woman in the presence of a timid and fabulous beast. One sudden movement and the widow might turn abruptly away from the subject, begin to speak about the weather.

"I felt for her," Mrs. Kinsley continued. "She seemed to me a woman utterly abandoned by the world, left without a single soul who cared for her. She came to see me for tea or for supper, just as you do, and we spoke of all manner of things. Town gossip, the antics of her students, poetry, politics. But she did not like to speak of her life outside of Lowry Bridge. Whenever the subject arose, she would fold in on herself. Make herself smaller and plainer and quieter, like a child hoping to escape the notice of some dreadful thing. The monster under the bed, or the bogeyman in the cupboard." She hummed, taking·a sip of cordial. I watched her set her tumbler down, the faint ringing of crystal against mahogany very loud in that still, dark room. "You say her mother wrote you a letter. What impression of her did you take from it? The mother, I mean?"

Slowly, thinking carefully about each word before it escaped my mouth, I said, "It seemed to me that she wanted her daughter to be a sort of . . . of live-in servant, to cater to her whims. That she didn't care about whatever trouble Miss Webster might be in and only cared that she might bring scandal upon her. She does not know what became of her child and does not want to know — she thinks of her as a burden, an embarrassment. The poor spinster daughter that no one wanted to marry. The woman was writing her letters about seeing and hearing things, dreadful things, and all her mother could do was complain that now there was no one to read the paper to her!"

My voice grew loud as I neared the end of this little speech. The final words rang through the library, making me flinch. Mrs. Kinsley, however, did not.

"You sound," she said, "as if you hated her."

I thought about it, remembering the trembling hand in which the letter had been written, the nasty, querulous tone throughout. "You know," I said, rather blankly, "I think I do. Isn't that strange, to hate someone that you have never met?"

The widow regarded me, her pale eyes lit with dancing flames.

"Amelia hated her too," she said. "She never told me so in as many words, of course. She took 'honour thy father and thy mother' as seriously as any Puritan. But beneath all that good breeding there was fire — so carefully banked that it was scarcely more than embers, but fire nevertheless. I saw it flash up in her eyes sometimes when I asked her about her mother,

her childhood. The poor girl was so hemmed in by the way she had been brought up that she could scarcely bring herself to look a grown person in the eye. But when she did . . . oh, then you could see it burning, the hate, and the fear, the love that had twisted and spoiled into something sickening."

She said this with a kind of vigour that made me tremble, and yet, I had to hear more.

"Did she tell you about . . . about what she saw? The things that her mother mentioned in the letter?"

"Not at first. At first, she simply seemed troubled and distracted, much as you did tonight. But as the weeks went on, she would refer to strange dreams — a shadow glimpsed from the corner of her eye — the conviction that someone was calling her name. She grew thin, frightened, tearful. Her students noticed this, of course, and became unmanageable; that made her more nervous than ever. I watched her become more and more preoccupied, less and less sure of herself, until one night last spring . . ."

Here she trailed off for a few moments, as I recall, and gazed thoughtfully into the fire, her chin propped up on one graceful hand. One slender finger tapped idly at her cheek. I noticed for the first time that she did not wear a wedding ring.

"One night?" I prompted eventually, unable to bear the silence. I had to know. I had to!

Mrs. Kinsley took another sandwich, taking a bite and chewing so slowly and thoroughly I thought I might scream. "It was late," she said after she swallowed, "almost more morning than night, and Rebecca woke me in a panic. She said that there was someone waiting for me in the library — that she herself had woken to the sound of someone pounding on the door, and a voice calling my name beyond it. When I came downstairs, I found Amelia sitting in the armchair — the very chair, my dear, that you are sitting in now — dressed as though for a long journey, her carpetbag full to bursting at her feet. When she saw me, she sprang to her feet and grabbed at my arms, gabbling desperately. It spoke to her, she told me, it knew her name. She had not slept for three days, she could no longer bear it, she had to leave Lowry Bridge and never return. She'd snuck out of the Griers' house after they had both retired, leaving a note that said her mother was sick and needed nursing. All the letters she had received from that fine woman contained enough belly-aching and misery that no one would doubt this explanation. If I could just drive her to the train station at Portsmouth, if I could just get her out of Lowry Bridge, she would do anything. Anything!"

Anything. Anything. I shut my eyes for a brief second, overwhelmed. I almost hoped that when I opened them it would be to a different scene, one friendlier and less oppressive, but of course all that met them was the library, the fire, Mrs. Kinsley's penetrating gaze.

"I soothed her," she said, "as best I could. I called for Rebecca to bring us tea with brandy, and put my shawl across her shoulders, and told her that of course I would drive her to the station — that I would hitch up the team at the first light of morning. She didn't care for that. She wanted to leave then and there. 'I cannot stay here one more blessed night,' she said — I remember the phrase exactly. She was panting like an animal in a snare, wild to free itself. But I told her she was too distraught for me to take her anywhere, that she had to sleep and calm herself before we could begin our journey.

"I had Rebecca make up the bed in the guest room for her. I tucked her in as a mother might a child, though there were scarcely five years between us. I even kissed her forehead, the way my mother had kissed mine when I was a girl. I left a candle burning on her bedside table. She did not want to be in the dark, she said. She was so terribly, terribly afraid."

Mrs. Kinsley stared thoughtfully into the fire, as though she might divine some wisdom from its leaping shape. The light played across her face, deepening the shadows under her eyes and in her cheeks. She looked like a perfect ghoul, a skeleton grinning from the depths of a cave.

"I had strange dreams myself that night," she said, and her voice was quiet now, with a curious sing-songy rhythm to it. "In all of them I saw that same grey dog that had come to me years ago, standing on the bank of the river, watching me, but now I saw Amelia standing at its side, her hand buried in its silver fur. She wept, just as she had wept in my arms that night, and yet she smiled, too, and laughed. I recall that in one dream she lifted her hand to me, as though in salute, and then she turned and walked into the shadows under the trees, the dog padding softly by her side.

"When I woke properly the next morning, the guest bedroom was empty, the back door open. Miss Webster was gone."

Very suddenly, she stood up, and I flinched at the unexpected movement, but she was only going to a little cupboard in the bottom of one of the bookshelves. Unlocking it with a small brass key, she reached inside to pull something out and returned, placing the item upon my knees.

"She left this," she said.

It was a carpetbag, old and clearly well-used, with a worn leather handle that seemed on the verge of falling off. After a moment's hesitation, I pulled the mouth of the bag open until it gaped obscenely in my lap.

What did I expect the bag to hold? Something horrible, something to match the ugly visions that have plagued me these last few months. Instead I saw a jumble of spinsterish belongings: faded underclothes, a patched shirtwaist, several pairs of woollen stockings, a calico nightgown. At the bottom was a meagre little hoard of coins, the amount that might be left to a woman after surrendering most of her earnings to a greedy third party, and a battered wooden hairbrush. When I lifted it out, I saw long, fine hairs twined around its sparse black bristles. Most of them were grey, but a few were a rosy colour that might have been auburn.

I pictured the gaunt, wet-eyed woman of my idle daydreams with strands of auburn threading through her prim bun, and a strangled cry tore itself from my throat. I thrust the hairbrush back into the bag and pushed it away. It fell to the floor and onto its side, its contents spilling onto the library rug.

After some moments had passed, I said, "Do you think that she . . . that she killed herself? Or . . ."

I did not know what the "or" might suggest. Was the possibility of self-annihilation not hideous enough?

"I have walked these woods many a time since she left this house," Mrs. Kinsley said. She watched me struggling to regain my composure with a certain sympathy, but her eyes, I saw, were dry. "In all those excursions, I have never found a body. Nor has anyone else in this town. She may have gone on to Portsmouth and simply taken a train to someplace other than her mother's house. Who knows?"

Her face was as smooth and placid as ever, but her mouth . . . her mouth twitched just a little, haunted by a smile.

I said, my words coming fast on the heels of the thought that spawned them, "You know, don't you? You know for certain."

Norah Kinsley smiled in earnest then. It was not sinister, not the broad grin of a villain or a fiend. We might have been talking about anything.

"I think," she said, "that she heard that voice again. I think that it pulled her from her bed and down the stairs, through the back door, out to the edge of the woods behind my house. I have pictured her many times, rumpled and dazed from sleep, staring into the darkness. Bare-headed, empty-handed. She walked slowly, I imagine, and reluctantly. She probably tried to turn back. But she couldn't. It was calling her, you know, and she had to go. Sooner or later, she had to go."

"When you say *it*," I said, "what do you mean?"

Mrs. Kinsley reached across the little table between us and laid her fingers on the back of my hand. Their tips were startlingly cold.

"My dear Ada," she said, her words a caress as much as the gentle movement of her fingers. "You know."

Yes. I know.

The rest of the visit to the summer house is a blur. The remainder of our conversation, the entirety of my walk back to the Griers', it has all disappeared in the face of that horrible vision of Amelia Webster walking slowly out the back door of the summer home and disappearing into the woods. Did she cry, or drag her heels in the ground? Did she call out for help, beg Mrs. Kinsley to wake up and come hold her back?

The Grier house is quiet. A mouse moves in scuffling bursts in the wall behind my bed, the bed in which Amelia once slept, dreaming of horrors. Amelia, and the Grier boy, too, in his final delirium. Both gone, eaten up by whatever lives on the other side of the bridge.

No. Surely not eaten. But *taken* — yes.

Amelia Webster owned stockings, and handkerchiefs, and clothing she patched herself. She loved poetry and hated her mother. She carried a carpetbag with a broken handle. She had been real, and now she was gone — but where? To what?

Into the woods, never to return. Into the arms of that unseen, waiting beast that called her name. Her name, and mine.

Is that to be my fate, as well? Shall I, too, walk into the woods and never emerge again?

March 27, 1902

 $\mathcal{I}$ have not slept more than an hour or two together this week, and it has become obvious to the world at large that I am not quite right. I start and twitch, look wildly back and forth as though beset on all sides by demons.

My own students, the children I have been nurturing for the last half a year, are beginning to see it. They have recently started to look at me strangely — to whisper when my back is turned — to stare at me insolently when I call on them for answers, and stay stubbornly silent when I raise my voice. This afternoon, when I asked Effie a question about the French Revolution, the girl sat there and looked at me. Just looked, her pretty blue eyes swimming with disdain, and crossed her arms, and shrugged.

"I asked you a question, Effie," I said, and if my tone was a little harsher than usual, if my face a little angrier than the situation warranted — well, who could blame me? "If you do not know the answer, be kind enough to say so."

And still the girl sat, her expression so contemptuous and cold that I found that feeling rising in me again — the bright, suffusing heat of shame.

"Miss Byrd," she said, "you ought to have a bath. You smell awful."

She said this, and across the room, another student — which one I did not know — let out a little horrified giggle.

To have that dreadful girl insult me so brazenly was more than I could bear. Striding back to my desk, I snapped open the desk drawer that housed the dreaded switch. I had not had to use it all year — I had not wanted to use it — but now my fingers itched to take it up and hear it crack against the wretched girl's smooth pink palm.

"Come here, Effie," I said.

Some of the bravado went out of the girl's face when she saw the rod, but to her credit, she did not crumble or weep. Nor did she stand. She remained in her seat with her arms folded, defiant and disdainful, and waited.

Something caught me in its teeth then, a howling monster made of nothing but rage and vengeance. I crossed the room in two broad strides — I reached down to grab the girl by the shoulder and haul her up — and she twisted out of my grasp with a shout, her composure finally broken — and my other arm came down in a furious arc, lashing out toward her face. The sound the switch made as it struck her face was as loud, in that suddenly quiet room, as any gunshot.

Effie turned to look up at me, stunned. On her left cheek was a long, ragged laceration, already beaded with blood. I had missed her eye by less than half an inch.

I could have blinded her, had the blow fallen a fraction higher. Or I could have scarred her permanently — a fate perhaps as dreadful for a pretty girl as the loss of an eye.

I sent her home. I sent them all home. And I spent the rest of the afternoon sitting at my desk, staring at that hideous instrument, which I still held in my left hand. There was red on it, from Effie's cheek, drying to a rusted brown. I am trying to feel some measure of shame for my loss of self-control, but I cannot. In that act of violence, I briefly became not Ada Elizabeth Byrd, spinster, schoolmarm, fallen woman, former sister, and forlorn daughter, but some other category of being entirely.

I did not keep hold of the switch because I was frozen with guilt, but because I liked the feel of it in my hand. My thumb rubbed against the rough grain of the wood, and I saw again the blood beading on Effie's pretty cheek, and I felt myself shaking with something that was not exactly hunger.

How horrible that seems now that I have written it down. And yet, it is true — it is true!

At the supper table tonight, I was quiet, barely responsive to overtures of conversation. As though to cheer me up, Mr. Grier told me that there will be another dance at the town hall at the end of April. He is going to play the fiddle again. He seems to be looking forward to it.

"You ought to come, Miss Byrd," he said, too kindly. I suspect that he and Mrs. Grier have been whispering together at night, their heads close on the pillow as they discuss me in murmurs, careful not to let their voices carry down the hallway. "It might be good for you."

Good for me! I snorted and did not bother to conceal it, and he was clearly hurt and let the subject go. For the rest of the evening, he looked distinctly downcast, and answered all of Mrs. Grier's questions in single syllables before leaving the house. To "feed the pigs," he said, although I had already seen him do so earlier that day.

Effie was right. I do smell awful. I have not been able to make myself bathe these past two weeks. I thought at first to cover it with Agatha's rosewater scent, but smelling her at all hours of the day proved to be too much. I poured the scent into the dirt and let my stench billow about me, moving within it like a bird in a cloud.

April 4, 1902

"*L*ook at her! Sitting there bold as brass, after nearly blinding that poor girl!"

The voice that said this on Sunday was one I half-recognized, a woman's. It came from behind me in church. The Easter service, pews bursting with repentant sinners eager to rejoice in the resurrection of Our Lord. (Or, perhaps, rejoice in their new spring bonnets — certainly there were more than a few new hats floating in that congregant sea.) The Griers had to shuffle farther and farther down the pew to make room for latecomers, leaving me to be gradually flattened into the corner like a lizard in a press. I sat with my hands carefully folded into my lap, trying to follow the Reverend's sermon, resolutely refusing to look at his wife at the organ — for Agatha is finally well enough to return to her duties, and I cannot meet her gaze without recalling, all unwilling, the taste of her.

And then that insinuating whisper, a current of sound that made me clench my fists, and on its heels, another in a voice more familiar still:

"Well, what can we expect? A woman like that . . ."

I turned in my seat, heedless of decorum and Mrs. Grier's quickly indrawn breath, my eyes raking the crowd behind me for the source of the voice. I found it quickly: it was the voice of Mrs. Elijah Castle. I stared at her, my mouth slightly agape, and the woman stared back at me, not in the least bit abashed. The lady seated next to her, whose name I learned once but do not remember, shook her head and leaned over to mutter something in Mrs. Castle's ear — something that made her snort with very un-Christian laughter.

No other whispers reached my ears that day, but I snuck surreptitious glances around the church throughout the service. On more than one occasion, I caught a glimpse of a man or woman looking my way — wary, hostile, suspicious. All averted their gazes as soon as my eyes met theirs. It was my arrival in Lowry Bridge all over again, but inside out. Where there had been curiosity, there was now contempt. Where there had been warmth, there was now a barren cold.

It happened again a few days later, during Wednesday evening's prayer meeting. Mrs. Grier and I arrived at the Castle house a little later than usual, and almost all the seats in her parlour were taken. I managed to squeeze in gratefully next to Mrs. Aloysius Benson, the mother of my students Arthur and Winifred — a small, dumpy housewife with a ready smile, nothing like her surly tomboy daughter. She is a woman with whom I have only ever exchanged the barest of pleasantries. But no sooner had I sat next to that gracious lady than she sprang up, body rigid with distaste, and went to stand by the parlour door. There she stayed for the remainder of the meeting, staunchly refusing to meet my eyes.

A change had come over the room. Although the other ladies, like Mrs. Benson, looked only at their prayer books, their bodies had all turned subtly away from the settee — from me — and toward Mrs. Castle, whose face was a veritable picture of triumph as she led us all in a prayer for the heathen abroad. Hot blood pounded in my temples as I chanted soullessly along, my monotone a contrast to the colour and fire in my distressed heart. I tried to catch Mrs. Grier's eye, wanting to derive some reassurance from her expression, but she kept her eyes fixed firmly on her book. Even in the lamplight, I could see the agitated flush that had risen to her cheek and neck.

Mrs. Castle stopped us on the porch before we left. She spoke to Mrs. Grier, but her eyes were on me.

"You may have noticed that Mrs. Agnew was not here this evening," she said. "She sent word that she wouldn't be coming — that she mightn't be along for some time, in fact, unless membership changes."

Her meaning was unmistakable. So was the triumphant little smile she gave me as we turned, stunned, to start the long walk home.

A bath again tonight. This time I did not even dampen my face or hair, and I saw Mrs. Grier mark it when I emerged from the kitchen, the water undisturbed in the little tin tub.

April 7, 1902

At supper this evening I saw Mrs. Grier's nostrils flare. The movement was subtle, delicate, like that of a well-bred cow. She did this every time she passed by my chair to refill my teacup, leaned in closer to pass the cream pitcher, offered me a slice of apple cake. Every time she caught a whiff of me, out they went like a pair of widening eyes.

Mr. Grier declined to sit in the parlour with us, claiming to have wrenched his back that day on the farm — and he did hobble very stiffly up the stairs, wincing with every step. Mrs. Grier watched him go with that look so common to wives that watch their husbands, an expression of amusement, affection, and annoyance, all commingled.

"My husband," she said, once we had settled in the parlour for the evening, "is not so young as he once was. It is high time he hired some hardy young thing to help him on the farm. Otherwise he'll keep injuring himself until he can't walk at all,

303

and I've already told him I won't be carrying him up the stairs in his old age."

In ordinary circumstances I would have chuckled dutifully. But now all I could see was her flaring nostrils, the disapproval with which she inhaled my scent.

And so I said, all sweetness, "What a pity that you never had a son!"

The woman was mending a pair of Mr. Grier's trousers when I said this, those busy fingers of hers pushing the needle in and out of the cloth so quickly I could scarcely follow it. The brisk movement faltered, and Mrs. Grier swayed just a little in her seat, her eyes widening. She looked, I thought, as though she had just been shot. My tone had been wholly innocent, but when I met her eyes, I knew that she knew what I was really saying.

"Ah," she said, a deep, hissing intake of breath, and I felt absurdly victorious knowing that she would not be able to avoid my smell. Her lungs were full of me.

Her needle began to move again, more slowly. From the settee she regarded me as one might a dog with its hackles raised, watching for an attack.

"Someone told you, then," she said finally.

I nodded. We sat in silence for several minutes, listening to the patter of the rain on the window, the crackle of fire in the grate, the barely audible purring of Cat as she stretched luxuriously out on the faded carpet to warm her plump little belly.

Mrs. Grier's needle went in and out, in and out, slowed, stopped.

"We tried," she said abruptly, shoving her mending aside. It slid off the cushion beside her and fell in a crumpled heap to the rug, offending Cat, who got to her feet and stalked haughtily to the door. "Glenn — Mr. Grier — and I, we tried for so long to have a child. Year after year, and nothing. It almost happened once. There was a little girl . . . but she was born early. No fingers, no toes. Blue. Never even cried. We named her Ann, for my mother, and buried her, and that was that.

"After that we thought . . . we thought it could not happen for us." Her hands were tangling together now, folding and unfolding as if in prayer. Perhaps she could not help it; perhaps idleness was so foreign to them that they had to busy themselves somehow. "We prayed about it, begging God to bless us if He saw us fit, but I suppose He didn't, for nothing came of it. We gave up after some years, put the thought of a family out of our heads. It was only hurting us. But I kept dreaming of . . . of holding a little warm crying thing in my arms." She paused, a little smile blooming on her mouth. "Then Jeremiah came — came like a dream. He was a surprise, a wonderful surprise. They gave him to me, and he opened his eyes and looked at me right off. Blue, blue eyes, like paint. The most beautiful boy in the world."

Jeremiah, then. Not John or James, as Agatha had thought.

"He was perfect," she said, and the smile deepened. "So good, and so handsome, and so clever. I suppose all parents feel that way about their children."

"No," I said before I could stop myself. "They do not."

Again, that look of wariness, a pause while she waited to see if I would bite.

"I thought it would be difficult," she said, "raising a child. A boy, at that — I had no brothers, growing up, only sisters. I knew nothing, really, about boy-children. But Jeremiah was the sweetest boy alive. Never pulled the cat's tail, never drew on the walls or threw his supper on the floor. I never had to spank him — but

305

I don't think I would have been able to, anyway, not even if he'd set the house on fire."

Her eyes were far away now, dreamy. She had been besotted with her son, I realized, was besotted still, the way some women are with their first loves years after they have gone to the grave.

"How old was he?" I asked.

Mrs. Grier blinked, the dreaminess clearing from her eyes. "Six," she said. "I suppose you know about that too?"

For the first time there was a note of reproach in her voice, and I felt a little prick of shame.

"I know he was sick," I said.

Mrs. Grier's face changed. Recollection had softened it, love had made it young, but now her eyes hardened, her mouth set, her fists clenched themselves tightly in her lap.

"Sick," she said bitterly. "That is what they say, of course."

"And what do you say, Mrs. Grier?"

The rain on the windows, the crackle of the fire, those noises were still in the room. But there was another sound: Mrs. Grier's breathing, quick and ragged.

"I sent him out to play," she said. "He'd been inside for days — the weather had been bad, but then it was bright out for the first time in weeks. I told him to put his wraps on and go play outside. He didn't wait for me to tell him twice — just put on his coat and burst out the door, whooping as he ran up the road. I was . . . I was glad to see him go. He'd been underfoot all week, whining about being cooped up. With him out of the house, I could finally get some work done."

Oh, the grim little chuckle that escaped her lips at that!

"I got the work done," she said. "I made supper. I had it on the table and waiting before I remembered that he was still out playing, and so I went and shouted for him. He would always wander home when he got hungry. But I called, and called, and he didn't come.

"At first, I was angry. Threw his supper in the pig trough and decided that he would go to bed hungry. He'd always been such a good boy, never given me reason to worry, and I didn't want him to start now. I wanted to keep loving him just as hard, always. I was terrified that something would happen to take the shine off him.

"By the time it grew dark, that anger had turned upon myself. I told myself I'd been a fool to let it go so long, that the child was lost and cold and hungry, that if anything had happened to him it would be my fault. Mr. Grier kept telling me to calm down, boys would be boys, but I knew better than him. I was his mother. I think I even told him that — shouted it, rather. That hurt him. I didn't care.

"He went around town with the team to ask folks if they had seen him. Told me to stay put in case Jeremiah came home. I didn't, of course. I couldn't stand the thought of waiting for him in the warm when he could be anywhere. As soon as Mr. Grier was gone, I put on my coat and ran outside.

"I knew he wouldn't be in any of his usual places — the garden, the little stand of birches behind the house, the wood-pile. I checked them anyway, just in case. Then I took to the woods, wading through cold muck and rotting leaves, calling for him all the time. I must have been at it for three hours, going in amongst the trees and then back onto the road, screaming like a madwoman. I had a lantern with me, and it was a foggy night. I remember the light looked funny, how it sliced through the mist. Solid, like a knife through a loaf.

"I was across the bridge when I found him, in that thick part of the woods far from the river. My voice was nearly gone by then, but I kept calling his name in a hoarse kind of yelp, praying that it would reach him somehow. And then I heard something. Not a word, but a whimper — like a beaten dog. It wasn't the kind of sound I'd ever heard my son make before. That didn't matter. I knew who it was.

"When I finally caught up to that little noise, he was lying on the ground, clutching himself so tight it seemed like he was scared he'd fall apart. His clothes were covered in dirt, torn and wrinkled, as though he had been gone for days instead of hours. There was blood at the corners of his mouth, and in his ears. His eyes, his pretty blue eyes . . . they were gone. Just a red mess in the sockets. Like they'd been clawed out.

"He was so cold when I touched him, but he moved a little, and looked at me. He couldn't see me, of course, but he looked anyway, and reached up to touch my face. He said, 'Mama, I want to go home.'

"That was the last time he knew me."

She stopped speaking for so long that I thought she must be finished her story. I was about to open my mouth to say something — anything to break the silence — when she suddenly continued.

"He lasted three days," she said, her voice brusque now, all business. She was no longer lost in her memories, but simply laying out the facts as she knew them. "Pneumonia, they said. We don't know for sure — we sent someone to Portsmouth for a doctor, but he didn't get here in time. Jeremiah would not take water, or broth, or milk. He was cold the whole three days, his teeth chattering all the time, and he kept waking up and seeing . . . well. I don't know what he saw. It wasn't me. It wasn't his father. There was someone else he spoke to that whole time, someone in the room that neither Mr. Grier nor I could see.

"He would say, 'Go away! You're not my mama, I don't like you!' And 'I'll tell my papa, and he'll come fight you!' And 'Why won't you let me go home?' He murmured something once that I could not quite make out, something about gifts. It was coming up his birthday. I thought perhaps he was thinking about that, mulling over what kind of presents he might get.

"The last day I knew he was going. I'd been in denial until then, I believe — thinking that if I just nursed him closely enough, he would pull through. Mr. Grier suggested otherwise at one point, very gently, and I went wild. I told him to get out, that just because he was too stupid to know how to care for his son didn't mean that I was. He's forgiven me that since, or says he has.

"It was early in the morning when it happened. I remember hearing the clock strike four, counting the chimes, and then looking at him — his little face so thin, the freckles faded into nothing. His empty eyes, just the lids stretched over the sockets.

"I hated the sight of him then. I'd been happy enough, you know, without children. I had my flowers and prayer meetings and company and a husband who suited me. I would have been fine. And now . . . now I'd had the thing I wanted, and it was being taken away from me. It's worse than not having it at all, having it and then not having it.

"I was sitting there by his bedside, so tired, so angry, when he took in a very deep breath. He called out — no words at first, but that little whimper, the one I'd heard out in the woods. And then he said, 'Help me.' He sounded . . ."

Here she paused again, and I could see that there were tears in her eyes, for all the forbidding tone of her voice. She was trying to keep herself together, I realized, for fear of flying into too many pieces to reassemble.

"He sounded old," she said. "Like a little old man. My father had sounded like that on his deathbed. I reached out to take his hand and that seemed old as well. His fingers were just bones. I could feel his pulse, and it beat as light and faint as a little bird's heart.

"He said it again, almost too quietly to hear, and then he sighed so long and deep that I knew the breath was going out of him. And then the sigh stopped, and it never started again."

She reached down to the floor to retrieve her husband's trousers, smoothing them carefully over her lap. With exaggerated care, she drew the needle out of the fabric and began to sew once more, tiny, even stitches in a pin-straight line.

"Why didn't you tell me?" I asked finally. She let loose a little squawk of laughter, though her expression was still grim.

"Tell you! Was there a reason I should tell you, Miss Byrd? Was the truth a thing I owed you, as well as room and board? My duty is to give you three meals a day and a roof over your head. Nothing more."

"You put me in his room," I said, and Mrs. Grier make a *tch*-ing sound in the back of her throat.

"It is not his room, Miss Byrd, any more than my own bedroom belongs to Mr. Grier's father. He died here, too, you know — died the year after the two of us were married, in the very bed we sleep in now. Should I have told you about him as well? Should you have told me all that has happened to you before you came here? I am not stupid, you know. A woman with your connections would never have taken a job here if she'd had any other choice, if there wasn't something she was running from. If I owe you my past, do you owe me yours?"

Her voice was sharper than I had ever heard it. I had opened my mouth to make some indignant reply but found that I had nothing to say. I closed it again, very slowly. Mrs. Grier looked up in time to see me do it and nodded.

"Just you mind, Miss Byrd," she said. "Every woman is full of tragedies. She is obliged to share them with nobody but God."

Which God? I wondered.

With one last tiny stitch she finished her mending, shaking the trousers out to inspect them, her movements as crisp and brisk as any soldier's. Apparently satisfied, she folded them neatly and stood.

"I'm off to bed now," she said. "Mind you take your candle upstairs with you when you go."

There was nothing in her voice that had not been there before, no change to her ordinary no-nonsense tone. Even the words were familiar to me — she had said the same thing to me many times before upon retiring for the night. But from the way that she looked down at me, I knew that something had changed. There was a sort of fatigue that infused every inch of her, a weary resignation that made her look much older than she was. Her eyes were empty. She was not worried for me, as she had been before, nor was she afraid of me, as she had been for weeks. Over the course of less than half an hour, she had ceased entirely to care for me.

Perhaps it was that which gave me the courage to say, as she made for the door, "Mrs. Grier? When you found your son in the woods . . . where was he?"

I was thinking, in that moment, of Amelia Webster, waking in the middle of the night and striding out into the woods alone. I was thinking of myself, the black eyes of the hare, the curled claws of the chickadee.

Mrs. Grier turned slowly to look down at me. A shadow was cast over her eyes from where she stood beneath the lintel of the parlour door; I could not see if the look in them changed.

"They did not tell you all of it, then," she said. "I found my boy on Norah Kinsley's land, Miss Byrd — in the woods less than one hundred feet from her house. Strange, isn't it, that he could be so close to her, crying so pitifully, without her hearing and coming to help?"

Her nostrils flared one more time.

"You ought to take a bath, Miss Byrd," she said. "You stink."

And with that she disappeared up the stairs, her shadow bobbing out behind her.

April 10, 1902

*E*ffie has not been back to school since the day with the switch. A few days ago, I found a note shoved under the schoolhouse door from her mother, severely chastising me for "injuring" her daughter and threatening to "bring action" against me. (Action of what sort? Surely there are no lawyers in Lowry Bridge.)

She is not the only one who is gone. Eugene Castle and the Perley brothers did not attend today either. The schoolhouse has begun to echo curiously every time I speak.

It is a matter of time before the other older girls stop coming. They do whatever Effie does, and none of them — save Clara, perhaps — care a fig for their education. If they stop coming, Caroline will stop coming too, and then Arthur in deference to Caroline, and all the boys that look up to Arthur, and soon I will be alone in the schoolhouse, at the mercy of whatever prowls the other side of the bridge.

One of the Griers' cows dropped two calves this spring, and the time came this week to butcher the superfluous male. Veal for supper tonight, the slices on my plate leaving rosy-red smears on the white porcelain. When the Griers were not looking, I used my index finger to sop up the juice, hardly able to stifle a moan when the first drop hit my tongue.

April 17, 1902

God

I

A Friday. Only nine in class. I tried to teach — to read aloud —
to call on the younger ones for their spelling — but every lesson
faltered and trailed away into nothing. Every time I spoke, I was
aware of my students' eyes on me, the way they whispered when
my back was turned, the occasional giggle drifting out from the
thinning ranks.

To stay inside, burdened by the weight of my own gloom,
was repulsive to me. After the children came in from their dinner
hour, I told them that we would be going on a nature walk for
the remainder of the afternoon, an announcement they received
with relative enthusiasm. I warned them that there might be
little enough to see, that most spring flowers will not bloom
until later in the season and many animals will still be sluggish
and shy from the winter, but of course the children did not care.

Their desire was less for any kind of scientific exploration than for an excuse to run around in the watery sunshine, filling their lungs with the smell carried by the wind in springtime, a heady combination of damp earth, new leaves, and melting snow.

I led the class down the road in a meandering line, calling over my shoulder my observations about the few birds we saw flitting from tree to naked tree. These were mostly starlings and blackbirds, but we spied a few blue jays hopping about, and once a flash of red I could have sworn was a cardinal. The younger children made note of those few plants beginning to poke themselves out of the soil, including, as we got closer to the riverbank, the tight green coils of newly sprouted "fiddle-heads" — a sight that pleased my older students to no end, for fiddleheads, they assure me, are one of the most delicious treats of early spring, when properly harvested and cooked. Ordinary sights, ordinary marvels. We encountered nothing that could not be attributed to the unremarkable miracle of spring. The brightness of the sun, the freshness of the breeze, the feeling of change and potential, all seemed to lift the dense cloud of misery in which I have been living these past few weeks, and the relief of it was akin to ecstasy.

You fool, Ada.

I was about to dismiss the children for the day when Winifred came running up to me, her square, stubborn face very pale.

"Miss," she gasped, "I can't find Lilly anywheres."

When I questioned her, the girl could hardly give me any more information. Lillian had been holding her hand when they left the schoolhouse, certainly, and had been in her grasp for some time after that, but when exactly she had relinquished the hold of her protector and disappeared was impossible to gauge. Before the cardinal? After the fiddleheads? Close to the school, or to where we were now? Winifred could not say, and her face was screwed up so tightly against the urge to cry that I could not continue to interrogate her. Calling the other children in close to me, I let my gaze sweep from one pair of eyes to another and asked, had anybody seen—? Did anybody know—?

Shaking heads, frowning mouths, winces of concern, little huffs of impatience and disdain. And then, a voice:

"She went into the woods, Miss."

I turned to look at Muriel. She stood apart from the other children as she always did, her arms crossed in her threadbare boy's coat, her fairish hair spilling onto her shoulders. She met my eyes brazenly.

"Into the woods," I repeated dully. I could have demanded to know why she had not stopped the child, or at least called out to me, but such questions would have been useless. I knew.

Muriel nodded, a slight smile bending her mouth. "That way," she said, and pointed to the left side of the road, into a dense thicket of pine and scrub.

I had to go and find her. A teacher must act in loco parentis for all her charges, especially the youngest and most vulnerable among them. But oh! How I longed to run in that moment, to leave Lillian to her own devices and hope that she found her way back home herself!

Jeremiah had not found his way, I reminded myself. Neither had Amelia Webster.

"Winifred," I said, "take everyone back to the schoolhouse. All of you, sit at your desks until I return. She can't have gone far."

Or so I prayed as I dashed into the woods.

The snow has still not entirely melted, and I found myself slipping again and again on piles of slush and ice obscured in the shadows of the trees. Once I fell, catching myself bare-handed on a rock and scraping the skin off my palms. Shaking my hands as though that might throw off the sting, I kept blundering forward into the green-grey dim of the trees, calling Lillian's name in tones that only increased in volume and agitation. The edges of my skirt became heavy and dark from dragging through dirty puddles of meltwater, and at one point a low-hanging branch snagged my hat and pulled it askew, leaving its brim tilted into my field of vision.

Perhaps this was why I did not see Lillian immediately — or perhaps I was only blinded with panic and fear. In any case, I nearly fell over the child before seeing the bright red splash of her knitted hat against the white of the remaining snow. She stood with her back to me, her woollen coat the same dull grey as the bare tree limbs that surrounded us. Under her arm, she clutched her doll, its golden curls considerably grubbier now than they had been at the beginning of the year.

"Lillian!" I cried, kneeling and seizing her shoulders. She gave a start and a hiccupping sigh, turning in my grasp to look up at me. Her round eyes were so wet and wistful, so full of that odd, unfocused longing so common in little girls, that I had to close my eyes against a sudden surge of rage so strong it left me weak at the knees. The nerve of the little devil, toddling away into the woods and drawing me in after her! "Why did you leave the road? What on Earth is the matter with you?"

I said this in my harshest growl, speaking in the voice of a thousand spinster schoolteachers and a thousand maiden aunts. I expected the child to cry — I believe I *wanted* her to — but instead she lifted a chubby finger to her lips and whispered, "Hush, teacher! Look."

And she turned around again and pointed through the trees. My gaze followed the pointing finger up and up, beyond the thick stand of nude birches by which we knelt, and then I saw it.

The doe sat comfortably in the last of the winter snow, her pointed ears twitching, her black nose quivering as she took in our scent. We were scarcely ten feet away from her, and yet she did not get up to run. There was no fear in her black eyes beneath their girlish lashes, no nervous shivering in her delicate limbs. I could smell her droppings, her musk, her sun-warmed fur. *Odocoileus virginianus*, a white-tailed deer. Although she was thin enough for me to see the outline of her ribs, the contours of her elegant skull, her belly was hugely swollen. I looked and saw it tremble like a shaken bowl of water.

"Look," I said to my student, my anger quite forgotten. "See how round her stomach is, Lillian? She is going to drop a fawn soon — the first of the season, I suspect."

As soon as the words were out of my mouth, I regretted them. In my experience, once a child learns that an animal is in a delicate condition, they will not rest until they learn how that condition came to be, and I was mindful, still, of Mrs. Castle and her letters to the board. But Lillian did not pester me with questions about the hows and the whys of the thing. She stood there quietly, still in my rather wicked grasp, taking in the scene with the solemnity of a priest.

The tremors in the doe's belly increased. Still staring at us, she shifted in place and turned to nose intently at her hindquarters, a grey-pink tongue snaking out to touch the soft white fur there. Her back legs slowly rose, her tail lifting, and I realized that her fawn was not coming soon, but *now*. Dismayed, I reached down to cover Lillian's eyes with my hands. After all that had occurred with Mrs. Castle and Effie, I certainly did not want to deal with Mrs. Morice charging the schoolhouse and demanding to know why I had corrupted her daughter.

But Lillian would not submit to blindness. She wiggled away from me, tiptoeing with exaggerated care a foot or two closer to the doe. I tried to grab hold of her again, but she was out of my reach. There was no way for me to protect her, no way to soften the blow of knowledge.

A thin little whining moan wound through the chill of the morning air, a sound much like the creaking of a door, opening slowly. The animal's flanks were now fairly convulsing, ripples disrupting the smooth brown of her fur. Her neck strained as the muscles in her hindquarters clenched and relaxed, a dribble of red running down between her legs. Her mouth opened in a desperate pant, and I could see past her teeth down into the black column of her throat. I fancied I could see beyond that, into her guts, her lungs, her fluttering heart.

The trickle of red became a stream, a gush, a torrent. The doe's moan grew louder, higher, and her dark eyes rolled back into her head until I could see a fingernail of white in each one. From the trembling hind of the deer emerged not the expected spindly legs of a new fawn, but a kind of *mass* — pulpy, gore-purple, expelled from the animal in shuddering bursts of flesh. Her head lifted, her mouth gaping open to show a crescent of small white teeth, the deer collapsed onto the melting snow, the white underside of her tail stained crimson. Her sides heaved twice more, then stilled.

The woods were, suddenly, very quiet.

The wages of sin. Father's voice, loud in my ear, and the bright, sharp ache in my belly, the smell of that thing falling out of me and into the dark of the privy.

Lillian let out a shivering cry, more of a sigh than a sob. "Miss," she said, turning again to look at me, "what happened? Is she asleep?"

I did not reply. I could not.

Pushing the child behind me, I stepped toward the crumpled brown heap of animal. Her eyes remained open, but the shine that had made them look so bold and human moments before was gone. Her mouth gaped open, her tongue lolling onto the snow. Her smell was overpowering up close, the stench of blood adding depth and horror to the perfume of her unwashed body, her stink so like my own that I felt a wounding throb of kinship. I looked at her ears, waiting for a twitch to indicate that there was life still in her elegant body. They did not move.

"Is there a baby, Miss?" Lillian called. She stood exactly where I had left her, her face frightened and uncertain, but eager, too, for good news, a little fawn to pet and exclaim over, soft and gentle as a newborn kitten. "Can I see?"

I did not want to look. But I could not leave her wondering.

Slowly, reluctantly, my eyes travelled down the doe's body. Here was the curve of her neck; here were her dainty shoulder blades; here were her pointed black hooves and her legs with their bones straining against the skin. Here was her tail. And here

here was

The thing in the snow was not a fawn. On first glance, it scarcely seemed to be anything at all, an unarticulated mass in lurid shades of red. I looked at it as one might a cloud, struggling to see any sense or shape in that amorphous pile of blood and flesh. For a moment I thought — I hoped — that it had no shape at all, that it was simply some mysterious excretion, the last sign of a sickened animal. But then I saw, all unwilling, the enormous bulb of a head, the little blooming hands with their tiny finger-buds, the bulging suggestion of an eye.

This was what I hadn't seen that day that I hunched and panted in my father's stinking privy. This was Agatha's miss, and all my almost-siblings, and Mrs. Grier's poor, half-formed little Ann. This was Florrie's demise.

Is there a baby, Miss?

The thing on the snow moved, a helpless, twitching spasm that made me jump back in horror. Its wide slit-mouth opened, a bloody tongue protruding to taste the bitter chill in the air. For the second time that afternoon a moan rose up through the trees, this time in a human voice, one so heavy with dismay that I scarcely recognized it as my own.

Yes. There was a baby.

April 14, 1902

*O*nly seven today. I dismissed them early, muttering some excuse about having a sick headache. It was almost true — the blood in my head seemed to be pounding, each vein throbbing in time with some unearthly beat. Sitting wearily at my desk, I folded my arms and let myself slump forward until my forehead touched the wood. I stayed there until late in the day, adrift on a grey fog.

Everything that I had hoped for when I first came here seems to be crumbling around me. Everyone is watching me, telling tales, waiting for me to stumble. Even if I somehow press on until the end of the school year, the board will not reassign me to another school after the Mrs. Castles of this town are through with them. When I look to the future, I see nothing, just as I had after Florrie's death. And yet, my nerves are steady. Ever since my encounter with the doe, I have felt myself possessed by an unholy peace, a stillness that leaves me untouched by the world around me.

Lillian was one of the children missing today. I wonder if she was too frightened to return. She had not seemed frightened when I led her back through the woods after the incident with the doe, only confused and curious. But perhaps what she had seen has simmered and thickened since in her little mind, turned into something bigger and stranger.

(And what, precisely, did she see? Was it only the animal expiring? Or did she glimpse, as I pulled her away, the shape of the thing in the snow? Does the thing in the woods that plagues me with these ugly visions afflict her also?)

When was the last time I slept through the night without starting awake in terror? Weeks, or perhaps months. What hideous thing will I be shown next? Nothing but questions and no answers.

Another letter from Father today, and one very official-looking one from the school board, addressed to me. Both went into the cookstove, unopened.

April 19, 1902

"Begin at the beginning," the King said gravely,
"and go on till you come to the end: then stop."
— *Alice's Adventures in Wonderland*

The fog is thick tonight, pressing close against the glass in my bedroom window. When I look outside, I can see nothing beyond the very beginning of Mrs. Grier's vegetable garden. The world ends there in a solid wall of grey, forbidding as the rampart of some grim castle.

It had already started when Mrs. Grier and I left to go to the dance at the town hall. Mr. Grier had left immediately after supper, his fiddle case tucked tight under his arm; he walked down the lane with a noticeable spring in his step. Mrs. Grier smiled to watch him go. At one time she would have turned to me and said something fond about the man, but she no longer speaks to me unless she absolutely must. We cleared the table and washed the dishes in perfect silence, exchanging not even the smallest pleasantries. The only thing that good woman said as we prepared to leave was:

"Are you sure you wouldn't like to wash before we leave, Miss Byrd?"

Over the last few days, I have stopped cleaning even my face and hands. There are black lines of grime beneath my fingernails, dirt worked into the fine lines beneath my eyes. When I look in the mirror, I can see a fine, greyish pallor creeping over my cheeks. This is how I imagined prisoners might look when I was a child and read books about suffering captives, languishing in tiny cells. Edmond Dantes, Amy Dorrit, C.3.3. My smell is sour and ripe, like a sweating cheese.

"No, thank you, ma'am," I said. This she accepted, and we made the walk to the town hall in mutual solitude.

The doors to the hall were thrown open again, and light streamed out into the damp twilight, gaining brilliance and intensity in the gathering dark. I could see only shadow puppet people milling about inside, their features wholly obscured in silhouette. It was not until we stepped into the spill of light that they resolved themselves into human beings. Familiar faces, familiar voices, all the townspeople who have made up the background hum of my life this past year. Everyone wore their Sunday best, some with little flourishes added here and there to make them particularly festive — a new collar, a freshly trimmed hat, a locket. I wore my grey poplin, but it was wrinkled and damply stained under the arms. The rank odour of my body seemed woven into its very fabric.

Mrs. Grier disappeared as soon as we entered the hall, whisked away by some acquaintance or other. This did not bother me;

I knew she was anxious for better company than mine. I kept to the back wall, pulling my limbs in close so I would not accidentally touch anyone. From there I could see Mr. Grier, standing on a box and fiddling away, lantern light glimmering in the sweat on his bald crown, surrounded by the other musical men of Lowry Bridge. Several pairs of eyes wandered to me only to snap away almost immediately. Perhaps they were ashamed to be caught staring — or perhaps they were made uncomfortable by my dishevelled appearance, my dirty face. Mrs. Castle narrowed her eyes at me from her place across the hall, turning to whisper something pointed to a neighbour. Several yards away, Effie and Anna gazed at me with open hostility. One leaned over and whispered something that made the other whoop with laughter.

Effie's cheek seems to be healing nicely. It will likely bear only the faintest of scars.

Mr. Grier and his compatriots fiddled, the townspeople danced and laughed and gossiped, and I stood with my back to the wall, my hands folded neatly before me, watching as a polka turned to a jig to an English chain to a clumsy quadrille. No one approached me to request me as a partner; no one tried to coax me into any of the group dances. I was the still centre of a storm, the rock on which ocean waves crashed and broke.

"Hello, Ada."

Ada. I heard my name first as it had been whispered through the door of the schoolhouse, in the snow outside of the church, but I realized that the low, smooth voice was familiar to me, as was the cool hand that came to rest on my shoulder. I could feel the chill of it through the poplin.

"Hello, Norah," I said, turning to her. The dress she wore was the blue of the sky as the last light fades from it. The silver in her hair caught the light and winked. "I did not expect to see you here tonight."

Mrs. Kinsley smiled at me. What a warm thing her smile can be — so at odds with her dignified, patrician looks. "I am like a lost handkerchief, Miss Byrd. I turn up when I am least expected." She nodded her head at the colourful, swirling crowd. "You do not care to dance?"

"I have not been asked."

I thought of the turn I'd taken with Agatha back in the autumn, the wild thundering of my blood as we'd danced the schottische. She was not there tonight. I looked for her.

Mrs. Kinsley hummed in the back of her throat, gazing at the dancers. Now that she had joined me, even more heads were turned my way. One of them, I registered with little surprise, was Mrs. Grier's, who was standing halfway across the room. Her eyes flicked from myself to the widow and back again, her expression a complicated melange of emotions.

"It seems that I am making you infamous," Mrs. Kinsley whispered, and I started at the closeness of her mouth to my ear. The heat of her breath pulled a shiver through my body. I felt it in my bones, my teeth.

"Not at all," I said, rather too hastily; I saw her smile again, as though understanding precisely why I had denied her so quickly. "I am making *myself* infamous, Mrs. Kinsley. Do you not see?"

I gestured to myself, the sweep of my arm taking in not only the disarray of my person but the sweat and stink of it, the burning pressure of the roomful of eyes on me.

The lady did not respond to that directly, but looked me up and down slowly, thoughtfully. Her expression was one of frank consideration, as though I were food and she not yet certain of her appetite.

"Since you will not dance," she said, "will you walk with me? I came here tonight because I thought the music and the light might rouse me, but I find, now I am here, that I do not care for it."

She offered her arm, and after a moment's hesitation, I took it. As she led me out of the hall, I spared a single glance over my shoulder at Mrs. Grier. Her expression was less complicated now: she looked at me with the flint-eyed stare of a person who has begun to feel the first dark stirrings of hatred.

The air outside was bitingly chill, and I shivered violently for a few moments before the blood really began to circulate through my body and warm me, driven by my moving feet. Mrs. Kinsley gave my arm a companionable rub, as though to encourage the heat.

"What a glorious night!" she said as we turned together onto the road. We could see only a few yards ahead of us, the fog so thick that a buggy could have run us down without seeing us at all. When I breathed in, my lungs felt wet and heavy. "I've always loved misty evenings like this. They are like watercolour paintings, all the layers of grey swirling and shifting on top of each other. Don't you agree?"

I had no particular feelings about either fog or watercolours, and said so. She laughed, and the sound, in the way of sound on very thick nights, carried strangely. We walked together quietly for some time then, the silence broken only by Mrs. Kinsley humming a tune under her breath. What the song was I do not know, although it sounded maddeningly familiar.

"John loved music," she said after a time, and it took me a moment to remember who John was. Her husband, of course — the late, elusive Mr. Kinsley. "He came to the dances here every time they put them on, even though he hated to dance. All he wanted to do was stand at the back of the hall and listen, tapping his feet."

She paused, that hum rising in her throat again, and then she said:

"Did I tell you how he died?"

No, I replied, she never had.

"He was not young." Mrs. Kinsley's tone was as steady and measured as her steps. "There was a difference between us of nearly twenty years, and I was not young myself when we were married. Still, no one expected it, least of all me. Some people have such zest that it is unimaginable to think that they shall ever die."

Florrie, her hand in mine. Florrie, her pencil flying over paper as she sketched a bird in flight. Florrie, bright-eyed and flushed, falling in love with her own demise, the man who would love her roughly and ruin her.

"How did it happen?"

"The coroner said it was a heart attack." Her mouth twitched into a strange half-smile for the briefest of moments, like the flutter of curtains in a slight breeze. "I was with him. I watched him die."

Any response to a statement like that is bound to feel inadequate. Still, I offered her my condolences, which she brushed away with a dismissive sweep of a hand.

"It was our seventh summer here," she said. "John was so excited on the journey — he loved Lowry Bridge more than any other place in the world. Probably he loved it more than me." Again the little half-smile, there and gone within the space of a blink. "On the second day, he made me get up early. We should go for a picnic, he said, so eager, so boyish. I couldn't help but indulge him. It was easy to give him everything he wanted; he was that kind of man. So I packed a basket with bread and butter, and a pair of little cakes, and a jar of tea, and off we went. Into the woods."

The mist was so thick that I could scarcely see more than twenty feet ahead. A horse and cart approached us head-on through the dim, the sound of its hooves flat and muffled. Mrs. Kinsley waited until it had passed before continuing.

"The day I met John," she said, her voice flattened by the press of the fog, "I was wearing a bonnet that was nearly five years old, so patched that it looked more like a quilt than a hat. When I married him, suddenly I had everything I could have wanted, a hat for every day of the week and two extra for Sundays, a wardrobe full of beautiful clothes, a pantry full of food, horses, servants . . . All my life I'd had to pinch and scrape to get by, and now, if I wanted anything, my husband would press the money into my hand with a kiss and a wink. 'Anything you want, Noddy,' he would say, 'all you must do is ask. Your happiness is mine.' I was sure that someday I would wake up and discover that it had all been a dream, that I was due to get out of bed and go teach again."

Where were we going? It occurred to me only then to wonder as we kept on together down the road. She had said *walk with me*, and I had thought that we would wander, but although her pace was slow, it was purposeful. Her stride was sure, her arm steady where it secured me to her. My hand nestled in the crook of her elbow, safe as a baby bird.

"In a way, I never stopped teaching. John was a wealthy man, and he had a certain kind of intelligence, but he did not have the patience for education as a boy, nor the discipline for it as a man. The books in our library were there because he thought a man of means ought to have them, but he did not read them. Instead, he liked me to play the schoolmarm for him whenever we walked together — to take charge, and lead him around like a child, and give him lessons on Ancient Greece, or geometry, or French grammar. It amused him to hear the odd, broad array of things I knew about. 'My little polymath,' he called me — after I'd taught him the word.

"I can't recall what I was teaching him that day, but whatever it was, he found it engrossing enough to keep me at it for hours, even after we had already sat down and had our picnic lunch. It was not until well after that, when we'd brushed the crumbs from our jackets and started off in what we thought was the direction of the summer house, that we realized we were lost.

"Before that day, if anyone had asked me if it were possible for either of us to get lost in Lowry Bridge, I would have laughed. My husband fancied himself an outdoorsman, although his business was in textiles, and I myself liked to ramble across the land that came attached to the summer house, nothing but forest as far as my eye could see. At night, after John had gone to bed, I would find myself drawn to the door, the dark, the moonlight. We knew the woods. But that day we wandered for hours, thinking first *here* was north, now *there*, and succeeding only in walking ourselves in circles.

"It felt like a game at first, a kind of joke. We laughed about it, made jokes about what poor woodsmen we were. But as the afternoon wore on and the light began to fade, our good humour went with it. First we grew quiet, then snappish, then angry, and we quarrelled over whose judgment had led us astray. John insisted it was my fault, that I had distracted him too much. But I had only done, after all, what he had asked of me . . ."

She trailed off, and the two of us were quiet together. The night around us was very still. In the distance I could hear, faintly, the distinctive hoot of a barred owl. "Who cooks for you? Who cooks for you-all?" is how its cry is usually transposed, but I have always heard it as "Who looks for you?"

"Norah," I said, "where are you taking me?"

For taking me she was, I realized — leading me, gently and firmly, in a certain direction down the road. Toward the river, the "wrong side" of the town. The woods.

Norah Kinsley looked me in the eye, then drew her arm from mine. Facing me, she stepped backwards, then backwards again. Her footsteps made at first the wet and heavy sound of shoes hitting damp earth, and then, as she continued to back away, they rang differently. Thinner, sharper, louder. It was the sound of feet on wooden planks, of a woman trip-trip-trapping over a bridge.

"No," I said, but I found myself stepping forward anyway, desperate to keep her in my sight. If she walked too far away from me, she would be swallowed by the mist. She would disappear forever, and I would be alone in the dark.

The sound of my feet striking wood was scarcely louder than the sound of my blood rushing in my ears. Beneath us ran the Slade River, swollen from the excess of melted snow and spring rain. I could have leapt off the rails and hardly had time to breathe before the water carried me away. Mrs. Kinsley kept walking backwards, and I continued to follow her, until she found solid ground on the opposite bank. There she stopped, and I did too, my own feet still firmly anchored on the bridge.

If I stayed there, I thought, I would be safe. It could not cross the river.

But how sure was I of that?

"It grew dim while we quarrelled," the widow said. Black branches stretched across the road above her head, still naked from the winter. Pale and stately she was, glowing like a thing

333

carved from alabaster. *Athena*, I thought. *Parthenos*. "The shadows were thick, but I could still see all around me. I have good eyes in bad light, like a cat, and so I was able to see the way John's face changed as we kept wandering. He was afraid, and fear made him ugly. It twisted him up, made him rage and snarl, made him curse me louder and louder as we turned first this way, then that. At one point I snapped back at him — something a wife should never do, my mother always said, but I could not help myself.

"He raised his hand to me then. I stepped back, out of his way, but he kept coming with his fist thrust forward, as though he meant to strike me in the face. He never had before. I could hardly imagine him doing it, could hardly think that the silly, boyish man I'd married could lay an ungentle hand upon me, but I saw his expression and knew not only that he could, but he *would*. His polymath. His schoolmarm. His little Noddy. He would put me back in my place, now that I had stepped out of it.

"And then, for the first time in my waking life, I heard it say my name."

Ada. From the thick mist behind her came the voice, the one I'd heard so many times before, crooning out the two syllables of my name with the ardour of a lover. I said nothing, and nor did Mrs. Kinsley, but between us there passed a look of such perfect understanding that I had to bite my lip to hold back tears of sudden, joyous relief.

She heard it too. My God, she heard it too!

"It was not gentle with John," she said, "when it saw him raise his hand. It loved me even then, you see. It would not see me come to harm."

"You said that Mr. Kinsley had a heart attack."

"And so it was declared when the body was examined."

I opened my mouth to ask a question, but it was swallowed by the sound of rushing wings, a sudden wind and a rustling in the trees. The branch above Norah Kinsley's head was bowed under the weight of a bird. A barred owl, the same kind I'd heard calling only minutes before. To step forward for a closer look at such an animal was instinctual. My foot had already made contact with the dirt before I realized that the creature was
it didn't

It had no head. The owl ended at a ragged stump of throat, ruffed with a thick collar of feathers. Out of the feathers emerged a slight white protrusion of vertebrae. The dark bars on its breast were all but obscured by a sanguineous bib of gore. In the dim light, it looked black as its own eyes would have been, the eyes that were not there, the eyes that must have long since rotted away or been consumed by some lucky scavenger. I could *smell* the thing, suddenly, that familiar reek of wild animal overtaken by the rusty odour of old blood.

The owlet skull, nestled comfortably on my desk in its little jar. Here was the rest of it, come to pay its respects. My feet scrabbled backwards of their own accord, onto the safety of the bridge, and I felt the whimper rising in my throat.

It looked at me. God help me, it had no head, so how could I tell that it looked at me? And yet, it did — I saw it move slightly to track my footsteps, saw it shift and resettle itself on the branch in response to my movements. Its body leaned slightly toward me as I backed away, perhaps trying to decide if I was worth the effort of a killing strike.

Who looks for you? Who looks for you-all?

"Why is it doing this?"

At first, I was not sure that Mrs. Kinsley heard me. She looked upwards at the owl, one hand reaching up as though to touch it.

"The grey dog gives you gifts," she said, and her voice was a caress from a hand in a velvet glove. "Just as it gave Amelia gifts."

"Gifts?" The word was so shrill with confusion and fear that it sounded as though it had been torn from another woman's throat. "These horrors I have been seeing, the awful things that have come after me in the dark, the voices, the . . . You call these *gifts*?"

And then Norah Kinsley did a curious thing: she stepped toward me, back onto the bridge, and placed one slender hand upon my jaw. The tip of her thumb rested gently on my lips with their persistent scabs. I felt the cool of it against the heat of my own flesh. The urge to open my mouth came upon me like a sudden fever, and I looked away, waiting for it to pass.

"You are such an innocent, Miss Byrd, in spite of everything," she said, and removed her hand. The way she said this made me flush, for it was with a pointed kind of knowingness. As if she knew I was no innocent at all. "Can you not recognize when you are being wooed?"

Wooed. The tightly curled claws of the chickadee, the black triangle of the crow's wing on the step, the straining neck of the doe as she emptied herself out onto the snow. The baby. The hare. The tail. The owl, that silent watcher on the branch above her head.

"It chooses the objects of its affection carefully," she said. "Like all lovers, it has a particular sort for whom it burns. *You* are that sort, Ada; it began to pine for you as soon as you set foot on this side of the bridge. I knew the moment I saw you sitting in church, so meek, so well-behaved, but with such fire burning behind your eyes! Just like poor Amelia. That is what it likes, the things beneath the surface, the fury of a river's current under a film of ice. It makes love to its chosen ones as sweetly and ardently as a boy. It whispers our names, tries to draw us out, seduce us. It shows us that which it thinks will bring us pleasure—"

"Horrible things," I said, but Norah Kinsley shook her head.

"Is it horrible when a cat drops a mouse at its mistress's feet? Is it horrible when a hound drags in a rabbit for its master? No, Ada. It sees what is inside of you. Your little jars, your books of dead flowers, animal bones and bloody sisters and the smell of rot. It gives you what it thinks you want."

Again I thought of the skull on my desk at the schoolhouse. When I looked at the branches above Mrs. Kinsley's head, I was not surprised to see that they were empty, the owl gone as though it had never been.

"What about you, Norah?" I asked. "Were you one of that 'particular sort' too? Did it woo you as it woos me? Or are you its . . . its servant, bringing women to it when it takes a fancy to them? Are you its *procuress*?"

I meant this to sting, but Mrs. Kinsley only smiled. She did not answer.

"I know about the Grier boy," I said. My voice sounded curious to me, thin and vague, as though it were a thing of air and water, the sound of the rising fog.

"Jeremiah." She nodded, the movement of her head elegant as a diving bird. "It knew that I wanted a child, and so when the boy came upon the grey dog when he was playing in the woods, it brought him to me. A gift, like your animals. But, of course, he was frightened, and he fought. It does not like to be fought."

337

Mrs. Grier's recounting of her son's words, uttered in the midst of a delirium, came back to me in a rush. *Go away. You're not my mama, I don't like you.*

Why won't you let me go home?

"It was a bad business." The regret in her voice seemed genuine, but how on Earth could I tell? "He put his own eyes out, you know, with his nails. So few can look upon the grey dog and live. He simply could not stand to see it. The poor lad."

Fall on your knees. The shepherds in their fields, hiding their eyes, overwhelmed with terror and with beauty, angels crying "fear not" in voices like tolling bells and baying hounds. My skin itched as I imagined the boy in the woods, weeping into the snow, blood coming from his mouth and from his ears. His eyes, the blue, blue eyes that Mrs. Grier had remembered with such love and longing, torn from his face by his own hands.

My mouth was very dry, despite the thickening wet in the air. In a curiously raspy voice, I asked:

"What should I do, Norah? I don't understand what it wants."

The fog pressed close against us as she replied, her face very kind and her voice very soft:

"You, dear Ada, are what it wants. Your body, your heart, your soul. Every inch of you. And it will not stop until it has you."

She held on tightly, her aristocratic fingers digging deep into my flesh, then let me go.

Dawn is coming. I can see the fog lifting outside the window. The Griers came home hours ago; I heard them treading carefully up the stairs, as though afraid to wake me. They are asleep now. Only Cat and I are awake, her green eyes glowing at the foot of my bed. Her stomach is flat again now, her kittens nowhere to be found. Mr. Grier went down to the river the other day, carrying a wriggling sack over his shoulders. All her little darlings, drowned before their eyes opened. I never even saw them. I wonder if she did.

What, precisely, is the grey dog? What manner of creature, if it is a creature at all — what species, what genus, what *type* of thing is it? I wish there was a way for me to find out, a book of some kind to consult. I long for the mooring comfort of facts, the certainty of knowledge, the objective and the rational. I want to *know*.

You, dear Ada. It wants you.

Amelia Webster walked out the door of the summer house and into the woods, unable to resist. She disappeared forever into the dark.

What did it show her? What did it offer that poor woman that made her walk into the woods to find it?

Who looks for you?

I feel the gaze of the owl on me still, and that of poor Jeremiah Grier, his eye sockets torn to bloody shreds, crying alone in the dark.

No matter if I plug my ears it
still calls to me

If Mrs. Kinsley is telling me the truth, the horrors I have seen are the creature's gifts to me, just as this black book was Florrie's, and the late jar of rosewater scent was Agatha's. Like a paramour desperate to win a girl's fickle heart, it offers tokens of its love to make me love it in return. This is not like my dishonouring in Willoughby, that nerveless seduction that left me aching and empty. It is not like my kiss with Helen, curiosity transforming in a heartbeat to revulsion, eagerness twisting into shame. This is something different.

I am being wooed.

I have never been wooed before.

April 23, 1902

When I sleep, I hear it calling. I wake up, still, with no memory of my dreams, and yet I know that it creeps through them, its breath hot upon my neck.

People avoid me now. The other day I saw Mrs. Morice coming up the lane, leading little Lillian by the hand; when that good woman saw me, she blanched and scuttled to the other side of the road, dragging her daughter with her. Poor Lillian didn't seem to understand why. She turned round to stare after me as she was pulled away, her round eyes full of wonder. She did not look afraid, only curious.

"Miss smells like a doggy," I heard her say to her mother, in her carrying child-voice.

She was right. My stink has gone beyond that of an ordinary, unwashed female body. It has become an entity unto itself, the powerful reek of an animal at the height of summertime. A crust of grime has formed around my navel, imbued with a rich and earthy smell all its own. The Griers no longer pretend that they cannot smell me. This evening, Mrs. Grier told me after supper that she would prefer me not to sit in the parlour with them.

"It has been warm of late," she said, by way of explanation, "and one of the windows won't open. The air in the room gets to be too close." She said this firmly, without a hint of apology.

So here I am, banished to my room like a naughty child. I have spent the evening pacing back and forth, occasionally looking out the window in hopes of seeing something — anything — to distract me from myself. I am as restless and volatile as a cat. Cat herself seems to have noticed this, for she keeps well away from me now, and will no longer sleep at my feet. I am too agitated in my bed, these days. I kick.

Five students left in my class. I teach little. They learn nothing. Muriel watches me every day with the eyes of a woman, smiling to see me struggle for words. I see the movement of the trees outside the window, jump at the movement of shadows on the glass.

April 30, 1902

He came again. The bastard. The wretch.

When I looked out the window today after dismissal, I saw an unfamiliar team of horses, hitched to a worn little buggy that looked to be from a commercial livery stable. So bleary and addled was I from the lack of sleep of these past few days that at first I thought I was seeing things. Perhaps the grey dog had finally sent me as mundane a gift as it could find.

I put them out of my mind and set to completing whatever I could for the next day's lessons, although I have so few children coming to school now that it scarcely matters if I prepare or not. It was not until a gentle cough interrupted me that I looked up from my desk and realized that I was not alone.

Three men stood at the back of the classroom, framed by the still-open door. It took a moment of squinting before they resolved into familiar figures. Two of them were Gannis and

Ammerman, those illustrious members of the board who had attended the winter examinations. The third, looming behind them like a black oak stripped of leaves, was Father.

"Good morning, Miss Byrd," said Mr. Gannis. He favoured me with a kindly smile.

I stammered some kind of reply, not even meeting his eyes. How could I, when *he* stood right there, gazing sternly at me from beneath his thick black brows?

"We hope that this will not unduly inconvenience you," said Mr. Ammerman. They approached the desk, all three of them, and fanned themselves out before me, a row of tin soldiers. "But we thought it might be best to speak with you before you leave for the day. No, no!" — this because I had risen confusedly, thinking perhaps to go around the desk and shake their hands. "No need to get up. Please, do remain comfortable."

He smiled, very pleasantly, and I felt my stomach turn to lead. I have been a teacher long enough to know that impromptu meetings with board members are signs of trouble, and when they smile — that is when a girl must beware.

"We understand," said Gannis, "that you have recently had some . . .. difficulties."

Difficulties! All the events of the past few months seemed to jostle for position at the forefront of my brain. Dead animals, virgin snow, the shadow of the woods. The word "difficulties" seemed so inadequate as to be absurd. A little hiccup of laughter burst from my lips before I could stop it.

A woman laughing is always a disturbing thing for a man to witness. Gannis shifted, looking acutely uncomfortable beneath his luxurious moustache, and Ammerman shot him a glance from the corner of his eye, paired with an eloquent twist of his expressive face. Father did not partake in this shared confidence but continued to glare steadily at me.

"No," I said, once I had gotten the urge to laugh under control. "No, sirs, no difficulties. I assure you, I am healthy as a spring lamb."

My voice rang false even in my own ears. Once again Gannis and Ammerman glanced at one another.

"I am glad to hear that you have not been ill," said Gannis. He spoke gently, delicately, as to a child whose wits were not quite about him. "But that is not the sort of difficulty to which we are referring."

Ammerman reached into his jacket and pulled out a number of folded papers, their creases softened from much perusal.

"I have here," said he, "letters from concerned parents in Lowry Bridge regarding your conduct. Several of them are from Mrs. Elijah Castle, and many of her complaints . . . well, let us say that much of what she takes issue with is unobjectionable. However, several other letter writers have taken exception to incidents which are, perhaps, less innocent, and have told the board that they have withdrawn their students from your school as a result. A Mrs. Hamilton Agnew claims that you struck her daughter in the face, leaving a wound that will scar and affect the girl's prospects. A Mrs. Theodore Morice says that you showed her young daughter an animal giving birth. Many parents have complained that you have led the children into the woods to collect bits of stick and bone—"

"Oh, but where is the harm in that!" I cried. "Surely it is a worthy endeavour to instill in children a love of the natural world. We are all creatures of nature, sirs, and the best curriculum is that which is derived from—"

Gannis coughed meaningfully into his hand, cutting me short. "That may be so, Miss Byrd," he said — oh, very diplomatically! "But these are farm children, country children. They need to know how to read and write, how to do their sums. Anything more than that will only sow confusion. They will not go on to attend college or universities, nor even high school for the most part. What use to them are the life cycles of worms and frogs when they have families to raise and farms to run?"

"The value of knowledge," I said, "is self-evident, Mr. Gannis. It does not need to be justified by utility."

This was saucier than I have ever dared to be with a member of the board. Gannis blinked in surprise. Ammerman cleared his throat, stepping forward a little and shuffling through his soft stack of folded papers.

"I am afraid, Miss Byrd," he said, "that there are other complaints of a less . . . pedagogical nature, specifically regarding your conduct and character."

If I had not been watching Father's face very carefully at that moment, I would have missed the little sneering twist to his mouth. It appeared and disappeared in the space of a moment, like a spark.

"We understand," said Ammerman, "that you had some . . . regrettable experiences at your last post. This position was given to you in hopes that you would not have any such indiscretions in Lowry Bridge. It was a second chance, Miss Byrd, a fact that I believe you knew when you accepted it. But here we have" — he shuffled through his little pile of letters again, frowning, until he found the one that he wanted — "a report that you are keeping company with a woman whose reputation is known to be dubious, by the name of Norah Kinsley."

"Norah Kinsley is a clever, educated woman," I replied, rather too quickly. "We have much in common. Is it not permissible, sir, for a teacher to have a friend?"

Gannis made a humming noise in the back of his throat. "As to that," he said, "we have another letter from a person in town, a highly respectable person, claiming that you have begun to demonstrate signs of . . . what was it, Mr. Ammerman?"

Ammerman thumbed through the letters again, pulling one out from the sheaf of them. Even from that distance, I recognized Agatha's loopy, delicate handwriting.

"'Mental and emotional disturbance,'" he read, his flat, pleasant tone somehow rendering the words more hurtful, "'that may be on the verge of derangement.' This woman, Miss Byrd, claims that *she* is your friend, yet even she declares that you are unfit for your position. What do you say to that?"

Agatha.

Agatha Iscariot.

"Mrs. MacPherson," I said, my voice not altogether steady, "was unfortunately witness to a — a moment of trouble I had. She may have misunderstood it."

Ammerman shrugged. The letters fanned out in his grasp, a winning hand of cards. "Perhaps," he said. "And perhaps not. But we also have here in these letters various remarks about your deportment, your hygiene, your language, as unbecoming to a woman meant to be a shaper of young minds. Indeed, even standing here now, Miss Byrd, I regret to say that your appearance, your dress, and — forgive me — your odour speaks to a certain . . . lack of care. What sort of example are you setting for your students, my dear? No example at all, I would say, especially the young ladies." He shook his head. "It will not do, Miss Byrd. It simply will not."

Gannis reached out and gently plucked Agatha's letter from his colleague's hand, as delicate as a girl picking a daisy. "There is another issue raised in Mrs. MacPherson's letter," he said, squinting down at the paper in his hand. "She claims that, on one occasion, you had some kind of fit and attacked her, threatened her. Bruised her arm. You were wild with rage, she says, and she feared for her safety. She seems to think that you are . . . well, that you may commit some violent act, by and by."

The memory of that feverish fight with Agatha filled my mouth, the taste of her tears and the softness of her flesh. I felt myself flush, then turn pale. Gannis, watching me, nodded as though he had seen all he needed to see, and Ammerman sighed gustily.

"It simply will not do, Miss Byrd," he said again. "Even if the claims made here are false — and some may be — we must think of the reputation of the board, of the school. We must guard the physical and moral safety of the children of this town."

I looked from one face to the next. Gannis looked sympathetic; Ammerman looked disdainful; Father was as unmoving as a stone. Was this how Jane Grey felt on her way to the block? Did she, too, search the faces of her executioners for any sign of mercy, and find none?

"What is the purpose of your visit, gentlemen?" I asked.

They did not answer this right away. Ammerman shifted his weight from one foot to the next.

"We must tell you, Miss Byrd," said Gannis eventually, his expression rather pained, "that after this term comes to an end, you will not be invited back. Indeed, the board has decided that it would not be . . . seemly to offer you further employment anywhere in the district. We have discussed it, and the decision is unanimous."

Snow White is said to have died with a bite of poison apple lodged in her throat, only to have it dislodged later by her rescuing prince. In that moment I felt as though I, too, was struggling with a bite of some poisonous fruit, trying and failing to choke it down. A great, unmelting lump blocked my gullet, making my eyes water and my face turn pink.

"I suppose that is your right," I managed to say at last. "And I suppose that there is nothing I can do to change your minds."

At this response Gannis and Ammerman visibly relaxed. What, I wonder, had they expected me to do? How had they thought I might respond to such news?

"You may finish out the year," said Ammerman, as though giving me a gift that I did not quite deserve. "It would not be possible for us to find another teacher at this late date. But we will be attending the examinations in June, and if your students do not perform to our satisfaction, we will be forced to consider disciplinary action — possibly in the form of wage garnishments." He hesitated, then added, "Your father, I believe, sent you notice of this possibility. He says you have not been answering his letters."

I nodded bleakly, staring down at the desk. The ravaged blond wood had never looked so ugly to me as it did then. My heart was gripped with a fierce longing to grasp it by its edge and flip it over, scattering jars and books and papers from one corner of the room to the next.

Instead, I breathed in deeply, imagining my lungs inflating and deflating like wet pink balloons, then looked up at the three of them. My smile seemed to take more effort than anything I had ever done. "Might I speak with my father, gentlemen?" I asked. "Privately, I mean?"

Gannis and Ammerman were quick to say yes, of course, and fled the scene. I think that they were more than happy to get away from me, and from whatever terrible storm was about to break.

Father and I looked steadily at one another for some time, his face as distant and grave as ever. As a girl, seeing that face loom over me had made me twist and writhe with guilt; it meant that I had done something terrible, even if I did not know what that something was. It had the same effect on me as recently as last autumn, in the Griers' parlour. But today I felt nothing of the terror that had gripped me as a child as I stared up at him. It occurred to me for the first time how old he looked, how thin and grey. My teeth found my lip on reflex, began to bite.

And then, miraculously, stopped.

At length he said, "You do not look well."

No translation was necessary now. We would both say exactly what we meant.

"I am *not* well, Father," I replied. "Isn't that what you and your two chums have come here to tell me? That I am ill, that I am 'mentally deranged'?" Agatha bent over a piece of paper, writing those words. My eyes closed against the image. I breathed in deep to gather strength. "Tell me, was this visit their idea, or yours? How many letters did the board receive before you convinced them that I had to be removed for the sake of public safety?"

"I am thinking of what is best for you," he said. His voice was devoid of any emotion, as was his face. He might have been a plank of wood, with whiskers painted on.

"You have never thought of what is best for me. Only what is best for you."

He blinked with surprise, and no wonder — I can count on one hand the number of times I have contradicted him. Those thick black brows of his lowered just a little. I watched them move and felt a sort of deadened jubilation overriding my despair. I was no longer a child. He could no longer whip me; even if he could, he certainly would not do so with two associates waiting outside of the schoolhouse. Let his brows lower, let his mouth twist, let him turn scarlet and burst forth with angry vulgarities! What power had he over me now?

Speaking seemed to take a great deal of effort, for his mouth worked noiselessly for some time before he formed a word. He said, his voice no longer as smooth as it had been, "It pains me to see you so changed. It pains your mother, too, to think of you falling into bad company and worse habits out here in the back of beyond. I hate to think of the influences that have been at work to make you—"

"You do not think that any influences have been at work on me." I dared to interrupt him! I dared to cut him off! "You have never felt anything for me but contempt. Well, now I have made myself contemptible. You called me a dirty little beast, and I have become as dirty and beastly a woman as ever there was. What you see before you is what you always, in your heart, thought to see one day. You may say otherwise to those gentlemen, to keep your name from being dirtied by the mud of me, but you do not truly believe that anyone is responsible for what has become of me but my own self. The *wages of sin*, sir."

This last I said to him in his own voice, imitating how he had intoned those words as I'd dragged myself back from the privy all those months ago. His brows lowered still further. Perhaps he recalled that ugly blot in front of his chair in the parlour, that shadowy reminder of the thing that had grown so briefly and disastrously inside of me.

"You are not yourself, Aidy," he said, and I stood, pushing my chair out from behind me. The groaning squeal of its legs as they scraped against the floorboards made my teeth ache.

"*Do not call me that!*" This came out in a snarl, a single, ferocious sound barely shaped into words. "That was Florrie's name for me. I can't stand to hear you say it. And I am more myself, Father, than I have ever been before. You think that I am not myself because I am not meek or mild, because I am looking you in the eye instead of gazing down at my shoes. But that was never my true self. You pruned me into that self as a gardener might prune a bush into the shape that pleases him most."

Father put a hand up to his whiskers, stroking them with fingers that appeared to tremble. "Sometimes pruning is necessary," he said, "to keep a garden in order."

And then — such a curious thing! — I felt a smile start to bloom on my face. It was not my ordinary smile, that weak and faltering grimace that I can hardly stand to see in the mirror, but a broad, bold grin that spread slowly from the corners of my mouth, baring all my teeth.

I smiled, and Father flinched. Just once — just a little — but it was enough to thrill me.

"I am no garden, Father," I said, emerging from behind the desk. There was a grace to my movements that had not been there before, a warm fluidity like that of a panther padding out from the shadows. He took one step back from me, then another. "Have you not guessed it yet? I am not a place where nature can be weeded and tamed and kept in order. I am tree roots — and dark hollows — and ancient moss — and the cry of owls. I am not a thing that you can shape, not anymore. I am no garden, but the woods, and if you ever come near me again, every bit of wildness in me will rise up to bite you. I will tear your throat out with my teeth."

Would I have done it? I do not know. But in that moment, I felt that I could have snapped my mouth around his neck and ended him with one vicious shake.

Father had continued to retreat, and now his back was nearly pressed against the door. His eyes blinked rapidly, and a droplet of sweat fell from his brow to the edge of his whiskers. In other men these things might be nothing, but I knew my father.

I had frightened him.

How wonderful that felt!

"First we lost her," he said, his voice markedly unsteady, "and now . . . now we have lost you. To madness, or something worse. I should never have let you out after Willoughby; I should have locked you up, kept you safe from yourself. If you think, after this, that your mother and I will have you back in our house—"

"I do not intend to come back to your house."

I had not guessed that I would say such a thing until the words flew from my mouth, but as soon as they did, I felt a lightness steal along my limbs, as though I might lift off the ground. Of course I would not come back! Of course I could never return to that miserable house and its miserable inhabitants! My smile grew wider. It almost hurt.

Father stared at me, his face no longer blank but dismayed, confounded, horrified. I reached behind him, and he flinched as though I were a viper about to strike, but I was only opening the door.

"Your friend was correct," he said, even as he backed over the threshold. For the second time in my life, I saw what seemed to be tears in his eyes. "You are deranged. My daughter has turned into a person I hope to never encounter in the dark of night."

On that parting note, he turned, clearly thinking that he had landed a devastating blow, but all I could do was smile as I watched him climb into the buggy behind the other two.

For the first time in my life, he understood me.

May 2, 1902

*F*ather and his cronies must have informed the Griers of their visit. Mr. Grier has not been able to look at me for the past two days, while Mrs. Grier walks about with a curious expression — a mingling of guilt, vindication, and defiance. Her voice, when she speaks to me, is too sweet; her eyes, when they meet mine, are hard and cold as iron.

She must have been one of the ones who wrote to the school board. I wonder what she said. Was her letter the one that complained of me keeping company with Mrs. Kinsley? Or did she report my dirtiness, my fit outside of the church, the increasing oddness of my behaviour? Or the things that she read in this little book?

I ought to be planning. I have lessons to create, examinations to prepare for; beyond that, I must think to my future, such as it is. For the past ten years I have moved from school to school within the district, trying to build a life and reputation for myself that would ensure my independence. That is gone now. I am no more employable as a teacher than the meanest beggar on the street.

What can I do? Move to another district, where my name is unknown, and hope that no one asks too many questions? Take my chances in a city, where anonymity will be a friend to me? Can I continue to make a living as a teacher, or would it behoove me now to try my luck as a shopgirl, a clerk, a seamstress?

The prospect of being hanged, it is said, sharpens a man's mind most wonderfully, so the prospect of unemployment ought to sharpen mine. But my thoughts move as sluggishly as a river in a drought, and I think of the years to come with only the barest interest.

When I walked home from the schoolhouse this afternoon, I found my feet taking me along that part of the road that branches and runs by the church and the manse before rejoining with the main thoroughfare. The church sat drowsing in the warm spring sunshine, the manse crouching some ways behind it like a stalking animal. There was no sign of Agatha in the garden, nor at the window, but as I stood there at the fence, gazing up at the house, I felt that I saw the white curtains in the window flutter just slightly, as though someone stood behind them, watching me anxiously. It could have been the wind.

Four students in today. Soon there shall be none at all.

May 4, 1902

I was wrong. I was wrong about it all.

In an effort to avoid dreaming, last night I tried my hardest not to fall asleep. Instead, I sat up in the uncomfortable chair by the window, reading *Introduction to Entomology* by the weak light of my little candle. Every time my head began to droop, I stuck my finger into the flame. The flesh there is thick and white now, blistered and full of fluid, but it was no use — at last I nodded off, slumped back against that terrible chair. There, my chin pressed to my chest, I dreamed.

In the dream I stirred — woke — got to my feet and tiptoed carefully out of my room, down the stairs, out the front door of the Grier house and into the chill night air, barefoot and wearing only my limp flannel nightgown. "Night air is poison," Mother always said, and I used to have nightmares about that, imagining putrescent toxins curdling in my lungs and blood while I slept.

But now I breathed deep. The moon was full, the world around me flooded with silver.

Graceful as a ghost, I wandered up the road and across the bridge, stopping only a moment to gaze into the river before moving on. The dread that seizes me every time I cross the river in my waking life did not take hold of me. There was nothing but peace in my heart as I padded along, lingering here and there to look at a newly budded flower, to delight in the piercing call of a whip-poor-will.

The world is beautiful at night. I had forgotten this, these past few months.

The widow stood at the gate to her home, smiling at my approach. Reaching for my hand, she placed a gentle kiss upon the knuckles. Her lips were petal-soft, warm and damp.

"Come," she said, and led me across her yard and into the woods beyond it. The trees were thick and draped with spider-webs. New saplings whipped merrily at my exposed ankles. I could smell the heady tang of sap, feel the cool squelch of mud between my toes, hear the distant singing of crickets.

I thought of Amelia Webster, that last night she'd spent in the widow's house, the image I'd had of her being pulled inexorably across the grass and into the trees. Perhaps, I thought, she had not been pulled at all. Perhaps she, like me, had been taken by the hand.

Mrs. Kinsley turned to face me, moonlight gleaming on her skin like the flash of the sun on a coin. I realized suddenly, as one does in dreams, that she was naked, her body striped with shadow, the dark thatch between her legs in stark contrast to her bloodless flesh. Her hair was loose from its pins, and I shuddered at its sinuous length, the snaky coils of it tumbling down her shoulders and back. She wore her immodesty as easily as another woman might wear a tailored suit.

"It is coming," she said. "It smells you on the wind, it hears the thudding of your heart. It wants you, Ada, so very badly."

She reached down to grasp the billowing edge of my night-gown. Gently, carefully, she pulled the garment over my head, discarding it in the dirt. I let her do it. Stepping back, she looked me up and down, her pale eyes taking in every inch of me. She did not seem to mind my smell, the dirt that crusted me like a second skin.

The ticklish sting of a blackfly bite on my arm made me shiver and start, looking down at myself. My plump belly and dimpled thighs bared to the world. The vermin of the forest had free range over my body, from the crown of my head to the heels of my feet. In waking life, I might have swatted them away, but in my dream — ah! I was overcome by the most voluptuous feeling of pleasure, a feral carnality that made me long to sink into the earth. I wanted to dig my hands into black soil and let the worms slide between my fingers. I wanted to invite the swarming mayflies to land upon my breasts and dart into my open mouth. I wanted to spread my legs and watch the black wolf spiders creep along their length, seeking with their spindly limbs some dark crevice to call home. A little sound, a moan or whimper, escaped me at the thought of it, and Mrs. Kinsley smiled.

"This is what it will feel like," she said. "This is how it will be every day — every moment — if you only let the grey dog take you."

"What does it look like?" I asked her. How odd, that I had never thought to ask before. I had never wanted to know.

Mrs. Kinsley closed her eyes, as though against the enormity of the question. "It is beautiful," she whispered, "beautiful as moonlight on the river, beautiful as the mist that rises from the ferns, beautiful as the shadows under the trees."

Looking at her face, rapt and luminous, I wondered what gifts the grey dog gave to her. What visions had it plucked from her mind and fed back to her, made stranger and crueller by their time in its hands? My mouth had opened to ask the question, but what came out instead was "I'm afraid."

She laughed, a sound as simple and lovely as water over stones.

"No," she replied, "you aren't."

And she was right. I knew that I had been afraid, that I should be still, but there was no room in my body now for fear. My whole self was pulse and nerve, rippling flesh and thundering blood.

She reached out both her hands to me again. I found my arms lifting toward her, straining to close the distance between us.

Procuress, I had thought her, but now a different word came, unbidden, to my mind: *liberator*.

Something rustled in the trees behind her. A shadow fell across us both, stemming the flood of moonlight. Mrs. Kinsley lifted her face to the wind.

"It is here," she said, and our fingertips touched.

That was when I woke, panting, sweating, trembling all over with a strange and unsubstantiated longing, an ache rooted in every atom of my body. The candle on the windowsill had burned down to the nub, sputtering to death in a little molten pool of itself. My lungs burned for air. I had been holding my breath in my sleep, I realized, waiting for whatever it was to appear behind Norah.

Inhaling deeply, I waited for the shaking in my limbs to subside. The room was dark still, but with that greyish dimness that means morning is fast approaching. The clock in the

Griers' parlour called the hour, four chimes splitting the silence with the violence of an axe.

It was then that I realized two things, both of which are still true now as I write this by the light of the rising sun — for I have not slept any more this night. Perhaps I shall never sleep again.

The first was that my nightgown was gone, leaving me bare in the growing light.

The second was that my arms were speckled with the bites of blackflies.

(later)

At about half-past nine, perhaps just realizing that I had not come down to breakfast, Mrs. Grier came to wake me for church. I saw her stand there in the doorway, staring with some confusion at my well-made bed, before turning and clapping eyes on me in my chair. She gave a little muffled shriek of surprise and alarm — for I had not moved to clothe myself and sat there with the spring sun streaming through the window onto my bare skin.

"Miss Byrd," she managed, her face a mask of distaste and unease, "I did not know if you were awake."

I did not answer. It was not the kind of statement that called for one.

"Mr. Grier and I are getting ready to go to church," she said, and her eyes roved from the bed to the wall to the washstand, trying desperately to find anywhere to land that was not my naked flesh. "Perhaps, if you would like to get dressed . . ."

A blackfly bite on my right breast had become red and swollen in the night. I reached down and scratched it, sighing with relief as the itch faded. Her eyes followed the movement against her own will, and her mouth turned to that familiar thin line.

"Really, Miss Byrd," she said, "I can't say that I understand what you are doing in this state. Sitting here naked as a babe, and my husband awake downstairs! Just suppose he comes up and sees you?"

I stretched voluptuously. Those Dionysian dream-feelings still thrummed through me, and I hummed pleasurably at the smooth brush of my seat against my skin, the cool air flowing over my limbs. *Just suppose*, she said, and I took a moment to imagine it, Mr. Grier stomping up the stairs and freezing in the doorway behind his wife, his mouth open as he took in the expanse of my uncovered body. The sight of my flesh piling up against itself, the smell of old sweat draped over me like silk, the deep shadow between my legs.

I would have shrunk from anyone seeing me unclothed before, rushed to cover myself and let forth a torrent of apologies for the sight of my naked flesh. But now I pictured the whole town parading up the stairs to my little room, all of them standing there gawping at me in my immodesty, and I smiled with delight.

This was what Jenny Carpenter had felt, all those years ago. She bared her flesh to the world and laughed.

"Call him up if you please, Mrs. Grier," I said. "Throw the front door open and shout out to all who pass that there is something to be seen in your upstairs bedroom. Put an advertisement in the papers, hang a notice on the board in the general store, send a telegram to the King of Spain alerting him to the news — it is all the same to me."

A part of me would have shrunk from these insolent words, even the day before. It did not shrink now. Something in me had changed. I remembered again the feeling of the earth beneath my naked feet and sighed with pleasure. At the sound of it, Mrs. Grier took a step back from the doorway, retreating into the shadow and safety of the hallway.

"I have been your defender, Miss Byrd," she said, her voice unsteady. "You know, I suppose, that folks have been saying horrible things about you. There have been wild tales about your conduct and your habits, things that might be attributed to a lunatic, or a heathen. Anyone who said such things to my face has gotten an earful from me, for when I first met you, you were a good woman. You might be a good woman yet, in spite of everything. But this behaviour . . . you are not *well*, you are not right."

A good woman. How odd that the phrase has such a particular meaning. One might say "a good man" and mean anything — there are as many ways of being a good man, it seems, as there are of being a man at all. But there is only one way to be a good woman. It is such a narrow, stunted, blighted way to be that I wonder any woman throughout history has been up to the task. Perhaps none of us ever have.

I stood and noticed the way the light moved over my body, so heavy and warm that it had an almost tangible presence, like a blanket. At my movement Mrs. Grier backed up just a little more, wary, watching. Prey.

"You are wrong," I said. I took one step toward her, then another, and she scuttled farther back into the hall, away from me. I followed, my bare feet sliding over the cool floor. She was nearly at the top of the stairs now, in her haste to put space between us. "I am not a good woman, Holly Grier, not anymore."

And thank God for that, my heart cried out, an unheard echo of my spoken words, thank God, thank God, thank the God of outside!

Her feet rested nearly on the edge of the top stair. I could have reached out and pushed her, watched her topple head over heels down to the first-floor passage. Just as I had imagined that parade of observers trooping into my bedroom, I imagined her falling, her skull striking every tread. I could hear the meaty thump of her skull as it cracked, over and over, brutal and beautiful as the beat of a drum.

My hand flexed by my side, as if preparing for that final shove. Mrs. Grier saw it, her eyes fixing on my twitching fingers, her little body tensing in anticipation. But I did not do it. Instead, I watched as she grasped the railing firmly, backing down the staircase properly, her eyes on me all the while. She did not feel safe enough to look away from me.

"I am no garden," I murmured, remembering the way my father had retreated from me, the way his eyes had widened as I advanced on him. Mrs. Grier seemed to hear this and paused on the landing, still gazing up at me. Her mouth worked for a moment, as though she could think of many things to say to me. None of them, however, were anything a good woman could make herself say.

"Heaven help you, Miss Byrd," she said instead, her face set in grim, firm lines, before turning at last to disappear into the gloom at the bottom of the stairs. I heard her speak to her husband in low and measured tones; a short time afterwards, they left for church. I listened to the rattle of the buggy until the noise thinned back into silence. I am alone now.

No, that is not true. Muriel said it, all those months ago when we met in the woods. You are never alone out here.

(later)

I put my dress on before I left the house, my poplin. That much of a concession I made. But no stays, no shoes, no hat. I wanted as little between my skin and the air as I could manage.

Church had just let out when I stepped outside, this book tucked under my stinking arm, and I passed many people on the road as I crossed the bridge. Faces stared incredulously at the movement of my unbridled flesh, the sinking of my bare toes into the earth. A few shouted after me, as though trying to capture my attention. A pair of little boys whose faces I did not recognize skipped beside me for a while, shouting gleefully and throwing stones. Most missed me, but when one struck my foot, splitting the nail on the largest toe, I let out such a loud bark of laughter that they startled and fell behind, staring after me.

"Loony! Loony!" I heard one of them shout, and I only laughed more.

Just as she had in my dream, Mrs. Kinsley waited for me at the summer house. Not at the gate, but on the front step, and not bare, but clad in a white dress, but she smiled at me in that same eager, easy way and reached out to take my hands in hers. I felt the faint calluses on the fingers, the smooth chill of her skin.

"Welcome," she said, her voice soft as a shudder. Her thumb stroked softly at my palm. My eyes closed, my lips trembled.

How good to be touched. How good to simply *feel*.

Mrs. Kinsley kissed my cheek, leaving a warm imprint of saliva, and pulled me into the shadow of the summer house. She led me down that dark, grand hall to the warm sanctuary of the library, a fire burning in the grate. Athena looked down at me from her place on the mantle, unyielding and disapproving.

Mrs. Kinsley's pale eyes took on the colour of the flames, the red velvet. Her hands were tender as she turned me around and began to undo the buttons of my grey poplin, one by one. They strayed, now and then, to my skin, stroking gently along the curve of my spine, as though I were a cat she hoped to soothe.

I closed my eyes and let myself come apart under her hands.

(later)

I can say her name now. Norah. Norah Belsey, who became Norah Kinsley, who became the beloved of the grey dog, its helpmeet, its trusted lieutenant. I say it over and over again, in a kind of mantra.

"When will it come?" I asked her in those first, fervent hours, but she only laughed and cupped my face in her cool hands. She told me to be patient, to wait. It will call me, and I shall go. Like she did. Like Amelia did.

And others, I wonder? Were other women called to its heart, other women flattered by its gifts and its love?

My dress lies in a sweat-stained heap on the carpet, flattened by the congress of our bodies in front of the library hearth. She breathes in deep the stink of me, licks the salt from my skin like a deer. Rebecca has left food outside the door for us, meat and fruit, soft bread, little round cheeses. We feed each other with our hands, drink deeply from the same cup, sleep together in a pile. Like the kittens Cat had but never kept.

(later)

*I*s it still Sunday? I cannot tell. We have the curtains drawn.

Norah has shown me all the books in her library, and so I have shown her this one in return. When she read my description of the dream, she met my eyes.

"*Was* it a dream?" I asked, but she did not reply, only smiled.

She is reading this now, over my shoulder, as I write it. She is pouring me a glass of strawberry wine, red as blood, thick as tar.

(later)

*T*he grey dog is not a dog, Norah tells me. It looks that way to her in dreams, and so that is the name she gives it, but it will look differently when it comes to me. I may know it by another name.

"How long has it been here?" I ask.

As long as the land itself, she says. As long as the stars. As long as time.

"Where was it before that?"

Everywhere, she says, and nowhere. It has existed for far longer a span of time than our paltry race. It rose from the sea, from the primordial muck; it walked out of the darkness before creation and into the shadow of the woods.

"How long shall it love me?"

Forever, she says. Forever. Just as it loves her, and Amelia, and all the women who have come before it, a long line of paramours disappearing over the horizon into the past. Its love is not the same as mortal love. It does not wither, even when we do. It blooms and lasts.

(later)

*T*here have been knocks at the front door, people asking for me. I heard Mr. Grier's voice; I heard the Reverend. I swear I even heard Mrs. Castle, and Gannis and Ammerman, in tandem. Each time, Norah sends Rebecca to tell them I am not there. We press against the door of the library, listening to the low murmurs of their voices, Rebecca's sharp, thin replies.

"They don't believe her," I told Norah after the last one was turned away, and she shrugged.

"They may believe her, or not," she said. "It does not matter. They cannot come in."

Her hand found my throat as she said it, resting gently against my pulse. My blood beat against her fingertips. I was not afraid.

(later)

*O*n the edge of sleep — true sleep, unmarred by dreams — I asked Norah why she did not disappear when the grey dog chose her, why she did not walk into the woods and never return.

"John always said, 'Your heart is cold, Noddy. Beneath that skin of yours, there's only ice, not blood.'" Her voice was very far away. One of her hands stroked through my hair, nails digging pleasurably into my scalp. "He was right. My love is always an arm's length away. The grey dog likes its lovers desperate, hungry. It likes to know that those who come to it come because they must. Whereas I . . . I have my house, my books, my little habits. I live comfortably; I have money; I want for nothing. There is no desperation in me. When it first called to me, I knew that I would be more useful to it as its *procuress*" — she used the word with an ironical little smile — "than as its paramour. I knew that I would not give up my ordinary life entirely."

"But I will give up mine?"

I opened my eyes to her smile, her pale blue eyes. Her hands cupped my cheeks, so cool, so strong. Those fingers had been in my mouth. I could taste them still.

"That," she said, "is your choice, Ada, and yours alone."

My choice. I tried to imagine turning back, taking up an ordinary life as an ordinary woman. Choosing to live the rest of my days as a schoolteacher, a spinster with no prospects, a sad and pitied failure of a woman. *Impossible*, I thought, *impossible*.

I cannot go back. I won't.

(later)

I told Norah what happened in Willoughby, how I had mapped *her* face onto *his*, the dreams I'd had in my sad little bed. I felt no shame. The time for shame has passed away.

When I finished, she reached out to cradle my face in her hands. Our silhouettes sprang together and then apart, melted into one and then separated.

"That was a shadow," she said. "A shadow on the wall of a cave that you mistook for the truth. Soon, sweet girl, you will know love."

Pallas Athena watches us from on high. Wisdom. War. We are beyond such things. We are teeth and skin, spit and hair, bones and blood.

(later)

Deep shadows, swarming insects. We ventured out into the moonlight, to the edge of the woods behind the summer house. Silver on our skin and the cool night air, not poison at all but life itself, vital and clean. Norah offered me the flesh of her arm to bite, and I did so, gently, as a puppy might gnaw on his master's hand. Her sweat does not taste like Agatha's, it is heavier, more subtle. A light burned in the house behind us, and I saw the dark and indistinct shape of Rebecca at the window, watching.

"Does the grey dog speak to her too?" I asked Norah, and she turned to look at the window as well, squinting through the dark.

"Rebecca keeps her own counsel," she replied. "If she hears it, she has never said."

"But Muriel does."

I do not know why the girl sprang to my mind in that moment. Perhaps it was the ragged treeline, the darkness of the pines thrusting into the pale moon. It reminded me of the day I met her in the woods, the day I'd been so sure that something stood behind me, watching. As it had. As it does.

Norah turned to me and smiled, shadow lying queerly upon her face. Her hands were open to the wind, her hair blowing

369

back and forth behind her. Lovely, uncanny, hands open to the wind, hair blown wild and free. A Maenad, pausing in her frenzied raptures. From the trees behind her, I heard again the call of the barred owl, that eternal question echoing through the night.

Who looks for you?

"Not yet," she said. "But soon."

We did not go into the woods, despite my pleading. Patience, Norah croons, patience, wait until it calls, but I have so little patience left.

(later)

There are foxes laughing in the dark. I can hear them.

(later)

Agatha came to find me. This time Norah went to speak to her herself, and I crept to the library door to listen alone, pressing my ear against the crack.

"No," I heard Norah say, her tone as calm and modulated as ever. "I am afraid she is not here, Mrs. MacPherson."

The words of Agatha's response were lost to me, but I could hear the rise and fall of her voice. I could picture her standing on the front step, staring anxiously into the darkness of the summer house, her hands tangling together as she strained her eyes to get a glimpse of me.

Did I want to see her? Could I stand to look upon her lovely face, now that I have become what I now am? Would she even recognize me?

"No, I understand," Norah said then, and I could picture her too, tall and erect in a respectable blue dress, not a trace of the bacchante about her now. Just a woman, barring another entry to her domain. Would Agatha try to force her way in? "If I hear from her, I shall let you know."

"Please do," was Agatha's reply, pitched rather loudly as though she hoped it would carry into the depths of the house. "We are so worried about her. She isn't . . . I fear she is not well."

We laughed about that, Norah and I, when she returned to the library. I am well. I have never been better.

(later)

She made me a bed of dead leaves. I felt the cold muck of rot on my skin as I lay there, watching the moon spin in the sky above me.

I imagined myself standing under that silver moon and walking into the woods, one quiet foot before the other. Barely a rustle of leaves, a breath of wind. Just the quiet and the dark, the trees parting before me like curtains, drawn slowly back to reveal the creature that has been pining for me all these months.

What will it look like? "Beautiful," Norah had said, nothing more. I saw the fairy-fragile ivory of my owlet skull, a pair of red-brown eyes, soft hair gleaming in the lamplight. Cool lips meeting mine in the dark. The flash of a kingfisher skimming across the river. The sound of crickets, singing mournfully into the night. I saw myself walking toward it with my arms out-stretched, eager to be embraced.

I want its flesh to merge with mine. I want it to engulf me, swallow me, obliterate me with its love. I want annihilation.

When Norah pulled me from the leaves and into the summer house, I sobbed like a child, like Jeremiah Grier on his deathbed.

(later)

Norah has told me what the grey dog has shown her, the gifts it laid before her to draw her close.

"You must take this to your grave," she said, and ran a finger over my lips, as though sealing them with wax. And so I would, I promised her, so I would!

(later)

And what, after all, was Amelia's fate? What happened after she surrendered herself to the woods?

Norah smiled and leaned in to whisper at my ear, hot breath and mirth, low voice tangled with insinuation.

"It found her," she said, "and it took her. As it took me. As it will take you, Ada."

I write this as she sleeps next to me, stretched peacefully across the library floor, her dark head pillowed on her arms. She has told me to be patient, that it will find me at its leisure. But I find I have no patience left.

In the morning, I shall rise and dress for the first time in what feels like years. I will go to the schoolhouse and wait. It found me there before. It will find me there again.

May 9, 1902

I know the date, because I asked Rebecca before I crept out of the summer home at dawn, leaving Norah asleep on the carpet. A clear, coolish day. Blue skies. Insistent winds. My poplin pulled once more onto my body. Already the feel of cloth against my skin feels wrong, a perversion of the natural order.

Only five days gone. How can that be? It ought to be more.

I made my way down the road to the schoolhouse as the sun rose, slinking in the shadows. That I was seen, that some curtain-twitcher spied me from the safety of her front window, I do not doubt, but no one approached me, no one gave chase. That was all that mattered.

The world has a different taste to it. The air is purer, the wind more bracing. When I stopped and scooped up a handful of water from a puddle to quench my thirst, its cool, sweet slide down my throat made me reel with bliss. The trees reached out to me with their branches, eager as an army of lovers, calling me to the edge of the road, into the shadow of their embrace.

I had expected the schoolhouse to be empty when I got there, and yet, when I opened the door to see Muriel Melville sitting at her desk, waiting with the air of an animal that knows it will soon be fed, I was not surprised. She turned in her seat to look at me, nodding a greeting. That knowing smile, that sylph's smile.

"The Reverend's wife came round to all the houses," she said, waving a hand at the empty desks. "She said we all ought to stay home for now. That you were too sick to manage, and you needed to get well. Most people were going to stop sending their kids anyhow. There are a lot of stories about you, Miss."

For the first time, she uttered that honorific without seeming to sneer at it. Her eyes were steady as they met mine, neither darting away nor rolling with scorn.

In the pale morning light, the schoolhouse seemed new to me. I looked from the left to the right, drinking in the sight of dust motes drifting in sunbeams, the dirt on the floor, the ghostly remains of last week's lessons on the blackboard. The owlet skull in its little jar beckoned me forward with its eyeless gaze, and I approached the desk to pick it up. Turning it about in my hand, I watched the shadows play across the yellowed surface of the bone.

"Do you remember the day that you found me in the woods?" I asked Muriel, my back still turned to her. "You told me that no one was ever alone here."

The girl did not answer. After a few quiet moments, I turned around to look at her, setting the skull down again. Her gaze was steady and unblinking. The shadows fell upon her face, obscuring her expression. She no longer looked like a little girl at all.

"It's been calling you," she said. "Ain't it?"

"Yes," I replied, just one word that I felt with my entire body, my skin and nerves and blood and bone singing with *yes*.

Muriel watched me for another long moment, then stood. She approached my desk with care — not the care that so many have taken around me these last few weeks, the care a man might show a dangerous animal, but the care one wild thing might show another as they cross paths in the shadow of the forest. My knees trembled at her approach. I let myself sit upon the edge of my desk, grateful for the support of that ancient wood beneath me.

"The widow told me that it took a shine to you," she said, "ages and ages ago."

The picnic. Her eyes seeking me from the shade beneath the maple tree, hard and fast. Mrs. Kinsley's finger, pointing.

"I knew before that, anyhow." The girl stood in front of me now. The pale sun caught in her dark gold hair, making it shine. Haloed, saintly, suffused with the knowledge of something not of this Earth. "That day I met you, when you was so jumpy and nervous, looking all around. I knew it then. I knew with the last one too, that Miss Webster. You get so you can recognize it — that look someone has when it likes them enough to talk to them."

"Mrs. Kinsley said that it does not speak to you." *Not yet*, she'd said. Not yet.

Muriel shrugged. With that motion she looked just like herself again, a sullen girl who had not yet lost her struggle with womanhood. "When I was small," she said, "it was like the wind in the trees, or an animal moving around in the brush. You know there's something making the noise, but it's just *noise*, not something you can follow. The older I got, the more I found that there'd be something else in there too, something that was almost words. Like how sometimes you hear something in French, and it almost makes sense, but it don't sound right enough to really mean anything."

I remembered the way the wind had howled and battered the schoolhouse, how its wails had finally settled down into intelligible words. *Open the door. Come outside.*

"I told the widow about it," Muriel said. "I knew she wouldn't laugh. She told me that someday the words would come clear. She said that if it wanted to speak to me, it wouldn't do me any harm. That maybe one day when I was grown, it would call me to it, the way it called her, and you, and Miss Webster. Now I can hear it all the time. Faint, sometimes, like when you call someone from far away, but it's always there, wherever I am. It makes it easier, sometimes, when it gets difficult at the house, or with Dad. Knowing that it's out there makes the other stuff less . . ." She paused and cleared her throat, as though embarrassed by her own train of thought. I remembered that awful little house, her father's hideous chuckle, and understood. "I heard it this morning, in the barn. I sleep there sometimes, to hear it better. And to . . . to get away. It told me to come here and wait for you."

The girl reached out then and laid one sunbrowned paw upon my shoulder. The weight of her hand startled me. There was something damp upon my cheek, something cramping in my guts.

"It has another gift for you," she said. "Just one. Go into the woods, Miss. Go there, close your eyes, and wait."

With a nod of her fair head, she turned to quit the schoolhouse. I sat in my chair for the longest time, looking at the spot where she had stood. I am here still, even though the clock reads half past one. The shadows have grown and shrunk in my time here, and will do so again.

I will do as she said. I will go into the woods.

(later)

$\mathcal{I}$ walked into the woods barefooted, bareheaded, just as I'd walked out of the summer house. Made my way carefully into the trees behind the schoolhouse until I found a flat-headed stump to sit on. An inhalation, an exhalation, slow, careful.

"I am here," I said aloud into the quiet. And it *was* quiet, I realized, the way it had been quiet right before the crickets set upon me on the road. No birds, no wind, no humming insects. The world was holding its breath. "I am listening."

I closed my eyes, and I waited.

It began as a whisper, too faint to make out even in the hush of the woods. The same beguiling tone that had called to me that long, terrible night in the schoolhouse, pulled me from the church into the snow. My hands spasmed by my sides, clenching fistfuls of my skirt as my heartbeat gained speed and urgency. Sheer will kept me upright and steady on my makeshift seat as the whisper grew louder, my bare toes curling into the dirt. I did not have to see my arms to know the hairs on them stood on end. Every atom in my body thrummed with urgency, every breath quickened my lungs with need.

The soul of the woods themselves calling me. My faithful hound, my paramour, my sweetheart of the shadows and the sap.

I heard the words as clearly as though they were murmured directly into my ear.

Open your eyes.

Bright sunlight, sweet as honey, warm as blood. And I saw my final gift.

It was Florrie. It was Florrie, standing not ten feet from me, looking as she must have in her last living moments, her white nightgown caked with blood and shit, reeking of birth and death. I saw the bruise like a stain at her temple. Her curly hair was matted to her head with sweat, her face pale and strained, but still she smiled, and reached out a hand to me, beckoning. My breath caught in my throat, the rasp of it the loudest thing in the still, still woods.

My bridal gift. The grey dog had chosen well.

I could not move. I could not speak. All I could do was stare at the apparition before me, blinking my tears away fast so that I could have a clear view of my sister, the person I had loved most in the world. There was blood between her teeth, from where her husband had struck her, or from where she'd bitten through her tongue at the end of her labour. Her mouth moved, but no sound came; all I could do was try to guess what she said, imagining the merry sound of her voice, the teasing lilt it always had when she mocked me for being too serious or too skittish.

Nervous, nervous. And here she was, spooking me one last time.

My sister stepped closer to me. Had I reached upward, I could have touched her face with my hand. I could have stood and embraced her, one last time. She stretched out her hand, palm up, the same hand that had so often shaken me awake from nightmares, pulled me out of the dark.

I had pictured this moment so many times, wished over and over again for one last look at her, one last touch. I had thought that I would have one thousand things to say. But as I sat and gazed up at her, I could think of nothing.

Her mouth moved again. This time I watched more carefully, and I understood then what it was she was saying to me.

I reached up then, finally, needing to place a hand on her flesh — what did I care if it was cold from the grave, or so soft from rot that it gave way beneath my fingers! I had to touch her, one last time. The other half of my soul, split and stolen from me. The best, the bravest, the most magnificent of sisters, the girl I'd always wished that I could be.

Our fingertips drew closer. I could almost feel her.

But before my hand could grasp hers, she winked out like a candle flame, just as all my other gifts have, and I was left with only the words she had mouthed to me.

The God of outside waits for you.

The grey dog. The God of outside. They are one and the same.

Twilight has begun to fall over Lowry Bridge. My stomach growls, my head aches. Norah must surely have missed me by now. But here I sit at my desk, writing by the last light of the day. When I close my eyes, I see my sister's face, the smile that bloomed there when she saw me. I can hear her voice, as I could not before.

It does not matter if the gift was real or not, if she really stood before me or was nothing but trickery and smoke. I saw her. That is enough.

Florrie, this book was your last present to me, and I am coming now to the end of it. There are very few pages left now beneath my right hand; soon their number shall dwindle to nothing, and I will have nothing else to write on. That does not bother me. I have nothing left to say.

The God of outside waits for me, and I must go to it. I shall

(later)

A knock, interrupting my thoughts, pulling me suddenly out of myself. I looked up, my breath catching in my throat as I remembered the sound of the schoolhouse door rattling in the dead of a winter night, the knock on the door of the manse.

What would it look like? What would I do?

"Come in," I called. My voice rang out clear and true.

The door swung open, slowly, quietly, and revealed not the unholy, unknowable thing I had half-expected, but a figure I knew well — oh, very well indeed!

"Ada," Agatha said. The light from the doorway did not reach her face, and she stood in blackened silhouette against the grey-violet murk of the evening. The crickets had already begun to sing in the distance. "May I come in?"

I did not answer, only stared. She hesitated a moment on the threshold before stepping inside anyway, closing the door behind her. In the dim, she looked half-finished, a wooden doll whose face remained uncarved. She wore the boots she'd had on the day we met, the ones she used while working in her garden.

"I wondered if you might be here," she said. She sounded wary, exhausted. "Mrs. Grier came to the manse the other night, asking for you. She thought perhaps you might have come to see me."

When I did not respond, Agatha continued, "The Reverend and I could hardly understand her at first, she was so agitated. I got her to sit with us, and have a cup of tea, and then it came out that — that your behaviour has been curious lately. She said that . . ." She paused. I imagined the blush creeping over her cheeks, red as a skinned hare. "She said that on Sunday before church you came into the hall without a stitch on, and that you seemed not to care if anyone saw you do it!"

My shoulders hitched in a shrug. "I am sure the two of you had much to say to one another," I said. "Perhaps almost as much as you had to say to the board."

My voice, strangely enough, was not angry. The memory of her betrayal seemed very far away, a melting dream that had left only a vague feeling of unease in its place.

Agatha took a deep, sharp breath at that, her hands folding tightly in on each other. It looked as though she was gathering herself up to turn and flee.

She should have. The fool. The beautiful, treacherous fool.

Instead, she squared her shoulders and stepped toward me, into the fading light that still drifted in through the window. Her features gained clarity as she approached, and I could see the shining eyes, the delicate nose, even the scattering of freckles.

"Ada, I did not say any of those things to hurt you," she said. Her nostrils flared. I knew that she was drinking in the hideous stink of my body. Even from where she stood, she could not fail to notice it. "I have been praying for you, these past weeks. It was not my intention to—"

Even now, I do not know if the deep, grating sound that came from my throat was laughter or something else entirely. A warning growl, perhaps — a scream so warped and mangled by my attempt to repress it that its nature had been wholly changed.

"Intentions," I said, and how changed my voice from the faltering, halting whisper it had once been. The air was heavy with the ring of it. "Prayers. Useless to me, Agatha. It's all useless. I am beyond it now, you see."

Slowly, as though the burden of her confusion and reproach made her limbs too heavy to easily move, Agatha shook her head.

"Ada," she said, barely speaking above a whisper, "what happened? Won't you tell me?"

There was real anguish in her voice, real pleading. It did not matter.

"Who sent you here?" I asked, and she closed her eyes against the blow of my words. "The Reverend? The Griers? My father? Who told you to look for me?"

Agatha made an abortive little sign with her hands, up in front of her breast, her heart. A push, a fending off.

"No one made me come, Ada," she said. "Not Mrs. Grier, not my husband, nobody. I have been ill, thinking of you. I was terrified that, wherever you were, you had come to some terrible harm, perhaps by your own hand. I left Douglas asleep in his cradle to find you. God knows why — I should have left you to your madness. Look at you! Look at the dirt on your face, how filthy your hair is, how badly you smell! This is not my friend before me, this is not Ada Byrd at all — this is an *animal*!"

She spat that last word at me with the ferocity of a hissing cat, trembling with emotion. The twilight caught in her hair, turning it from red-gold to deepest bronze. She gazed down at me from what felt like an infinite height, as beautiful as I had ever seen her.

The taste of her. My teeth against her cheek.

I knew what I wanted. It had taken me so long to know it.

I moved almost before I had made the decision to do so. Over the desk I vaulted, sweeping this book off the table and into the corner in my haste, and leapt for her, clutching her thin shoulders with both hands. The shriek that tore from her throat was almost as wild as the one that came from mine. Stumbling backwards, she tried to throw me off, but she was weak, still, from the winter's miss, and my grip was too strong — she managed only to pull us both down to the floor, my body pressing close on top of hers. The fall knocked the breath out of her, and she wheezed desperately as she scratched at my arms, struggling to gain traction against me.

Now it was I who looked down at her, marvelling at the sight of her beneath me, her wide eyes with their spilling wet, her soft mouth open and gasping for air. The smell of her billowed heady and powerful as steam from hot wine, soap and cotton, sweat and sweet rosewater. Her legs kicked frantically beneath me, her boots scrabbling against the floorboards. That sound burst forth from me again. I put my mouth to her throat and kissed it, a gentle act incongruous with the violence of our position, and felt her stiffen under me.

"You pretty thing," I murmured, and let my tongue trace the soft ridges of her throat. She shuddered, in pleasure or in horror — I did not know — I did not care. I let my mouth wander where it would, up the lovely column of her neck to the soft place where it met the angle of her jaw.

There I stayed for a long and beautiful minute, savouring the beat, beat, beat of her pulse against my tongue. The jugular throbbing under my mouth, the carotid further beneath that, blood rushing feverishly toward her brain.

Agatha drew a deep breath, still gasping faintly from the roughness of our landing, and croaked out, "Ada—"

And then I bit.

I bit, just as I'd dreamed of doing.

No break in the skin at first, and Agatha screamed and thrashed once again, kicking furiously at my shins. But I was too strong — the taste of her spurred me on and gave power to my limbs — she could not shake me off. Moaning rapturously,

I bit again — and again — and again, until I felt her spurting into my mouth. My eyes spilled over, our salt mingling once again, her blood, my tears, joined forever as they slid down my throat. She bucked once more against me, an unbroken horse fighting the bridle, and then fell still.

Those beautiful eyes had already clouded over when I pulled back to look, the pupils expanded so that the grey barely showed. The shredded flesh of her neck spurted once more, weakly, and then tapered off into a slow, languorous drip.

I breathed in deep, swallowed a mouthful of hot meat.

The schoolhouse is a wreck. The desks are splashed with a crimson so dark it is almost black. My dress is a crumpled heap in the corner, stinking of gore and woman-sweat. Agatha's body lies cooling, her eyes open and unseeing. Once or twice I have paused in my writing and walked over, meaning to close them, but every time I have decided against it. I want her to see me as I am now, clad in nothing but her life's blood. My mouth stained, my hands crusted with scarlet. Beautiful, in my eyes, in the eyes of that which watches me.

It is dark now, very dark, and it will only be a matter of time before the Reverend misses his wife. He will raise the alarm to his neighbours, who will raise it in turn to theirs, and one of them, somewhere along the line, will volunteer that they saw Mrs. MacPherson walk toward the schoolhouse this evening, and wasn't she friends with that teacher, that spinster, that madwoman, once upon a time?

The lamp is burning now, filling the room with dancing orange light. It will be the work of a moment to knock it over as I turn to leave the schoolhouse; it will fall on the floor and shatter, and its flame will catch on some papers lying there, upon which I have spilled (oh, quite by accident) a quantity of lamp oil. When I lock the door for the very last time, it will be on a school full of merry flames, unruly pupils leaping and licking at the wood.

That life is done. A new one awaits me beneath the trees, in the damp muck of the underbrush, in the places where worms writhe through the dirt and predator chases prey, and I shall turn to meet it. I shall walk into the woods, bare and open to the rush of the wind, washed with moonlight and shadow, and there I shall await the grey dog.

The End

Acknowledgements

$\mathcal{I}$ have been writing the acknowledgements for my first book in my head since I was about eight years old. It feels awfully strange to finally write them for real. Dozens of people have been involved in the creation of this novel, and I am tremendously grateful to each and every one of them.

Over the years, my life has been changed by the dedication and empathy of many wonderful teachers. Elaine LeBlanc, thank you for taking a chance on me. Clara Dugas, thank you for telling me stories, and sorry for never returning your typewriter. Dr. Paul Grant, thank you for encouraging me to think deeply about language, and for teaching me how to pronounce "Nabokov." Dr. Stephanie McKenzie, your passion for Canadian literature was so infectious that I finally caught it. Steffany Marynovska, your careful guidance and rare insight made me believe in my story. Paul Headrick, your honest analysis helped me understand my book in a way I hadn't before. I will expand the narrative. I will dramatize the affect.

I would be remiss if I did not give special mention to Jen Sookfong Lee, my Writer's Studio mentor, current editor, and stalwart supporter. Your compassion, enthusiasm, and belief in the power of every writer's voice kept me afloat during the initial writing process and the many drafts that followed. Thank you for seeing something in this book, and for helping me to see it too. Aside from my mother, you are probably my biggest fan.

A million thanks to Rebecca Chan-Gill, Judy Dercksen, Colleen Doty, Hugh Griffith, Uttara Krishnadas, Angela May, Fred Sahyouni, and Anya Wyers, my comrades from Simon Fraser University's Writer's Studio program. Your thoughtful comments, questions, and criticisms have shaped this book, and I have grown as a writer through knowing you all. WTF Crew for life.

To my post-grad Writer's Studio friends Teminey Beckers, Becky Block, Julie Gordon, and Libby McKeever, thank you for coming with Ada on her journey, even on days when I wanted to dump her in the woods and leave her there. I will treasure your kindness and reassurance forever.

Thank you to the amazing team at ECW Press, with a special shout-out to the many Jens who helped along the way. Without you, this book would still just be a long Word doc full of typos and square brackets that read PUT SOMETHING GOOD HERE.

To my beloved friends, thank you for cheering me on, and for answering my weird questions even when they sound like something a serial killer might ask. ("This is for a story, I swear!") A special thanks to William Dicks and Quinn Arruda, my intrepid first readers. I am eternally grateful for your late-night proofreads, perceptive feedback, and ability to drag me out of the Anne Shirley–est depths of despair.

To L.M. Montgomery, despite her faults, I owe a debt of gratitude. My early discovery of the Emily Starr novels showed me how to experience the world as a writer and encouraged me to start thinking of myself as one. Thank you for climbing the Alpine Path and for inspiring me to do the same.

To my parents, Pamela and Stephen Kenny, your love and support helped me become the person I am today. Thank you for turning me into a reader.

To my sisters, Kerrin Rafuse and Stephanie Kenny, thank you for your wisdom, your patience, and your unwavering faith. Kerrin, I'm sorry I hit you in the mouth with a Frisbee that one time. Steph, I'm sorry I mooned you that other time.

To my late sister Cael "Caylee" Kenny, thank you for your strength, your brilliance, your bravery, and your gentle soul. I wrote this book before we lost you, and I didn't know how prophetic those passages about wanting a sister back would become. I miss you every single day.

And, finally, to Amy Beck. My teammate, my scientist, my heart's other home. You were here at the beginning of this story, and you are still here at its end. Thank you for loving me.

PHOTO BY WILLIAM DICKS

ELLIOTT GISH wants to creep you out. A writer and librarian from Nova Scotia, she has published short fiction in *The New Quarterly*, *Wigleaf*, *Prairie Fire*, *The Baltimore Review*, *Vastarien*, *The Dalhousie Review*, *Foglifter Journal*, and many others. She was a finalist for the 2018 Wigleaf Mythic Picnic Prize and nominated for a 2022 Pushcart Prize. Elliott is a 2020 graduate of the Simon Fraser University Writer's Studio program, and later participated in the program as an apprentice fiction mentor. She lives with her partner in Halifax, a city full of rain and ghosts. *Grey Dog* is her first novel.